A Thousand Suns

A Thousand Suns

Suns

Alex Scarrow

First published in Great Britain in 2006 by Orion Books
an imprint of The Orion Publishing Group
Orion House, 5 Upper St Martin's Lane, London WC2H 9EA

1 3 5 7 9 10 8 6 4 2

A CIP catalogue record for this book is available
from the British Library.

ISBN-13 (hardback) 978 0 7528 7254 4
ISBN-10 (hardback) 0 7528 7254 0
ISBN-13 (trade paperback) 978 0 7528 7255 1
ISBN-10 (trade paperback) 0 7528 7255 9

Typeset by Deltatype Ltd, Birkenhead, Merseyside

Printed and bound in Great Britain by
Mackays of Chatham plc, Chatham Kent

The Orion Publishing Group's policy is to use papers that are natural,
renewable and recyclable products and made from wood grown in sustainable
forests. The logging and manufacturing processes are expected to conform
to the environmental regulations of the country of origin.

www.orionbooks.co.uk

For you, Frances, this one is for you.

The following is encrypted for *your* eyes only:
MWTCDH YDK ENAEXGV FT TI MWTI IPKIR, AHCZ PZD.
BIL QXTG IAT UTLI XXZWMTXC RTTGL.

I am Vishnu, become death
Destroyer of worlds,
Shatterer of worlds,
The Mighty One
A thousand suns
Bursting in the sky.

On 29 April 1945 the Allies secretly surrendered unconditionally to Nazi Germany. Four hours later, the surrender was withdrawn.

Herons Cove, Rhode Island

30 April 1945

At a distance it had looked like a tangled ball of fishing net and seaweed. It rolled in the breaking surf and settled a little further up the shingle as each succeeding wave surged up the beach and then drew back with the hiss of thousands of pebbles tumbling in the froth.

The two young boys ambled down through the sand dunes crowned with tufts of coarse grass and descended onto the pebbled surface of the beach. The eldest boy studied the objcct for a long while before putting raw fingers to his numb lips. He attempted a whistle, which was all but lost between the crash and rumble of the waves and the gusting wind.

A moment later a large German Shepherd appeared on top of a dune, panting noisily, its long pink tongue flapping like a pennant.

'Over there, Prince!' he said pointing towards the dark object on the beach. Prince set off at a sprint, passed the boys, showering them with kicked-up sand and flecks of saliva.

They watched the dog as it quickly crossed the beach, correcting course once it had sighted the object for itself.

'Don't let him roll in it,' the smaller boy called out, 'you know your dad hates him rollin' in beached catch.'

The dog splashed through the surf and reached the object as the boys clattered across the pebbles and onto the soft sand, slowly approaching the dog and the discovery.

Twenty yards away from it, the older boy slowed down. 'That ain't a fishin' net,' he said uneasily.

Prince pawed at the object and buried his nose in it, noisily snuffling and oblivious to the boys as they came to a halt a few feet away.

'Oh boy,' he muttered under his breath, taking an involuntary step back.

A wave rolled the object over. Prince began to lick the exposed pale face of a young man, a blond fringe plastered to the brow with dried blood.

'Is that man dead, Sean?' the smaller boy whispered, looking up at his older friend for confirmation. 'He's dead, ain't he?'

Sean moved reluctantly towards it, aware that Danny was holding back and looking uncertainly to him to take the lead. He was only a year older than Danny – thirteen, to his twelve – but that was enough to confer an unambiguous seniority on him.

He approached the body and leaned over it, studying the face intently, 'Think so. He's not moving a whole lot.'

Danny gasped.

He watched each wave lift and move the dead man's arms up, and the retreating ebb pull them back down again. In a bizarre way it looked like he was trying to fly.

'When a body dies it goes all stiff,' he said matter-of-factly. Danny had the stern face of an undertaker. 'Do you think he's one of the fishermen?'

The dead man looked like he couldn't have been over thirty years old. Sean knew most of the men who worked on the trawlers in Port Lawrence; they were all much older. Most of the young ones in Port Lawrence had long ago left these shores for the war in Europe.

'I don't think so. I don't recognise him. Anyway, those don't look like oilskins.'

He slowly reached out a finger and lightly prodded the corpse's chest. 'Yeah, reckon he's dead all right,' he announced with growing confidence. 'Maybe he fell overboard from one of the cargo ships.'

Danny nodded gravely. 'He must've fallen,' he added soberly.

Sean, encouraged that the corpse wasn't about to spring to life, grew bolder and started to pull away some ribbons of seaweed that had wrapped themselves around the body. Prince resumed licking the dead man's face.

'He ain't going to wake up, Prince, he's gone,' said Sean. He had pulled away enough of the seaweed to reveal the clothes on the corpse's body.

No oilskins, no slicker.

'That ain't a fisherman,' he said suddenly. 'That's a flying jacket. He's an airman, one of our boys.'

The pair of them stared with renewed awe at the dead man rolling with the rhythmic pattern of the waves.

'Gee . . . reckon we should bury him?' said Danny. 'We could make him a nice cross from some driftwood. There's plenty of it lying around.'

Sean considered the idea, but he knew this kind of thing required the intervention of grown-ups, and someone official to 'square the box and nail the lid', as his mom used to say. 'We should really go tell the deputy, or my dad, or someone. He's one of our fly-boys, Danny – that makes him important. You go and get my dad and tell him, I'll see if he's got a name tag.'

Danny nodded, relieved to have an excuse to step back away from the body. He turned around and ran back across the beach towards the sand dunes and the small village of Port Lawrence beyond, casting one last glance back at Sean as he knelt down beside the body.

Sean watched Danny go before turning back to the body. He wasn't that keen to touch it any more than he had to, but he knew it was the right thing to do. The man had a name, and no doubt a mom and a dad, and a missus who needed to be told where he'd ended up.

Sean knew the body would have something with a name on it . . . a dog tag, or a name-badge on the chest or something. He knew all the fly-boys had some way to identify them.

With one hand only and a barely concealed look of distaste on his face he slowly peeled back the lapel of the leather flying jacket and prepared to slide his fingers under the wet tunic and hunt for some tags. Sean was fully aware that he might just make contact with the dead man's cold flesh, and his bottom lip drew back with disgust at the thought.

But he needed to probe no further.

His eyes widened when he saw the object lying under the lapel of the flying jacket and upon the man's still chest.

'Oh boy,' said Sean.

Three Miles off the Coast of Rhode Island

Present day

The sea was as flat as a tabletop. The failing light of an overcast evening sky painted it a dull, featureless marble grey.

Jeff sat on the aft deck smoking and looking back over the stern gunwale at the pale wake of suds trailing behind the trawler as she made a steady six knots south. Undisturbed by the calm sea, the wake extended off towards the horizon, where one drab grey merged seamlessly into another.

When it was like this, so calm, so quiet, he found it hard to believe that they were on the open sea, and not in some sheltered lagoon or inland lake. The North Atlantic wasn't often like this. He was used to the sea off Rhode Island and Connecticut being choppy along the Sound at the very least, and the salt spray from broken waves stinging his skin. But this evening it was subdued, unnaturally calm, like a scolded child sulking. If it wasn't for the rhythmic thud and sputter of the trawler's diesel engine, he knew it would be utterly silent, except for the lapping of water against the hull.

No way for the Atlantic to be.

It wasn't right. It felt like the calm between two pressure fronts, the sort of calm that had you hauling in your nets and securing down every loose thing on deck. But there was nothing to get excited about, no major weather heading their way; just the ocean having an unsettlingly quiet day.

The net lines stretched from thirty-foot outriggers either side of the trawler's pilothouse into the water. He could tell by the limp way the lines hung and the reduced drag on the boat that there was precious little catch in the voluminous net beneath the surface, trailing several hundred yards behind them.

It had been a poor day.

All in all it had been a pretty shitty week. By a rough reckoning of the last five days' haul he had maybe broken even on the diesel they had burned cruising up and down this stretch of the banks off the New England coastline. Then there was the cost of the food for the three lads he had aboard.

Maybe he'd break even, if they could pull in something decent. Four tons of catch, be it mackerel, cod, herring, tuna, swordfish, whatever . . . was break-even point roughly. If it were mostly tuna, you could say three tons. It would be impossible to weigh the haul until they returned and offloaded it, but Jeff could guess the weight from the space taken in the ice lockers. They needed another ton before they could start thinking about turning a profit.

One last run this evening and then I'm taking her home.

He hoped this last roll of the dice would end his week-long run of bad luck. It would be a good way to draw a line under their profitless trip, to pull out a full net tonight and end on a good note. Even if all it did was cover his costs instead of leaving him hundreds down on the whole trip.

It wasn't exactly the easiest way to make a living.

He took a final pull on his cigarette, watching it glow brightly in the gathering dark, and then tossed it out into their churning wake.

It wasn't the easiest way to make a living for his lads either, that much was for sure, but then it had to be better than wearing a stupid paper hat, a plastic name tag and serving fries.

The boys on his boat were young. All three of them were under twenty. Jeff took them on instead of the more experienced crew because they were happy to work for a percentage only, instead of a retainer and a percentage. Young fellas, not one of them had properly finished school, leaving them all with few options to choose from. Round here it was either catching fish or stacking shelves. And catching fish paid better.

He remembered when he was twenty: no bills to pay, no family to provide for and little to lose. Percentage-only worked just fine. A good trip and his boys saw good money, far more than is decent for a kid without a high-school diploma. A good trip, three to five days away from home, could bring in up to 2000 dollars each after Jeff had subtracted overheads.

A bad trip? . . . well that's the way it works. Some good, some bad, you throw good dice then you get the super-big dollar prizes, you throw lame dice . . .

Well, look at it this way; at least you've been out in the fresh air.

Jeff smiled. That was something his old man used to say.

That's the only game going round here, and them's the rules.

That was another.

All three of the boys still lived at home with their folks as far as he knew. All the money they made was pretty much fun money. Booze, bikes, smokes, whatever.

Ritchie Bradden, a lad who used to crew for him last season, called it his 'screw you' money. He'd taken five days' sick leave from his seven-dollars-an-hour job at Wallders, only to come back at the end of the week and walk off Jeff's boat with nearly 3000 dollars in his back pocket. His first stop was Wallders to say 'screw you' to the store manager. Since then Ritchie had stuck with fishing.

Percentage-only worked just fine.

Jeff watched the line descending from the outrigger silhouetted against the last light on the horizon. It twitched and began to pull backwards with a creaking that could be heard above the chug of the engine.

'Hey! We got a catch!' one of the lads called out.

Jeff watched as it tightened. A school of mackerel could do that. They were dense, tightly packed. You knew it when you scored them.

The net suddenly drew fully taut, and the port outrigger bent alarmingly.

Jeff jumped to his feet and hastily leaned over the port side. He could hear the twang of nylon fibres stressing and snapping.

The net was beginning to tear.

'Stop the boat! It's ripping!' he bellowed towards the pilothouse.

The trawler's engine kept the same monotonous note. The outrigger looked like it was beginning to buckle.

'Shit! Tom! Stop the goddamn boat!'

The trawler continued at a comfortable six knots.

The young lad at the helm turned wearily around, and raised his eyebrows questioningly at Jeff as he wrenched the door to the pilothouse open and stormed in. He angrily pulled the boy aside and immediately grabbed the throttle and threw it into neutral. Tom pulled his headphones down off his ears and Jeff could hear the irritating sibilant hiss of rock music played too loudly.

'What's up, Skip –?'

'Dammit Tom! How many times have I said no music when you're on the wheel? . . . Huh? How many?'

The young lad fumbled for his Walkman to turn it off. Jeff reached for it, tucked into the gathered swathe of the slicker tied up around the boy's slender waist. He pulled it out and threw it on the floor. Its cheap plastic casing stayed in one piece, but from the internal rattling sound it made as it slid across the floor of the cabin Jeff didn't think Tom would be getting much more rock music out of it.

Tom opened his mouth to complain.

'I wouldn't worry about your tape recorder if I were you. That's the least of your worries.'

He grabbed the boy's shoulder, turned him round and pointed at the buckling portside outrigger. 'If the net's screwed, I'll fucking throw you over the side.'

'I'm s-sorry, Skip . . . I –'

He watched the young man's mouth open and close silently as he struggled for something useful to say.

Jeff turned abruptly and left the cockpit, cursing his stupidity and weakness for promising to take the boy on. Clearly the fool would much rather be at home (in the warmth) with his feet up on his mother's threadbare furniture and staring lifelessly at the drip feed of daytime cable.

But a promise was a promise.

Tom's mother had pleaded with him to take the lad along, with a beseeching smile that seemed to promise a little more than gratitude for his troubles.

She'd wanted to shake the idle waster out of the rut he'd comfortably rolled into. She was confident that a few days of hard graft rewarded with several hundred dollars of his share on the catch, maybe even a full thousand for him to play around with, would be the kick in the pants he needed.

Next time, you idiot, Jeff muttered to himself, *let the Big Head do the thinking*.

Outside he walked across the aft deck towards the portside outrigger, where the other two members of his young crew were leaning out studying the net with the aid of a torch. Ian and Duncan were cousins, or second cousins or something. They seemed to come as a pair, neither prepared to crew without the other. Which was fine. They were both good workers, he'd taken them on over a dozen trips before, and they'd made good money on all of them.

'Net's rigid, Skip,' said Duncan as he passed the torch to Jeff.

Jeff shone it on the outrigger, which was bent like a fully drawn bow and buckled near the end. That was going to cost a little to straighten out or be replaced.

He panned down to the net. It was as taut as cable wire and beginning to fray.

'Shit, we better back up a little before something gives.'

He turned towards the pilothouse to see Tom standing in the doorway, shuffling from one foot to the other guiltily awaiting instructions and, it seemed, eager to make amends.

'Put her in reverse . . . gently', he shouted. Tom nodded eagerly and went back to the helm. The trawler shuddered as gears engaged and the gentle diesel rumble changed to a rhythmic chug. Slowly the boat eased back, the outrigger swung with a metallic groan and the net slackened.

Jeff waved his hand at Tom, and the rhythm of the engine changed again as she went back into neutral. The trawler drifted a few more feet backward under its own momentum and then came to a rest.

On the calm, mirror surface of the sea, the boat was unnaturally still.

'Shall we try and pull in the net, Skip?' asked Ian.

'Yeah, but go gently . . . I don't want any more damage done if it can be helped.'

Ian reached for a lever beside the base of the starboard outrigger and pulled it down. With a clunk and a rattle the motor on the hydraulic winch whirred to life and began winding in the net. Jeff watched the fibres of the net begin to stretch and the winch's motor began to struggle.

'It's not coming in,' shouted Ian above the noise. He looked at Jeff and placed a hand back on the lever, ready to put the motor out of its misery.

'Nope. Damned thing's snagged. Shut it off.'

The lad slammed the lever down and the motor on the hydraulic winch sputtered and died.

Jeff was looking at losing a hundred dollar net if he didn't play his cards right. A hundred dollar net, four days of cruising diesel, the cost of groceries for four hungry mouths . . . and a less than stellar haul on ice, below decks to pay for it all.

It was getting too dark to see anything. 'Tom!' He barked towards the pilothouse. 'Put on the floods.'

Twin beams bathed the aft deck with a powerful white light, and all of a sudden twin 1000-watt halogen bulbs obliterated the last, faint glow of dusk. It was officially night.

'Whad'ya want to do, Skip?' asked Duncan.

Good question.

Jeff headed back inside the pilothouse. He looked sternly at Tom and tapped the depth sounder display with his knuckles.

'You been watching this, right?'

Tom nodded. 'Sure.'

'All the time, right?'

'Uh, yeah. It's been nothing but flat bed for the last hour, Skip.'

'Yeah? Well obviously it hasn't because we've snagged our nets on something, and it sure as hell ain't cod.'

Tom's jaw flapped ineffectively again, his Adam's apple bobbed in sympathy.

'Don't say anything boy, or you'll just piss me off even more. Put this boat in reverse and let's retrace our steps.'

'Sure, Skip.'

'And this time keep your eyes on the sounder. Reckon you can do that for me?'

Tom nodded vigorously. Jeff left the pilothouse once more and found himself muttering under his breath yet again.

Somebody else can take his sorry ass out, next time.

Outside, Ian and Duncan were awaiting orders.

'Okay, Ian . . . you're on the winch. We're going to carry on reversing, and I want the slack on the net pulled in as we go.'

The boat began to shudder again as the engine engaged reverse gear, and slowly they started backwards. Ian operated the winch, intermittently slamming it on and off to recover the net as the tension allowed, and Jeff studied the wet folds of braided nylon netting for damage as it slowly built up on the aft deck.

Ten minutes had passed when he heard Tom calling out from the pilothouse.

'What is it?' he shouted back.

'I think you should see this, Skip. Not sure if I'm reading this right.'

Jeff threw down the net and started towards him.

So NOW he sees something.

Tom turned towards Jeff as he entered, and pointed towards the green glow of the sounder's display.

'I umm . . . didn't notice that there before –'

Jeff looked at the ghostly image on the display screen, a grainy rendition of the seabed in profile. Flat from left to right, but with an unmistakable spike building up on the extreme right.

'Didn't notice? How the hell did you not notice that! . . . or maybe you just weren't looking? That's the shitting thing that's going to ruin my net.'

• 11 •

'I'm sorry, Skip . . . I just didn't see it –'

Jeff angrily waved a hand to shut him up. He studied the green screen as the spike slowly progressed towards the middle of the display. The spike was followed by another and then the line became a plateau at a new height for forty, fifty feet, then dipped back down again.

'Stop the boat,' Jeff ordered. Tom slammed the engine into neutral. Whatever that thing was, it was directly beneath them.

'I can't believe you didn't spot that first time round,' Jeff said shaking his head with incredulity. Tom ashamedly lowered his gaze, anticipating another roasting. He knew he wouldn't be going out on Jeff Westland's boat again.

The door to the pilothouse swung open, and Ian entered. 'The net's not moving, Skip. I reckon we're on top of whatever we're caught on.'

Jeff nodded at the sounder display. 'A wreck, I think, we're sitting right over it. Genius here didn't notice it.'

Tom's cheeks turned crimson as Ian stared silently at him.

Overheads settled before shares paid out. That's the way it worked. With the net totalled, the outrigger damaged, and the crappiest haul of the season on ice down below, Ian could see a lean fortnight ahead of him, until the Skip was ready to take his boat out again.

Tom realised he'd be best avoiding the bars in Port Lawrence for a while. At least until Ian and Duncan had been out again, and found themselves flush with money once more.

'If we lose the net we lose the evening haul,' Ian said bitterly.

'Leave him be,' said Jeff, 'I've already spoken to him.'

Ian studied the display carefully, trying to comprehend the three-dimensional shape described by the two-dimensional profile on the screen.

'Is that a shipwreck, Skip?'

'Yeah. There're no rocks out here. This section of the banks is nothing but sixty miles of flat silt. It's just great I find the one shipwreck out here when my net's down. Just fucking great.'

Ian continued to study the form on the sounder. It was fifty feet long and pretty flat, peeking at one end with a tall spike.

'That's a wreck all right, Skip. Reckon maybe that spike there's a mast or something?'

Jeff looked closely. 'Maybe.'

Tom pointed at the screen. 'It doesn't look like a ship.'

The other two turned to look at him.

'I said I don't think it's a ship.'

'Well, I don't care whether it's a ship, the body of Moby Dick or the lost city of Atlantis, the damn thing's got my net and it's going to chew it up pretty good before I get it back.'

Tom's cheeks continued to burn under their withering gaze. But he knew that wasn't the profile of a boat. It was obvious if you looked at it right.

'So,' said Jeff tiredly, the force of his anger spent leaving him feeling only exhausted resignation, 'given that this is the seabed we're looking at, if it's not a ship, what the hell do you think it is?'

'It's a plane,' said Tom with a voice he'd hoped would sound certain and confident, but in fact came out as little more than a whisper.

Chapter 1

The Assignment

Chris Roland adjusted the arrangement of photographs on the table in the conference room. He had spent last night in his hotel room at the Marriot reviewing the contact sheets and from this he had carefully picked out several dozen of the most striking images. He'd developed and printed them in the en-suite bathroom through the early hours of this morning.

He was exhausted.

He caught a glimpse of himself in one of the glass partition walls that separated the conference room from the rest of *News Fortnite*'s open-plan office. A tall and gaunt apparition stared back at him, his weather-tanned forehead at odds with the fish-belly white of his recently shaved chin and topped off with a marine buzz cut. Chris shook his head and smiled. He looked like the top half of his head had been zapped by a ray gun.

His coarse brown hair had grown long, and he'd developed a full beard while on the last assignment, a wildlife shoot on the island of South Georgia. He'd begun to look like one of those hairy geeks they wheel out from time to time to talk about the good old pioneering days of the computer industry. Guys who looked like they could do with a little help-me-out cash but whose handful of gratis Apple or Microsoft shares are worth billions.

After clearing immigration at JFK, he'd headed for a barber, yearning to feel the smoothness of his chin once more and lose the dead weight of his long, greasy hair tied up carelessly in a ponytail.

As the interminably itchy and aggravating facial hair was whisked away by the barber, Chris had been shocked by how thin his face had become. The last few months of existing on a basic hi-sugar diet and spending all day long in the freezing winds of the South Atlantic seemed to have robbed his face of any spare fat. He knew if his mother could have seen him then, she'd have scolded him for not eating properly.

Chris's focus extended beyond his reflection in the glass towards a trim, silver-haired woman moving swiftly. He watched her weave her slight frame across the open-plan floor of the Features Section through a labyrinth of shoulder-high partitions towards the conference room. She was moving quickly and purposefully towards him, not a woman you'd ever want to risk keeping waiting, he fancied. Clearly she was running late with her own strictly imposed schedule. Chris had time enough to hurriedly straighten a couple of the pictures before Elaine Swisson, the deputy editor of *News Fortnite*, pushed open the door to the conference room and entered.

'Hey, Chris, how's my favourite little cockney urchin doing?' she said with a no-nonsense Brooklyn accent.

Chris had once described Elaine to a friend by asking him to visualise Susan Sarandon's older, more aggressive sister. He wasn't sure whether the actress even had an older sister, but if she did, Elaine should be her.

But that was perhaps a little unkind. Sure, he'd seen her chew out a member of her staff here at the magazine once before, and she had a reputation for being an incredibly harsh negotiator with his agency, but for Chris, she seemed to find a warmer centre, inside the sharp edges of her business persona.

'I'm fine, a little tired . . . but otherwise fine,' Chris answered.

'Yeah?' She appraised him. 'You look a lot like shit. Bad flight back?'

'It was okay. It didn't crash, which is always a good thing.'

Elaine smiled. 'Cute. How was South Georgia?'

Chris could quite happily never go there again. Cold, wet and rough. It really hadn't been one of his better assignments. 'Weather wasn't particularly great,' he answered flatly.

'Oh, surely no worse than an English summer?'

Chris smiled. She wasn't exactly the world's most ardent Anglophile. Elaine had spent several years in London working for a sister publication. As far as Chris had worked out, the only thing she'd liked about her time in the city was the money she was being paid to tolerate it. There were many things over there that she casually described as 'second-rate' or 'third-world' to the irritation of her English colleagues, such as the ineffectual London Underground, the blandness of pub grub, the appalling cost of living and, of course, the miserable bloody weather, moans that any self-respecting Brit would happily indulge with her, if it wasn't for the fact that she was American and quite happy to go on to say how much better things were back home.

Chris had first met her while he was tentatively starting out on his freelance career after five years of relatively secure employment for *MetroLife*, one of the seedier, freebie-tabloids in the capital. After delivering promptly on a couple of assignments, she had begun requesting him by name through the agency Chris had signed up with. After she had returned to New York, he still found she was specifically requesting him and putting a decent amount of work his way, despite having any number of good photographers on her doorstep to choose from.

Somehow she had managed to erase from her mind the fact that he was one of those wet-fart Limeys. It had probably helped that he'd moved away from the east end of London, used a New York-based agency and worked on watering down his estuary accent a little.

Or maybe she just wasn't as anti-Brit as she made out.

Elaine smiled warmly at him.

Or maybe she just wants to mother me.

Chris hadn't failed to notice he tended to bring that instinct out in the older women he worked with.

'It's good to see you again, Chris. Shall we take a look-see?'

She leant over the conference table and studied the spread of pictures. There were images of a whaling station abandoned in the 1920s. Fantastic images, some in black and white, some in colour but desaturated and monochromatic. Images of beached whaling ships, their plate metal hulls rusted, exposing ribcages of corroded steel. Images of the station itself, interiors such as the dormitory huts and the canteen, complete with tin plates and cutlery laid out on a communal table ready for a meal that was never to take place.

Nature, it seemed, had wasted little time in commandeering the station, and eighty years of undisturbed invasion had produced stunning compositions of lichen-covered toilet seats and beds and whale-rendering equipment playing host to communities of terns and puffins.

Some in colour, some in black and white, but all of them beautiful. Elaine made no comment until she had viewed all the images on the table.

'These are stunning Chris . . . absolutely remarkable.'

'Thanks.'

'I think we can easily syndicate these. I can think of three other periodicals off the top of my head that will take 'em. They're gorgeous.'

'Thanks. It was a pretty good assignment,' he said, momentarily forgetting the cold, miserable discomfort on the island.

Elaine looked up from the photos. 'Tired?'

'I am a bit. It was a long flight yesterday, and then I was up late working on these.'

'You need a break?'

'I'd love a break. But then I guess the assignment you're going to tell me about would have to go to some other young, hungry freelancer who might just do a better job.'

She laughed. 'That's how we like you guys, paranoid and competitive.'

'Yeah, well, I guess we can't afford not to be.'

'So, you sure you're ready for another?'

'I just need a couple of good nights' sleep, a few warm baths and I'll be good to go.'

'Okay, well, the good news is it's not the other side of the world this time, it's local.'

'And the bad news?'

'The bad news is . . . it's another cold one,' Elaine stuck out her bottom lip in sympathy. 'I'm sorry it's not a photo-story in Florida or LA, but, if it's any consolation, I think this one could be a reputation-maker for you. You want to hear about it?'

Chris nodded.

'We tend to comb through local newspapers for our human-interest stories, which is how we came across this one. It was in the *Trenton Herald*, which is a local rag that serves Newport and a few towns up the Rhode Island coast. There's a small seaside town, Port Lawrence. No big deal, a few thousand people, a couple of diners and a few seasonal attractions. They've got a small commercial fishing fleet that still operates out of the town. It's the real Amityville deal, old shutter-board huts, quiet inbred locals who view the rest of the world as outsiders, fishing nets strung across cobbled streets . . . you get the idea? Anyway, one of their trawlers snagged its nets on a wreck some five miles out from the coastline –'

'Wreck? Are we talking an underwater shoot?'

She nodded. 'Why? . . . are you not keen on that?'

He'd done underwater before, several times, but always within the luxury of warmer latitudes. After his spell on South Georgia, throwing himself into the bitter cold of the Atlantic, albeit insulated within a dry suit, simply didn't appeal to him right now.

Pass up this job, and they could easily find someone else.

Chris winced at the thought.

'No, underwater is fine. Go on.'

'Good. Anyway, so one of these trawlers snagged its nets on a wreck. Turns out it was a plane. A big one.'

Chris's interest was piqued.

'Yup. Oh, we're not talking missing commercial airliners or private Lear jets or anything.'

'No?' Chris tried to contain his disappointment.

'No, it's better than that; a World War Two bomber. One of our B-something-or-others, you know? The big ones we used to flatten the Rhineland with. Some local propeller-head expert on wartime planes identified it from an item of debris they pulled up in the net.'

'Has anyone been down yet to look it over?'

'You're thinking "anyone" as in, any other news mag? No, I don't think so. It's not a big story. Some wartime plane goes down due to bad weather or some component malfunction. It's not like we've found the remains of the *Marie Celeste* or anything. I think we've got this story to ourselves for now.'

'That's good to know. How intact is it?'

'They reckon it's in one big glorious piece. I think this is going to make one hell of a compelling photo-story. I want to go with a kind of "time capsule" slant on it.' Elaine's eyes widened like an excited child's as she visualised the spread within the covers of *News Fortnite*.

'The cold waters will have preserved it quite well, I'd imagine,' added Chris.

'Exactly! If you can get some pictures that make the plane look as if it dropped out of the sky last week, that'll be the angle. You know? "The plane time forgot!" kinda deal. You know what I mean?'

Chris nodded.

'Focus on the small things, Chris, the little things. I don't know, the navigator's box of Lucky Strikes, the pilot's picture of his sweet-heart ... the ... ah shit, you know what I'm after, you're the photographer.'

Chris was glad she'd noticed. He smiled at her. 'So when would you want me to head out and do this?'

'Well now, there's no real sell-by date on this story. If it's waited fifty years to be discovered it can hang on a little longer for its moment of fame. But all the same, I'd like to think we could get some pictures in for next month's issue. We've got a pretty weak line-up for that one . . . needs a bit of juice.'

Chris weighed things up. Frankly he could well do with a week up on the blocks, get some serious down time. Despite catching the wave of Elaine's enthusiasm and surfing the momentary buzz of excitement, he was really beginning to feel like he needed some R&R.

'What if . . . what if I got out there by next week. Would that be soon enough?'

Elaine stroked her chin. 'If you think you can deliver before our next issue, that's fine by me. I can't afford it to miss, though. That issue really needs this story, or we risk losing subscribers.'

She looked at Chris with the eyes of a worried mother. 'You need some time to catch up on your sleep? Enjoy a few comforts?'

'Yup, something like that. And anyway, I'll probably need to source some equipment for deep sea –'

'Oh, it's not that deep. The article says the plane's sitting under only seventy-five feet of water. I'm no diver, but that doesn't sound too far down. Is that deep, Chris?'

'Deep enough that I think I'll need to make some calls. Reinforced camera casings, dry suits and cold-water diving equipment and some other stuff. It'll take a few days to organise that anyway, but I could be on my way up there, say, middle of next week?'

'You sure? I imagined you were thinking of taking two or three weeks out of the loop.'

I was, goddammit.

'No, of course not. A few days should see me right,' said Chris with a chirpy 'I-can-take-anything' smile.

'Great. Well I'm glad you can say yes to this one, Chris, I really am. You've got a good eye for visual poetry. I think you're going to come back with some great images. Maybe some of the best you've ever done.'

'Yup. It sounds good.'

She draped an arm around his narrow shoulders. 'Excellent! Listen, go back to your hotel and get some zeds. Give me a call tomorrow and we'll sort out the details and expenses. Okay?'

Chris nodded, finally aware that he had been a straight thirty-two hours without a moment's sleep. She led him from the conference room onto the noisy open office floor, and patted him gently on the arm.

Chris was uncomfortably aware that a few heads were turning their way.

Christ, I hope they don't think I'm her bit of sugar.

She winked at him. 'I want you in bed, okay? Get some rest, you look like death warmed up.'

Chris winced, knowing that those members of her staff with the keenest hearing had only heard the first part of that sentence.

Chapter 2

The Coast Road

The late-afternoon sun shone through the silver birches lining the coast road and cast a steady procession of hazy beams across the road. Alternate strips of light and shadow dappled the windscreen of the Cherokee, and Chris found himself squinting from the intermittent and distracting glare.

He pulled a pair of sunglasses out of the glove compartment and slipped them on.

'Giving you a headache?' asked Mark, sitting beside him in the passenger seat.

Mark Costas was a good diving instructor. He'd known Chris back when he'd trained him for a PADI certificate. Like the best of teachers, he easily inspired trust from his pupils, and that was mainly because of the calm, unflappable demeanour of the man. His darkly tanned face, framed with a lush black beard and topped with a Yankees baseball cap, was a picture of measured ease.

Along this part of the coastline there were a number of small villages perched on the seafront. Quite a few of them seemed to service small fishing vessels of one sort or another, and many of these were beach-launched, from trailers reversed into the water, and retrieved in the same way. Once upon a time most of the boats along this stretch of coast were part of an industry; now the vast majority were used for sports fishing.

On the right of the road it was becoming cluttered with the detritus of generations of nautical activity – abandoned, weatherworn wooden hulls riding high on grass-topped dunes shored up with wooden pallets, and an endless mélange of crates and washed-up freight spillage garnished the roadside. They passed through a village that consisted of no more than an old boat yard, three houses, and a gas station-cum-diner, an isolated sign of habitation amidst a rolling montage of coastal wilderness.

'It looks like something out of a Stephen King novel,' said Mark in a rumbling, deep voice.

'I know, beautiful isn't it? I could live in a place like this.'

'Uh-huh.'

Chris drove in silence. It really was magnificent, inspiring and solitary. His recent sojourn in the southern Atlantic wilderness had changed him. After so many months being alone out there, he'd found the aggressive noise and haste of New York a little overpowering. He frequently had found himself back in his hotel room relishing the comparative peace and quiet, happy to have the echoing wail of police sirens and the harsh rattle of urban noise muted to nothing more than a subdued rumble seeping through the double-glazed window.

New York these days felt like a town under siege. Every subway train and bus station was manned with cops checking IDs. Having olive skin, or even just having a dark beard, seemed to invite suspicious inspection from every passer-by.

It wasn't just New York. London was the same. Cities twinned by their paranoia, waiting for the next big bang.

Chris shook his head; it was becoming an ugly world, one waiting, spoiling for a fight. Those months away from it all, away from people, photographing terns and penguins, that had been a refreshing antidote. But on coming back from his months of solitude, the whole Muslim–Christian hate-thing seemed to have gotten worse. The news seemed to be fuelled by this alone these days.

He felt old. He certainly couldn't face doing another 'hot' assignment. A year ago he'd done some work in northern Iraq for *News Fortnite*, documenting the appalling and bloody tit-for-tat killings between the Kurds and the Sunnis that was still going on even now, years after the second Gulf war. A few years ago he might have been able to dispassionately shut out the worst of it on this kind of field job, but that last one had finally got to him.

From now on, he would be happy to stay away from the hazardous stop-and-drop assignments like that. It was going to have to be terns and penguins, or he was going to have to find a new way to earn a living. The world was becoming too ugly a thing to study through his viewfinder.

'So how long are you planning on staying out here?' asked Mark, disturbing Chris's woolgathering.

'I don't think we'll need to be too long here. I can probably do the shoot in one dive if the water's clear and we have a good day for the weather.'

'The water here's pretty cold this time of year. I'd say not far off zero degrees down below. It'll have to be a short dive, no more than thirty minutes tops. You think you can get all that you want in that time, Chris?'

'Well, if not, then we can do a second dive, I suppose.'

'It's been a while since we did any together. How are you with diving on wrecks? How many have you done?'

'Only one . . . that time with you in Florida. When was that? Two . . . three years ago?'

Mark looked a little unhappy. 'Okay, so tonight we'll go over the safety rules again. It seems like you could probably do with a refresher course. It's a dangerous type of diving, especially with all the added complications of a cold-water environment. But then you know all this, don't you?'

'That's why I hired you, mate. So you can do all the worrying and fussing.'

The last of the evening's light was fading quickly as they entered Port Lawrence and parked up near the wharf.

It was a small fishing town, with a population of five and a half thousand. On Fridays and Wednesdays it pulled in people from all over the county for the market, and in the summer, townies came from as far away as Boston and New York to enjoy the odd long weekend of provincial charm. Outside of the vacation seasons and market days, it was a ghost town.

There was plenty of space to park along the wharf, and Chris rolled the Cherokee up beside several delivery trucks facing the wharf's edge. He looked out of the windscreen at the row of trawlers tied up like horses outside a saloon bar.

Most of them were stripped down and tarped up for the winter. They would sit like that, not earning money for their owners for only a couple of months, the worst of the gale season, and be out on the sea again by the end of January.

The bigger boats headed out Nova Scotia way, towards the Grand Banks for trips that lasted four to six weeks. They were fifty- and sixty-foot Sword boats with crews of up to seven, which could sometimes bring in nearly sixteen tons of catch. They were mostly owned by cartels of investors, their skippers and crews on retainers and smaller shares.

The few smaller boats lined up were mostly independent operators that fished nearer home, boats that were owned or part-owned by their skippers and trawled only a few miles out from the coast, up and down the silt banks for only four or five days at a time. They couldn't afford two months tied up, and fished pretty much all year round.

Chris and Mark climbed out and surveyed the boats.

'I told you,' said Mark. 'You should have chartered from somewhere else. There's no way we're going to find a suitable boat down here.'

'Yeah, looks like you might be right,' Chris sighed reluctantly. He had gambled on finding a motor launch or a leisure boat. The place was a tourist town as well as a fishing port, after all.

It was going to have to be one of the smaller fishing boats. Halfway along the wharf he could see a single light mounted on the pilothouse of one of them.

'There, that would do us. And it looks like someone's home.'

Mark followed his gaze. 'It's a trawler, Chris, not some leisure cruiser. You'll be lucky if they'll take you out.'

'I'm sure the rustling of a little dosh will help some.'

'Dosh?' asked Mark. 'Money, right?'

Chris nodded.

Mark looked quizzically at him. 'Just how much money do you get paid for this kind of assignment anyway?'

Chris smiled. 'Enough, and then some . . . shall we go and charter us a trawler, then?' He headed across the diesel-stained concrete of the wharf towards the solitary light without waiting for an answer.

Mark watched him go. 'Enough and then some, eh?' he muttered, and then he found himself grinding his teeth. Chris could be an annoyingly cocky punk sometimes.

'Come on, mate.' Chris called back.

Chris approached the trawler's stern. 'What time do you make it?'

Mark pushed up a sleeve revealing a Rolex nesting in a luxuriant bed of dark forearm hair. 'Seven-thirty.'

Chris leaned over and rapped his knuckles against the hull. 'Hello? Anyone home?' he shouted. They heard some movement from inside the boat.

'Jeeeez, Chris! You know how rude that is?' Mark said.

'What? . . . knocking on the boat? It's not as if it's got a doorbell.'

'She's a "she" not an "it". All sea-going vessels are "shes", okay? You don't want to get the owner pissed before you start your shmoozing, huh?'

They heard the clunk of a bolt sliding, and a crack of light appeared on the foredeck as a hatch lifted a few inches. They could just make out the shine of a balding head framed by a thatch of grey whiskers.

'Yes?'

Chris absent-mindedly swung the torch on him.

'Hey! Get that goddamn thing out of my eyes!'

'Sorry,' he said sheepishly. He flicked it off.

'Whad'ya want?'

'Hi, we're looking to hire a boat for a day, maybe two days. Yours looks like it won't sink if we untie it.'

Chris's laugh quickly died in his throat as the old man stared at him in silence.

Mark shook his head in the dark. *Not the best start, Chris ol' buddy.*

The old man scowled and finally said something. 'Are you Canadian? 'Cause if you are, you can get the fuck away from my boat.'

'What? No! I'm English ... I just –'

'Shine that torch of yours on yourself, so I can see you.'

Chris fumbled with the switch, and then turned it on himself and Mark.

The man studied them for a few seconds. 'Yeah, you look English,' he said, pushing the hatch fully open and pulling himself with surprising agility out onto the foredeck.

Chris turned back to Mark. 'I *look* English? How the hell is an Englishman meant to look?' he muttered.

'You lack American cool,' Mark smirked.

'You boys want to hire this boat for a couple of days?' The old man interrupted, scratching his chin.

They both nodded.

'Of course we'll pay top dollar,' added Chris.

'You'd have to. This is a workin' boat. If she's busy takin' you boys out on a pleasure cruise, then she ain't workin', and that's gonna cost.'

Chris nodded gravely, 'I understand.'

The old man looked them over again. 'This'll be about the wreck out there, won't it?'

'The plane wreck, yeah,' Chris admitted reluctantly. He had hoped the story would still be relatively unknown, but, it seemed, Port Lawrence was a small town.

'So ... you boys don't look like tourists. Where you from?'

Chris pulled out a business card and handed it to the old man. 'I work for a magazine. I want to photograph the plane. I'm doing a story on it. The name's Chris by the way.' He gestured at Mark. 'This guy's Mark. He's a diving instructor and he's here to hold my hand when we go underwater.'

For a moment he wasn't sure whether the old man was going to take that literally.

The old man appeared mildly impressed with the press card. 'What magazine? Not the *Enquirer*, I hope. I can't stand that kind of rubbish.'

'God, no! ... I work for *News Fortnite*, it's a bit like the *National Geo –*'

The old man snapped his fingers, 'I know it. I got some of those.' He looked at Chris for the first time with an expression one step up from contempt. 'Do the pictures, huh?'

'Some of them.'

'Good pictures in the *Fortnite*.'

'Thanks.'

'The name's Will by the way.'

Mark and Chris nodded. 'Hi, Will.'

The old man studied Chris silently. The tall, thin English guy with the toothbrush hair seemed good for easy money. His type always seemed to have it. His boat, *Mona Lisa*, was booked in to Winston Macies Marine to have her refrigeration storage units overhauled soon for the first time in nearly ten years and that would take a week or more and cost a small fortune. He could really do with some extra greenbacks to cover that.

'So?' said Chris.

Will donned an expression of painful reluctance. 'Well, now. On the subject of hirin'. The *Lisa* here is a fishin' vessel see ... shrimps, herring, some cod when we can find it. That's what we catch round here. We go out in the mornin' and return late. Sometimes we'll stay out overnight. I can't take you out tomorrow, because I got men who work on this boat for the share they get on the sale of the catch. So they can't afford to miss a day's work. If you want to hire this boat ... it's gonna have to be at night.'

Chris turned to Mark and spoke quietly. 'At night, are we okay with that?'

'No difference really. It's virtually night seventy-five feet down anyway. The question is, are you going to be comfortable with doing that?'

Chris took a long look up and down the wharf. There really wasn't a great deal of choice in the matter.

'Sure. If you're happy it's okay and safe, I guess I am. You're the pro here,' he replied.

'You sure you don't want to look around? Maybe go find a proper chartering agency?' asked Mark.

'Hmmm, that's going to cost a shit load more dosh.'

'Yes. Your call, Chris.'

Will watched the two men talking quietly. He decided they needed a little extra nudge.

'You'll find it's the same with any of the other workin' boats in this area . . . 'cept I'm ready to sail.'

He smiled for the first time and added, '*And* I can give you the full ten-cents tour. A little local history, a few stories, eh?'

'Okay. How much?'

'Five hundred dollars should just about cover it.'

'Five hundred!'

'You gonna' tell me how much you're gettin' paid to take them pictures? I bet it's a lot more 'an five hundred. That's the price . . . an' if I hear back from some other skipper that they offered you cheaper, well, more fool them.'

Chris looked up and down the wharf. There really was only Will's boat that looked good to go.

'Looks like a seller's market. I don't think you're going to be able to haggle him down any,' said Mark under his breath.

Chris turned back to Will. 'Four hundred and you got a deal.'

The old man waved at Chris. 'Been nice talkin' to you.' He headed back towards the hatch on the foredeck.

'Bollocks,' Chris muttered. 'Five hundred, then.'

Will turned back round to face them. 'I'll take that in bills, if you don't mind. We don't do American Express round here.'

'Cash? Yeah, I guess I can do that. So what time can you set off tomorrow night? I'm pretty keen to get over and see the –'

'Settin' off *tonight* sound good to you boys?'

Chris and Mark exchanged glances. 'Sure.'

'Be back here at nine o'clock then, and bring my five hundred dollars.' Will winked at Chris. 'Pleasure doin' business with you.'

Chapter 3

Heading Out

At nine-thirty the trawler finally chugged noisily away from the wharf and passed Leonard's Spur, a small rocky island about an acre in size and linked to the mainland by a sandy spit. A single flashing beacon on a tall metal spire marked it out.

Will hugged the channel tightly and passed close by the wet rocks of the spur that seemed to twitch and move with the pulsing flicker of the beacon's light.

Chris watched Port Lawrence slowly recede, shuddering at the thought of the freezing dive ahead of him. He looked at his watch.

Say, forty-five minutes out to the buoy marking the wreck, half an hour underwater and forty-five minutes back.

He'd be soaking in a warm soapy bath in a little more than two hours' time. Of course, it was never that easy. It would probably take a little longer to get out there, the dive might only take half an hour, but Mark would insist on a thorough equipment audit before and after. And then there was the task of checking the quality was there on film: process a contact sheet and print one or two of the shots large, and if he hadn't got the shots he was after, they'd have to go out and do it all again.

One thing was for sure; when they got back later he was definitely going to have a bath. He was glad they'd ended up checking into the motel up at the pricey end of Devenster Street. It was a little more, and he was paying out on Mark's room too, of course, but it was better than the couple of guesthouses they'd sneaked a look at. One of them only had one shared bathroom between ten guest rooms, whilst the other could offer only one room with its own shower, and that had looked pretty shabby.

Chris watched Mark on the aft deck. He was already at it, unpacking and checking the diving gear. He worked with a quick, silent efficiency, laying out the apparatus carefully in a deliberate order and fitting together the regulators and tanks with a precision that reminded him of a marine assembling his trusty M15.

'Just like those ol' navy SEAL days, uh?' joked Chris.

Mark carried on oblivious, focused on the pre-dive drill.

Chris watched him for a while longer before making his way forward to the pilothouse. It was dimly lit by a single bare bulb in a wire cage that rattled with the vibration of the engine. Will had the helm in one hand and held a mug of something hot in the other. Ahead through the window he could see the foredeck brilliantly lit by a searchlight on the roof of the pilothouse. It cast a thick beam into the night ahead of them picking out the white suds on the water.

'Hi,' said Chris. 'I assume you know which way the buoy is?'

Will turned and scowled at him. 'I been fishin' these waters for nearly thirty years. I know every nook and spit along this shoreline for twenty miles either way –'

Oh boy, I've hit this guy's squawk button.

'– I can tell you. Hell, I could even tell you how far our from shore we are right now just by listening to the rhythm of the water.'

Will slapped the engine into neutral and turned it off. The boat drifted silently for a while.

Chris was a little bemused. 'Uh . . . are you going to turn that back on now?'

'Shhhhh . . . Just listen to that, do you hear it?'

Chris could hear nothing but the sound of Mark outside working on the aft deck and the gentle slapping of water on the hull. He saw Mark stand up and come forward to the pilothouse. He opened the door and stuck his head in. 'What's going on? Why's the engine gone off?'

Chris shook his head and shrugged. 'I think Captain Salty's listening to the water,' he said quietly.

'You hear that?' Will said eventually, 'you can tell by the ditty she sings just how far out you are. I reckon we're about a half mile out.'

Chris was impressed. 'You can tell that just from the lapping sound? Sheeez, that's pretty cool . . .'

Will smirked and shook his head; he turned the engine back on and slammed her back into gear. 'Of course, it helps if you got one of these little babies.' The old man pointed to a small digital Nav-Sat display beside the helm and snorted with laughter.

'Oh, I see. Very funny.'

Mark slapped Chris on the shoulder. 'Reckon he got you a good one there, buddy.' He headed back outside to the aft deck and resumed checking the gear.

A little after ten o'clock, Will dropped the engine into neutral and panned the searchlight over the still water until he spotted the buoy that marked the wreck. He brought the boat slowly over towards it and let it run the last few yards on momentum only as he left the pilothouse and leaned over the side to scoop up the buoy with a gaff and bring it aboard. He tied it off on a cleat, wrapping it round in a figure of eight and a half hitch for good measure.

'Here you are, boys, delivered safe and sound.'

Will had been quick finding the buoy; it had only taken them half an hour. A straight beeline out from Port Lawrence, Chris guessed they were about five miles out.

Chris and Mark sat on the aft deck in the neoprene dry suits Mark had brought along. Chris winced as he adjusted the tight-fitting rubber; it was pulling on his leg hairs.

'Christ Mark, it's like going for the world's worst waxing.'

'How would *you* know?'

'Ah well, you know what it's like, gotta keep the bikini line nice 'n'tidy.'

Mark snorted, typical Chris. The guy would last about five minutes with the sorts of ex-navy jocks he spent a lot of his time with, before being branded a faggot, or a geek, or maybe he would just get off being branded 'weird English guy'. Mark liked that about him, though, you got a little bit more than just locker-room humour out of him.

'These are smart,' Chris said picking up one of the diving helmets.

'Yeah, I thought you'd like these, rather than the usual. This way we can talk to each other instead of sign. I think this'll be better for you. If you lose sight of me you'll still be able to at least hear me.'

'Not planning on deserting me down there, are you?'

'Don't worry. I'll be on your back all the time, watching you do your thing.' Mark gestured towards Chris's underwater camera.

Will finished up in the pilothouse and joined the two men on the aft deck.

'You got a lot of expensive-looking toys there,' he said.

Mark absent-mindedly rested a defensive hand on one of the helmets. 'Yes, some of this stuff is pretty expensive.'

'How much are those funny-lookin' space hats, then?'

'The best part of five thousand dollars each,' said Mark.

The old man pursed his lips in surprise. 'Lotta money for a goldfish bowl.'

'Hang on, that reminds me,' said Mark, ignoring the jibe and delving into one of his canvas kit bags. A moment later produced a small black box and handed it to Will.

'Oh, you shouldn't have, it's lovely,' the old man said sarcastically. 'What is it?'

'Radio receiver. It's just for safety. You can listen in on us talking. This way, if something does go wrong, you'll be ready when we surface,' he said. Chris looked up anxiously. 'Just a precaution,' Mark added.

Will turned the black box over in his hands. 'How does this damn thing work?'

'It's just a receiver. Switch it on at the back,' said Mark. Will did so and grimaced as he was met with a warbling shriek.

'Damn thing's broken.'

'No it's not. It just needs to be tuned in. Give it to me.'

Will passed it back to Mark. 'So, this plane you're goin' down to see . . . old wartime bomber, eh?'

Chris nodded. 'One of your B-17s.'

'You reckon on findin' any of the crew?'

'Don't know the story yet, whether the crew bailed out or went down with it.'

Will nodded. 'Well if you do find them, treat them with a bit of respect, eh? The waters here have claimed a lot of souls. Ain't just your plane down there. There's a lot of older wrecks, sailing ships and the like.'

'Uh-huh, we'll be respectful, Will, okay?'

'They say when a squall whips up, it's the dead below reminding the living to tread careful.'

Chris looked at Mark and gave him a discreet wink.

'Look, Will, uh . . . you've caught me out once already with the ol' salty sea dog routine –'

The old man glanced sternly at him. 'I don't joke much about dyin' at sea. There's many a bad story from this stretch of water, without me making stuff up to add to it.'

They were preparing to go down to the graveside of some poor souls, and despite the photographer's assurances, they were going to disturb it, poke it and prod it. He was uneasy. It felt a little too much like grave-robbing.

'Let me tell you something that happened out here.'

Chris looked up at Mark, who was smiling.

Here comes the ten-cents tour.

'– there was a ship come over from England, this is way back ... eighteen hundred an' something, back when England was as tainted with the slave trade as we were. This ship was called the *Lady Grey*; she was due for Charleston, but winds had blown her up north a ways.'

'She was carryin' a few dozen payin' passengers and two or three hundred negro slaves. She hit ice comin' in. She was only half a day's sailin' from shore. They had a small hole, but water was comin' in faster than they could bail it out. She was goin' down all right, but slowly. Still, they got within a mile from shore when they decided to call it a day and abandon ship. The crew, the payin' passengers, even pretty much most of the more expensive items of cargo, were ferried in row boats from the sinkin' *Lady Grey* to the shore. All the while she's slowly goin' under.

'People from Port Lawrence gathered on the beach kind'a helpin' out, maybe even helpin' themselves to a few choice things. This ferryin' went on for the best part of the day, and all the while you could hear it from the shore, the hammerin' of hundreds of palms against the inside of her wooden hull, and hundreds of voices wailin' and screamin' to be let out. Finally the question is asked of the captain, "What about them negro slaves locked up below decks?" He says, "Leave 'em. The condition they're in, them negroes would be worth more on shippin' insurance than sold at a slave market." He says the valuable cargo's already been saved. People up here hadn't much to do with negroes back then, many had never even seen one. They were pretty shocked at the captain's answer.

'That evening, the *Lady Grey* finally lists to one side and quickly then she jus' slides under. All the while the people on the beach could hear the hammerin' and screamin'. The story goes, you could still hear them slaves for a while after she'd gone down.'

The old man struck a match and lit his cigarette.

'I presume there's some hackneyed moral to that tale?' said Chris, a little uneasily.

'They say them slaves are still down there screamin'. When folks go missing at sea round these parts, they say "the slaves have got 'em".'

Chris nodded sincerely. 'Right, okay . . . I'll keep my eyes peeled for them, then.'

'You hear that distant hammerin' and screamin' and you're in big trouble, boys.'

'If I hear hammering and screaming down there, trust me, Will, I'll be back in this boat and halfway home before you can say scooby-doobie-doo,' said Chris, smiling nervously.

Mark shook his head. 'No you won't, you'll be spending five minutes decompressing with me on the way up. Then you can run away.'

Chris nodded at Mark. He was right, and now wasn't the time to be goofing around.

Will smiled, perhaps reassured that his little story had sobered things up some. 'You enjoy your dive, boys. And mind you treat that wreck with the respect it deserves.' He headed back towards the pilothouse and poured himself a steaming mug of something from a thermos flask stashed beside the helm.

Chris shivered. 'He could have offered us one, the tight git.'

'I guess that would cost extra.'

'Yup. On that note, care for a swim?'

Mark pulled his helmet on and twisted it until it locked with a reassuring clunk. Chris did the same.

'You hear me okay?' Mark's voice sounded tinny over the helmet speaker. Chris gave a thumbs-up.

'You can talk, you idiot.'

'Oh yeah, I forgot. Okay Mark, you can take point.'

Mark rolled off the stern of the trawler and splashed into the Atlantic.

'Here goes,' said Chris as he followed suit and disappeared into the ink black water, leaving behind a circle of splash suds that were quickly washed away.

Will turned off the floodlight that bathed the aft deck and turned on a fan heater and his FM radio. It was tuned to a station that played classical. The soothing melody of *Cavalleria Rusticana* quickly eased away some of his misgivings as he watched the faint glow of submerged torchlight slowly recede.

Chapter 4

The Wreck

The reinforced-plastic diving helmet felt infinitely less claustrophobic and uncomfortable than a regular diving mask and regulator. They were Mark's latest equipment purchase, his pride and joy.

It's like being an astronaut, going EVA.

Chris looked around. He was immersed in total darkness. Above him there were only a couple of flickering shards of light from the trawler. Suddenly a strong blue shaft of light cut the world in two in front of him as Mark aimed his torch upwards.

'You might want to turn your torch on,' Mark's voice hissed out of the speaker. Chris fumbled for the switch on his torch and found it.

'Whoa, that's bright,' he said, panning it around, admiring the power and length of the light beam.

'Two hundred-watt halogen bulbs,' said Mark proudly. 'Only got about forty minutes charge time on the battery pack, though.'

Mark shone his torch at the buoy's line.

'Okay. We're going to follow that down.' He kicked his legs out and began to swim down, holding the line in one hand and torch in the other. Chris followed suit, keeping an eye on the dwindling beam of Mark's torch below.

'Not so fast, mate,' he said with an edge in his voice. 'You're leaving me behind.'

'Relax, I'm just down here. You can see my torch, can't you?'

'Yup.'

Chris kicked his legs and pulled himself down the buoy's line. Mark was waiting for him, treading water.

'See? I'm here. Stay calm, okay? Things go wrong only when you lose your cool and start getting worked up. We've got half an hour, remember. So we haven't got a lot of time.' He checked his depth gauge. They were thirty feet down. 'It's seventy-five feet down, you said? We should see it soon.'

Mark resumed swimming downward with slow strong strokes. Chris followed, struggling to keep up and breathing harshly with the exertion. For a few moments all that he could hear over the helmet speaker was the even, relaxed, rhythmic breathing of his partner. It was strangely soothing, like a heartbeat or the ticking of a clock.

'Ahh here we go . . . I think I see something down there.'

Chris pushed hard with his legs and a moment later he was floating alongside Mark. Below, their two torch beams picked out the unmistakable oval silhouette of a wing tip. The beams worked their way along the wing, passing over the bulge of an engine casing, then another, and finally coming to rest on the cylindrical form of the plane's fuselage.

Chris turned to Mark. 'Bingo.'

They swam down the last few feet and settled with a gentle bump on the wing. Chris reached out and ran a hand along its surface. Only a slippery coat of algae covered the sheet metal. It belied the years underwater. His fingers danced over rivets that had experienced only a small amount of corrosion.

'Isn't it bloody beautiful?'

'Amazing. This is a *big* plane,' said Mark.

'It's a B-17, nicknamed the Flying Fortress. Looks in fantastic shape.'

Mark studied the ghostly grey giant. 'Yup, it is. But then it's a cold, low-salt water environment.'

'No, I don't mean corrosion, or marine growth. I mean there's hardly any impact damage. It's like it was just gently placed here.'

Chris pulled out his camera and took a couple of shots. The flash on the camera flickered like a strobe. He swam along the wing towards the inner port engine.

'Look at that,' he gestured towards the propeller.

'What am I looking at?'

'The propeller blades are intact. Do you know what that means?'

Mark shook his head. 'Not really.'

'It means this particular propeller wasn't spinning when she touched down on the ocean. If it had been the blades would be bent to buggery.'

'Oh.' Mark watched as Chris photographed the engine and the prop. He checked his watch; they had been down five minutes. Twenty-five left.

Chris swam back to the fuselage and slowly drifted down the side towards the rear. His torch eventually picked out the barrel and small opening of the portside waist-gun.

'Come and look at this!'

Mark followed the glaring beam of Chris's torch and found himself staring at a long line of bullet holes that ran diagonally up the fuselage side towards the waist-gun's porthole.

'Looks like she's seen some action. Maybe that's why she ditched?'

Chris shook his head. 'That would make some sense off the coast of France or England.' He looked at Mark, 'but off the coast of Rhode Island?'

Chris took a couple of shots of the bullet holes and the waist-gun and then pulled himself closer to the opening and shone his torch inside it. He could see little past the corroded barrel of the old machine gun.

'I want to find a way in.'

Mark looked at his watch. 'We've used six minutes. Twenty-four left. If we find a way inside, we give ourselves a clear ten minutes to find our way out. Okay? That means you get fourteen minutes from now to do all the inside stuff you want, and that's all.'

'Okay, Mom. Listen . . . you work your way to the back of the plane and I'll work my way to the front. There's bound to be some hatch we can prise open to get a look inside.'

'No way. I'm not leaving you on your own. You're paying me to –'

'Mark, I appreciate you're looking out for me, but time is limited, I've got to get a shot inside . . . okay?'

Mark wasn't convinced.

'Please, I promise I won't go inside without you, we're just looking for a way in, that's all.'

'You'll be okay, if we lose visual?'

'Yeah . . . I'm getting braver.'

'That's what's worrying me.'

Mark headed aft, one hand dragging along the rough metal of the fuselage for guidance, the other panning his torch up and down in search of an opening. Chris headed the other way, towards the front of the plane.

It didn't take him long before he came across the plexiglas canopy of the cockpit. He shone his torch across the panels hoping to catch a glimpse of the inside, but they too were coated in a thin layer of algae.

Swimming down, he found the front end of the plane was raised enough to swim underneath her belly. And then he found what he was looking for.

'Mark! I've found a way in.'

'What have you got?'

'It's a hatch leading up into the cockpit. It's open. I'm going to stick my head up inside.'

'Be careful! I don't want you knocking that equipment, or even worse, puncturing your tank. No squeezing through anything, okay?'

'Okay . . . okay, no squeezing.'

Chris shone his torch up through the belly hatch into what looked like the bomb-aimer's observation blister. The torch beam slid across the plexiglas panels and metal struts of the canopy, throwing them into sharp relief and sending phantom shadows dancing across the confined space. He could see a short ladder leading up from the blister into another area above.

The cockpit?

Chris studied the width of the hatch and decided it was wide enough to climb through. With a tug on the hatch rim he pulled himself up. His helmet thudded noisily against a cross strut inside. 'Shit!'

'What's up?'

'Nothing, I'm fine.'

'I'm *fzffzf*ing forward.' Mark's transmission crackled. Chris silently mouthed a curse. He must have given the radio a knock. There'd be a lecture coming his way when they went topside, and Mark discovered the damage.

Great.

He shone his torch down inside the fuselage. There was a bulkhead six feet back and a narrow doorway. The light picked out a cloud of floating debris hanging in the space between the blister and the bulkhead. Shreds of paper, a pair of headphones, several life jackets.

'Some of this stuff looks like it could have been left here a couple of days ago.'

'Yeah? I'll be ther . . . a second.' Mark's signal was getting worse.

Chris took another couple of shots and then reached out for the short ladder leading up to what he guessed must be the cockpit. He studied the size of the opening, it was narrower, but still just wide enough to get through. Chris, much more carefully this time, pulled himself up through the opening. He heard his air cylinder scrape noisily against the edge of the hatchway and cringed at the thought of the scratches it would leave.

Mark was going to kill him.

He shone his torch around inside the cockpit. There was a lot less space than he'd imagined, and he found himself bumping and scraping on all sides. His torch panned up and across the co-pilot's seat.

He lurched backwards. 'Oh Jesus!'

'What . . . it?' he heard Mark call.

He took a few deep breaths to steady himself and then trained his torch back on the seat.

'I . . . uh . . . think I've found one of the crew,' he said pulling himself closer to get a better look.

The skeletal remains, long since stripped of soft organic material save for a few fibrous strands, seemed to be held together and in place by the body's clothes and the seat's harness. It was all there, a complete human form except for one of its hands. Chris spotted a leather flying glove on the cockpit floor. He picked it up delicately by a fingertip and a cloud of organic mush floated gently out, followed by a cluster of small white bones that see-sawed down through the water and settled on the grey, silt covered floor.

It looked like the remains of a KFC dinner. Chris felt his stomach churn ever so slightly at that thought.

He heard his helmet speaker crackle. '. . . found?'

Chris tapped the radio casing with his torch. It crackled and hissed in response.

'Mark? Can you hear me? I've found one of the crew.'

'Jeeeez, glad you found him and not me.' Mark was coming through clearly now.

Must be a loose wire, then.

'Yeah,' he replied. 'He's not a pretty boy. I'm going to grab a couple of shots.'

'Okay. I'm coming up over the other side of the fuselage. I can't see any tears or breaks or any way to get in. How do I . . . in up there?'

'Hatchway right under the nose.'

'Okay, see . . . in a second.' The signal was breaking up again.

Chris continued to study the corpse. He was amazed at how intact the clothing and equipment was. The only concession to sixty years of undisturbed submersion was a thin coat of grey sediment that seemed to have settled on everything. The leather flying cap still rested dutifully on the body's skull, a solitary tuft of pale blond hair poking out from beneath it, and its radio mouthpiece dangled from the end of a short length of coiled rubber flex beside the lower jaw of the skull. The jawbone had at some point fallen away and now rested on the collar of the thick, fur-lined flying jacket.

Chris reached out slowly for the jawbone, careful not to disturb too much of the sediment. Hc lifted it up and placed it back as it should be and then pulled the radio mouthpiece in underneath to hold it in place.

He felt a passing twinge of guilt for messing with the body. But, it *did* make for a better picture, having the skull and jaw reunited again. Without the jaw it simply wasn't a face. Chris had learned from freelancing in several war zones in the last ten years that you needed to have a face in the shot when photographing a body. People always look for it, look for an expression on it. Perhaps as a way of understanding what death must be like, what emotion is drawn at the moment it occurs.

Without a face, a body is just a bundle of clothes.

Chris unhooked his camera and aimed it at the long-dead pilot.

'Say cheese.' The flashlight of the camera strobed again as he hit off a few shots.

He heard Mark's voice. 'I can li . . . out seeing the . . .' The popping and whistling on the helmet speaker was driving him mad. He tapped the radio housing.

'What's that, Mark? Your signal's breaking up again.'

He tapped it again, this time much harder, hoping his big-mallet repair philosophy would deliver the goods. The low-frequency, almost inaudible buzzing that had been constant since locking the helmet down and turning on the speaker suddenly stopped. The only sound he could hear now was his own breathing reverberating inside the plastic bowl of the helmet.

'Mark? Can you hear me?'

Nothing.

It's not just a loose wire now, you muppet; you've broken the bloody thing.

Mark was going to be pissed at him for that. He decided he'd offer the guy money to replace it. He could afford it.

He turned back towards the body of the co-pilot and took a few more shots. The camera flash strobed again, throwing a blinding white light at its fleshless face. He half expected the skeleton to angrily reach out with its one remaining hand and snatch the camera from him.

Professional guilt. Ignore it and finish the job.

Movement.

An eel shot out through the opening in the bulkhead; a silvery streak headed straight towards his face and thumped against the glass plate of his helmet. Chris, startled, dropped both the camera and his torch. The torch landed face down in the silt. The light inside the cockpit was suddenly gone, leaving it in absolute darkness. He could sense the eel thrashing around in the cockpit with him, disturbed currents of water, disturbed sediment floating once again.

'Shitshitshitshitshit!'

Chris felt himself beginning to panic. The damn thing was going crazy. He felt its long and strong body bump against him several times, each time anticipating the needle-sharp teeth slicing through the neoprene of his dry suit and into his flesh. It passed between his legs, and then with no warning he felt it clunk against the glass of his helmet again.

A hard clunk, not a soft thump. That was the sound of a tooth hitting the glass.

And then suddenly it was gone.

Chris could feel the water around him quickly growing still once more. He waited for the eel to return, to renew its attack on him. Seconds passed.

It was gone.

He bent down carefully and let his hands fumble along the floor, desperately seeking the torch.

'Mark? I'm in trouble. Mark?' He heard his voice beginning to break. It scared him even more.

In absolute darkness, in this cockpit with a ridged floor and all manner of debris and silt sitting on it, he was not going to find his torch by touch. That simply wasn't going to happen.

'Oh shitshitshit,' Chris found himself muttering.

Mark's coming, should be here any second. For fuck's sake calm down.

A faint light turned the world outside the plexiglas cockpit from black to a deep blue. It flickered brighter and darker, but over time it was growing steadily stronger.

Chris sucked in a big breath and puffed out a sigh of relief.

He saw a dark form through the algae-fogged glass of the cockpit. It was treading water outside. No doubt Mark was calling for him on the radio and probably getting worried that he wasn't receiving an answer.

Chris found himself smiling with relief. The cavalry was here.

Bless you, Mark.

He could see Mark's foggy form moving across the cockpit plexiglas, the torch came up and he shone it into the cockpit. The bright halogen beam shone into his face. Chris gestured for Mark to aim it down to the floor of the cockpit, hoping he would be seen through the thin film of scum on the plexiglas.

The beam changed direction and tilted downwards.

Immediately Chris could see the outline of his torch and the camera. He reached down and picked them both up.

But his eye was drawn to movement ahead of him.

The light from Mark's torch shone through the bulkhead into the radio operator's booth and beyond down the inside of the fuselage to the waist-gun stations. Manning these positions, silently looking through their gun sights, stood two ghostly young men in flying leathers. They remained motionless, squinting into the darkness awaiting the inevitable swarm of enemy fighters.

My God!

One of them turns towards Chris as if finally aware that he is being watched. He nods.

And that was the last thing he clearly recalled. The rest was a jumble, Mark entering the cabin and pulling him out, the slow ascent, the short pause for decompression halfway up . . . and him babbling away to Mark about ghosts in the machine.

Will begrudgingly handed him a mug of coffee. 'There you are. This'll help.'

Chris took it gratefully and held it in both hands savouring the warmth seeping through the chipped enamel to his fingers. 'Thanks.'

Mark was already out of his dry suit and back in his clothes and starting to pack away the diving helmet. 'How are you feeling now?' he said.

'Like a bloody moron,' replied Chris.

'You were saying all kinds of strange stuff coming up.'

'Yup, rambling like a fool no doubt.'

Mark smiled. 'Kind of.'

'Nitrogen narcosis . . . I know, I know.'

'Yeah. You were all over the place when I pulled you out. What got you so worked up?'

Chris looked guiltily at Will. 'I was taking some shots in the cockpit and I guess the flash must've spooked an eel or something similar. It knocked me for six on the way out. I lost the torch and the camera, and I suppose that's when I started losing it.'

'Yes, you sure did. You gave me a pretty nasty scare back there.'

'I was sitting in the dark, no radio contact. I lost it . . . you know, panicked.' Chris shook his head, angry with himself.

'Don't beat yourself up over it.'

He looked up at Mark. 'Thanks for coming in and getting me. That was nasty back there, it really shook me up.'

'No sweat. Diving on wrecks, those confined spaces . . . shit like this happens. It's easy to get rattled when you're boxed in.'

Will was ready to start up the engine and take the *Mona Lisa* back to Port Lawrence. 'You boy scouts done for the night?'

Mark answered before Chris could get a word in. 'Yeah . . . No more diving for us tonight.'

Chapter 5

Missing in Action

Chris looked out of the window of the coffee shop. It was pouring down, and the wind was gusting. The rain smacked angrily against the glass as if frustrated at the missed opportunity to soak him and the two other solitary patrons inside.

Real Brit weather, that's what Elaine would say.

Chris smiled; she wasn't wrong. There was many a day as a child he'd been taken down to Southend-on-Sea for a fun-filled bank holiday at the beach only to spend it in a greasy café looking out at the rain and sipping tepid tea.

Same deal today, only it was tepid coffee.

Chris checked the time, it was nearly half-nine in the morning. Time to get to work.

He pulled out several prints he had made first thing this morning; an image of the engine casing and the propeller, an image of the waist-gun port and the bullet holes stitched diagonally across it, an image of the nose of the bomber and the plexiglas canopy to the cockpit and the observer's blister.

And the plane's ident.

Chris squinted. It wasn't as clear as he had hoped and he held the glossy paper closer to his face as he tried to make it out. It was a picture of a near-naked lady, smiling wickedly with an arm coyly covering ample breasts. Her hair looked like dreadlocks.

Dreadlocks?

Below the image, faint and peeling, a single word that made sense of the woman, her improbable hair and the mischievous, impish face.

Medusa.

Below that, stencilled in formal USAAF style, were three letters. Chris noted them down on a napkin and then dialled a number he'd pulled off the Internet a couple of days earlier.

A woman answered.

'Hi,' said Chris quickly adopting a more authoritative BBC accent. 'I wonder if you can help me? I'm making a documentary on the United States Air Force based in England during the war. It's really a programme that follows the fortunes of the crews of several planes, you know? How they coped with the war, their personal experiences of it. That kind of thing. Are you with me?'

'So far,' the female voice replied.

'I need a little information on the identity marker of a particular plane. Where it served, which squadron it was in, who its crew were . . . can you help me with this kind of infor—?'

'I'll put you through to the Crew Reunion Helpline.'

Chris shrugged. The old BBC documentary ruse wasn't necessary, then.

'Crew Reunion Helpline, what's your Regimental Designation?' said another female operator.

'My what?'

'Regimental Designation.'

'Would that be the letters on the plane?' asked Chris hopefully.

'Yes.'

'The letters are L, then beneath that GS.'

'Okay . . . just a second . . .'

Chris could hear the clacking sound of fingernails on a keyboard and in the background the sound of other voices and phones bleeping.

'You get a lot of calls like this?' asked Chris casually.

No answer. Obviously not part of the script.

'Hello. The L denotes the 381st Bomber Group. The GS was the squadron identification code for the regiment. GS was Squadron 535. They were stationed in England from April 1943 to January 1945 and then in Germany until the squadron was disbanded in 1947. What was the plane's name?'

'Do you mean the nickname?'

'Yes sir, the nickname.'

'Medusa.'

'Medusa? Like the snake lady?'

'That's it.'

Chris heard the clacking sound of nails against plastic keys again. A pause. Then something else being typed. Another wait. Chris thanked God they hadn't modernised their switchboard to employ an 'on hold' musak system.

'Oh,' said the female voice.

'What's the problem?'

'Not a problem, sir . . . it's just never happened before. That record is flagged. I'll need to talk to the supervisor. Can you hold?'

'Yeah, okay.'

The line went silent. Chris looked out of the window again. The rain was easing off slightly but still coming down enough to drench him if he was going to have to walk back down the coast road to Port Lawrence. Mark had borrowed the Cherokee. He'd wanted to take the damaged helmet radio downtown to find a Tandy or a Radio Shack. He was convinced it would be a quick and easy fix, although when he was due back was anyone's guess. 'Downtown' was twenty miles away.

There was a click, the call was being transferred.

'Hello? I believe you were enquiring about a plane serving with the 381st called *Medusa*?' A male voice.

Chris confirmed the name.

'I'm sorry about the confusion,' he sounded flustered. Like somebody unaccustomed to this kind of conversation. 'The records show this plane went missing in a raid over Hamburg in 1944.'

'Missing over Hamburg?'

'Yes. Hamburg, Germany.'

Thanks for that.

'The plane crashed?' Chris asked, lowering his voice.

'Probably sir. Most MIAs were assumed to be crashes.'

'So she wasn't recovered?'

'Well, no, of course she wasn't. Like I say, the records simply list the plane as missing.'

'What about her crew? Were there any survivors?'

'The records show that all nine of them were also reported as MIA.'

'None resurfaced after the war as POWs?'

'I'm sorry sir; all I can give you is what is printed here. We can send you a copy of the records we have for a nominal fee of ten dollars. Would you like to give me your name and address?'

'Uh? . . . no don't bother.' All of a sudden he felt the urge to end the call very quickly.

'Can I ask *why* you're enquiring about this plane?' the man on the end of the phone asked.

Chris hung up. Almost immediately he wished he'd attempted to slide out of that conversation in a casual, easy manner, rather than panicking as he had. Even more so, he wished he'd thought to withhold his number before dialling in. It left him feeling jumpy.

Coffee.

It's one of those things that become increasingly insipid the more you have of it. The first mouthful of the first cup of coffee of the day was always sublime, after that it all goes downhill. Chris curled his lip at the bitter-sweetness of his fifth since lunchtime. It was black to boot, which didn't help. He'd exhausted the supply of cream cartons from the guest room's wicker basket of courtesy refreshments, but the coffee and the sachets of sweetener were still going strong.

He turned out the light on the bedside cabinet and carried his mug across the room in total darkness to the bathroom. He pulled open the bathroom door and entered the crimson twilight of yet another impromptu developing booth. The sink was an inch deep with developing fluid and on the floor in a shallow plastic tray was some fixative. Strung across the bathroom, dangling from a length of twine like an unlikely laundry line hung photographs of the B-17. Chris ducked underneath it on the way to the sink, and placed his mug of coffee on a toiletry shelf above. He pulled out several sheets of photographic paper that had been exposed to the negatives he'd selected to print.

Chris was pretty sure that *News Fortnite* would pass on these prints of the co-pilot; they were too grim for their regular readers.

He slid the sheets of photographic paper into the sink and gently separated them in the fluid. Silently he counted to sixty as the sheets of paper slowly darkened and form and definition emerged from the white.

The first shapes to make sense were the symmetrical round black holes of the co-pilot's eye sockets. Chris watched as the detail slowly emerged. A row of vertical lines that slowly became teeth, the lower jaw slightly askew where Chris had placed it last night.

The second sheet of paper revealed an image of the body taken from further away, showing off some of the cockpit, the steering yoke and the plexiglas canopy. It was a better composition in his opinion. It helped tell more of a story, placed the body within a context, grounded it within a simple visual narrative.

But it was the third sheet of photographic paper that really caught Chris's eye.

Mark was sitting on the bed fiddling with a soldering iron and the guts of the damaged helmet radio housing when Chris entered his motel room unannounced.

'Fancy going for a beer?'

Mark jerked, and a blob of solder missed its target. 'Jeez, don't you knock?'

Chris looked suitably apologetic. 'Sorry. What are you up to?'

'I'm just trying to work out where the loose connection is on this damn radio. It's definitely a loose wire.'

Mark picked up the carbon-fibre casing for the radio and turned it towards Chris so he could clearly see the nasty gouge.

'Are you sure you didn't bang it on anything last night?'

'All right, already, maybe I might have accidentally clumped it on the way inside the plane. Listen, I'll pay for the damage, okay? It's the least I can do. Come on, let's go get a pint and I'll buy some dinner too, since it's getting on for supper time.'

'A "pint" eh? Why not?'

'And I want to show you something ... I want a second opinion.'

Mark looked intrigued. 'What is it?'

Chris smiled. 'First, beer.'

It was actually a lot more pleasant inside than it promised to be from the outside. 'Lenny's' was an old converted shutterboard boathouse, just down the street from the motel they were staying in. At some time in the past its timber walls had received a cheerful coating of sunflower-yellow, but the paint had flaked off in many places, exposing wood so old it could tell a story or two. A single flickering neon sign fizzed over the doorway asserting that the hut was a 'Bar & Grill'.

Inside, Mark and Chris could have been in any sports bar, in any town, in any state. A juke box, a pool table and carved wooden Indian standing guard outside the toilets. Nothing changes, thought Chris. Hell, there were faux American sports bars in every new town, in every county in England. Which was even worse. Sports bars populated by spotty young Essex boys pretending to be American.

A TV in the corner above the bar was showing some football. Chris was no big NFL fan, but Mark was.

'Good choice. You want to sit up at the bar?'

Chris shook his head. 'Nah, not my sport.'

Mark laughed. 'I forget, soccer's your game, isn't it?'

Chris shook his head wearily. 'It's known as "football" around the rest of the world. Anyway, listen, I want to show you something.'

'You can show me up at the bar, can't you?'

'Discreetly, if you don't mind.'

Mark nodded. 'Oh, okay. I'll go find us somewhere comfortable and you can buy me that beer and dinner, then.'

Chris went up to the bar and ordered a couple of Buds and two Steak Royales from a chalkboard menu that seemed to favour fish. The Royales were described as 'grilled and seasoned with Lenny's secret blend of herbs and spices and served with jumbo jacket fries'.

He looked round the bar as the barman pulled a couple of ice-cold bottles out of a fridge and shouted the order through a hatch into the kitchen.

It wasn't particularly busy, perhaps no more than a dozen drinkers, mostly regulars by the look of them, all staring vacuously at the TV. There was no doubt that it was mid-week and out of vacation season.

Chris took the beers over to a little wood-panelled booth that Mark had found. He smiled when he realised Mark had still managed to keep the TV set in view.

'Who's winning, then?' he said as he set the bottles of beer down.

'The Dolphins,' replied Mark chugging a mouthful directly from the bottle, leaving some suds on his beard. 'Ahhh, I needed that. Thanks.'

'I got us some grilled steaks and fries to wash the beer down.'

'Great. So, Chris . . . what's this thing you want a second opinion on?'

Chris slipped off his shoulder bag and pulled out a manila folder. He set it carefully on the table between them and opened it to reveal a dozen black and white photographs.

'Ahhh, you've developed them already.'

'Just some.'

Chris spun the folder round so that the pictures inside were the right way up for Mark. He studied them intently for a few moments, spreading them out across the table.

'They look good.' He pointed to a group of three images of the body aboard the plane. 'Nice, you definitely caught his best side.'

'I want you to look closely at these three pictures.'

'At what?'

'I'm not going to say just yet. I don't want to bias your opinion.'

Mark studied the grim images of the pilot. Chris definitely knew his craft. The photographs were high-contrast. He knew enough about the way Chris worked to know that this was deliberate. The contrast pushed the images away from various greys towards decisive whites and blacks. It made every little detail, every little bump and groove stand out.

'Well, what do you want? A judgement on the composition?'

'Of the de-composition more like,' said Chris. 'Sorry, go on.'

'Okay ... they're striking, but I wouldn't think they'll make their way onto any kitchen calendars or Mother's Day cards. You think your employers will go for them?'

Chris shook his head. 'What, *News Fortnite*? Nah ... It's a little too visceral for them. This is the kind of scat image that some sick website would love.'

Mark looked back down at the images of the skeletal face. He was right. If it were just a skull it wouldn't be quite so bad. But the few strands of organic debris clinging to the bone still looked like flesh. And the tuft of blond hair poking out from beneath the leather cap, the vertebrae of the neck descending into layers of clothing all came together to produce an unpleasant portrait of decay.

'Let me help you a little here. Take a close look at this one,' he said picking up a photo and handing it to Mark. It was a close-up of the body. An image that showed the skull and the vertebrae of the neck descending into the leather flying jacket and uniform tunic.

Mark looked it over carefully. 'No, I can't see what you want me to see.'

Chris pointed to a metallic object half-obscured by the lower jawbone and radio mouthpiece.

'Well, now, that looks like, what? A medal or something?'

Chris nodded. 'It's a medal all right ... but it ain't a Purple Heart.'

Mark looked at it again. 'It looks a bit like—'

'An Iron Cross?'

He looked up at Chris. 'Yes.'

'Look at the pilot's tunic, the collar.'

The tone of the tunic appeared to be dark, and amidst the hard-to-read chaotic pattern of high-contrast blacks and whites he could just discern the collar and on it two barely distinguishable oak leaves.

'You telling me, you think the pilot was a Kraut, Chris? A Luftwaffe pilot?'

A waitress arrived with their grilled steaks and waited irritably for them to tidy away the photographs and make space on the small wooden table between them. Chris ordered a couple more beers before she departed.

'Yeah. So what do you think?' Chris asked eventually.

Mark took his steak knife, cut a slice of grilled rump and tucked it into his mouth. His jaw worked on the piece of meat for over a minute before he replied. 'I'll tell you what I think. I think you may well have one helluva story waiting for you down there.'

'Yeah. There's something there, but I don't want to get too excited yet. There could be a hundred and one reasons why that corpse is wearing what he's wearing, and any one of them could lead to a dull story . . . and we won't know unless –'

Mark could guess where he was going with that. 'Unless we go take another look.'

Chris nodded. 'I might go and see if our friend Will's around after we've finished dinner.'

'We're not diving tonight if that's what you're thinking.'

'Why not?'

'Because we've both eaten dinner, consumed alcohol and I've still got to finish fixing the radio. It can wait until tomorrow.'

Chris threw his hands up in a gesture of resignation. 'Okay, okay . . . you win. Tomorrow night, then, that is if I can get that old bugger Will to agree to take us out again.'

Chapter 6

File n-27

It had been asleep for sixty years, file number n-27, a dusty file, containing reams of yellowing paper in a faded and dog-eared cardboard cover. Once upon a time n-27 had occupied dozens of cardboard covers, which in turn had filled several filing cabinets. But over the years, 'liabilities' had died off and the unnecessary documentation had been stripped away – old records to do with these long dead liabilities . . . details of movements, copies of bills and invoices, bank statements, phone bills, discreet liaisons, sexual peccadillos, all of these had been peeled out of the folder and destroyed, no longer useful or relevant. What was left was a barebones file, the skeletal remains. One last, persistent name at the bottom of a list of approximately two dozen on the inside of the front cover had survived the merciless sweep of a black marker pen.

One of them remained alive.

File n-27 had spent its entire life residing in a windowless office off the duty corridor on mezzanine floor 3, beneath an anonymous government building in Washington. More than half a century ago, all of the rooms on this floor had been occupied by staff belonging to this department, which had been hastily assembled and granted a black budget in the final days of the Second World War.

The anonymous men who had once worked here had only ever referred to this place as 'the Department'. A long, long time ago it had been busy for several frenetic months, then, over the ensuing five years, it had gradually been pared down to a maintenance staff responsible only for collating data from the routine low-key surveillance operations carried out.

In the early years of the department's life, at any one time, roughly half of the names on that list were being watched discreetly, from a distance. However, over the decades, there were fewer names as Mother Nature had whittled their number down, and in turn the head count on the department's payroll had slowly dwindled too as the data to collate correspondingly decreased.

To be fair, from time to time, the department's personnel had temporarily grown. There had been other very special files over the years that had been entrusted to the department to look after. These files had come to join n-27, like reluctant house guests. In particular, file 759-j had arrived in '63, and had stayed in its own filing cabinet for over thirty years. Its arrival had once more restored, if only for a little over a decade, some semblance of life to the duty corridor. A second water-cooler had even been installed against one lime green wall, and a poster of Marilyn Monroe had mysteriously appeared one Monday morning. But the years passed, Marilyn's print faded, the corners and edges of the poster scuffed and ripped. In the mid-eighties, file 759-j was eventually closed and its paper contents incinerated. The second water-cooler was removed as staff became reassigned and n-27 once more slumbered fitfully alone. And as the second millennium came to an end, the department became all but a shell. A single office, a single phone line, a trickle-feed black budget no longer topped-up but allowed to slowly spend itself out and one solitary clerical officer, counting off the last months until his retirement . . . and just one sleeping file.

That all changed with a small clipping from a local newspaper, arriving by internal post in a plain brown envelope.

The clerical officer read it quickly and understood its importance instantly; his traditional mid-morning cheese and bacon bagel was forgotten for now.

The Medusa *has been found.*

The clerical officer knew what to do.

There was a protocol to follow; a protocol originally written with a fountain pen sixty years ago, and again on a typewriter ten years later, and when the ink on that had finally faded, rattled off on a dot matrix printer . . . and that too was fading now.

The clerical officer read through it and finally located in faint grey dots the name he was after.

He dialled the number, hoping that it was still current. If not, he wasn't sure whom he would have to call next . . . there was no one else's number to dial.

He tapped in the number, surprised at how edgy he was. After so long, file n-27 had come back to life.

Chapter 7

McGuire

It had been raining all day.

Chris finally decided to venture out of the coffee shop and head back to the motel as the dull grey of the afternoon was darkening with the approaching evening. Normally he would have grumbled and cursed the mean-spirited weather, as the fresh wind pulled at his clothes and the rain stung his cheeks, but right now his mind was on that aborted phone call to the museum and the very odd way it had ended.

The shortcut from the coffee shop led him down from the coast road, through dunes of sand peaked with wild grass, to a small, deserted cove. Across the cove he could see the bright quayside lights of Port Lawrence.

There were numerous boats at rest on the shingle, many of them little more than dinghies or just the stripped-down remains of larger vessels. All of them eroded by the elements, many worn away to exposed ribcages of ageing timber. Littering the ground between these dead and dying hulls like scattered body parts were ropes, tackle, anchors, cleats . . . the loose detritus of several dozen boats. A man could make a fortune selling this sort of junk in the right place to the right kind of people. A trendy little boutique in Greenwich Village, catering for dim-witted rich people seeking a slice of 'traditional' to slot inappropriately into their modern homes.

The shower was easing now, nothing more than a few willful spots.

It was then that he heard a cough behind him. Not an honest, out-loud-bark, but a short, brittle grunt that sounded smothered.

He spun round. Amongst the dimly lit silhouettes of dead hulls around him, he could make out nothing. He debated whether to call out a challenge. But he knew his own voice would unsettle him even more. He held his breath, and listened intently for any noise other than the tide on the pebbles and the occasional clatter of wind-borne debris. A few seconds passed, and Chris was prepared to believe it was his over-active imagination playing the devil when he heard the clatter of pebbles and the crunch of a clumsily placed foot.

'Okay, who the fuck is that?' he growled in a voice he hoped sounded menacing.

He heard another footfall, and then, his eyes growing keener, he picked out an indistinct form moving slowly between two of the beached vessels.

'You're the news man, aren't you?' said a voice coming from the dark shape; an old man.

News man? Chris found himself grinning in the dark. The natives were gossiping.

'Yeah, I'm the news man.'

Chris heard the crunch of feet drawing closer, and the dark form grew until he could make out a lined and weathered face framed by the hood of an old canvas raincoat.

'My name's McGuire,' he said. Chris could see by the fading light of the overcast afternoon that he was holding out a hand.

He grabbed it awkwardly. McGuire's grip was surprisingly strong.

'You're here about that plane out there, aren't you?'

Chris wondered whether to play it dumb, but then Port Lawrence was a small town. Undoubtedly old Will must have been spreading the news about his two passengers, like some old dear in a salon.

'Yeah, you got me.'

'I can tell you a story or two about that,' said McGuire as he pulled out a crumpled pack of cigarettes and offered one to Chris.

'No thanks. I'm five months quit.'

The old man laughed, a wheezy cackle that degenerated into a rattling cough. It sounded like something loose and leathery rattling in a cage. 'Five months quit, eh?' he said finally. 'Not bad, but you know, you're never "quit", you're just resting between smokes.'

Resting between smokes just about summed it up perfectly. Chris was tempted, but resisted the urge to reach out for one.

'Don't mind if I poison myself, then?'

'No. Poison away.'

McGuire sheltered his cigarette and lighter from the wind and lit up. From the flickering glow of the flame Chris could see his face. It was long and narrow and weathered. He suspected the old man looked ten years older than he was.

The wind gusted and Chris shivered.

'So? You going to tell me what it is you know about that plane, then?' asked Chris.

McGuire took another long pull on his cigarette. 'We found the pilot of that plane out there, on the beach just along the way from here. Found him on the sand rolling in the waves . . . pretty much in the last week of the war that was, if I recall correctly.'

'How do you know it was the pilot of that plane?'

'Well, it was Sean who got a good close look. Sean said he was an airman, one of ours. I went off to town and found Sean's dad and told him we'd found the body of one of our boys down on the beach. Then, within only a few hours, they arrived.'

'Who?'

'Goddamned near everyone by the look of it. Army first, then later on some navy ships and still more army. They closed off the beach and spent several days out there looking for the plane that poor lad had come from. They never found it, though. Those navy ships trawled this way and that way out to sea for near on a week. Then overnight, in fact, the night before VE day was announced, they just disappeared. Ships, army, barbed wire, everything . . . just vanished into the night.'

'And you're certain they were looking for the plane?'

'Yessir, that's what it looked like. They sure as hell wanted to find that plane out there. And I figure I know why.'

Chris nodded. 'Go on.'

McGuire smiled. 'You planning on putting this in a book or on the TV or something? Cos if you are, I guess I'll be due something, right?'

'Sure, if I quote you, you'll get something. That's how it works,' replied Chris with a reassuring smile.

McGuire seemed satisfied with that. 'I'll tell you, I think there was someone real important aboard the plane that pilot was flying; maybe a general, a government man or something. I mean, there was a lot of top brass and big hats heading over the sea at the end of the war, you know? All heading over there to see what beaten Nazis looked like, and slice up that country with the Ruskies.'

'And the British,' muttered Chris quietly.

'Oh, yeah, you Limes were in it at the end too, weren't you?'

'I'm sure we had something to do with it.'

McGuire nodded. 'Maybe you did. Anyway, so I think it was top brass who crashed out there, and they were looking for his body. And he must have been real important, because I never heard nothing on the radio or read anything in the papers about it. I reckon it was someone *too* important, if you know what I mean? Too important to tell everyone he'd been lost in a plane crash.'

'And you think I might find out who it was out there on that wreck?'

McGuire cast a long glance out at the grey sea and raised his hand to point. 'They were right out there, where that trawler snagged her nets. Just out there, a few miles out. I'll bet the barn, the wreck out there is the one they were lookin' for.'

Chris stood silently for a moment, following the old man's gaze. Then he turned back to McGuire. 'This body . . . you're sure it was one of yours? An American airman?'

'Hell, yeah. Didn't look like a Limey to me. Sean got a better look, though.'

'Sean?'

'My friend, he was a little older than me, he got a closer look; turned the body over an' all. He was looking for a name on the body.'

'Could I speak to him?'

McGuire shook his head. 'Doesn't live here any more. Shit, I don't know if he's still alive any more. He moved away with his dad not long after the war. Never seen him since.'

'What was his surname?'

'Grady, Sean Grady. His dad was . . . Tom Grady, I think,' McGuire smiled, 'it's been a long time. The old memory ain't what it used to be.'

'Do you think Sean found out the pilot's name?'

McGuire shrugged. 'Don't know, didn't get a chance to speak with him again. He took all the damned credit for finding the body when the army came. I don't think he bothered to mention once that I'd found it too. The army and government men made a big fuss of him while they were down there in the cove. Then, not long after, Sean and his dad moved away.'

McGuire spat a plug of phlegm on to the beach. 'Sean and his dad got some kind of reward. That's what happened. Or maybe you might want to call it go-keep-it-to-yourselves money . . . either way, all of a sudden, Tom Grady didn't need to carry on scratching a living round here any more. No, sir.'

Chris cursed under his breath. If he had a name, it would go a long way towards making some sense of this story.

'You didn't speak to this friend of yours? Not ever again?'

'No. I was too angry with him at the time. I know the bastard never mentioned me. I never got any goddamned money. To be honest, I never gave him, nor the body, nor all those ships and people a second thought until the other week when that trawler found the plane wreck. Then I figured that was the plane those ships had been looking for all that time ago.'

'Right.'

'You find out who it was on that plane out there, and you got yourself a story. That's what I reckon.'

Chris nodded. Maybe this old boy was right. Maybe there was a body out there in that plane that was going to make sense of what he knew so far.

'And you get some money for this,' McGuire continued, 'then you come looking for me, 'cause you'll owe me some. I ain't missing out on this story two times round. You understand?'

Chris nodded. 'Sure. Presuming there is some money to be had, where would I find you?'

'The Fisherman's Club in town. Just ask for Danny McGuire.'

'Don't worry, I'll do that,' said Chris.

The last of the pale afternoon light was rapidly fading, and the old man was little more than a dark silhouette. Chris saw the old man raise his arm again. McGuire was pointing up the beach towards a small cove.

'You know, I went back to the cove some weeks later, after all the soldiers and ships had gone. I went back to where me and Sean found the body, and I made a cross out of driftwood, you know, out of respect an' all for the dead pilot. I guess that cross would be still there if you looked for it, back in the dunes.'

Chris nodded. *I might do that . . . might make a good photo.*

'Okay, I'll have a look for it.'

McGuire nodded. 'I'm getting cold.' He studied Chris intently for a moment. 'Don't go forgetting that money, now,' he muttered before turning away and disappearing amongst the dark forms of the beached hulls around them.

Chris shook his head. 'Now this is just getting silly.'

But he knew this was something he might have to follow up. If this friend, Sean, had indeed been *bought off* somehow, then he surely had something interesting to say on the matter. That is, if he was still alive after all this time. Chris made a mental note of the name: *Sean Grady, son of Tom Grady*.

That was a lead he could think about following up later, after he'd had a chance to take another look around the wreck of *Medusa*.

But this next time, despite Mark's inevitable over-zealous cautionary warnings, he wanted to go right down inside the bomber. He knew the answer was there. It had to be.

Chapter 8

The Second Dive

They descended down along the buoy's rope in silence, the last flickering rays from the trawler's floodlight quickly dwindling to nothing. Once again, at about fifty feet down, their torches picked out the wing tip of the B-17.

'There's *Medusa*. You beautiful thing, you,' said Chris. This time around he didn't want to waste any precious dive-time – straight inside was what he wanted; straight inside, hopefully to find something, or perhaps the remains of someone. Either way, he was almost certain he'd stumble across a *find* of some sort in the next half an hour.

Mark pointed his torch towards the front of the plane. 'Let's not hang about, then. You want to make straight for the cockpit, right? I'll go in first this time, okay?'

'Thanks. You can shoo out any critters in there for me.'

'And like I said to you this morning, this time we're staying together. Okay?'

'You're the boss, Mark.'

Mark swam towards the cockpit and Chris followed him down to the seabed beside the nose of the bomber. He shone his torch at the open belly hatch. 'Right, Chris, gently does it this time. Okay?'

Chris nodded as he floated beside him.

The big American stuck his head up through the hatch into the observation blister and shone his torch round before pulling himself in carefully.

'Okay. No eels in here. I'm going up the ladder into the cockpit.'

He moved slowly up the short ladder, feeling the edges of the hatchway catch on his air cylinder. He backed down, leaned forward and rose again slowly, listening unhappily to the gentle metallic scraping sound of the cylinder on the hatchway as he pulled himself up inside the cockpit.

He shone his torch around, coming to rest eventually on the body.

'I'm in the cockpit, no eels here either,' said Mark. 'You can come up.'

'Roger that.'

'I'm going to move to the back of the cockpit to the doorway, there should be room for you to enter. Be careful on that hatch from the observation bit into the cockpit, it's much tighter than the first hatch.'

Chris pulled a face, remembering the damage he'd done to Mark's equipment.

'I'll go slowly. Promise.'

Chris eased himself up inside the plane with extra care this time, and then climbed the ladder and squeezed tentatively through the even tighter hatchway into the cockpit.

Mark was waiting beside the bulkhead leading back into the fuselage. 'Hi there.'

Chris nervously shone his torch down through the opening, half expecting a rerun of his ghostly hallucination. The beam of light picked out the navigator's desk and the bomb bay.

He then turned his torch on the body. 'Okay, I want to make sure this guy wasn't just a souvenir-wearing Yank, sorry, no disrespect, Mark.' He reached out and peeled back the leather of the flying jacket. It tore like tissue paper and a cloud of soft debris billowed out.

'Gross,' said Mark curling his lip in disgust.

The debris took its time to settle. Chris stared at the tattered shreds of the dark tunic beneath. The silver eagle on the right of the tunic was remarkably untarnished thanks to the leather that had been covering it for the last sixty years.

'Okay, he's either a German or he's someone who took souvenir-wearing a little too far.' Chris took a couple of shots of the exposed remains of the Luftwaffe tunic.

'Seems like you really have got a genuine story on your hands,' said Mark.

'Let's go in further. Somewhere back there we'll find the story, the reason why this plane's here.'

'I'll take point again.'

'Be my guest,' said Chris with a jittery, anxious grin.

Mark pulled himself through the bulkhead with an agility that reminded Chris of this man's impressive experience in wreck diving. He followed through behind him, flippers clumsily disturbing a cloud of silt from the floor.

'Go easy on the flipper action, Chris. There's over half a century of undisturbed sediment sitting on every surface in here.' He was right of course. The less motion they produced, the less time they'd waste waiting for it all to settle.

Mark panned his torch around the navigation booth. The beam picked out a small desk. He reached out a hand and very gently swept the silt off a corner of it. It billowed up into a small mushroom cloud that took a dozen seconds to settle to the floor.

'See how I did that? If you sweep it off *gently* it settles down really quickly.'

'Gotcha.'

Mark looked down at the corner of the surface he'd exposed.

'There's a map here.'

Chris glided over. He reached out to sweep away some more of the silt.

'Gently . . . if that's paper it'll shred with the slightest touch. Here, let me.'

Mark lightly wafted his hand above the surface of the table. The sediment began to rise into a cloud. He stopped moving, and gradually it settled elsewhere, revealing a large section of the map detailing the coastline of New York State.

Chris looked up from the map. 'They were heading for New York . . . or on their way back from a trip there?'

'Jeeez.'

'Mind your eyes.' The camera flashed brilliantly as he took a couple of shots. 'Do you know the story of Rudolf Hess?'

Mark shook his head. 'No. A Nazi, I guess.'

'Yes, a pretty senior one. I forget when it was, sometime after they'd kicked our arses out of France, near the beginning of the war . . . but this guy sneaked over to Scotland without Adolf's permission to negotiate a peace deal with Churchill. He came over by plane.'

'You think we might find the body of some other high-ranking Nazi, uh? Doing the same thing? Doing a Hess?'

Chris smiled. 'Be one helluva great story, wouldn't it?'

'Don't forget your old buddy when you're rich and famous.'

'Mark, if this turns out to be half the earner I think it's going to be, then trust me, I'll put a smile on your face too. Shall we press on?'

Mark checked his watch. 'Yeah, we should. We need to be making for the surface in twenty minutes.'

Chris led the way. The space narrowed ahead as they passed through empty bomb racks on either side of a narrow walkway above an open space below.

Chris pointed down at it. 'Bomb bay.'

'Wow, there's space for a lot of bombs on these racks,' said Mark.

'Yup. They carried a pretty impressive amount of ordnance.'

Chris shone his torch down into the open bomb bay. He could see past what looked like an immersion heater through the open hatch to the sea floor. The outer bomb bay hatch must have been open when she ditched, or perhaps ripped off by the sea on impact.

That's an interesting shot.

It was a nice twist on the classic 'bombs away' image he'd seen in countless WWII documentaries. The only world visible through the frame of the bomb bay was the sea floor. It was what Chris considered a concept shot; it summed things up nicely.

'Mind your eyes.' He took a couple more pictures.

They pressed on, making slow progress between the racks as their equipment frequently snagged and scraped on the metal spars. Mark looked anxiously at the racks. This kind of environment could trap a diver easily, especially with reduced visibility. He decided to reduce the dive time by five minutes to allow them some additional contingency. If they overran for whatever reason and had to come back through these racks in a hurry it would be inviting trouble, especially with Chris being so inexperienced at wreck diving and so easily disorientated, as the other night's episode in the cockpit had clearly demonstrated.

Disorientated? Scared shitless more like.

Mark had been involved with a team of marine archaeologists who had discovered a U-boat off the coast of Gibraltar. It had attracted a lot of experienced divers with a passion for WWII wrecks, and he'd been on site as a safety watchdog. One father-and-son team had pushed deeper into the sub than they should have and not allowed themselves a safety margin of air. They'd managed to kick up a lot of debris and lost their way in a blizzard of sediment and flakes of rust. The more they panicked the worse it had got. Mark pulled them out several hours later, quite dead. He had found them with the father's regulator still in the boy's mouth. The boy's air must have run out first and the father had sacrificed his life to buy the lad a few more minutes.

On the far side, the plane opened up again and they came across the waist-gun ports.

Mark shone his torch down at the cabin floor. 'Jesus, look at that.'

Mottled green cylinders the size of cotton reels littered the floor.

'Spent shell cases. You see how many there are? This plane saw some pretty heavy action on the way over.'

'The plot thickens, eh?' said Mark.

'Yup. Eyes.'

Mark closed his eyes as Chris's flash popped with the succession of half a dozen shots. He stopped for a moment and looked up at Mark. 'Here's a question for you. Who was this plane fighting on the way over?'

'Americans?' ventured Mark.

'Or Germans?'

'Germans?'

'Yeah. Maybe there was some rocket scientist looking to come over to join you guys and the Nazis didn't want you to have him. How's that for a story?'

'I think you're reaching.'

'Okay, so I'm just getting a little excited here.'

'Shall we continue, Chris? I give us nine minutes, and we'll have to squeeze back through those racks again on the way out.'

'Yup, let's go on.'

Both men began to head further down the plane when they picked out a second body on the floor of the cabin. It was completely buried by the silt, but the recognisable contour of a prone body was unmistakable. Chris swam closer and gently brushed some of the sediment away exposing another skeletal face.

'Well?'

Chris looked up. 'He's dead.'

'Very funny.'

He waited for the cloud of mud to settle before brushing away some more to expose the body's clothes. Chris saw the faded yellow oak leaves on the collar.

He aimed his camera. 'Another Luftwaffe guy. Eyes.' The flash popped several times. Mark pulled himself over to look at the body.

'Two guys only so far. I thought these big planes had big crews?'

'Well, they did, about nine or ten I think. But you could get somewhere with just two, a pilot and a navigator.'

'You think there were any more? Maybe some escaped from the plane when it ditched.'

'Possibly,' Chris answered, recalling McGuire's story about the body on the beach.

Mark checked his watch. 'We should quickly check the rest of the plane then start heading back out.'

Chris nodded. 'Fine, let's do it.'

They glided up to the tail-end of the bomber, briefly investigating the belly-gun hatch and the tail-gun. There appeared to be no other bodies aboard the plane.

Mark announced they had to start heading out, and Chris was happy to agree. He patted his camera, convinced that there was a big story sitting comfortably on the roll of film nestled inside it. What exactly the story was he had no idea. It looked like it was going to take some unravelling, and he wondered whether one place to start would be with this young lad and his father who supposedly vanished after the discovery of that body on the beach.

Chapter 9

Sean Grady

Chris had done this kind of thing once before, nearly fifteen years ago: attempting to track down the location of a young man, still a kid really, only fifteen, for his mother. The boy and a dozen or so other men, old and young, had been rounded up in a village in southern Bosnia by a small unit of armed Serbian militia and whisked away, never to be heard from again.

With hindsight, many years later, it was obvious that they, like many others who had *disappeared*, had met with a grisly end. But, at the time, Chris was willing to believe that the boy and his companions were either being drafted or taken to some hastily assembled prisoner of war camp, and that they could be tracked down. His efforts, of course, had led him nowhere.

This was hopefully going to be a little easier.

He had a name, two names, Sean and Tom Grady, and that was all. The first thing Chris thought to do would be to establish that the old man, McGuire, for lack of another name, had in fact been telling the truth, and that there had been a Sean Grady and his father living in Port Lawrence during the Second World War.

He left Mark to his own devices once more, tinkering with the diving equipment, while he headed out in the morning to visit the local church, perched on a small hill overlooking Port Lawrence. The preacher he managed to speak to there was only in his thirties and although very helpful and friendly couldn't assist Chris at all when he mentioned the names. He suggested the Fishermen's Social Club as possibly being of some use. If Tom Grady had worked on one of the fishing boats then he almost certainly would have been a member of the club. And, the man added, back then that was pretty much all they had for work round here, fishing, so it was more than likely that he would find this man's name in their member register.

Chris thanked the young man and headed back into town, down towards the jetty end of Devenster Street, where he eventually tracked down the old weathered barn that still functioned as the Fishermen's Social Club, as well as being used as a community centre.

He let himself in through a small door at the front. Inside, he found himself standing in a small hall, dimly lit by several strip lights that shone coldly down onto a tired and scarred linoleum floor, and a small wooden stage upon which were stacked dozens of orange bucket seats. At the far end of the hall, he saw a small bar, which, surprisingly at this time in the morning, was open.

If it was anything like the working men's clubs his dad had taken him into when he was just about old enough to shave, Chris imagined there were no formal opening times for the bar; it just opened when any member of the Fishermen's Social Club decided it was about time for a drink.

Perched on one stool was a young man in his twenties, staring languidly at a small TV on a counter behind the bar. Another man, old enough to be his grandfather, was stacking bottles of beer in a fridge.

'Can I help you?' the older man asked, his voice echoing down the hall.

'Hi, I wonder if you *can* help me actually.' Chris walked over towards the bar. 'Somebody suggested I try this place, so hopefully you can. I'm trying to trace someone who lived here a while back. I've got a name, but that's all I have.'

'How far back?' the younger man asked.

'Oh, 1945 . . . war time.'

He shrugged. 'Too far back for me, sorry.' The young man resumed gazing at the TV opposite.

The old man behind the bar sauntered over to stand opposite Chris. 'What name have you got?'

'Grady, Tom Grady.'

He stroked his chin as he pondered the name. 'Hmm, Tom Grady. Can't say the name rings any bells.'

'He had a son, Sean Grady.'

The old man's face lightened up. 'Sean Grady, now that . . . that, yes . . . I remember Sean Grady. Yes, he was a lad in the school. A year above me if we're talking about the same Sean . . . he was, a character, there's no doubt about that.'

Chris sat down on one of the stools. 'Do you think his father might have been a member here?'

'Easy enough to find out, young man. I can have a look at the member register. Just give me a moment.'

The old man came out from behind the bar and wandered across the hall to a doorway. He let himself in and closed the door behind him.

Chris nodded a greeting to the lad propping up the counter beside him. 'All right?'

'Sure.' The lad studied Chris for a moment. 'You Canadian?'

'English.'

'You the reporter guy come to look at the wreck?'

The question took Chris aback. He wondered if there was anybody left in Port Lawrence who still *didn't* know about the wreck and Chris for that matter.

'Yeah, that's me, I guess. I'm just looking up a relative for a friend of mine back in England. They lost touch during the war.'

'Right,' the young man responded, uninterested in Chris's tacked-on cover story; once more his dull gaze transferred back to the TV behind the bar.

The door opened and the old man returned with a large, dog-eared, leather-bound book.

'Yes, we did have a Tom Grady as a member. I think that's the one you're looking for. Here –'

He set the register on the bar and ran a finger down a column of handwritten names.

'He was a member at the club for about ten years. Ahhh, I can see he left owing us a subscription!'

'Would you have any details on his next of kin, or, I dunno . . . his employer, or bank details. Perhaps a forwarding address?'

The old man laughed. 'This is a social club, not a census bureau. That's all we have I'm afraid.'

Chris cursed under his breath.

'But, I do recall they had family not so far away. Up the coast about fifty miles, a place called New Buxton. If you can find them, maybe they can help you.'

Chris looked up New Buxton on his road map when he got back to his room. It looked like a small town, and that was good news. If they were family on the father's side, he was in business. Otherwise, that would have to be the end of the trail. If he was lucky there would be a few Gradys living there, and he could ring them up in turn. But first, he needed some numbers to ring.

He knocked on Mark's door and let himself in.

'Can I have a quick go on your lappie?'

Mark looked up from the laptop. Chris could see from the flickering screen he was mid-session in a game of *CounterStrike*.

'For work?' he sighed.

Chris nodded. 'Yes, for work. Sorry, mate, I'll be as quick as I can.'

Mark quit the game. 'Here you go, all yours,' he said, sliding the laptop across the bed. 'Chris, how much longer are you thinking of staying up here? I know it's easy money you're paying me, but I'm sort of getting bored.'

'Hmm, not much longer. Two or three more days I guess.'

'Do you think you'll want to do any more dives down on that plane wreck? You do, I've got to go and restock the cylinders, and that's a drive.'

'Right. I think I'll probably want to do another one and that's probably it. But I want to fill in a few more of the blanks first,' he said. As an afterthought he added, 'Bear with me Mark. This feels like a bloody good story, I just need to snoop around it a bit more.'

'Ah well, have fun. I'll go sort the air tanks out, then. See you later on. We'll get a beer this evening?'

'Sounds good. Here –' Chris tossed him the keys to the Cherokee.

Mark closed the door behind him, and Chris listened to the heavy sound of his feet down the hallway before firing up Explorer. He tapped in the address for *NeighborSnoop*, a handy, if somewhat shady, search engine he used to make use of all the time during his paparazzi days to track down the details of his latest quarry. He had a surname and a town; more than enough to flush out the phone numbers of anyone living there under the surname Grady.

Five minutes later, he had three phone numbers to call, and had decided, and quickly rehearsed, how he was going to handle them. The first number he dialled was engaged. The second answered after three rings.

'Hello?' a woman's voice answered.

'Hi, this may seem like a very odd call, it's not a sales call, though, okay?'

'Who is this?'

'My name is –' it occurred for the very first time to Chris, that it might be wise to start being a little bit more careful '– Jason Schwartz, I'm from the New England Fishermen's Union. We arrange, from time to time, reunion gatherings for crews, and get-togethers from various social clubs. I'm trying to track down one of our members, his old crew are looking to meet up, you see . . . so I'm trying to get hold of Tom Grady. I was told he had family living out in New Buxton. But I've got no record of his current address see, so . . . there you go, hence the call.'

There was a pause as the lady absorbed Chris's story, and in turn Chris held his breath in anticipation. It had sounded okay in practice, but just now it had sounded forced, as if read from a script. Chris reminded himself not to rehearse next time; busking this kind of thing always ended up sounding more natural.

'Tom Grady? That's a name I've not heard in a long, long time.'

'Ma'am?'

'Tom Grady was my uncle.'

'Was? Oh dear, I'm sorry –'

'Oh, don't be. I don't know if he's passed on, young man, I haven't seen him in sixty years. I guess he probably must be dead by now. He moved out of state with his son. I guess that was . . . not long after the war. I think only a few days after the war, thinking about it.'

'Oh . . . why do you think he moved away?'

'I heard he came into some money, but I think that's just hearsay. More likely he knew, with our boys coming home soon, that they would fill up the places on the trawlers once more, and he'd have trouble finding work any more. There's not a lot else to do in Port Lawrence, other than fish, you know? I guess that's still the way?'

'Yes, ma'am. Fishing, and processing fish, that's pretty much what we got over here,' replied Chris, wary that he was exaggerating the drawl too much. He decided to try another angle – after all it was always his mum who was the one who bothered to write out and send the Christmas cards each year.

'Did you ever hear from Mrs Grady?'

'Oh, there was no Mrs Grady, Mr Schwartz. My aunt died some years earlier, before the war.'

Shit.

'Well, I must say it is a surprise to have someone ask after Tom and his boy after so many years,' she added after a moment or two.

'You never heard from them again?' Chris probed.

'Well, thinking about it, yes. I think it was a year or so after they disappeared, we received a letter from Tom. He said that they'd moved to

Florida, and he was working again and they were happier down there, and not to worry, that he would be in touch again when they had settled into a home.'

'Do you have an address?'

'No, not any more. I replied to his letter, but he never wrote again. I think they must have moved home once more and just . . . well, you know how it is with family. Sometimes they just give up on each other. Tom and I were never that close, not even when we all lived in Port Lawrence.'

Damn. This was feeling like a dead end.

'Well, I'm sorry to hear about this. I'll have to let Tom's crewmates know he can't be found. I do apologise for disturbing you.'

'Not a problem, young man.'

He said goodbye and hung up.

The woman seemed, at least to some degree, to have confirmed McGuire's little tale. That his childhood buddy, Sean, and his father had been gently *hustled* out of town . . . and probably with enough shut-up money for them to start over very nicely, thank you very much. And that, along with McGuire's tale of navy ships at sea and the cove cordoned off with barbed wire and soldiers, that . . . and the fact that there were two Luftwaffe bodies lying off the coast of New England, inside a B-17 riddled with bullets. When it came to writing up the story, the old boy McGuire might well prove useful – he'd definitely get something out of it. But it was a shame he couldn't track down this boy, Sean . . . an old man now, of course.

Chris decided following up on Sean Grady could wait until he was done with the diving up here. Then that was a line of enquiry he could pursue later on . . . just to add a bit more meat and gristle to the story.

Chapter 10

Contemplation

Somewhat oddly he was thinking about the Department when it rang him. He had been thinking how best to deploy what remained of the legacy budget. There was just under 300,000 dollars left, and it was arguably approaching the time when he could look to start wrapping things up. Bob Palantino, the last man left on the payroll, was approaching his mandatory retirement age. Bob had been a good desk man, reliable, discreet and very organised. When Bob served up his last day, he wondered whether it would be wise to bother enrolling a replacement. The old guy knew most of it.

But not everything.

Bob knew enough, but then he had worked down there on that windowless mezzanine floor for a long time now, nearly forty years. If he took on a replacement to continue as the 'caretaker' after Bob hung up his hat, then it would mean bringing someone new in on the secret, and that meant introducing an unnecessary element of risk. The fewer in *the know* the better, especially now, after such a long time. After all, the secret, 'Truman's legacy' as he sometimes liked to refer to it, was very nearly dead and buried.

Or so he had thought.

Then there had been that damned call from Bob. After all this time it looked like someone had snagged their nets on the bomber, *Medusa*.

He had spent some time pondering what to do over that.

Well, now, what it *didn't* require was a rushed, ill-considered response . . . absolutely no need to panic here. It was just the wreck of a wartime plane sitting at an acceptable depth in uncomfortably cold water; hardly the sort of destination for casual holiday snorkellers, and not exactly a big story; just a small item of interest in a local rag.

But, he reflected, it would need to be dealt with in due course. It would need *tidying up*.

He had enough money left in the budget to hire in some freelancers. A couple of divers hired in to go down there and collect the offending item. No questions asked. Probably ex-servicemen, ex-agency bagmen, professional enough to just get on and do the task and leave the 'whys' and 'wherefores' to someone else.

That would wrap it up nicely. He would have them retrieve it *carefully* and have them take it out into deeper waters and drop it there.

He had begun to discreetly organise this 'tidy-up' job, once more returning to DC and the dark dungeons of the Department floor, at least for a few days, providing old Bob with a bit of company while he set about making the necessary calls to start the wheels turning when, as an old acquaintance of his had the habit of saying, *the proverbial hit the fan*.

He discovered there was some damned journalist poking around in the town near the crash site. Poking around and asking questions. God knows if the nosy shit-stick had access to diving equipment and been down below to take a look at the plane.

He hoped to God that this guy hadn't.

Agitated and unnerved by the thought, he distractedly rubbed his temple, attempting to ease away the tension building up there. He didn't need this. Not now. After so much hard work on his part, for so long . . . so much dedication, it could all unravel if this nosy sonofabitch managed to spot what was down there in the plane. If he sat back and did nothing, there was just enough out there to be pieced together. There was enough there to tell the tale; enough goddamned skeletons to crucify the Department.

What the hell – not to put too fine a point on it, to crucify him.

He took a deep breath, still gently caressing the side of his head, trying to massage his headache away and clear his mind, and decided the next move.

This needs to be handled carefully, gently, my friend. Observation first; find out how much he knows, see what he's got, if anything, and then take it from him. Most important . . . find out the exact location of Medusa, *and remove what's down there.*

He picked up a phone.

He needed a small team of freelancers, ones with street surveillance experience and enough smarts to stay invisible. And, of course, the dive team.

And that was pretty much going to clear out the last of the Department's budget.

Chapter 11

Finding KG-301

11 April 1945, east of Berlin

The road leading into Berlin was a logjam of vehicles, mostly trucks, he noticed. What was left of the Eastern armies had precious few armoured vehicles left, and those that hadn't been torn apart by T34s or enemy artillery were being mustered for one of several rearguard actions being hastily thrown together along the Potsdam River.

Leutnant Höstner shook his head. This ragtag procession of men, trucks and the occasional horse-drawn cart wasn't an army any longer. It didn't deserve that kind of description, that kind of word. It didn't deserve any word that conveyed the concept of order, discipline or structure. This was a disorganised rout, little more than a shambolic stream of refugees, united only by a shared desire to leave behind a war they had lost months, if not years, ago.

It certainly wasn't an army. Not any more.

The road had been used as one of the principal supply arteries leading east through Poland towards Russia. It had been widened and resurfaced to facilitate the movement of vehicles and supplies and had been a superbly efficient channel down which thousands of trucks had passed effortlessly since '41 to supply the rapidly advancing eastern front. But now it was riddled with potholes and craters and caked with a thick layer of mud.

Höstner scanned the trucks as they passed by his parked VW Kubelwagon and the spare supply truck he'd commandeered. The men in the convoy stared contemptuously at him as they rolled past, seeing his uniform and instinctively reacting with thinly veiled hostility. Several men spat in his direction. Most of them were too tired to offer even that gesture. A year ago his SS uniform would have been intimidating to these men, four years ago it would have inspired admiration from many of them. Right now, Höstner felt like he was wearing a big bloody target.

It was cold. He'd been standing here for well over three hours, since first light, waiting for the column to arrive. He wasn't sure exactly when it had 'officially' turned up. Since dawn he'd watched a sporadic trickle of soldiers on foot shuffle pass, which had gradually over the last few hours developed into the column of vehicles before him that extended as far as the eye could see. How the hell he was meant to find the men he was after amidst this flowing river of defeat he didn't know. It was like trying to find a needle in a haystack. No, worse than that, this particular needle was on the move and could already have passed him by.

Höstner decided it was time to flag down one or two of these trucks and ask some questions.

Be careful of these men, Jan Höstner.

Höstner subconsciously felt for his gun holster, and allowed his gloved hand to seek reassurance from the grip of his Walther.

Things were beginning to fall apart. The authority of the junior officer ranks was rapidly failing amongst the enlisted men. They were far less worried about them and any issues of insubordination than they were about the Russian army snapping at their heels. These days, an officer was likely to have an order obeyed only if it coincided with the interests of the soldiers it was given to. It was unspoken amongst the men, but they all knew the war was just weeks away from ending. The threat of a pending court martial meant nothing now.

He watched them pass by, a procession of drawn, empty faces. Most of these men were veterans, professional soldiers who had spent the last two years fighting the most barbaric campaign of this war. And they had lost badly. Right now, there was no enmity between the men and their officers. After all, they had all suffered hell together. These men simply viewed what was left of the command structure now as, at best, irrelevant.

The SS, however, that was something different; they were still worth despising. Höstner was acutely aware that his uniform was going to cause him problems.

He made his way carefully down the muddy bank at the side of the road towards the slowly moving column. He watched several trucks rumble and clatter past, splattering his boots and the bottom of his greatcoat with mud. He could see the faces of the drivers through grime-speckled windscreens, drivers who Höstner could imagine were wrestling with the temptation to swerve their truck enough to 'accidentally' roll over him. No one here would care that much, accidents happen.

He decided he was tempting fate standing on the road side inches away from those large churning wheels and quickly clambered up onto the running board of the next truck that rumbled past. The driver cracked open his window an inch, careful not to lose too much of the body heat he'd built up inside the cabin.

'What do you want?' The driver shouted through the gap.

Only a few weeks ago Höstner would have scolded the man for such an insubordinate response. He bit his lip – those days were long gone.

'I'm looking for some Luftwaffe men. I'm told some men from KG-301 have joined the column.'

'We've got men from all over.'

'Have you got any in your truck?'

'I don't fucking know! Men climb aboard if they can see any space. I don't have a clue who's back there.'

Höstner decided the driver could tell him nothing useful. He jumped down off the truck onto the muddy road, and the truck slowly rolled away. He probably wasn't going to have much luck with any of the other drivers.

As the next one trundled past, Höstner grabbed the tailboard and pulled himself up. He lifted the canvas cover at the back. Inside, sitting in darkness there were about thirty men. The smell struck him immediately, a mixture of body odour and infected wounds. The men nearest the open flap shivered with the blast of incoming air.

Höstner mustered his most commanding voice. 'Any men from KG-301 in here?'

No one replied.

'Has anyone seen *any* Luftwaffe personnel?'

The men remained silent. Höstner knew he carried little, if any, authority here. Chastising or threatening them would achieve nothing. He sought a different approach.

On your hands and knees, Jan . . . and talk to them at their level.

'Look, I've got to find some men, Luftwaffe lads. No one's in trouble, I just need to find them or else I'll be in shit.' He hoped he sounded like a common soldier, just carrying out orders, just trying to keep his head down and do as he's told.

'Why?' a voice from the back of the truck.

'I don't know. I'm just following orders. Help me out, please.'

'Yeah? . . . so that you bastards can shoot them?'

'No, no of course not. They –'

'Go on, piss off.'

Höstner pulled his head out from inside and let the canvas flap drop down. He jumped off the back on to the muddy road again.

This was a bloody nightmare. There was no way he was going to find these men like this. He decided to head back to his Kubelwagon, light up the oil heater he'd brought along, warm himself up and rethink his plan.

Höstner climbed the earthy bank at the side of the road to get away from the trucks. He walked slowly towards his vehicle, imagining how he would break the news to Major Rall that he'd been unable to locate the men despite his orders not to return without them. Surely the Major realised it was going to be a long shot, trying to find four men amongst tens of thousands?

He hadn't been wrong back there in the truck when he'd said he'd be in shit if he failed to find them.

A long convoy of open-topped trucks were passing by. Höstner looked at the men shivering in the back. Their faces said it all. Win or lose, we want this over.

Maybe they had the right idea.

In a few weeks' time, maybe even days, it would all be finished. So why not join them? Why not just lose the uniform and join the men heading back to Germany? Many of these men were no doubt contemplating finding American and British units to surrender to, once they were near enough to them to make a dash for it.

It was tempting.

He knew the Allies would be sifting their German POWs for SS. But amidst the hundreds of thousands of men he could easily hide. And if worse came to worst and he was uncovered as ex-SS . . . Well, Höstner could not recall being directly associated to some of the more disturbing activities of his colleagues. He had only been an intelligence officer. That was all.

Very tempting.

An open truck with Luftwaffe personnel in the back passed him by.

Höstner instantly dismissed his nebulous thoughts of desertion and descended the earth bank at the double, landing with a messy splash in the ankle-deep muck once more. He raced after the truck, his smooth-soled boots slipping perilously a couple of times, and reached out for the tailboard, only just managing to get a hold of it. With a gasp of exertion he pulled himself up.

There were twenty to thirty men huddled on the back and exposed to the open air. Few of them had winter coats, most of them shivered in just their uniform tunics. Höstner addressed the group of Luftwaffe men.

'Do you men know if there's anybody in this column from KG-301?'

One of them looked up at him. 'Yeah, there are a few of us here.'

'You're from 301?'

'Yeah. There's a few ground crew in the truck behind. I don't know where the rest are.'

Höstner sighed with relief. He was getting somewhere.

'I'm trying to find an Oberleutnant Max Kleinmann. According to my records he was commanding Staffel 109f. Do you know if he is here, in this column somewhere?'

The man looked at him with suspicion. 'What do you want him for?'

'It's none of your business.'

'In that case I don't recall seeing him. Now do the decent thing and piss off, Leutnant, before we throw you off.'

Höstner felt anger welling up inside him. He'd taken just about enough shit this morning. He instinctively reached down for his gun and pulled it out. 'This is still a fucking army, and you are –'

'Put the gun away, unless you've got enough bullets in there for all of us,' the man said quietly. Höstner looked around at the soldiers on the truck. They looked like they'd beat him to a pulp if he tried using it. Tense seconds passed by as he weighed up whether to risk continuing to assert his authority with the help of his handgun. The men in the truck weren't even looking at it; they'd had their fill in recent weeks of agitated junior officers waving their guns menacingly and threatening death and damnation.

Höstner placed it back in his holster, and managed a conciliatory smile. 'Look. I'm sorry . . . I –'

'There, wasn't so hard, was it? Treating us with a little courtesy. You're after Max Kleinmann?'

Höstner nodded.

'Then you've found him. I'm Max Kleinmann.'

One of the other Luftwaffe men turned to face Max. 'What the fuck –'

'Relax, Pieter, the bastards'll track me down one way or the other.'

The SS officer looked at the other Luftwaffe men. 'And these men are your crew?'

The second Luftwaffe man, Pieter, turned to two of the other men and shared a silent nod before turning back to Höstner. 'We are his crew.' He looked at Max. 'We stay together, right, boss?'

Max nodded grimly. That was the deal. 'Okay, Pieter.' He turned to

Höstner and nodded. 'You heard him,' he gestured to Pieter and two other Luftwaffe men huddled next to him. 'These sorry-looking fools are my crew.'

Höstner smiled. 'Thank God! I've been freezing my balls off here since first light. Gentlemen, will you come with me please?'

'Why? What's this about?'

'I don't know. I'm just following orders.'

Max sat up stiffly. 'We're not going anywhere until we know why.'

'There is nothing to worry about, Oberleutnant. Listen, I have a truck parked nearby, with an oil heater inside . . . and a flask of soup. Huh?'

Pieter and Max looked at each other, and shared a glance with the other two.

'That'll do nicely,' said Max.

Chapter 12

The Telephone Call

Chris kneeled uncomfortably on the hard tiles of the bathroom floor, counting out a forty-five-second photographic exposure, his familiar crimson studio-world temporarily obliterated by a blast of white light from the enlarger's small fluorescent tube. He wore red-eye goggles to preserve his dark-adjusted vision.

His mobile phone started to bleep the *Simpsons'* theme tune.

'Shit!'

It was in the bedroom. He let it ring out, desperately trying to keep track of his countdown as it ran through the irritating ring tone three more times.

'Three ... two ... one.' He snapped off the light and covered the exposed photo-paper before lurching out of the bathroom to catch the phone before it rang off. He knew it would be his agency. Chris had been expecting them to get in touch to confirm receipt of the advance from *News Fortnite*.

The mobile predictably went silent as he grabbed hold of it.

'Bollocks.'

Chris checked the number of the caller. It had been withheld. That was almost as irritating as answerphone messages from people who identified themselves with 'It's me' and expected him to know who to phone back. Only Chris's mum could get away with that.

He loitered by the phone for half a minute before deciding that whoever it was had either dialled a wrong number or reckoned whatever it was could wait.

He was reaching out for the bathroom door when it rang again. He was quicker this time and interrupted the first bar of the tune.

'Hello?'

'Good evening,' The voice of a man. No one he recognised.

'Who's this?'

'Uh . . . my name is James Wallace.'

Chris quickly trawled through his mental list of business contacts; the name meant nothing to him.

'Sorry, mate, I'm not –'

'I used to work for the Office of Strategic Services during the war.'

A pause. Chris vaguely recalled that organisation from some documentary he'd seen on cable; the OSS was the precursor to the CIA. Wartime intelligence.

'And after the war ended, the United States Airforce Intelligence. I'm retired now, of course. I have friends there still, but now I spend too much time watching daytime TV.'

The old man paused, presumably anticipating a muted laugh.

'Go on,' said Chris.

'I . . . this is a little awkward over the phone . . . I gather you enquired about a certain wartime plane with the USAF museum over at Dayton? A flying fortress that went missing over Hamburg?'

How the –? Chris took a second to compose himself.

'Yes, I was asking about a plane called –'

'Please . . . It's best if we don't mention the name. Let's just refer to her as "the find" for now, okay?'

Chris felt an adrenaline spike, and not for the first time in the last few days cursed the fact that he was on the cigarette-wagon. He reached out for a piece of chewing gum from the bedside table. If there *had* been a packet of cigarettes within reach, it would have been game over for this year's attempt to quit.

'How the hell would you know that? Hang on . . . how did you get my number?'

The elderly voice wheezed a small, knowing laugh. 'Let's just say I have a few old friends still in Airforce Intelligence, and those old dogs know a few clever tricks. I'd like to arrange a meeting with you, if that's not any trouble.'

Not for the first time Chris felt his stomach stir uneasily. All of a sudden, his little scoop was beginning to attract a bit of attention. Was it the sort of attention he wanted, though?

'Why? What do you want from me?' he said, trying to keep the tension from his voice.

'I know you are investigating a certain "find" discovered off the coast nearby. I thought maybe we could exchange some information about it. If it *is* the same plane, then I know a little about how she might have ended up there, and in return, I'd be curious to hear anything you might have discovered about her. A mutual quid pro quo. Does that sound of interest?'

Christ, what the hell am I getting myself into?

The missing father and son, true or not, was one thing. An old wartime intelligence spook emerging out of the gloom was very much another. Unsettling, but then Chris reminded himself he had exposed himself to far more worrying situations in the past, in the pursuit of the all-elusive cover-photo . . . Rwanda, Sarajevo, Iraq . . . This was, so far at least, nothing to get too jumpy about. Not yet anyway.

'I suppose we can arrange a little show and tell,' he answered.

'Good. I'd prefer we had this little mutual show and tell in person rather than over a phone, if you understand me.'

'Uh . . . I'm not sure I –'

'Relax. If my motives were sinister, I wouldn't be asking your permission to talk with you, would I? You could just say no, and that would be that. But I suspect you're just as curious about this plane as I am.'

True.

Chris wondered if he was being too cautious. Whatever tale lay behind this plane nestling on the seabed off America, it was sixty years old. The only men in dark suits who might come looking for him would be packing zimmer frames.

'And anyway, I'm wary that ears are still listening out there, if you get my drift. Best to be safe than sorry.'

'Okay, then,' said Chris. 'Where and when?'

'Now that's the thing. I'd like our meeting to be discreet. It's probably best if I were to come over to you. I presume you're on or near Rhode Island somewhere?'

'Port Lawrence. It's a small place, very quiet right now.'

Chris was cautious about telling this man where he was staying; he decided it might be best to arrange a public, but not too public, meeting place.

'There's a little bar and grill place called Lenny's. We can meet there if you like. I've been there a couple of times. It's quiet and empty. We can talk discreetly there.'

'Good.' The old man sounded relieved. 'What's your name by the way?'

A first name couldn't do any harm; you've got nothing with just that.

Chris decided to let him have that. 'Chris. Listen . . . how did you get my number?'

He heard Wallace chuckle. 'You didn't withhold your number when you called the Museum, did you?'

Chris could almost have smacked his forehead. But then, to be fair, he hadn't anticipated the call to Dayton would be anything other than routine when he had started dialling.

'Don't worry,' Wallace added, 'it's just me that has your number. Would tomorrow be okay with you?'

'Tomorrow evening? Yeah that's fine. Seven p.m.?'

'Nineteen hundred, that's fine. How will I identify you?'

'I look English, apparently.'

'I . . . I'm sorry?'

'Tall, slim, short light brown hair, pretty nondescript . . . look, sod that, I'll carry a camera, okay?'

He heard Wallace sigh. 'Please be discreet, Chris. Tell no one about this for now. Like I've said, old ears might still be listening. After all, I found you, and I'm hardly a professional now.'

Wallace's words gave him pause for thought. Just how careful was he being? It seemed pretty much every bloody living soul in Port Lawrence knew what his business was.

'You're right, I'll keep shtum. Look, forget the camera. Lenny's is pretty quiet, you'll find me easily enough, I'll be the only bloke who *doesn't* look like a fisherman.'

He heard a gentle wheeze from the old voice on the end of the phone. Wallace was laughing this time. 'Good. Tomorrow at seven, then,' he added and the line went dead.

Chris sat down on the end of the bed and stared at his mobile phone, worried that it might ring again with some other shady spook from the past enquiring about his comings and goings.

God, I could really do with a smoke.

Chapter 13

Another Truck

11 April 1945, twenty miles south of Stuttgart

*A*nother *truck, another journey.*

At least this time he and his men had the truck to themselves, an oil heater to keep them warm and several flasks of potato soup to share between them.

Oberleutnant Max Kleinmann watched a tableau of misery pass by with a cold, impassive face. It was still a young face, but one prematurely aged by battlefield stress, fatigue and a poor diet. The eastern front hadn't turned boys into men; it had turned them into old men. Those few that survived, that is.

It hadn't taken him long to learn the single most valuable survival technique a soldier can learn.

To not care. To give up all hope and accept death as inevitable.

Not caring was what had saved him; because it seemed like those who desperately wanted to live, to get home to wives, sweethearts and newly born sons and daughters that they'd yet to meet, those were the ones who never made it. It was as if God or some other omnipotent, all-seeing bastard, was hunting down, one by one, the few men left with a burning desire to live on and live a life beyond this squalid, barbaric hell. So Max decided he wouldn't care one way or the other. Death could come for him at its convenience. Thus he had carried on surviving. The stupid, unkind logic of war.

He pulled on his cigarette; his gaunt unshaven cheeks drew in. Max was twenty-nine but sometimes, when he saw his face reflected, he saw beneath the pallid, grey skin a dead man trying to get out.

They had been going for fifteen hours. Progress had been painfully slow, as the truck had to pick its way through many rubble-strewn and cratered roads. He was horrified at the amount of devastation that had been wrought on Germany since he had last visited home. It had seemed that virtually every town or village they had passed through had taken some degree of bomb damage. Much of this destruction he guessed was accidental, Allied bombing runs that had drifted off target. But then he had heard that had been happening less in recent months. The carpet bombings had suddenly become *very* accurate. There was a rumour running around that the bombers were using multiple radio signals from England to pinpoint their positions. The ability to navigate from visual reference points was no longer a necessity. And so the waves of bombers were coming under the cover of night and dropping their bombs from altitudes well above the effective range of their flak.

If they'd had a system as accurate as that of the Allies back in the summer of 1940, the British airfields would have been pulverised into submission in a matter of weeks. Instead, navigating by sight only, they had simply pulverised many an empty field and marsh and suffered appalling losses at the hands of those lethal Spitfires for their troubles.

One of Max's commanders had once told him that this was a war of technology and the side with the best would win. It was that simple. War would never again be a measure of the will or courage or resolve of a people, but a measure of the efficiency of their men in lab coats.

'And if that is to be the future of war, Max,' he'd continued, his eloquence lubricated by a bottle of vodka, 'then how can a victory ever again be seen as something to be proud of? To be on the winning side after a battle, a man used to be able to say he won because he was smarter, braver, better than the other side on the day. Not any more. From now on those men that win their battles will have nothing to take pride in, merely that they've been given the better tools for the job.'

Major Lemmel that had been, he was a man who had cared passionately about things, and desperately wanted to survive the war. Max guessed by now God had tracked him down and finished him off.

The truck rumbled through a small town where the main street of shops was marked only by the hollow outlines of their eviscerated foundations. Several dozen corpses caked in plaster and dust were lined up at the side of the road awaiting collection and burial. They were bloated and distorted, scorched skin like tanned leather – taut, inflated by the gases of decay within. He had seen so many bodies like these in the ruins of Russia. Swollen corpses fit to burst, poking from the plaster and rubble of the world about them. That was the terrain that Max had grown used to over the last two years ... rubble and charred flesh, charcoal and meat. He had seen grand-scale devastation from close up on the ground, where the smells and visceral detail had once upon a time turned his stomach inside out, and he'd seen it from afar, from the air.

He had seen Stalingrad. Mile upon square mile of complete, total, devastation. As if God himself had reached down from heaven and tried to vigorously scrub the land clean of this city. It had been truly chilling to witness for himself how much destruction they had brought to bear on this one place ... how much raw destructive power mankind could summon at will. Too much power.

Our capacity to destroy has exceeded our capacity to create.

Max shook his head. When this was over, mankind would need to find another way, other than war, to resolve its petty disputes ... or mankind would end up totally destroying itself – turning the world into one relentless Stalingrad.

Of that he was certain.

As the truck rumbled past the bodies, he watched two old men collecting the corpses in their cart, and they passed by a large ditch where the dead had been stacked like sardines in a tin, head to toe.

That's what a defeated country looks like. A landscape of shattered ruins, dust, debris ... and carcasses stacked like timber.

Pieter passed him a tin mug of steaming potato soup. 'Here you are.'

'Thanks.'

He sat beside Max and stared miserably out at the passing landscape of rubble. 'It's all over now, isn't it?'

'Soon. Weeks, maybe days.'

Pieter lowered his voice. 'Days would be better than weeks.'

Max mumbled agreement. It would be better to end it now while all three of the Allied nations could claim an equal stake on Germany, rather than let the war run on. The Russians were covering ground at a far greater pace than the Americans and British. Having lost so many of her people to the Germans over the last few years, the Russians were a little less concerned about their casualty rate in this final chapter of the war. The Americans and the British, however, seemed more cautious in the way they were finishing the war, reluctant to lose too many more men to a struggle they considered all but over.

Max looked around at Pieter and the other men, Hans and Stefan. They were all ready to walk into an American or British POW camp. All three men had fought with him on the eastern front for the last year and a half, flying JU-88s, dropping supplies to the beleaguered 6th Army – a futile endeavour that had achieved very little and cost too much in lost men and machines. For the last four months, their role had been reduced to moving their plane back from the frontline; a concerted effort to keep the few remaining bombers out of the hands of the enemy. Finally, two weeks ago, when the fuel supply had finally dried up, they'd been forced to destroy what was left of the squadron and take to the road . . . and that was when KG-301 had ceased to exist and became nothing more than a few hundred men scattered along the retreating column.

These boys had done their bit, flying for whatever it was they believed in, the Fatherland or the Führer. Now all they wanted to do was to find a way to survive the next few weeks until someone decided enough was enough and called a halt to the bloodbath.

'That SS shit didn't give you any clues what this is about?' asked Pieter.

'No, but if I had cigarettes to bet, I'd wager this is a regrouping exercise. Someone is attempting to pull together a counter-offensive.'

'A counter –? With *what* for fuck's sake?'

Max shrugged. '*We* know there's nothing left to fly, but whoever's organised this truck probably thinks 301 is still operational.'

Pieter's face drained of colour. It was a response Max hadn't seen from him in a long time. His co-pilot had begun to believe he was going to make it home.

'I'm not going on any more raids. I can't –'

Max reached out and placed a hand on his shoulder. 'Don't worry, there aren't any more planes left. There is no more Luftwaffe, there's nothing more they can ask us to do. Whatever morons are behind this, they'll find out soon enough, and then I suppose they'll go and find us something pointless to do until the war ends.'

Pieter nodded.

'Just be grateful that this particular screw-up has given us our own truck, heater and food.'

'Yeah, I suppose you're right, one of their better screw-ups.'

'Exactly.'

Chapter 14

Major Rall

As the light of dusk was failing, the truck rumbled through the outskirts of another shattered town and out into an open area.

Max stirred as the truck shuddered to a halt and he heard a muted exchange of voices in the gathering dark. He turned to Pieter, but he was fast asleep, as were the others, comforted by the warmth of the oil heater and exhausted from days of deprivation.

He leaned over and lifted the canvas at the back of the truck to look out. The last light of day was now no more than a dusty grey strip on the horizon. They were in an open field. He could only see the irregular outlines of trees against the sky.

Max could hear the driver talking to someone. The conversation ended, and the truck proceeded, bouncing across an open stretch of grass. A guard hut passed by and they were within a chain-fenced perimeter. Max spotted the unmistakable outline of an aircraft hangar. It was an airfield.

His heart sank.

The truck came to an abrupt stop moments later and he detected movement out in the dark. A torch momentarily snapped on and shone into his face.

'Oberleutnant Kleinmann.' It was Höstner. 'Get your men ready and follow me. Quickly.'

The torch snapped off again.

Max turned back to his men; they were beginning to stir. 'Okay, boys, we're here.'

'Where?' asked Stef sleepily.

'I don't know. Get your stuff, we've got to get out.'

The four men wearily got to their feet, shuffled to the back of the truck and climbed down into the night.

The torch snapped on again and shone into their faces.

'Follow me, please.'

A hand appeared from behind the torch and wrapped over its end, dampening the light to an orange glow. The muted torchlight began to move away. 'Come on, hurry!'

Max nodded to his men and they followed him as he led them away from the truck.

'Where are we?' asked Pieter.

'An airstrip. God knows where,' he replied.

'Shit. I *was* right. Another bloody mission.'

Leutnant Höstner led them towards a low bunker they didn't see until the last moment. He rapped on a metal door with the torch, and almost immediately it opened a crack, revealing a faint light from inside.

'I have Kleinmann, and his crew for Major Rall.'

The light went out, and Max heard the door creak as it opened.

'Inside quickly.'

Höstner ushered them through, and once inside they heard the door slam behind them.

A dim ceiling light came on, a single bulb illuminating a featureless concrete corridor. Höstner held out a hand to Max. 'Sorry for bundling you out like that. I just wanted to get you men inside before any of their planes spotted the torch. They own the sky now.'

'What's this all about?'

'I'm sorry. You'll be seeing Major Rall soon. He will explain it all.'

'Then at least tell me where the hell we are?'

'Ulmsruhe, several hours south of Stuttgart.'

'Where are we going?'

'I have orders to take you to Major Rall immediately, sir.'

Max followed the man along the concrete corridor to a set of steps that took them downwards.

'What is this place, Leutnant?'

'A regional intelligence post. Well, it used to be until it was abandoned last week. Major Rall appropriated it a couple of days ago. So you'll have to excuse us if it looks a little messy.'

The steps descended into another featureless corridor. Several doors opened on to it. The SS Leutnant led them down the corridor towards a door at the end. They passed a room filled with banks of radios, and in the middle of the room was a metal crate full of ashes; the brown, unburned corners of papers still smouldered. The floor around it was littered with boxes full of documents waiting to be destroyed, but forgotten in the haste of departure. The Leutnant followed Max's gaze. 'When we're done here, we'll finish the job.'

He gestured towards another open door off the corridor. 'Canteen. Your men can help themselves to some food. I believe we even have some coffee too.'

Max nodded to Pieter. 'Go on. I'll be back shortly.'

Pieter led Hans and Stef in and they proceeded directly towards a steaming steel urn.

The SS Leutnant tipped his head towards the door at the end of the corridor. 'Come, please. Major Rall is waiting for you.'

'Don't forget to leave me a bit, lads,' said Max as he watched his men eagerly helping themselves to the coffee and opening several tins of pork.

Max fell in behind the Leutnant as he eagerly proceeded the last few yards down the corridor to the door and knocked gently on it.

'Major Rall?'

Max heard a muffled voice from beyond the door. 'Come in.'

Leutnant Höstner opened the door and gestured for Max to enter. He closed the door behind him, leaving Max alone in the room with Major Rall.

The room was a small, windowless, concrete cell. The walls had at one time been painted a dull 'waiting room' green. Scuffmarks and scrapes on the walls indicated this room had once contained a lot more furniture. Now a single desk and two chairs stood in the middle, and a solitary filing cabinet in a corner made the room feel a lot bigger than it was.

Major Rall stood beside the desk. He was a man of average build and height, but his face was instantly striking because of a burn scar that stretched from below his collar, up and across the left side of his face to his hairline. His left ear was little more than a hole with a small rib of skin around it, and his left eye glistened with excess moisture. Rall, it seemed, had made no concessions to his disfigurement and quite happily boasted a well-maintained moustache that disintegrated as it crossed his lip towards the scar tissue on the left.

Max was relieved that Major Rall wore a Luftwaffe uniform.

Rall picked up a manila file from his desk and opened it.

'Oberleutnant Maximilian Kleinmann?'

'Yes sir,' answered Max.

'Hmmm . . . you've served for the last two years on the eastern front, before that in France. You earned an Iron Cross, followed by a Knight's Cross. It looks like I chose well.'

Max spoke up. 'Permission to speak freely, sir?'

Rall smiled. 'Yes, of course.'

'My men and myself have been brought here and no information has been given to us. We have no idea what this is all about, sir.'

'No, that's quite right. Those were my orders . . . I'm sorry about that. It was a precautionary measure in case you were intercepted on the way here.'

Rall gestured towards the seat nearest Max. 'Please, make yourself comfortable. Would you like something to drink, a coffee perhaps?'

Max nodded eagerly as he settled down into the seat and Rall walked stiffly across to the door, opened it and quietly ordered a coffee. He returned to the table and perched informally on the edge.

'Nothing quite as satisfying as having an officer of the SS wait on you, is there?' Rall smiled conspiratorially.

'Never had the pleasure, Major.'

Rall took a deep breath. 'Right.' The small talk was over. 'I was passed your name by your previous commanding officer, Major Schendtler. You – and your crew – have a very impressive service record. You came highly recommended.'

'Thank you, sir.'

'It's rare to find a bomber crew that have been together for so long.' Max nodded; he knew Rall meant '*survived* for so long'. 'Which is why I took the enormous effort to find you and your men. It really wasn't easy, I can tell you. There seems to be very little logistical control over what's left of our boys.'

Rall fell silent for a moment, it seemed he was pondering what to say next. His left eye, surrounded by scarred skin tissue and bereft of any lashes, leaked moisture onto his cheek. He wiped it casually away with his hand.

'We've lost the war,' he said out of the blue. Max instinctively flinched. True words, but recklessly dangerous spoken aloud. 'We've lost, it's over. Things may rumble on for a little longer, but we all know right now that this is finished.'

Max carefully guarded his response, suspicious of Rall's candour. 'There's always a chance, sir.'

Rall smiled. 'Kleinmann, relax, I'm not fishing for a treasonous statement. It's just you and I, two airmen. Surely in these final days we can speak our minds freely, eh?'

Max remained silent, still wary of committing himself.

'It's over. The Russians are approaching the outskirts of Berlin and are settling in and making ready for an offensive to take the city. I'm sure they're expecting as stiff a fight as we experienced in Stalingrad. But I'd say we have two, maybe four, weeks of fight we can give them.'

Rall left those words hanging in the air. There was a gentle rap on the door, and Leutnant Höstner entered awkwardly carrying a tray with two steaming cups of coffee on it. He placed it silently on Rall's desk and left.

Rall waited until the door closed behind him before continuing. 'We have an opportunity to end this war on our terms. One opportunity, but we need to work quickly to make it happen.'

'A mission?' Max asked uncertainly.

Rall passed a cup of coffee to Max.

'Yes, a mission.'

Max looked down at the cup of steaming coffee, a delaying tactic; time to think carefully about what he had to say next to the Major. He owed that much, and more, to his men.

'Sir, there's no easy way for me to say this . . .'

Rall nodded. 'Please, feel free to speak your mind, Oberleutnant.'

'My men and I have fought in three campaigns. We have flown over three hundred sorties for our country . . . and maybe it's God's will or sheer blind luck that we're all still alive. With respect, sir, we all feel we've done our duty for Germany, and I . . . ' Max faltered, unsure how Rall would take his next words. 'I can't order my men to fly again, not with the end of the war only days away.'

Rall remained silent, impassive and motionless.

'I can't order them to. Sir, at the risk of a court martial, I won't,' Max added.

'I understand,' Rall said eventually, warming to the pilot's loyalty to his men.

'Which is why the mission is voluntary.'

'Voluntary?'

'Yes.'

Max looked up at Rall. The Major appeared to be sincere.

'This mission is too . . . how shall I say? . . . delicate,' Rall added, 'to be undertaken by men under duress. Only if you and your men are willing, is this mission going to proceed.'

'And this mission will end the war?'

'Yes, it will. It will end this war in a way that guarantees Germany survives, that the Russians stop, turn around and leave our soil.'

Max looked back down at his coffee.

An end to the madness.

Now that the Allies owned the skies, any mission undertaken would surely be suicide. He guessed that this endeavour, whatever it was, had probably been hastily conceived by some ambitious staff officer desperate to extract a little glory from the final days of the war. A pointless and reckless gamble with the odds stacked heavily against Max and his men surviving it. Max had learned to despise those commanders who led from the rear and casually bandied terms like 'acceptable losses'.

'Kleinmann, I want to show you and your men something. And then I will explain the mission to you in detail. I will tell you everything. I will tell you things that only I, and a handful of other men, know about. For a short time, you and your men will have the privilege of sharing a confidentiality with, amongst others, the Führer.'

Max wasn't entirely convinced his men could give a flying fuck about their Führer.

Rall smiled, realising the grim-faced veteran in front of him had been less than impressed by such a clumsy attempt to win him over.

'Let me show you what I have, and I'll outline the mission. Then, and only then, will I ask you and your men to volunteer.'

'And when they and I refuse?'

'You are all free to go.'

Max looked up at Rall, studying the man's wrecked face, searching for a sign of sincerity or guile.

'We are free to go?'

'You have my word. Like I said, this will only work if we have volunteers.'

Against his better judgement, Max decided to take this man's word, for now.

'Then my men and I will at least listen.'

Chapter 15

Medusa

On the horizon Max could see a flickering of light, the telltale sign of a distant bombing run over Stuttgart. The flashes of light in the night sky, like localised sheet lightning, were accompanied by an almost constant muted rumbling.

Major Rall led Max and his men across the pitted and rubble-strewn concrete of the airfield towards a solitary hangar. The airfield was unlit and in the darkness the men had to make their way cautiously or run the risk of twisting an ankle. Max used the sporadic flashes in the sky to study the treacherous ground in front of him.

Three Waffen-SS stood guard outside the closed sliding doors of the hangar. In the darkness, they only became aware of the approaching men from the clatter of debris unintentionally kicked across the ground in front of the building.

'Stop and identify yourself!'

'Major Rall,' his voice rasped.

A torch flicked on, and the beam flashed across the Major and the others.

'Turn that fucking thing off!' Rall hissed at the soldier. 'If you do that again I'll wrap it round your neck.'

The torch snapped off.

'Sorry, sir.'

'Just open the door.'

Max heard the metallic clatter of the door to the hangar sliding open. The intermittent flickering light on the horizon did little to penetrate the dark void revealed inside.

'Okay, Max, gentlemen, this way.'

Pieter tapped Max on the shoulder. 'What are we being taken to see exactly?'

'I don't know, he hasn't said yet.'

Rall entered the hangar and the others followed him hesitantly. The SS guards pulled the hangar doors shut behind them.

In total darkness they heard Rall's voice. 'The Allies bombed this airfield to hell and back two weeks ago. As far as they're concerned, this is now just rubble and craters.

'They came back the following day to drop a bomb on this hangar because it was still standing. Since then the airfield has been left alone. As far as they're aware it's no longer usable. And that's what we want them to carry on thinking. You see we've got something very valuable in here.'

Rall flicked on a torch and muted the light by placing his hand over the end. His fingers glowed red and faint amber light illuminated the hangar. Giant shadows cast from his fingers danced like enormous phantoms.

'Look.'

He removed his hand from the end of the torch and swung the beam of light towards the middle of the hangar. Taking up at least a third of the total floor space, stood a B-17 bomber.

'Magnificent, isn't she?' he said proudly.

Pieter gasped. 'My God, is it a real one?'

Rall laughed. 'Of course it is, go on, go and take a closer look.'

Pieter and the other crew members jogged over towards it and began inspecting it closely.

'Major, how did you manage to get one of these?' asked Max.

'It was a gift made to us, over a year ago, courtesy of the United States Air Force. It landed undamaged in a field in Holland. The crew had become disorientated through the night and lost their way from the rest of the bomber group. They ran low on fuel and ended up putting down in the field. It was rather amusing, you see, they believed they'd made it back to England and were putting down on friendly ground.'

Max nodded with a little sympathy. Stef, his navigator, had managed on occasion to misplace them by a few miles, but in fairness he'd always managed to navigate them to the correct country.

He wandered beneath the plane's giant wings and ran a hand over one of her Wright Cyclone engines. Rall stood beside him and watched the pilot caress the smooth steel plates of the engine casing.

'It really is an awe-inspiring plane, isn't it?' he said.

'What on earth convinced us we could win against a country that can produce machines like these in their thousands?' he said more to himself than the Major.

'Arrogance, foolishness. Didn't we all think we were invincible two years ago?'

Rall panned the torch across the fuselage towards the front of the plane. The light picked out the painted image of a topless woman, breasts held at bay by crossed arms. The woman smiled malevolently, while the hair looked unkempt, wild and almost alive.

'What's that?' asked Max

'Ahh, yes, the nickname the American crew had for this plane, very clever. A little more thought went into this one than most others.'

'What is it?'

'*Medusa*. The Americans called her that presumably in the superstitious hope that enemy pilots staring at the plane, at her, would turn to stone. Silly, hmm? But clever.'

Max could understand such a foolish notion. Superstition governed many of the little habits and rituals he and his men privately acted out before every mission. It was a good name.

Pieter approached the two men. 'Major, can we get a look inside it?'

Rall nodded briskly. 'Of course, take my torch with you.' He passed it to Pieter.

Pieter dipped his head formally. 'Thank you, sir.' He grinned and turned towards the belly hatch, leading Stefan and Hans up inside.

'Boys in a toy store springs to mind, eh?' Rall nodded and winked.

'It's too easy to forget they're all still young, Major.'

Max watched the subdued light from the torch flicker faintly through the Plexiglas canopies at the front of the plane and watched as the three young men clambered up into the cockpit and examined, with fascination, the interior.

'We've modified the plane in several ways. Inside the cockpit the instrumentation has been relabelled in German, the Browning M2 machine guns have been replaced with our MG-81s.'

'Why?'

'Shell calibre. We would need to manufacture our own supply of 50 mm shells to use them.'

'Of course.'

'And inside we've added additional fuel tanks to extend her range.'

Max looked quizzically at Rall. 'These planes have a long range already.'

'Yes, we know they have a range of four thousand miles; the extra tanks will give this one another thousand miles.'

Max turned back to look at Rall. 'She'll have a range of five thousand miles?'

The Major nodded.

'I presume my men and I have been brought here to fly this plane.'

Rall nodded again.

'Five thousand miles?' he said again. 'So where exactly are we going to fly her?'

The faint, flickering torchlight spilling from the bomber's cockpit lit up enough of Major Rall's face to show he was smiling.

'I think perhaps it's time you and I took a little walk outside, and then I can tell you about our little plan.'

Chapter 16

Watched

Chris walked out of the rear entrance of the motel towards the quayside parking area. He was halfway across the parking lot on his way towards the Cherokee, weaving his way between two 'Runcies Fish' delivery trucks parked side by side, when he saw them.

He surprised himself with his sudden paranoid decision to duck back into the evening shadows between both vehicles. That telephone call yesterday out of nowhere from the mysterious 'Mr Wallace' had definitely done a number on him. He was getting jittery. Another week in Port Lawrence and he could see himself hugging his knees in a closet and wearing his favourite tinfoil hat.

The two men stood beneath one of the bright floodlights that lined the jetty. A sharp pool of white light picked them out in stark clarity. His first impression was that they had the appearance of ex-military types. Both were physically fit. They looked like they had the kind of whippet-lean musculature that comes from decades of genuine fitness, not the bloated Mr Universe-like bulk that any fool can build up in a few months with the help of a fitness instructor and a supply of steroids.

He had seen idiotic thugs like that in virtually every bar in Sarajevo. Pumped up wannabee-John McLanes, some of them ex-soldiers, many more who had never been, all attracted like wasps to a Coca-Cola can, looking for mercenary work. Not for the money, but for the thrill. Most of them had signed up to fight for the Kosovans.

Chris had done an assignment with *FHM* magazine, for an article entitled 'The Shooting Gallery'. He had photographed quite a few of these thrill-chasers for the piece. Most of them had revelled in the attention, posing in their combat fatigues, brandishing their guns for the camera and enjoying the temporary celebrity status. They had boasted openly about the action they'd seen, their kills, or 'frags' as some of them casually euphemised the act of killing. They discussed their bloody business like excited trainee managers after a paint-ball game.

It hadn't taken him very long to work out that he was dealing with the *poseurs*, the weekend warriors, big boys playing at being soldiers, and he soon learned to take with a pinch of salt most, if not all, of their Hollywood-inspired combat claims.

He'd moved on to find the genuine mercenaries in that wrecked city and had the shit kicked out of him on one occasion when he'd pulled out his camera in a bar. The three men that had cracked several of his ribs, split his lip and trashed his camera, they'd been the real deal. They had worn smart casual clothes – sports-casual, not combat fatigues – and they'd looked a lot like the two men across the quay, standing patiently under the light.

Chris watched them. They were talking and looking around, looking for something or someone. There was no mistaking their furtive manner; no mistaking the fact that they looked like pros ... not just a couple of 'scroats', as an old police buddy of his used to refer to suspicious-looking civvies on the street, up to no good.

Chris found himself debating whether cowering here in the shadows between these two trucks was paranoia gone too far or a sound precaution. On the one hand, he felt there was already enough to this bomber story to speculate that even after sixty years some agency out there might want to ensure it wasn't splashed across tomorrow's newspapers. On the other hand, whatever happened, it all went off sixty years ago. Who would possibly care now? Who would care enough to send out a couple of heavies?

Chris shook his head. It probably was paranoia on his part, and he was glad Mark wasn't here. The bastard would relentlessly take the piss out of him for wimping out like this.

His phone chose this moment in time to vibrate enthusiastically and trill the *Simpsons'* theme.

In the relative silence of the jetty, it carried effortlessly across to the two men standing near the edge. They both spun sharply around.

'Shit!' Chris cursed as he fumbled to pull his phone out of his jeans and kill it.

He looked up to see the men walking warily towards the trucks. One of them gestured to the other to check out the right hand side of them, while he veered towards the left.

Chris, panic beginning to grip him, finally eased the damned thing out of his front pocket, only to let it slip through his fingers and clatter noisily to the ground.

'Oh, for fuck's sake,' he whispered as he squatted down and patted the gravel in search of it. The shrill theme tune came to an abrupt end, which was a small relief, but the damage was done. The two men were almost upon him. He looked under one of the trucks; there was enough space to slide beneath, but he dared not leave his phone on the ground for them to find. As they drew close enough to hear their footfalls, Chris redoubled his efforts, feeling the uneven ground for the phone.

But it was no good, and they were too close.

He quickly dropped to a prone position and crawled as quietly as he could under one of the trucks just as one of the men appeared as a silhouette in the space between both of the vehicles.

A shaft of bright torchlight illuminated the ground beside Chris, throwing into sharp relief the scuff and drag marks he had left in the pebbles; a telltale sign of Chris's hasty scramble for cover. Chris could now see where his phone was. It nestled just behind the front tyre of the truck opposite, half in, half out of view.

Shit.

All he needed now was for the previous caller to try his number again.

The beam of torchlight moved up and down the narrow gap between the trucks with a slow and steady thoroughness.

'No one,' he heard one of them say.

'Check in the drivers' cabs,' the other said.

The torchlight flickered wildly, and shadows leaped as the beam was aimed into the cabs of both trucks in turn.

'No one inside, but there's a phone up here on the dash. See it?'

'Yeah. Maybe that was it.'

'Shit, that was a loud ring.'

The torch snapped off, and he heard the crunch of feet on gravel as the two men slowly headed back down towards the jetty's edge. Chris watched them as they returned to where they had been standing, resuming, it seemed, a vigil.

They're waiting for Will's fishing boat to come back in, aren't they?

Yes, it looked like they were. Word must have got around that Will had taken out a couple of divers to the plane wreck; that's how McGuire had found out in all likelihood. The old boy had been talking for sure, then.

With great care, Chris eased himself out from beneath the truck and hastily reached out for his phone. His fingers quickly located it and before it could ring again he switched it off, letting out a sigh of relief as he did so.

It was nearly time to meet 'Wallace' at Lenny's. He looked anxiously back at the two men down by the jetty. If they really were here to keep things quiet, then not only he and Mark were potentially in danger, but this poor old sod Wallace too.

And hadn't he already sounded a bit uneasy on the phone when he'd called you out of the blue?

Wallace could be dangerous. He may be a harmless old man with the best of intentions to blow the whistle on some wartime secret, but if there were spooks like these watching him from afar, then he was leading them, albeit unintentionally, right to Chris.

Not exactly an encouraging thought.

Shit, Chris, you muppet. If the CIA or whoever wanted you dead, you'd be dead already.

Fair point. He made his way towards Lenny's, casting one last glance back over his shoulder as he crunched quietly out of the parking lot, and walked briskly up the dark cut-through between a couple of buildings and onto Devenster Street.

Chapter 17

Decision

Max finished explaining the details that he'd been given. Major Rall had described to him an outline of the plan, just enough to understand the enormity of the task they were being asked to perform, and the appalling risk.

And now his men knew too.

He swigged a mouthful of tepid coffee, relishing its bitter taste. The questions were coming, any second now.

His men sat around him in the bunker's canteen on document cases dragged in from the radio room. Chairs, it seemed, were a rarity down here. They sat in a circle, each of them savouring the coffee, and all but Stefan smoking the cigarettes Major Rall had generously offered the crew after they'd returned from the hangar. The blue-tinged smoke from the coarse Russian brand converged above them against the low concrete ceiling in a thick fog.

As Max watched each of them absorb what he had finished telling them, the silence lengthened. Faintly he could hear Rall moving around in his office, no doubt anxiously waiting for them to discuss the mission and decide whether they were willing to undertake it.

Pieter's lower jaw moved from side to side. Max knew he was grinding his teeth, an unfortunate habit of his when he was immersed in deep thought. His dark, full eyebrows were knotted in concentration beneath a lick of blond hair as he waded through the information, the repercussions, and the events that would follow if they went ahead with the mission.

Pieter was undecided.

Decisions like these were for leaders, generals, he argued wordlessly, not for the likes of him. It is the luxury of a soldier not to fathom why an objective exists, just to make sure it is met. Max had briefed them on the task, but then he'd also clouded the water with suggestions on how the Americans, Russians and British might react, and how the whole thing might play out in the next few weeks. He wished Max hadn't. It was a layer of detail too much for him and he was making no progress with it. He decided to sidestep these considerations by assuring himself that the top brass would have exhausted finer minds than his on the strategic repercussions of what they were planning to do. He limited himself to a simpler, straightforward question.

Can it be done?

He sucked on his cigarette, as he weighed up the risks. The mission sounded like a bastard. But you had to hand it to this Major Rall, it sounded like an audacious and impressive bastard. If it could be done, and the war won, then surely they *had* to do it. They had to at least try, surely. Pieter wasn't afraid to die – he'd passed that point a long long time ago – he just wasn't that keen on doing it pointlessly. If there was a fair chance for success – just a fair chance – they had to give it a go.

Max turned to study Hans.

The young man was nodding and tapping a finger on the metal rim of his mug, as if enjoying a tune no one else could hear. In his other hand he held his smoke, forgotten, burning steadily towards the filter. His blue eyes were unfocused and lost in the distance. Of all of them, Max knew Hans would have the least reservations and would probably be the first to volunteer. He wasn't one for careful deliberation by any stretch of the imagination; he was a bull-necked thug with a preference to thinking with his fists – a typical gunner. But here, now at least, he seemed to be indulging in some level of introspection about what could lie ahead. Even for Hans, the mission was too dangerous to blithely accept. But there was one thing Max was certain of: if Pieter voted yes, so would he. Hans although physically strong, was a follower, unsure of himself. He would always look to either Pieter or Max for a direction. Hans would follow Pieter on this.

And finally Stefan.

The young lad rocked gently from side to side; his eyes darted uncertainly from Max to Pieter to Hans. 'Baby Bear' was what Pieter liked to call him when he ruffled the boy's ginger hair. That was stupid. Stefan had done his share of growing up like the rest of them. He had been with them for over a year and flown on nearly a hundred sorties as navigator and radio operator; but being the youngest would always make him the pup of the crew. Stefan absent-mindedly pulled on the tuft of red hairs that had managed to grow on his chin. All of them were sporting bristles long enough to tug, it had been many days since they'd had the luxury of a razor, but unlike the others, who would happily pay a day's ration for a razor and some shaving oil, Stef took great pride in the meagre offering on his jaw.

'Okay, tell me what you lads are thinking,' said Max.

Pieter looked up at him. 'What do you think, Max?'

'I want to see what you boys reckon first. Whatever decision we end up with, it has to be unanimous, right?'

Hans cocked his head.

'Unanimous means . . . everyone has to agree,' Max added.

'Right.'

Stefan raised a finger, a classroom habit that he still hung on to. Max nodded. 'Go on.'

'We'll get fighter escort cover most of the way?'

'Across France and some of the way beyond, yes. They'll be arriving soon, some of the best fighter pilots in the Luftwaffe. You can't get a better escort than that.'

'How many?'

'As many as we can find planes for. Major Rall told me that they have managed to pool something like thirteen 109s, maybe some more can be put together between now and when we leave.'

'Thirteen fighters and a B-17 against everything they can throw at us between here and the Atlantic?' Pieter smiled. 'My money says we won't even make France.'

Max shrugged. 'I'm not going to lie to you. This is going to be a nasty one, the worst one we've flown together. But we have the element of surprise, we're flying one of their planes – they won't expect that, and we'll have a squadron of the best fighter pilots nearby watching and waiting to step in when we need them.'

'This is a one-way flight, isn't it?' said Stefan.

Max turned to the lad.

Clever boy, you've done the maths.

'Yes, Stef, the extra fuel tanks give us the range we need to get there and a little more, but not enough to come home. After we've done our job, we'll attempt to land, or bail out over there.'

Pieter snorted. 'They'll bloody well skin us.'

'If it all goes to plan, by the time we bail out or land, the Americans will be our allies.'

'And what if we say no?' asked Pieter.

Max shrugged. 'The Major says we can go.'

'And the Russians carry on with what they're doing,' added Stefan.

On that point they all looked at Max. He nodded slowly. 'Yes.'

All four men were fully aware of the savage revenge the advancing Red Army was exacting from their German foes. It was common knowledge that they were not taking prisoners. Rumours had spread of many atrocities that had occurred to straggling German forces, even the liberated civilians left in their wake. And now they were on German soil and hungrily advancing across the country, surrounding Berlin and spreading west and southwards. They knew Germany was to be obliterated and most of its people massacred, and when the war ended, the Russians would surely demand access to what was left of the Fatherland under Allied control to complete their bloody act.

'Fuck it, I say we do it. We've been running from the enemy for too bloody long,' Pieter said, the shadows of doubt banished from his mind.

Max looked towards the other two.

Hans stopped tapping his mug and looked up at Pieter and Max, still unsure.

'Come on, Hans, let's stick it to them,' growled Pieter.

'Yeah, okay,' said Hans looking to Pieter.

All three men turned to face Stefan.

'How about you?' asked Max.

The young man looked awkward under the gaze of his older colleagues. 'I've got family near Sprenberg . . . three sisters.' Stefan looked at Max with eyes reddened from fatigue. He didn't need to add any more to that, the men knew what fate awaited them when the Russian army arrived.

'I say yes, too,' Stefan added quietly.

Pieter reached out and punched the lad's shoulder. 'That's the spirit, boy.'

The men looked to Max for the deciding vote. 'And so, Max, what about you?' asked Pieter.

Max stubbed his cigarette out and drained his now cold coffee.

The men are waiting for you to say yes.

The plan was a good one. It could work, it really could. They had the element of surprise, and the American B-17 was the perfect conceit, the air was full of them. Crossing France would be the dangerous part of the mission. Beyond France, across the Atlantic, they would be home and dry. New York had no air defences, she had never needed to have any.

It could be done.

Manhattan Island was the target. Max knew very little about the city of New York, but Major Rall had informed him that the island was the commercial heart of the city, and it would be a Sunday morning when they arrived with the bomb. Civilian casualties would be minimised.

But, there would still be several thousand people who would inevitably die.

Rall had not discussed the bomb in detail, only that it was a new 'explosive formula' one thousand times more destructive than that being used currently by the American bombers. This one bomb would do as much damage as the combined payload of fifty of their B-17s.

Imagine, Max, it will seem to them as if we have the power to conjure four squadrons of heavy bombers out of thin air, anywhere we want.

He could see how frightening a thought that might be to the Americans, safe these last four years, on the other side of an ocean. It could possibly be enough to convince them to step in and save what was left of Germany from the Russians, if for no other reason than to prevent the communists from getting their hands on this magical, powerful formula.

And there is the key Max: mutual distrust between the Americans and the British on the one hand, and the Russians on the other.

It really could work. And if it did, there were many, many more German lives that would be saved by this than would be lost on a Sunday, on Manhattan Island.

There's a simple arithmetic at work here, Max. One or two thousand of them for God knows how many of us at the hands of the Russians. When they've taken Berlin, do you think their revenge will stop there?

Rall's faultless argument had boiled down to simple arithmetic. A few thousand American lives, to save millions of German lives. And on that basis, Max could see that they had to give this thing a go. There was no choice. But he was drawn back to the haunting image of total destruction that was Stalingrad.

'This really is to *end* the war?' he had asked the Major.

Rall had nodded. 'God help us if it doesn't. With such a bomb as you will be dropping, it would be insane for any further war after this to happen.'

Pieter, Hans and Stef were waiting for an answer. He knew they were all hoping for the same answer. He owed them at least that.

'All right, I will tell the Major we will do it,' said Max.

Major Rall looked up at the sound of rapping on his door. 'Enter,' he called loudly. Max walked in and saluted smartly.

'Oberleutnant Kleinmann, you have a decision for me?'

Max nodded. 'My men and I will undertake the mission, Major.'

Rall smiled. 'I was beginning to think you and your men had eloped after enjoying my coffee and cigarettes. Thank you, Kleinmann. I will have you and your crew properly billeted here in the bunker and supplies arranged shortly. You'll be pleased to know I can lay my hands on some more of that South American coffee, but first I have some calls to make. Please excuse me.'

Rall nodded as Max clicked his heels and departed. He picked up the phone on his desk and dialled a number he had been reciting in his head over and over for the last hour. The telephone rang once and was picked up.

'Yes ... Heil Hitler. This is Major Rall. Please inform him that the operation is ready to proceed.'

Rall placed the phone back in its cradle and listened to the faint rumble of the raid over Stuttgart, twenty miles north. His meticulously laid plans were now starting to roll forward; after so many months of organisation, fighting for a rapidly dwindling pool of resources, it was finally beginning to happen. Now that they had managed to pull in a suitable crew, the American bomber was fitted with enough additional fuel tanks to achieve the range they needed, and the weapon itself was approaching final assembly, it was time to activate the last component of the plan. He looked at his watch; it was 11.54 p.m. on the 11th of April. In little more than two weeks this would all be over.

'My God, it's actually going to happen,' he said aloud.

He looked at the phone, another call was necessary. It was time to track down the one remaining U-boat that was big enough for the job and still operational somewhere in the North Sea.

Chapter 18

One More Voyage

5 a.m., 12 April 1945, North Sea,
fifty miles off the coast of Norway

Captain Lündstrom checked the chronometer – it was 0500 hours. He banged his fist angrily against the bulkhead. They should have been on the surface making the most of the darkness to recharge the boat's flagging batteries, not skulking beneath the water; a stupid waste of the night hours.

'Shit,' he muttered to himself.

Time was running out for them. They needed to have at least another three hours on the surface running under diesel to give them enough charge on the batteries. Three hours' charge would carry them through the next day underwater using as little power as possible, and then they could run the next night on the surface to get the batteries fully charged up.

If they surfaced now, Lündstrom estimated they could run for one hour more before the light of day exposed them, then they were vulnerable for the other two. It was unavoidable, they had to come up, and they had to do it soon.

He cupped his jaw firmly in a hand. His fingers massaged the coarse bristles of his recently grown beard, making long, exaggerated, stroking movements. That was just for show, for the men. His palm was wedged firmly under his chin to stop his head from shaking, a nervous tick that he'd seemed to have developed in the last year. Often, if the shaking was too noticeable, he would blame the cold. It was a convincing enough lie given that the confines of the boat were always damp and he could utter it amidst a cloud of condensation. Nonetheless, it was a bad twitch for a commanding officer to get; a shaking hand could be tucked away in a pocket, or easily folded under an arm. He knew it was getting harder to hide . . . it was definitely getting worse. But then, everything was.

His mind returned to the dilemma at hand.

Surface? ... Wait? ... Surface? ... Wait? ...

The longer they left it, the longer they'd be exposed up there while they charged. Two hours on the surface in the daylight was a bad place to be these days.

Nine months ago, Lündstrom's boat, U-1061, a supply vessel, a 'milk cow' as they affectionately called them, had been servicing the U-boats that had been sent in to harass the supply ships feeding the Allied forces that had recently taken Normandy. Doenitz had decided, after months of marshalling what was left of his U-boat fleet, that now was the time to strike – to hamstring them while they were still vulnerable and literally just off the beaches. The attacks had been an unmitigated disaster. Lündstrom's boat had gone in close behind the attack boats. During the principal night of the attack they had sat at periscope depth on the periphery of the action, listening to the cacophony of depth charge explosions and watching the Royal Navy destroyers circling the sea in tightening loops like buzzards around a carcass. Several times during the night Lündstrom distinctly recognised the faint signature sound of steel buckling and collapsing under pressure, the death rattle of another U-boat sent to the bottom, another crew of boys buried within a twisted and compressed tangle of metal.

Of the fifty-six boats that had been sent in, the Royal Navy and Airforce had sunk twenty-six. The U-boats had only managed to sink nineteen Allied vessels.

That had been June 1944. Since then, the English Channel had continued to be a death trap, with Royal Navy patrols densely plotted along the narrow stretch of sea. The last of the U-boats were mostly holed up in Norway and the Baltic Sea, with a few venturing north around the Shetland Isles to the Atlantic to attempt the occasional daring attack on the convoys that now passed largely without incident from America to Britain. U-1061 met these few boats south of the Faroe Isles; they rarely seemed to require replacement torpedoes, just fuel and supplies.

Lündstrom didn't envy them. The best they could do was silently stalk the convoys. Any attempt to attack a ship was inviting disaster. The best they could hope for was to catch a ship that was falling behind and beyond the protective range of the escort.

They had been making good time yesterday evening, heading towards an arranged rendezvous co-ordinate south-west of the islands, cruising comfortably at eighteen knots under diesel power, when one of his men had spotted a Royal Navy destroyer bearing down on them. The bastards were getting too good at spotting them. They had dived, and within two hours a second destroyer had joined the first. Within four hours they had three Allied vessels circling above.

It seemed the Royal Navy had discovered this part of the North Sea was a rendezvous point and had ships in the area, patrolling it.

Lündstrom and his men had endured nearly eight hours of well-focused depth charging and as this particularly nasty game of hide and seek played out through the night, none of them had had a chance to sleep, even during the lengthy periods between bombardments of unsettling quiet.

There had been a lull now for well over two hours and the men anxiously looked at their captain, aware that time was running out and that he must be agonising over the decision to risk going to periscope depth for a quick reconnoitre.

Leutnant Holm ended a silence that had lasted a long time. 'Sir?'

Holm was reminding him tactfully. *We have to go up soon.*

Lündstrom turned to him.

'Okay, periscope depth.'

The Leutnant barked out the order, and almost immediately the U-boat tilted gently upwards. Lündstrom leaned into the angle of ascent. He looked around the young faces with him. Many of these boys were only seventeen; Hitler Youth hurriedly drafted and half-trained to fill the rapidly depleting ranks of the Kriegsmarine. By comparison, Leutnant Holm, aged nineteen, standing beside him with a face like a choirboy, was an old, seasoned veteran.

He felt the boat tilt further as her stern lifted and she began to rise steeply. He held on to the edge of the map table and looked around the bridge, watching his crew subconsciously lean into the ascent. It was a silly thing but often, when he was ashore and walking up a shallow hill or a ramp, he half expected to hear a rating counting away metres of depth.

The angle of ascent quickly flattened out and he watched and smiled as everyone in the bridge synchronously leaned back in response. The helmsman called out a depth of seven metres.

'Periscope depth, Captain,' Holm announced.

Lündstrom grabbed the periscope's handle and pulled it firmly up. It locked with a clunk into the extended position. He pushed his peaked cap back and hunkered down to look through the viewfinder.

He quickly spun it through 360 degrees, and then again more slowly, before pulling away from it and standing straight.

'Clear!' he announced loudly, almost shouting. '*Thank God for that,*' he whispered, allowing himself the release of those words. Holm, standing next to him, was attempting to suppress a tight-lipped grin. He'd heard. Lündstrom winked at him. The lad undoubtedly had been contemplating a phrase far more colourful.

U-1061 had been fitted with a snorkel, which could be raised to allow them to proceed at periscope depth using the diesel engines. It allowed them to suck in air for the engines and vent the exhaust fumes. But it was only of any use if the sea was calm, which wasn't often the case here in the North Sea. This morning, however, it seemed fortune was smiling on them. There was a light chop, enough to make it difficult for a plane to spot the snorkel's wake, but not so rough that it might be submerged by a wave and the air flow blocked. For the first time in eight hours he allowed himself a sigh of relief.

'Raise the snorkel and let's get the old girl going,' he shouted cheerfully. The ratings on the bridge cheered, and Leutnant Holm passed the order on at the top of his lungs. A moment later the submarine was filled with a rhythmic chug and a subtle vibration as the twin MAN diesel engines slowly came to life. There was a thud as the propellers engaged, and U-1061 was, at last, again under way.

It was twenty minutes later, while Lündstrom was enjoying a privilege of rank and taking a leisurely shit, that the radio message came through. It was swiftly decoded on their Kriegsmarine Enigma machine and within minutes of the message's arrival a rating tapped apprehensively on the door to the toilet.

'Captain?'

Lündstrom's voice sounded muffled through the thin plywood door. 'For Christ's sake, can't a man take a crap in peace? What is it?'

'Message from U-Bootflotille at Bergen, sir.'

'Well? What are you waiting for? Slide it under.'

The paper with their orders on slid under the panel door and he reached down and picked it up. He quickly unfolded the paper and scanned the two lines printed on it. What he read there made his heart skip. They were asking U-1061 to return to Bergen and remain there for further orders. He knew the war was now in its final phase, the end game. It seemed at last that someone up there at Admiralty, Doenitz perhaps, had decided enough was enough, that there was little point sending out any more U-boats. They were being recalled to Bergen to await the end.

Lündstrom found himself analysing his emotional response to the news. *How do I feel?*

The answer came surprisingly quickly and easily. Indescribable relief.

Once he and his men had safely navigated their way back to the pens in Bergen, the war would effectively be over for them.

He finished his business, flushed the toilet and opened the door. Outside, the rating was still tautly awaiting an order.

'Sigi, my lad, we're going home.'

Chapter 19

Wallace

Chris sat at the same table in Lenny's that he and Mark had used two nights ago. He checked the time; it was ten minutes to seven. He ordered a Bud to drink quickly before this Wallace chap arrived.

Just a little Dutch lubrication to ease things along.

Lenny's was as dead this evening as it was the other night, more so. Only three solitary drinkers stared vacuously at the TV above the bar. Tonight it was basketball. He tried watching the game for a few minutes. It would be the inconspicuous thing to do, in here, with a cold beer in his hand, he thought. But every time the door to the bar swung open, he glanced anxiously towards it, half expecting to see the two men he'd seen at the quayside enter.

His nerves got the better of him, and before long Chris had to go and take a leak. He hurried back as quickly as he could after relieving himself and, as he settled down in his booth once more, he felt a light tap on his shoulder.

'Chris, I presume?'

Chris jumped a little. He looked up to see a frail-looking old man standing beside his table. The man was short and the top of his back was rounded, forcing him to stoop slightly. He wore tan slacks that were hitched up too high on his waist and a red and black chequered shirt. On his head, perched awkwardly on thinning hair as white as the suds on a Bud, was a Yankees cap. A windcheater was draped over one of his fragile arms; in his other hand was a walking stick. Chris guessed he had to be in his eighties.

'Mr Wallace?'

He nodded. 'Trust me, I don't normally dress like this. I was going for the tourist, weekend-hiker look. I'm not entirely sure I managed to get it 'right.' He smiled awkwardly. The old man sounded like an asthmatic James Stewart, and his face reminded him a little of the old stand-up George Burns. It looked like a strong gust of wind could carry him away with little effort.

'Have a seat. Can I get you a beer or something?' he asked the old man.

Chris noticed Wallace cast an anxious glance around the diner before allowing himself to settle down, with some effort, onto the chair.

'I'm afraid I need to steer away from the stuff . . . I'm on medication. A cup of milky coffee would be good.'

Chris caught the attention of the waitress and ordered another beer for himself and a coffee. He waited until she had gone before he decided to talk.

'I've got to say, since you called me I've been a little bit jumpy. I hadn't really thought this story had any big angle on it,' said Chris.

Wallace nodded. 'We must be cautious. I was around when . . . well, when these events happened.'

'Can you tell me what exactly happened?'

'Well,' Wallace said, lowering his voice. 'What do you know so far?'

'Not a lot. There's a B-17 down there, it was flown by a German air crew. I think it fought its way over Europe to get to America. I also know that the body of one of the crew drifted ashore near the end of the war, and its discovery triggered a huge search off the coast nearby for a few days. I presume they were looking for the bomber. That's what I know. What I can speculate is that there was something or *someone* aboard the plane that the US government really wanted. How's that for starters?'

Wallace nodded. 'Very good – almost as much as I know. Tell me, have you been down to look at it yet?'

'Yup. I've done two dives down there.'

'How is she after all these years? How does the bomber look?'

'Amazing. The whole plane is intact, very little corrosion, very little marine growth.'

The waitress returned with the order and placed the drinks on the table between the two men.

'Can I get either of you folks somethin' to eat? A Surf Grill? Steak and Fries? BBQ Ribs?' Both of them shook their heads silently. 'How about maybe a snack? We do Fish Burgers, Hotdogs, Filled Bagels.'

'No. Thanks, honestly we're not hungry,' Chris answered abruptly, eager to send her away.

The waitress handed him an insincere smile. 'Fine. Well just you shout if either of you gents change your minds.' She turned and headed towards a couple of swing doors that led into the kitchen.

Chris watched her go, then looked back at Wallace. 'Let me show you something.'

He produced a cardboard folder from his bag and placed it on the table. 'Well, you see, I've made two dives on the plane, the second time was inside . . . I took a load of pictures.'

Wallace's eyes immediately widened. 'You have pictures of the inside of her?'

'Yeah, sure . . . in here,' he said, tapping the folder.

Wallace reached out a hand. Chris could see that it trembled slightly. He wondered whether that was attributable to old age, an illness . . . or maybe he was just as wired as Chris.

Chris quickly pulled the folder back from him.

'May I see those pictures?' Wallace asked eagerly.

'Sure, but let's slow down. I've got one or two hundred bloody questions I want to ask you first.'

'Let me look at the pictures first, please?' said Wallace. 'It'll almost certainly help me to answer those questions of yours.'

Wallace looked Chris firmly in the eye. In a face so pale and drawn, his eyes seemed to shine with a keen, intense, energy. 'Trust me. You show me what you have in that folder, and I can tell you how that plane ended up down there.'

He was right of course. It all boiled down to trust. Quid pro quo, Wallace had said on the phone.

Chris opened the folder and pulled out a pack of black and white photographs. After a moment's hesitation, he handed them over to Wallace.

The old man studied them intently, one after the other, his eyes widening with each new image.

'My God,' he whispered after a few minutes.

'What is it?'

Wallace looked up at him. His jaw quivered with excitement or fear, Chris couldn't tell which.

'It was for real,' the old man whispered.

'What? What was for real?' Chris asked.

Chapter 20

The Bunker

8.43 p.m., 13 April 1945, Berlin

The night sky pulsated like an erratic strobe light from the artillery bombardment; the flashes on the horizon threw the silhouetted remains of the buildings nearby into stark relief. Dr Hauser stood outside the staff car and took in his surroundings. A fresh breeze blew down Wilhelmstrasse, what was once a grand thoroughfare that linked the various buildings of government, the Air Ministry, the Gestapo Headquarters and the Reich Chancellery. It was accompanied by a moaning sound as the wind whipped in and around the empty shell of the Chancellery. One storey up a window frame, blown out and dangling from a cable, clattered noisily against the massive front façade of the building.

The rubble from the previous night's devastation had been swept aside to allow at least one lane of traffic to pass down. But there were no other vehicles on the road tonight, just his staff car, with a driver anxious to tuck the vehicle away in the concrete vehicle bunker two streets away.

Hauser was horrified by the ruins around him. His last visit to Berlin had been six months ago. This place had been a city back then, these buildings intact, the road awash with streetlights and bustling with activity. That had been the occasion Albert Speer, the Armaments Minister, had green-lighted the project, appalled at the lack of progress and the wasted resources thrown at Heisenberg's failed attempt. The proposal Hauser had submitted, quoted at a fraction of the cost, had promised so much more. It had been an easy decision for Speer to make.

Just six months ago.

Berlin is a dead city.

Hauser wondered why, when a place becomes nothing more than a few stacked bricks in a sea of dust, people continue to think of it as a city.

Stalingrad had looked like this once, and yet those bastard, in-bred peasants had died in their thousands to keep hold of it. Perhaps the Russians were asking that question of the Germans now.

A Feldwebel of the Leibstandarte, Hitler's personal SS bodyguard, approached him from the dark archway of the Chancellery.

'Doctor Hauser?'

Hauser nodded. 'Yes.'

'Come this way please.'

Hauser looked at the gloomy entrance to the Chancellery building. In the moonlight it looked like a yawning mouth framed with decaying teeth.

'Doctor . . . please, it's dangerous to stand out here in the open.' The soldier beckoned with a gloved hand. 'Follow me, we can enter via the basement of the Reich Chancellery.'

'He is really here?' Hauser gestured at the ruined buildings around them.

'Of course, but below ground, sir. Now please . . .'

A rogue shell from the Soviet bombardment landed only a half a mile away with a thud that was more felt than heard.

'All right . . . all right,' said Dr Hauser anxiously.

The soldier waved the staff car on, and it began to pick its way slowly down the cleared gap in the road, headlights off.

'The Reich Chancellery took several hits some weeks ago. It's no longer used, but we have cleared the access way to the basement. We have power and lights below, but until we get down there,' the soldier produced a flashlight, 'we'll have to use this.'

He headed swiftly towards the steps leading up between the twin columns of the main entrance. As he jogged up the steps, the bouncing flashlight made giant shadows from the columns dance across the enormous marble walls.

Inside, they passed a machine-gun post discreetly hidden within the shadows of the interior. Two more men of the Leibstandarte manned it; they nodded silently at the Feldwebel as he passed by with Dr Hauser following. They entered what was once the large marble-covered foyer. The torchlight picked out only the floor, covered in an inch of white plaster powder. As they walked swiftly across the floor of the foyer, they kicked up plumes of dust that the gusting breeze grabbed hold of and whipped up into little cyclones near the high ceiling.

'This way, sir.' The soldier led him towards a door that led to the mezzanine floor. He opened the door and the pair of them descended a metal staircase to a basement, which was full to the ceiling with wooden boxes.

'What's in these?' Hauser asked.

The Feldwebel reluctantly engaged the question and panned his torch beam across the stacks of crates and boxes. 'Documents, records from the Chancellery building. They moved most of the important things from the floors above us down here before it was hit.'

The soldier proceeded down the stairs, and they wound their way tightly through the floor of boxes to the entrance of the basement. The soldier pulled open the door and the faint yellow light from a wall lamp inside illuminated them. The soldier snapped off his torch.

They walked swiftly down a second flight of stairs to the basement, and along a narrow corridor, the walls painted a drab olive colour and lined with pipes and cables and yet more storage crates. The soldier pointed to the end of the corridor.

'Down there.'

Dr Hauser saw a solid-looking iron door guarded by two more soldiers. They sat behind a small wall of sandbags and jumped to their feet at the sound of the Feldwebel and Hauser approaching.

Dr Hauser pointed towards the door. 'Is that –?'

'Yes, that's the door to the bunker.'

The Feldwebel presented himself to the guards. 'I have Dr Karl Hauser, he's expected for a meeting at twenty-one hundred hours.'

One of the guards picked up a phone and carefully announced the name and meeting time. He listened to the response and nodded once before replacing the phone.

'You're expected. Door one is Matador.' The guard pulled back a bolt on the iron door and pushed it inwards. It swung slowly and heavily. Hauser could see it was at least a foot thick.

The soldier led Dr Hauser down a short flight of concrete stairs. At the bottom they stood in a corridor cluttered with stacked supplies of tinned vegetables.

'This is the Führer's pantry,' the soldier said, noticing Hauser's curiosity. They continued down the corridor, weaving through the pallets of supplies and stacked tinned foods, until they reached what looked like a submarine bulkhead. To one side was a red telephone handset. The Feldwebel picked it up.

'Matador,' he spoke quietly.

Immediately Hauser heard the sound of metal sliding against metal, and, with a heavy clunk, the door unlocked and swung inwards.

'I stop here. Go through and one of his personal staff will see to you,' the soldier said. He gestured for Hauser to proceed through the door.

The Doctor stared at the open bulkhead into the dimly lit corridor beyond. The concrete floor of the corridor inside had been covered with a thick rug, but the drab olive paint of the walls continued onward.

The corridor stretched for fifty or sixty feet and ended with a spiralling metal staircase. Off the corridor on either side he could see several wooden doors. On the right a door was open and he could see into what looked like a bedroom. A concrete windowless cell half-heartedly decorated with pieces of coloured paper stuck to the walls.

Children's drawings; a house, a tree, a horse, flowers.

He heard the voices of children coming from inside. With no warning the door opened fully, a woman came out of the room and headed up the corridor. Hauser could see the children inside, playing a card game, one of them lying on a rug on the floor colouring a picture with coloured pencils. She looked up at him and smiled.

Hauser took a deep breath.

These must be Goebbels' children.

He had heard that Goebbels and his family had only recently moved in, to be closer to the Führer at this crucial time.

With little warning it finally hit Hauser that somewhere in this maze of rooms was their leader, mere yards away from him, perhaps separated only by one wall, or a door. Spatially, he was closer now to Adolf Hitler than he had ever been, despite having been a supporter for nearly seventeen years. He had only ever dreamed of being this close.

Hauser imagined he could sense the magnetic power of the man, the aura, drawing him in, bidding him to step forward into his inner sanctum. Hauser momentarily resisted the urge, desperate to make this moment of delicious anticipation last as long as possible. To be shortly in the company of the Great Man, to have the Great Man, attentive, listening to him . . . to him! Hauser felt a tremulous shudder of excitement ripple down through his body. This was the reward for so many tireless years of devotion to the great cause.

Dr Hauser had been an active card-carrying member of the party since first he'd heard the Great Man speak. In his opinion, that made him part of the 'old guard'. He had even volunteered to join the SS at the outbreak of war, but his 'special skills' had proven an obstacle to joining. He had been refused on the grounds that his academic and research work could benefit the Reich far more than his physical contribution as a soldier could.

So Hauser, reluctantly and with some bitterness, had served his country living and working alone. He had worked in isolation on a chalkboard, in a ten foot by ten foot office in the Kaiser Wilhelm Institute for Physics, an annexe of the University of Berlin. He could talk to no one about his work and was given the task of checking and duplicating the notes and calculations of Professor Werner Heisenberg. Every day of the war he had spent a little time at a café nearby, reading about the spectacular victories of the Wehrmacht and the Waffen-SS, and cursing his role in the war as little more than a clerk double-checking the simple arithmetic of another mathematician. Hauser had grown to hate the slanted and florid writing of Heisenberg, the flamboyant tails on his Ys and Gs; the elaborate depiction of mathematic symbols suggested a man who was easy in the company of others, a man who could effortlessly climb the hierarchical ladder and speak with ease to those at the very top.

He resented the man.

Heisenberg was good, but not brilliant. His work was reliable and consistent, Hauser rarely found any mistakes in his calculations. But he was definitely not the genius he thought he was.

At the heart of Heisenberg's work was the task of determining the minimum mass of U-235 required to produce the chain reaction of fission. The man had produced this lengthy calculation several dozen times, and each time the answer had pointed to unfeasible masses of this substance, tons. And yet the fool Heisenberg had persisted, securing additional funding for his work, attempting to construct a small reactor in Straussburg.

Hauser hadn't been able to believe the utter stupidity of the man: the futility of the process was staring him in the face with every iteration of this same calculation.

Tons.

To produce a ton of U-235 one would need to extract a hundred tons, refined from 10,000 tons of enriched ore. Hauser wasn't even sure that the whole planet contained that much of it. By March 1944 Hauser had convinced himself that the process of nuclear fission having a practical use either as a weapon or a power source was a stillborn science, and he was beginning to suspect that Heisenberg was merely extorting funds for his own private use.

It was during 1944, one wet and overcast afternoon in March, that he uncovered the pre-war research notes in the archives of the University of

Leipzig of a Jew called Joseph Schenkelmann. He had been a student of Heisenberg's while he had been a Professor of Theoretical Physics there in the 1920s. Reading the man's notes and carefully following the path of his calculative trail, Hauser had been able to understand that something amazing was possible. The stupid and arrogant Heisenberg had repeatedly made the same mistake over and over.

The arithmetic was correct, but he had made several erroneous assumptions in his work.

If he'd had the humility to double-check his own work he might have seen that it wasn't tons of U-235 they needed, but only a few ounces. If the chain reaction could be accelerated enough at the beginning, that is. There was the trick, and this Jew Schenkelmann, this clever little Jew, had spotted that.

On that cold and wet afternoon everything had changed.

'You should go in now, this door needs to be sealed,' said the Feldwebel.

Hauser looked at the man in uniform; he had a soldier's face, bereft of intelligence or emotion.

Little more than a shaved monkey dressed in a black uniform.

Hauser felt pity for him, and the millions of other shaved monkeys on this planet that passed themselves off as *homo sapiens*. Amongst these retarded *homo erectus* creatures lived only a few people intelligent enough to deserve being considered genuine human beings. Hauser had known the Führer was one of these rare people since the very first sentence he had heard the man speak.

Hauser nodded and then stooped slightly as he entered Hitler's bunker. As he straightened up beyond the bulkhead, the soldier grabbed a handle and pulled the heavy iron door closed with a solid clunk.

The woman he had seen earlier returned down the corridor and entered the children's room. She closed the door and the chatter of young voices was instantly locked away.

'Dr Karl Hauser?'

He jumped a little. A smartly dressed young lady stood to the side of the door in a corner with the benefit of very little light. Her hair tied up in a bun and a slim build, Hauser guessed she was in her early twenties.

'My name is Traudl Jüng. I am one of his private secretaries. Will you come this way, please?'

Traudl led him down the corridor towards the spiral staircase at the end.

He passed by one of the paintings on the wall, a watercolour scene of a stream in a wood; in the corner was scribbled 'Adolf Hitler June '25'.

This is real, Karl Hauser . . . not a dream any more.

Traudl turned round to look back at him.

'He is in the map room right now, Dr Hauser, in a meeting. But he knows you are here and will see you in his private study shortly. It's this way.'

They reached the spiral stairs, and the secretary led, modestly holding the hem of her skirt to the side of her leg as she took the steps one at a time upwards. Hauser's eyes took in what was still visible of her stockinged legs. His mind so often distracted with numbers, he had had little time in his life to consider other matters, those things that it seemed most men's minds strayed from rarely. But watching the young woman's slender legs bend and stretch with every step, he felt the faintest charge of arousal.

The spiral stairs took them up one floor, and Hauser found himself staring along an identical corridor with metal doors on either side.

'It's on the left here.'

The woman tapped on a door. 'Ma'am?' There was no answer. 'Miss Braun?' Again, there was no answer. She opened the door slowly and entered.

Hauser followed her inside. The room was small and with little content. In one corner stood a coat rack. On it hung a leather coat, a cane rested against the base of it. To his left, a door was ajar and Hauser could see a bed. The touches here and there suggested it was a woman's bedroom. A German Shepherd was curled up asleep on the bed.

'Blondi! Off!'

The Shepherd's tail thumped guiltily against the bedcovers. She clambered off and curled up on a rug on the floor beside it.

Traudl wagged a finger at the bitch. 'You know you're not allowed on there. Ba-a-a-d girl.' Blondi's tail continued to thump guiltily against the floor and her ears tucked down.

Traudl noticed Hauser looking past her into the bedroom. She pulled the door shut with a disapproving frown and reached for the handle of another door ahead of them.

'Here, this is *his* private study. He will be along shortly, Dr Hauser.'

'Thank you,' he replied automatically.

Frau Jüng studied him for a few seconds before adding, 'He never conducts meetings in his study. *Never.*' With that she pulled the door open to reveal the small room.

Hauser found himself holding his breath as the door swung open to reveal the study. It was a volume of space privileged enough to witness the most private moments of the Führer.

A desk, a standard lamp, a leather chair, a second chair and, behind the desk, a bookshelf laden with bound notebooks. It was as Hauser would have imagined such a room: simple, uncluttered, a reflection of the Führer's brilliant mind with no space for unnecessary embellishments or decoration.

'Please take a seat.'

Hauser entered the study, a room no more than ten feet long and eight feet wide, and settled himself down on the chair in front of the moderately sized desk. The young woman nodded at him before leaving the study and closing the door.

It took him a few minutes to realise he hadn't experienced quiet like this in a long time, an almost complete absence of sound, except for the thudding of his heart and the faint and constant hum of a diesel generator in the bunker somewhere nearby.

The project had started only six months ago. Hauser had managed to pass on his discovery of the Jewish mathematician's work to the Armaments Minister, Albert Speer, and amazingly, with a little investigation, the Jew had been tracked down to one of the munitions factories along the Rhine, where he had been working for the last two years. In a matter of only a few days, Hauser swiftly found himself placed in charge of a fast-track project to produce the world's first atom bomb, while, to his immense satisfaction, Heisenberg's fruitless and expensive programme was immediately mothballed. Speer had visited Hauser's modest lab on a number of occasions to receive updates from him on the weapon's progress during this period of time, but with the construction of the bomb nearing completion, Albert Speer had asked to review the design papers once more.

Hauser had done his best to expunge from the documentation the Jew's frequent references to the risk of a *runaway chain*. But he suspected Speer must have found something in there somewhere. The Armaments Minister had attempted to raise the subject with Hauser; there had been a meeting arranged between them today to discuss his 'concerns'. But then, at the last moment, Hauser had been informed that the plans had been changed, and that the meeting was to be with Hitler himself. Speer was no longer to be a part of the project.

Hauser had both sighed with relief that Speer was gone and shuddered with elation at the thought of meeting the man.

The door handle rattled as someone outside took hold of it and began to turn it. He heard a muffled voice – two, a man's and a woman's. Hauser shuddered anxiously as he recognised the man's voice as unmistakably Hitler's. He heard both voices talking in lowered, soft tones, an exchange of pleasantries between two people, intimate. The muffled exchange ended and the door to the study opened.

Hauser immediately stood to attention, heart pounding like a piston engine in his chest. He brought his heels together in his best rendition of the formal military greeting. 'H-Heil Hitler.'

Hitler held his palm out beside his head, returning the salute tiredly. 'Yes . . . yes. Please sit down.'

Hauser did as the Führer asked. He sat down promptly while carefully studying Hitler as he settled himself in the leather chair behind his desk. He was wearing a white shirt and a black tie with his initials in gold discreetly stitched onto the tongue. His top button was undone and the tie had been loosened a little. Over the shirt he wore a beige, woollen cardigan with leather patches on its elbows. Hitler poured himself a glass of water from a decanter on the desk, his left hand trembling enough that a few spots of water splashed onto the desk.

Hauser was disturbed to see how tired and beaten he looked. The Führer looked nothing like the proud figure standing tall in the news pictures; it was a feeble old man that sat before him.

'Dr Karl Hauser, Albert Speer has been briefing me on your work. I have been following your progress.' He leaned forward, his hands gathered together under his chin. 'You must understand, time is the most important thing for us now. The Russians are very close and our men have orders to hold out till the last. This buys us a little respite, perhaps we have only two or three weeks before they reach the centre of Berlin.'

Hitler closed his eyes and his lips seemed to tremble ever so slightly as he prepared himself to ask the next question. 'Is the project on schedule?'

Hauser could see the anxiety in the Führer's face. Time, of course, was everything now, the only currency worth anything. 'The raw materials we needed have been produced, and the bomb is being assembled now. Nine, perhaps ten, more days, my Führer. It is exactly on schedule.'

The transformation was almost instantaneous. Hauser watched as Hitler suddenly beamed with joy and slapped his thigh merrily. 'Wonderful! Marvellous!' Hitler sat back in his chair, exhaling with obvious relief. 'Good . . . good. I knew that God would grant us time to salvage this war.' Hitler paused, reflecting for a moment. 'It saddens me that Speer has deserted us, now that victory is so close at hand.'

Hauser shuffled uncomfortably in his chair. *No mention of Speer's concerns about the design of the weapon. Thank God.*

Hauser had wondered whether, if the issue were raised, he should lie to Hitler or be truthful. After all, it was only a calculated risk, and not a certainty.

Hitler took a sip of his water and studied Hauser with small eyes that glistened with moisture. 'So tell me all about this weapon you have nearly finished building. Tell me first . . . how much destruction we can expect from it?'

Hauser smiled. *He will be pleased with this.*

'It is a small bomb, the size of only a ten-gallon petrol drum, but with it we can destroy an entire city, certainly dozens of square miles of complete annihilation.'

Hitler sat forward and clasped his hands together under his chin again, his index fingers forming a steeple beneath his nose. 'A whole city?'

For a moment Hauser wondered whether he should come out right now with the truth. *A whole city* was a conservative estimate. Even if the runaway chain, the infinite chain that Schenkelmann had panicked about so much, didn't occur, the destruction would be phenomenal.

'Yes, that's correct, a whole city sir.'

Hitler shook his head and smiled, 'More destruction than a sky-full of these Allied bombers. That is truly amazing. We will terrify them, and the Russians, with the incredible power of this weapon of yours.'

Hitler's smile quickly faded and his eyes narrowed as he addressed him. 'Dr Hauser, you have done an incredible thing. You alone have done more for Germany, more for me . . . than whole armies of men. It seems only your weapon alone can save Germany now. For that reason, I personally am indebted to you.'

Hauser felt a surge of pride that flushed his face with its intensity. 'I am honoured, my Führer, truly honoured by your generous words.'

Hitler shook his head. 'Lately, you know I have been let down by so many men,' he confided. 'Men who had promised me so much and delivered to me so little, and yet, Dr Hauser . . . may I call you Karl?' Hauser nodded eagerly. 'And yet you, Karl, in my most desperate hour, you have given me the victory that a room full of generals has failed to.' Hitler leaned forward over the desk and patted Hauser's shoulder in a paternal manner.

The Führer's gentle touch affected him profoundly. He fought ferociously to keep his voice steady, 'I am so proud to have been able to help you in this way, my Führer.'

'So, ... then, perhaps you are a little curious as to where, when and against whom the weapon will be used, hmmm?'

'I'm afraid I have no idea.'

'Indulge me, guess.'

'Russia, sir?'

Hitler shook his head and smiled. 'America. New York, to be precise.'

Hauser's expression caused Hitler to chuckle amicably.

'Yes. What a symbolic place to demonstrate your bomb, isn't it? Its tall, powerful buildings, that Statue of Liberty ... all reduced to ashes by a country thousands of miles away.'

'A country they have assumed is already beaten,' added Hauser.

'Indeed.'

'But why not Russia, sir? They're the ones who are all but above us now.'

Hitler reached out his right hand and rested it lightly on Hauser's arm. The other hand, Hauser noticed, was tucked out of sight beneath the desk. 'Their capacity to endure destruction and death is so much greater than the Americans. Losing a city wouldn't stop Stalin now, losing a dozen wouldn't. But New York?' Hitler winked at him. His eyes that only a few moments ago had looked moist with fatigue and despair now sparkled with an almost benign mischief. 'The Americans are already seeing the Russians as a threat. Imagine how terrified they will be at the thought of *them* getting their hands on your technology, Karl? Especially after this demonstration of ours. They will have no choice, no choice at all, my friend ... '

Hauser studied his face. Hitler was waiting for him to complete the sentence, to understand the implication.

'So ... America, will have no choice but to declare war on Russia?' he uttered in a voice, little more than a conspiratorial whisper.

Hitler nodded approvingly, as a mentor would to a student. 'They would have to push the Russians back, out of our country, to be sure of this?' added Hauser.

He squeezed Hauser's arm gently. 'Yes.'

'But why not just explode the bomb somewhere closer, my Führer. Like London, or maybe outside Berlin, where the Russian army is concentrated?'

'American presidents are weak, Karl. They rely on the will of their voters. The people over there need to be as frightened by this technology as their leader ... after New York has vanished, the President will have no choice but to push his soldiers forward from the west into Berlin to fight the Russians. It will be an easy decision for him to make. We will have forced it to be the *only* decision he can make.'

Hauser managed to look up again at the Führer's face, to meet those intense eyes. The relief was conspicuous. His demeanour was that of a man who had escaped the hangman's noose by an inch, or a second. He looked years younger, magnificent, almost the man who had led them to war in 1939.

'This is a brilliant plan, sir,' he managed to say.

'It is a little regrettable that our first bomb will have to be dropped on the nation that should have been our ally from the very beginning. There are many people in that country who would welcome us as friends. It is a shame.'

Hitler reached into a desk drawer and pulled out a bottle of brandy.

'I put this aside earlier today, for this little meeting. I'm not a big drinker, Karl, but I would like us to toast your genius. Dr Hauser, you are a German who has beaten the Jewish technicians in America at their own science.'

Hauser took the glass tumbler offered him, and Hitler awkwardly poured a dash of the liquor into his own glass and a much larger measure into Hauser's.

'To you and your wonderful bomb, Karl.'

'Th-thank you, my Führer,' he said, emotion thickening his voice.

Hauser smiled and drank his brandy. Hitler smiled and sipped his.

Chapter 21

Test Flight

5 p.m., 16 April 1945, an airfield south of Stuttgart

Major Rall stood on the grass outside the entrance to the bunker and watched a flock of seagulls swoop and circle the airfield.

'There must be a storm out at sea, that's what brings them inland,' he muttered to no one in particular.

Storms at sea.

He wondered how U-1061 was faring. The North Sea was becoming a dangerous place for the Kriegsmarine. There was a fair chance that the sub had failed to receive its orders, or worse, had been destroyed by a Royal Navy vessel. He had yet to hear from the U-Bootflotille in Bergen any news on whether the sub was on its way back. Of course, no news meant nothing, it was getting increasingly difficult these days to keep the lines of communication open between disparate elements of their armed forces. It hadn't been easy to get the order through to Norway, partly because it had not gone through the usual channels.

Worrying about the U-boat demonstrated quite clearly to Rall how fraught with uncertainties this whole operation was. The U-boat was just one small piece in the jigsaw. It was the only way of transporting a platoon of troops from Norway, north around the coast of Scotland and Ireland to a particular airstrip on the west coast of France. Intelligence reports indicated that the airfield was operated by the USAAF and staffed only by aviation mechanics and administrative personnel; a perfect place for the Messerschmitt escort planes to refill their tanks and continue escorting the B-17 beyond fighter range of France. No U-boat, no troops; no troops, no captured airstrip; no airstrip, no fighter cover for the bomber those first few hundred miles into the Atlantic – and that's undoubtedly where the Americans and British would converge to take her down.

And then there were the other uncertainties: would the bomb be ready before it was all too late? Could it be safely transported here without being accidentally intercepted by an Allied plane or ground troops?

He had received precious little information about the bomb from Speer since he'd been headhunted and assigned the task of planning its delivery all those months ago. Other than being informed that it employed a new explosive formula that allowed it to yield destruction well in excess of its size, there had been no information about its dimensions and whether the B-17's bomb racks would need to be modified to accommodate it. Nor had there been any information about the weight of this weapon, so the size of the extra fuel tanks had been guessed at. Although the brief he had been given by Speer, the Minister for Armaments, months ago had been very specific, the paucity of details about the bomb itself was causing Rall an immense amount of concern.

And then there was the fighter escort. He had two Me-109s in the hangar; they had both been flown in the previous night under cover of darkness. The pilots that had flown them in said it had been touch and go getting them across skies crawling with American, British and Russian aircraft. What about the other ten or so he had been promised? Would they make it here?

The seagulls lost interest in the airstrip and swooped away northwards. His gaze fell upon Max and his men playing football with some of the ground crew just inside the hangar. The dim light of the late afternoon made little impression on the darkened interior of the building where the B-17 and the first two Messerschmitts of the squadron were discreetly hidden in the shadows. He watched the men kick the football between them; each one taking turns to do a trick with the ball.

It was good to see them play like that.

The morale of the men seemed quite high here on the airfield. It had become a remote outpost where order still reigned, while beyond the solitary guard hut it was a turbulent sea of drifting refugees, running before a Russian tidal wave. On the airfield it almost felt like another time, the happy days at the beginning of the war when it appeared as if every campaign they embarked upon would lead inevitably to victory. Just a few days ago, all of these men had nothing else on their minds other than how to find American or British troops to surrender to safely. Now, once more, they looked like men with some fight left in them, some purpose greater than making it through the next few days alive. Rall found it hard not to smile. Even with grim defeat staring them all in the face, and an uncertain future ahead for them at the hands of their Russian conquerors, it seemed to take the smallest spark of hope to turn them once more into soldiers.

And, in all honesty, it was just that, a small spark of hope. Max and his boys would be lucky to make it out of German airspace, let alone reach the Atlantic or beyond. They had to know that too.

Damn, we should have won this war on balls alone.

The ginger-haired lad, Stefan, seemed to have a natural ability with the ball. He deftly flicked it up with his toe and kept it in the air alternately with both feet. Both Max and Pieter clapped him on, as they counted each touch.

Good men, both of them, older than most. Max was twenty-nine and Pieter, two or three years younger. They had experience and the calmness that comes with maturity in their favour, important qualities for a pilot and co-pilot. Both of them had already taken turns flying the bomber at dawn and dusk, and both had adapted efficiently to the abnormal size and handling of the plane.

Rall watched Max receive the ball, trap it and lob it to Hans.

Oberleutnant Kleinmann was an interesting parcel to unwrap. The personal records of the crew had been forwarded to Rall many months previously, when the project was in its infancy. Back then Rall had asked for the service records of the best, longest-serving bomber crews in the Luftwaffe. There had only been half a dozen sets of records forwarded to him, and by the time Rall had been able to start pulling in men for the operation, four of these crews had already been either captured or killed. Max's crew had a longer and far more impressive service history than the other remaining crew and so, by process of elimination, they were chosen. Max, being their pilot, was of course the most important part of the equation. Rall had been instructed to vigorously examine the records for the crew that were to deliver the bomb. The weapon, he had been told, represented a significant technological advance and could not be allowed to slip, intact, into the hands of the enemy. Thus there had to be no doubts about the crew and their loyalty. Their motivation had to be beyond question. It was for that reason alone that Rall had advised his superiors that the crew be offered the opportunity to volunteer for the mission rather than be ordered to carry it out. Max remained a small concern for Rall. The man had one black mark on his records. He had apparently questioned an order to release bombs on a retreating column of Russian soldiers. The column had contained civilians. His bomb load was eventually dropped but had missed the column. No disciplinary action was taken, but the incident remained an indelible mark on an otherwise exemplary record. Rall knew that Kleinmann was now prepared to drop this bomb on American civilians. He knew it hadn't been an easy decision for the pilot, but the rationale was there, and Max had acknowledged it made sense if this was to end the war. However, what caused Rall some degree of concern was that Kleinmann wasn't an automaton, he was a thinker, as demonstrated by this incident on record, someone prepared to think beyond the order. An admirable trait in anyone other than a soldier.

What else worries me about Max?

He was not a Nazi. It would have made things a lot simpler for Rall if he had been. The issues of motivation and loyalty could be taken as a given. He would carry out the mission unquestioningly for his Führer and the party; but Max had to be handled a little more carefully and his motives analysed more closely.

Rall had decided not to pass these niggling concerns up the chain of command. There was now no more time left to mess around finding another crew. Max had fought dutifully for the Luftwaffe for the last five years, whatever his reasons – loyalty to the Führer, the Nazi party or simple patriotism – and he had volunteered willingly. There was no need, or time, to doubt him now.

Max kicked the ball back to Stef and looked at his watch. It was half past five. The sky was overcast, and the pallid grey light had begun to make it difficult to see the football. It was time again. He looked toward the bunker and spotted Rall standing near the entrance. He pointed to the sky and Rall gave him a thumbs-up.

The old boy's got sharp eyes.

'Okay, lads, playtime's over. Time for another spin.'

The men headed back inside the hangar towards the B-17. Max ducked underneath the fuselage, hoisted himself up through the belly hatch into the bombardier's compartment and then climbed the ladder up into the cockpit. Pieter followed behind him, squeezing his stocky body awkwardly through.

'Max, am I flying this thing tonight?'

Pieter was desperate to get as many hours as possible on the bomber before the mission date. Both men had discussed the flight schedule of the mission and Max would be flying the plane through the most hazardous portion of the journey, across southern Germany and France. Once they were across the French coast and over the Atlantic, Pieter would take over and allow Max some rest.

Pieter needed more time at the controls.

'Think you can handle take-off?'

He grinned. 'Of course.'

'Well make sure it's a tidy one, the Major's got his eye on us.'

The pair of them slipped on their thick sheepskin flight jackets and flying caps and sat in their seats. Max lifted the oxygen mask to his face and spoke into the interphone. 'Hans, Stef? Are you boys dressed and ready?'

'Yeah,' said Stefan.

'Waist-gun port and starboard check, ready to go,' answered Hans.

Max fired up the engines and gunned the throttle several times. He turned to Pieter. 'Okay, let's run through this in order. Set the aileron, elevators and rudder trim tab controls to zero.'

Pieter found the tab controls easily and reset them. 'Aileron, elevators, rudder to zero.'

'Okay, test the wing flaps.'

Pieter tested both sides full up and full down. 'Check.'

'Okay Pieter, next?'

'Test the propeller pitch, test the super-chargers?'

Max nodded. 'Yes.'

The engines roared momentarily. 'Check.'

'Okay. You can take her out and taxi to the end of the strip.'

Pieter signalled to one of the ground crew and the chocks were pulled away from the wheels. The B-17 eased forward and rolled out of the hangar, across the grass and up onto the tarmac of the strip at a sedate pace.

'A little, faster, Pieter. The less time we're down here on the ground the better.'

He nodded, eyes locked firmly on the ground passing them by outside. He opened the throttles slightly and the bomber lurched as she picked up some speed. As the end of the strip approached Pieter eased back and swung the plane round.

Max patted his shoulder. 'Looking good. Now remember, 100 mph and we're off the tarmac, ease her away but get the speed up there as quickly as possible, all right?'

Pieter nodded and licked his lips.

'Relax. Now remember what do you need to do next?'

Pieter closed his eyes, recalling the take-off procedure they'd read from the translated USAAF training manual.

'Tail wheel lock to ON.' He fumbled for the switch and found it.

Max smiled reassuringly at him. 'Go on, Pieter . . . she's all yours.'

Pieter tentatively eased his foot off the brake and adjusted the manifold pressure. With a face locked with concentration he began to open the throttle. The four Wright Cyclone engines roared angrily and the bomber shuddered forward along the strip. Pieter kept one eye on the cockpit window, watching the concrete race past to ensure they were steering a straight line down the strip and not drifting to one side or the other, and one eye on the speed indicator. As the bomber approached a hundred miles per hour they felt the force of lift pulling the bomber up, and Pieter began to ease up on the control column.

'That's good, Pieter.'

The tyres swiftly cleared the ground, and the plane pulled up quickly to an altitude of several hundred feet in only a few seconds. Pieter retracted the landing gear and, a minute later, at an altitude of 700 feet and an IAS of 150 mph he eased the throttle back to 2300 rpm by adjusting the propeller pitch controls.

'Excellent. You're a natural, Pieter,' Max said generously. 'Much better than my first attempt.'

Pieter sighed with relief. 'I think I'd rather fly an H-111 than this huge bastard. She feels bloody heavy, like a Tiger tank wearing butterfly wings.'

Chapter 22

Koch

11 a.m. 18 April 1945, the port of Bergen, Norway

He watched the submarine as it gently came to a rest, parallel to the concrete side of the pen and about thirty feet out. On her narrow foredeck half a dozen men waited for a rope to be tossed over to them, and aft beyond the conning tower another six men waited. Their eyes were screwed up against the brightness of the day, and the crisp morning air had them rubbing their hands and stamping their feet to keep warm.

Koch watched as the ropes were tossed across and the men grabbed hold of them and began pulling. The U-boat gently began to drift towards the concrete wall of the pen.

The crew looked unpleasantly like so many tramps, many of them sporting scruffy beards, all of them wearing uniforms that were smeared with oil and sweat stains. Koch wrinkled his nose, even from twenty feet away the faint stench of their body odour reached him; it reminded him of a stale meat pie.

'Strange little mole-men, aren't they, sir?' said Feldwebel Büller, one of Captain Koch's men.

Koch nodded silently; he was reminded of the Morlocks in H.G. Wells' *The Time Machine* – pallid man-like creatures that lived below ground amidst a cavernous world of arcane Victorian technology. Actually the comparison wasn't a bad one. The Morlocks always stayed below ground, but every now and again they would surface to kill and cannibalise one of the beautiful, peaceful surface-dwellers. In the early years of the Atlantic war, these men had most definitely been the Morlocks, striking ships with impunity, dragging them down to the ocean floor. But now? Now they were being hunted like rabbits.

'Go easy, Büller, we've got to spend a week or two with these men. Let's remember to be polite,' said Koch.

Koch curled his lip in disgust, as the meat pie smell grew stronger. He'd endured a lot of things for his country, many hardships, discomforts and hazards. He certainly wasn't relishing the prospect of being jammed into this U-boat with fifty of these submariners and thirty more of his own men. It was going to be an extremely unhygienic and claustrophobic few days. The misery that lay ahead of them could be best conceived by considering one simple logistical fact. Eighty men . . . one toilet.

'Yes, sir, polite, sir.'

Koch found himself wondering if this was it . . . The Mission.

The Mission . . . the one that would make a difference, the one he'd been waiting for since signing up three years ago. He had been on perhaps a dozen important undertakings, all of them pretty dangerous. The worst had been in Greece, fighting in the hills and taking a heavily defended base camp of General Mavros' communist guerrillas. But that, and the others, were merely skirmishes in a campaign, one of many small-scale engagements that would have no real impact on events beyond it. This one . . . this felt different.

The war was at an end, and yet he had received these orders out of the blue.

Nobody now was being sent out to attack anything. Every command decision was about retreat and entrenchment. It had been that way for months, possibly that way for over a year. Koch and his men had, of course, been out on patrols since being pulled back into Norway, and, on several occasions, there had been a few minor brushes with Norwegian partisans. But essentially since returning to Norway, they had all been watching the war slip away from the comfort of their barracks.

And now these orders.

It had to be the one. The one he'd been waiting for.

He had only been informed that he and a platoon of handpicked men would be boarding a U-boat; that he was to present himself to the vessel's commander, and then both he and the Captain would be allowed to open their sealed orders. Even then, he had been told, the U-boat Captain would not be allowed to know the objective, only the location he had been ordered to take these men to.

Such secrecy.

Koch smiled proudly. Perhaps this would be another Gran Sasso? He wondered if this wasn't going to be the rescue of an important member of the Reich high command from Allied hands. He remembered reading about Skorzeny's rescue of Mussolini from the Campo Imperatore hotel, his daring arrival by glider on the slope in front of the building, and how, with a handful of paratroops, he quickly overpowered the Duce's guards and hustled him off the mountain in a Storch without a single shot being fired.

Koch found his young face creasing into a smile. He and his company had waited out the war for something like this. It was about time the Gebirgsjäger, the Alpine troops, had an opportunity to show what they could do, that they *were* an elite regiment, that they were every bit as good as the Fallschirmjäger.

The thirty men he'd selected from his company were as eager as he was to get on and do this thing, whatever it was, but he realised they were going to have one hell of a hard time coping with being boxed up inside this boat. These were lads who had spent their childhood in wide-open, natural environments, sleepy villages nestled on the side of glorious snow-capped mountains. Most of them were drawn from around Tyrol in Austria, some from Finland, even a couple of Norwegians. Two weeks in a submerged iron coffin was going to be tough on them.

The U-boat bumped against the pen wall with a dull clang and the ratings on the sub's decks secured the lines. One of the pen workers wheeled up a gantry and pushed it out so that it rested on the deck.

Out of the foredeck hatch climbed the submarine's captain. Koch watched him as he chatted to his men and exchanged a joke, clearly relieved to be stepping out of the cramped confines of the vessel. The men exchanged banter for a few moments before he turned away to step briskly up the gantry and onto terra firma. Koch let the man have a minute to adjust to the light, the air, the solid ground, the space, before approaching him.

'Captain Lündstrom?'

Lündstrom turned round to face him. 'Yes, who wants to know?'

'Captain Koch, 3rd Company, Gebirgsjäger regiment 141. I have some orders here for you.'

Lündstrom studied the young man. He wore the Eidelweiss badge on his cap, the elite Alpine troops, the Gebirgsjäger, a respected infantry regiment. The young man had a tanned face chiselled out of muscle and bone, and a sprinkling of freckles that crossed the bridge of his nose from one cheek to another.

So young for the rank of captain.

That was something Lündstrom had noticed becoming more and more commonplace these last two years, battlefield promotions. Officers were getting younger and younger. Soon it would just be boys leading boys into the meat grinder.

The young officer was patiently holding out a sealed envelope.

Lündstrom reached out for it and noticed Koch was standing awkwardly to attention.

'At ease, we're both captains,' said Lündstrom. Koch softened his stance and looked relieved.

'Recent promotion I'm guessing, Hauptmann?'

Koch nodded. 'Three weeks, sir.'

'You'll get used to not saluting other captains soon enough.' He looked down at the envelope in his hand; it bore the stamp of the Reich Chancellor's office.

'This has come directly from Berlin to me?'

'Via Kriegsmarine HQ, Bergen, yes.' Koch produced a similar envelope. 'I have one also. These orders came with the instruction that we're to open them together.'

Lündstrom closed his eyes and breathed deeply. With a heavy heart he realised the envelopes could only mean one thing . . . another trip out.

He looked at his crewmen finishing off the task of securing the submarine and readying themselves for a week of shore leave, perhaps even an indefinite sojourn ashore. It was going to be hard breaking the news to them. Very hard. They had travelled back to Bergen in the firm belief that they wouldn't be setting sail again.

'Well, then . . . I suppose you and I had better find somewhere quiet to open these and see what lunacy has been lined up for us.'

Chapter 23

Schröder's men

6 a.m., 25 April 1945, an airfield south of Stuttgart

By the gathering light of dawn Major Rall watched the B-17 as it banked around and made its final approach towards the runway, just a silhouette against the pale grey skyline. The bomber's immense wings wobbled slightly as her wheels came down. The plane steadied as she dropped the last few dozen feet and the tyres made a heavy first contact with the ground. She bounced high before making contact again. This time, the wheels stayed on the ground and gradually the weight of the bomber settled onto them and the plane was down.

'Kleinmann won't win any awards for that landing, sir,' said Leutnant Höstner.

Rall was irritated by his jibe. 'He won't have to land her, just flying her will do.'

The B-17 rumbled down the concrete strip, wheels passing smoothly over craters that had recently been filled in. Rall smiled smugly at a conceit of theirs. The strip had been repaired under the cover of dark, but large crescents of dark grey had been painted on the ground where the craters had been to fool the reconnaissance planes that flew over periodically.

The plane rumbled past Rall and Höstner and finally came to a stop at the end of the runway. It turned in a slow arc and began to taxi towards the hangar.

'Good lad . . . let's get her inside quickly.' Rall scanned the sky around the airfield. There were no planes to be seen.

The bomber taxied towards the hangar, and Max nodded out of the cockpit window at the Major as they trundled by.

'Do you think they'll be ready in time sir?'

'I think they already are,' Rall answered, dismissing the SS officer's question impatiently.

Max steered the bomber carefully towards the open door of the hangar, and a member of the ground crew guided them into the dimly lit interior. He brought the plane to a halt.

Pieter craned his neck to look out his side window. 'I see we have three more 109s in the family.'

Max shut off the engines and pulled himself up from his seat to look out. Lined up nose to tail and packed tightly within the limited floor space of the hangar were a number of Messerschmitt Me-109 fighter planes. Over the last few days several of them had flown in under the cover of darkness and two more had been brought in by trucks and assembled inside the hangar.

'That gives us a grand total of seven escort planes so far, not exactly an intimidating number,' he said to Pieter.

'Better than four,' Pieter replied.

'Well, yes, I can't fault your logic there, my friend.'

They both climbed down the ladder into the bombardier's compartment and out through the belly hatch. Hans and Stefan followed them out.

'I can't believe how much room there is inside her,' said Stefan.

'Don't forget that they pack ten American airmen inside a plane that size, whereas there's only four of us,' said Max.

Major Rall approached Max and his crew.

'Good landing, Max.'

'Uh . . . not really sir. I think it's going to take a few more attempts before I can put her down, no bounce.'

'How are you finding her?'

'She's a lot less manoeuvrable than I'm used to.'

'That's understandable, there's a lot more there to fly than a Heinkel.'

Max nodded. 'I notice we have three more 109s.'

Rall turned round to admire the tightly packed cluster of planes. 'Yes. They arrived only half an hour ago, flown in by the pilot who is going to lead the escort squadron, and two wingmen. Perhaps now would be a good time to affect some introductions?'

Rall turned to Höstner. 'Go and get our new arrivals, I want Max and his boys to meet them.' Höstner turned and headed towards the cluster of fighter planes in the corner of the hangar.

'The flight was unchallenged?'

Max nodded. 'We did a fifty-mile circular trip, attracted a little flak from our boys north of here, but there were no other unwanted encounters.'

'Good. For the foreseeable future, I think the Allies are going to be too focused on Berlin to bother us too much down here.' He smiled reassuringly.

At the sound of approaching footsteps Rall turned around to greet the fighter pilots.

The three pilots stood to attention and saluted Rall. They were still wearing their flying jackets. Rall returned the salute and then reached out a hand towards one of them.

'Hauptman Schröder, your reputation precedes you. It's an honour.' Rall pumped the pilot's hand enthusiastically. His scarred face turned crimson either from the exertion or the exhilaration.

Pieter jabbed an elbow into Max's ribs and whispered hoarsely. 'Why's the Major sucking this guy's dick so hard? He's just a captain, for fuck's sake.'

'I think he's a fighter ace. The name Schröder sounds familiar.'

Rall turned to Max and Pieter. 'Allow me to introduce Hauptman Klaus Schröder, one of the Luftwaffe's golden boys. He's our highest-scoring ace. Well, I should say the highest-scoring pilot we have left.'

'Highest-scoring ace still alive and yet to be captured, to be fair,' Schröder added.

Rall nodded. 'That's true. He is also a distant relative of Generalfeld-marschall Keitel I believe?'

Schröder smiled faintly. 'Yes, Major.'

Max caught a glimpse of his co-pilot's face hardening. 'Behave yourself, Pieter,' he whispered.

Pieter nodded reluctantly.

Rall finished with Schröder's hand and gestured towards Max and his men. 'This is Oberleutnant Max Kleinmann and his crew. These men will be flying the American bomber.'

Max prepared to salute the superior officer, but Schröder swiftly extended a hand. 'Oh, you don't want to be worrying about the rank.' Max uncertainly reached for his hand. 'A pleasure to make your acquaintance, Max, and I'm sure it will be a pleasure and an honour flying with you.'

Max was taken aback slightly at his enthusiastic greeting. The pilot seemed like the type of over-cheerful, confident, aristocratic fop that seemed to start in the Luftwaffe at an ill-deservedly high rank. Usually fools like that died swiftly. But this one hadn't. With a sky so dominated by Allied fighters, that made him a good pilot. He had the refined, almost feminine, Aryan features that one would expect from his aristocratic bloodline. His brow and lashes were blond, almost white, like an albino, and framed by a fringe that flopped down like a theatre curtain over one of his eyes.

'Hauptman,' Max responded formally, reluctant, and too weary, to match Schröder's jovial tone.

'So, I've yet to be told by the Major here exactly what fun and games lies ahead for us, but I understand it involves this brute of a plane?'

Max nodded. 'Yes, but I'm afraid I can't comment on the mission until you've been properly briefed by Major Rall.'

Rall stepped in. 'Max is correct, Hauptman Schröder. I would prefer to brief you and your men first before we discuss it openly out here.'

Schröder looked at Rall. 'Of course, my apologies for getting ahead of things there, Major.' He turned and smiled conspiratorially at Max. 'But I'm sure whatever it is the Major has up his sleeve will be an adventure, eh?'

Max smiled, unwilling to pass comment on the mission.

The two men finished shaking hands and Schröder offered it enthusiastically to Pieter.

Pieter stared silently at the extended hand a moment before reluctantly offering his. 'Hauptman,' he said drily. Schröder barely registered the coolness of the gesture before Major Rall decided to step in.

'Hauptman Schröder, and your men, come with me and I will introduce you to the other pilots who arrived last night . . . and then perhaps I think it is time for you and your new squadron to be briefed.'

Schröder and his two wingmen turned smartly and followed Rall out of the hangar into the pale light of morning.

'What the hell was that all about, Pieter?' asked Max.

'I just don't like his type. Bloody stuck-up arseholes, the lot of them.'

'Maybe, but he's a bloody superior officer first.'

Max could sympathise a little with him. The Luftwaffe had an appalling reputation for snobbery, preferring to pick its fighter pilots from the ranks of the aristocracy. Following the example Göring set, the Luftwaffe saw itself as the latter-day equivalent of an exclusive, members-only cavalry regiment. Pieter had joined the Luftwaffe and passed examinations that would mark him out as pilot material, but he was never going to find himself flying a fighter, not unless they ran completely out of men like Schröder.

'Take it easy, Pieter, we're all on the same side.'

Chapter 24

Lucian

26 April 1945, an airfield south of Stuttgart

Major Rall had billeted Max and his men in one of the vacated radio rooms. The room had once housed a nerve centre of intelligence-gathering equipment and personnel. Now it was little more than a grey painted concrete box. Several tables remained, and scuff marks and scratches on their surface hinted at the machinery that had once been there.

Rall had provided some blankets and a gas heater, which they gratefully fired up in the evenings when the cold seeped through the blankets on the hard concrete floor. The men had managed to make themselves at home in the room, spreading out their blankets around the heater on the floor. On the ground beside the heater there was a growing pile of empty food tins. The Major had certainly delivered on his promise to find adequate supplies for them. They hadn't eaten this well in months. Max decided that it was probably time they were gathered up and chucked into one of the other empty rooms. He'd get one of his boys to do it in the morning.

The overhead lights in the room had been left off; both Pieter and Hans were asleep. Stefan was still awake and sat hunched over the glowing heater with his blanket draped over his shoulders.

'You all right, lad?' asked Max.

'I'm fine, sir.'

Max sighed in the darkness. 'For God's sake, Stef, you can call me Max like the others, you know. You've been with us long enough now.'

'Sorry . . . Max.'

They sat in silence for a while listening to the soothing hiss of the heater.

'So, this is better than sitting out in the open, eh? Just think, we could still be sitting in the back of that truck.'

'This is much better. Just to be warm again is great. I can't remember the last time I wasn't cold.'

He couldn't agree more.

If he lived to be ninety Max knew the most enduring memory of his time on the eastern front would be that of a constant battle with the cold. Staffel KG-301 had been stationed up on the northern end of the frontline near Murmansk for a good portion of the last two years. Up there, even in mid-summer, it was an unforgivably cold place to live.

'Yes . . . warm is good,' he replied turning on his side to look at the amber glow of the heater.

Stefan sat hunched over it, a small, thin, ginger-haired youth with the pale skin of a child unblemished with the knocks and scrapes of life. He was nineteen, but he looked so much younger. He reminded Max of his younger brother, Lucian.

Lucian Kleinmann had been nineteen when he'd died. That had only been eight months previously. He had fallen in Poland, near the Vistula River, just east of Warsaw during the Russians' summer offensive, Operation Bagration. Max's parents had been given no details as to how his younger brother had died, just that he had been one of the casualties of the ill-equipped infantry regiment that had been placed in the way. There had been ten years between Max and Lucian, almost a generational divide. In many ways the age difference had made them more like father and son than brothers.

The news had almost broken Max, as it had his parents. A lot of the bitter anger he felt for the death of his younger brother was directed towards the Russians, quite understandably, but a little was also directed towards the German high command, for pointlessly throwing an infantry regiment in the path of a battalion of T-34s, a tactical decision born out of desperation, as they all seemed to be these days.

'Max? Can I ask you a question?'

'Of course, ask away.'

'What will happen if we *do* make it there and drop the bomb?'

Max spent a moment considering the question. Rall had suggested that there was a growing feeling amongst the American people that Stalin and the communists were becoming a dangerous force in the world, and potentially an enemy that they would end up fighting some time in the near future. This bomb would provide them the final incentive to change sides.

'The Americans will have no choice but to join up with us and fight the Russians.'

'And what will the Russians do?'

'They haven't the resources to take on America and Britain combined. Even Stalin isn't that crazy. They would have no choice but to turn around. I suppose we hope they will panic when they see the devastation this new explosive does and promptly withdraw.'

Stefan was silent for a moment, digesting Max's answer.

He had a good mind, thought Max. One that soaked up information quickly, but more importantly extrapolated from it, applied it and used it.

'If that happens, the Russians withdraw . . . will that be an end to it? An end to the war?'

Another good question.

'Of course, because they'll be out of our land, that's all we're after right now. I'm sure that would put an end to it.'

Really?

Max wasn't entirely convinced by his own answer. Would the war truly end? Maybe it would for a few years, long enough for Germany to replenish her resources. But then what? He wondered whether a leader like Hitler would simply settle for Germany's pre-war borders. After having conquered most of Europe, would he be happy with that?

Would he fuck. There would be another war.

Another war, a Third World War in ten, fifteen, twenty years? This time fought with planes and these super bombs. The world would obliterate itself with them. For a moment Max wondered whether the best thing to do would be to drop the weapon in the Atlantic when they reached it, where hopefully no one would ever find it and use it.

'Do you think we're going to do it, Max?'

'What?'

'Do you think we'll make it across to America?'

The troubling doubts instantly vanished to the darkest corners of his mind as he considered the audacious, ambitious challenge Rall had presented to him. It could most certainly be done.

'The Major's put together a clever plan, Stefan . . . of course we will.'

That seemed to satisfy the lad for a few moments, before he looked up once more from the heater and stared at Max. 'Why did you decide to do this mission? I know why the others did. Pieter I think because he believes in this country, Hans because he just wants some revenge, and me, I voted yes because of my family, my mother, my sisters . . . but you?'

So much like Lucian, always asking bloody questions.

Max suspected Pieter had volunteered because deep down he'd never stopped believing in his beloved Führer, something he would never admit to in public now. There was a lot that he didn't have in common with Pieter, their politics, their background, their basic view on life differed, and yet it was the shared experiences of the last three years that had forged a rock-steady partnership between them. They had seen three navigators and two gunners come and go, and most of the other original personnel of KG-301 had died, been wounded or transferred to other under-manned squadrons. He wondered, if both of them survived the war, whether they would stay in touch with each other.

Probably not.

They would have nothing in common to talk about other than their wartime experiences. Pieter's world was factory floors, beer cellars and women. Max's world had once been teaching, a long, long time ago in his pre-war life.

'I suppose I want my life back, Stef. I want to grow old in a quiet country village where I know everyone's face, and the most terrifying thing that happens to me every day is crossing the road.'

He turned to the young man. 'If the Russians take Germany, we can't expect an ounce of mercy, and I don't expect they'll show us any. If they take Germany, Stef, we're all as good as dead.'

'We have to succeed then, don't we, sir?'

Max nodded. 'Yes, we do, lad.'

Chapter 25

Schenkelmann

27 April 1945, a southern suburb of Stuttgart

Dr Hauser stood in the middle of the lab and stared at the device. It looked like a small beer keg surrounded by a frame of scaffolding.

This is my creation, MY creation.

Hauser felt the need to remind himself regularly that this thing was his work. Of course, the Jew had made a contribution, but in the end it was just a different way of calculating the same process, and it was obvious now, looking back. Hauser knew he'd have figured it out for himself sooner or later.

This was the fruit of all *his* hard work; the Jew had merely helped.

Without him the project would never have been put before Albert Speer and consequently received the go ahead.

To be fair, the Jew, Schenkelmann, and his two assistants had done a good job assembling the device, but Hauser had designed the mechanics of the bomb and had drawn out the schematic; after all, he'd spent enough time pouring over Heisenberg's bomb designs to know what the best configuration would be.

If he was going to be totally honest about the distribution of credit, the Jew deserved something for his calculations on accelerating the critical mass, but it was *he*, *Dr Karl Hauser*, who had really made this project happen.

Hauser admired the compact device, taking pride in the efficiency of the design.

Such a small, beautiful thing to cause so much destruction.

He approached *his* bomb and tenderly ran his hand along the metal casing, sensing the kinetic energy inside, the explosive monster lying inert, asleep, waiting.

'Dr Hauser?'

Hauser felt his skin crawl at the sound of the little Jew's voice. He turned round to face Joseph Schenkelmann. He was a short, slight man in his late forties, thick dark hair, greying at the temples.

'What is it, Joseph?'

'Sir, d-did you speak with the Führer?' the small man stuttered nervously.

'Of course I did.'

'And you explained the ... the p-problem to him?'

Hauser found his temper quickly fraying at the mention of the 'old issue'. He forced a smile at Schenkelmann and consoled himself with a little truth.

I won't have to put up with him for much longer.

'He is aware of the risk, but is still keen to have the bomb readied for removal tomorrow, Joseph.'

Schenkelmann looked incredulous. 'He knows? . . . and still he wants to p-proceed?'

'Yes, I explained the risk, and he and I agree it is marginal. Now if you don't mind –'

Schenkelmann seemed to turn a shade paler than his usual complexion. 'M-marginal? Please ... Dr Hauser, you've seen the c-calculations for yourself ... you've seen it. The danger of an infinite reaction is –'

'– is acceptable given the current situation. Now, we have discussed this I don't know how many times and I am growing tired of hearing –'

'The danger of the infinite reaction is f-fifty per cent. Dr Hauser, sir ... we are gambling the world on a one in two chance!'

Hauser felt something in him snap. He reached out and grabbed Schenkelmann by the arm and spoke in a low, menacing voice. 'Now listen. The bomb will be readied for the journey tomorrow and you will also prepare the arming codes tonight. There will be no more talk about this infinite chain reaction. Your calculations on this are exaggerated, and they always have been.'

Hauser knew Schenkelmann's figures were right.

They were right when first he came across the theory papers and they remained unchanged now. The theory, quite simply, was pure genius. Schenkelmann had shrewdly proposed accelerating the chain reaction by firing two uranium bullets at opposite ends of the mass. The advancing ripples from both ends would cause overlapping shockwaves to quadruple exponentially the rate of acceleration. A reaction like that would require so much lower a critical mass of U-235 than had previously been thought. Heisenberg had calculated that tons of U-235 would be needed; Schenkelmann's technique required only ounces.

The danger, as far as Schenkelmann was concerned, was that such an accelerated chain reaction might cause enough immediate energy to be released to split the nuclei of non-fissile material. The man's figures convincingly demonstrated the probability to be high, as much as fifty per cent, that the weapon would vaporise not only its target but also an unquantifiable range beyond it.

The mathematical implication was simple, an infinite chain reaction . . . a doomsday bomb.

'The figures are right, Dr Hauser.'

'If you do not shut up now, I will have you shot, Schenkelmann. Do you understand?'

Making the threat felt good, powerful. Like throwing a punch. For a fleeting moment he felt like following through on the threat and issuing the command to one of the guards, just to enjoy the thrill of issuing an order and seeing it carried out automatically, without question. He suspected he would have made a fine officer if his expertise hadn't prevented him from being recruited. He found giving orders so easy, so natural.

Hauser had been assigned half a dozen SS men to guard the small laboratory and keep an eye on Schenkelmann. It had been Speer's idea. He had been worried about Schenkelmann attempting to commit suicide, sabotage or even flee from the claustrophobic confines of the small underground lab. The men were always present inside and discreetly placed outside the inconspicuous corrugated doors of the building.

Hauser regarded the soldiers as his own private army, to command as he pleased. The novelty had yet to wear off.

The lab had been built into one of the arches of a railway bridge that ran parallel to a small cobbled back street. Behind this unassuming façade, which could easily have been the premises of any small, one-man business, the stairs descended to a cellar that had once been used to store wine. Here, in a space little bigger than a generous living room, Schenkelmann and two lab assistants had been given the task of assembling Germany's atom bomb. This cellar had been Schenkelmann's prison since the project had begun; the Jew hadn't seen daylight in months.

'P-please, Dr Hauser.'

Hauser felt his face flush with anger, first his cheeks, then his forehead and his ears. He knew he looked as crimson as a baby screaming for milk.

If threatening his life isn't going to work, then there are other alternatives.

'This conversation ends now, and you will proceed with preparing the bomb for tomorrow morning or I will see to it that your sister and your mother are visited by one of my men.'

Schenkelmann's family had been found working alongside him in the munitions factory. It had taken very little string pulling to have all three extricated from the factory and the women held in 'care' while Schenkelmann was put to work. With Albert Speer as the Armaments Minister providing the authority for these arrangements, there had been absolutely no red tape to cut through to move these three Jews. Equally, while they were useful to Speer and Hauser they would never be shipped off to an extermination camp, nor casually executed on the street by some over-zealous Gauleiter. With the rubber stamp of Speer, these three people were perhaps the safest Jews in Europe. They had been lucky to find his sister and mother alongside him in the factory, for now Schenkelmann was beginning to care little about his own miserable life; they still had the leverage of his loved ones to play around with.

Hauser smiled, aware that the threat had worked and that this troublesome little man had been silenced.

'There, I'm glad we have that unpleasantness behind us, Joseph. Let's finish the job here, shall we?'

Joseph Schenkelmann stared bleakly at the ground, aware that he had been a stupid, weak man for allowing the project to have progressed this far.

What have I done?

He knew his only consideration now should be to think of some way to sabotage this bomb before it was taken away from him and used in whatever way these barbaric animals had planned. He had hoped all along that the unpredictable nature of his bomb's design would eventually make it a redundant development. He had thought no one would be stupid enough to use a weapon like this, except of course that twisted man, Hauser. He'd known, from the first conversation with the German, that his tunnel vision would let him see nothing but the glory he would bathe in after its successful deployment. The risk of global devastation had been tidied away somewhere in his distorted mind behind some assurance that the risk was grossly exaggerated. Schenkelmann had been holding on to the hope that at some point someone higher up the chain of command would be made aware of the appalling risks of this project and put an end to it immediately. He'd desperately hoped that the meeting with Hitler, the one that Hauser had been dreamily looking forward to for days, would see the project abruptly terminated.

But clearly now that hadn't been the case. Hitler was as insane as Hauser.

He could perhaps attempt to sabotage the bomb somehow; God knew why he'd left such a decision so late. But he knew he hadn't the strength of will to carry out such a bold act; it would certainly guarantee the death of all that remained of his family. At least co-operation ensured their continued survival, and if the bomb failed to trigger the infinite chain reaction he so feared, then there was a chance that all three of them would emerge from this nightmare alive.

'So? Why are you still standing there? You have a lot to do tonight.'

'Yes, Dr Hauser.'

'The arming code for the altimeter trigger will need these values set.' Hauser handed him a manila envelope. 'The arming code is in there, and I *will* test the code when I come back later.'

'Where are you going, Dr Hauser?'

Hauser raised an eyebrow, annoyed at Schenkelmann's impertinence. 'I am arranging to have an escort for our little device.'

'Yes, Dr Hauser.' Schenkelmann watched the German leave. He looked around: a soldier stood at the top of the stairs leading down into the lab and one of the two technical assistants was working on sealing the uranium casket. The other one was asleep on a cot in the corner of the room. He looked down at the envelope, still open, and shortly due to be sealed.

He saw a possibility.

He tucked the manila envelope under his arm and approached the bomb. He picked up a notepad, clipboard and a pen.

The lab assistant looked up at Schenkelmann. 'Is everything all right, Mr Schenkelmann?'

'Fine thank you, Rüd, I'm just going to run through my checklist, before you and I finish assembling the altimeter trigger.'

Schenkelmann looked down at the notepad and the pen he held in his left hand. He realised the next words he wrote down would be the most important he'd ever written, or would ever write. With only a minute's thought, he began to scribble furiously, aware that Hauser might return at any time. This was perhaps the last window of opportunity he had left to try and undo his work.

To the one responsible for arming this weapon . . .

He wrote swiftly for over a minute and stopped only when he became aware of his assistant looking up curiously. Rüd was no Nazi, but he was German. Any suspicious behaviour exhibited by Schenkelmann now would be reported to Hauser. In fact, Hauser had probably asked Rüd and Jürgen, the other assistant, to keep an eye on him now that the project was reaching its end.

These few dozen scribbled sentences were all that he had to prevent this insanity progressing to its apocalyptic conclusion. Schenkelmann could only pray that the man who would activate this bomb, whoever he was, was someone capable of thinking beyond an order. And he prayed with all his heart that it wasn't some simple-minded soldier who would be activating this weapon, that it wasn't an insane creature like Hauser who would risk the entire world for his own twisted ambition.

He turned his back on the lab assistant and slid the note into the manila envelope, then, turning back to face his assistant, he pulled out a slip of paper with four digits handwritten on it. Dr Hauser's handwriting.

'The arming code and arming instructions,' he announced.

He read the four digits at the top and then slid the paper back inside and sealed the envelope.

'I will set the code on the altimeter now,' he said calmly to the assistant.

As he worked, he discreetly wiped away sweat from his brow, beads of fear and despair. If Hauser were to open the envelope and find the note, then death for certain faced Zsophia and Mother.

It is done. As long as the code tests correctly, he will have no need to examine the contents of the envelope.

Joseph Schenkelmann realised his attempt at sabotage was too little and probably too late, and doomed to failure if Hauser should decide to read once more his carefully worded instructions, but at this stage it was all he could think to do.

He completed setting the code on the altimeter, and then together he and his assistant Rüd began to prepare the bomb for its journey.

Chapter 26

Truman

27 April 1945, Washington, DC

He recalled those days vividly: the day that the ultimatum arrived, and then the chaotic days that followed.

James Irlam Wallace had been plucked from obscurity, studying for his post-doctorate in theoretical physics at Stanford, in his own little study. One day, out of the blue, several stern-faced men in plain suits had entered his study and, with little in the way of an explanation, had escorted him to Washington and the offices of the OSS to meet with Bill Donovan, then the head man of the recently restructured wartime intelligence agency.

Bill Donovan had recruited him then and there in the name of national security. And that had put an end to his academic career. From that point on, James Wallace was an intelligence asset.

There had been disturbing intelligence reports from Europe that the Germans, under the technical direction of Professor Werner Heisenberg, were going for the atom bomb. Donovan had explained to Wallace, after he'd signed a clutch of documents that threatened death and damnation should he utter a word of anything that was about to be revealed to anyone, ever, that they had only small pieces of the puzzle coming over as intelligence on the subject. The OSS needed someone with a keen mind, but more importantly a knowledge of the subject, to pull it all together and answer with some confidence whether the Germans had the capacity to make one yet. Donovan had added that Oppenheimer himself had mentioned Wallace's name, as a suitable candidate to analyse and summarise the German atomic effort, in lieu of providing one of his own team, now working at breakneck speed on Trinity, none of whom he could spare.

And so, after a hurried induction process, Wallace found himself answering directly to Bill Donovan and working in isolation, once more in a study of his own, on the tiny fragments of information that had been acquired thus far on Heisenberg and his team, and their progress.

It was six months after Wallace had started in this job that the event in question occurred. It was in the early hours of April the 27th that he was roused by a phone call from Donovan and told to meet him at the White House, where he would be waiting with an emergency security pass, to walk him through to meet with the President.

Wallace recalled that particular day with such clarity, the day he met Truman, the man who had been President for only a matter of days, a man who was struggling to find his feet in a role that had been thrust upon him with little preparation or notice in the wake of Roosevelt's untimely death.

Truman came in and sat down at the conference table without a word. He took a moment to compose himself and then held the telegram in his hand shakily and began to read it aloud:

> To The President of America,
> Germany has at her disposal a number of weapons of great destructive power. These have been completed and readied for deployment.
>> It has long been my belief that both America and Britain are our natural allies, and that the war we have been fighting since 1939 has been the wrong war. The real struggle should have always been solely against communism.
>> Now we have these weapons, we are in a position to correct this mistake.
>> You will cease all military action against Germany and declare war on Russia. Allied troops under the command of General Eisenhower in Germany are to be placed under control of General Keitel to assist Wehrmacht forces in the defence of Berlin.
>> These measures are to be carried out within 48 hours.
>> There will be one demonstration of this weapon for the world to see. Failure to comply to the requests made above will result in additional demonstrations. It is with regret that a demonstration is necessary.
> Adolf Hitler

The men around the conference table were initially as shocked as the President. After a few moments to absorb what the President had read aloud, Truman's cabinet, all of them, began talking at once.

'Stop, gentlemen, quiet please,' Truman muttered, unheard by everyone in the room. His assembly of wise men looked like little more than a class full of unruly children. He steadied himself, breathing deeply.

Here's the crunch, Harry . . . now it's time to act like a leader.

'QUIET!' he barked with a voice unused to being raised. The men around the table were instantly silent, finally aware that they had broken rules of conduct and behaviour that they would never have broken in Roosevelt's presence.

Truman sipped some water to settle his voice, and buy time to steady himself. 'Now, I need us all to think this through one step at a time. I have no idea what the potential capability of Germany is to produce a super-weapon. I had thought with all the bombing we've done in recent months, they were now incapable of producing *anything*,' he said looking pointedly at General Arnold, the Air Force Chief of Staff, then around the table, studying the brass name-holders on the conference table in front of each attendee.

He focused on Donovan.

'Colonel Donovan, you are head of our Foreign Intelligence. What do we have? What can you tell me about this?'

'Well, Mr President, sir, we do have a lot of information on this. Our aerial photos of the Rhineland show approximately ninety per cent of her manufacturing base is beyond repair. Germany does have other industrial areas, but these are piecemeal and many have already been overrun either by our troops or the Russians, sir.'

'So you're not convinced by this threat, then?' asked the President.

'I'm not saying that, Mr President, but I can't see there would be many places left in the country where a significant industrial process could be carried out . . . assuming of course that the threat being referred to *required* a significant industrial process.'

'Hmm, I see,' Truman steepled his fingers and looked around the table for another candidate to extract information from.

Wallace was one of the junior attendees and stood a few feet back from the table behind Donovan, as did several other assistants and advisors to the various department heads present. As the room remained silent, Truman took the time to familiarise himself with the names and faces around the table.

Donovan leaned back and summoned Wallace over.

'Sir?' whispered Wallace.

'You may need to present right now what you've put together so far, lad. Are you ready for that?'

'I . . . I'm not sure I –'

The whispered conversation between them wasn't missed by Truman.

'Young man, if there's information to be had, then I'd prefer it first hand.'

Wallace's face coloured as the room, full of older, senior military men and statesmen, stared at him.

'Given the severity of the situation, I really don't think I have time for opinions to filter their way through the correct channels. Please.' Truman spread his hands, inviting him to speak.

Donovan twisted round in his seat and looked up at Wallace, who was now swallowing nervously, his almost pre-pubescent Adam's apple bobbing like a cork. Donovan nodded and in a deep voice quietly said, 'Go on, son.'

Wallace felt the crimson in his cheeks suddenly drain away and his scalp prickle as an even greater wave of anxiety swept through him.

'Mr President . . . the ahhh . . . we believe the Germans could conceivably have a number of projects for weapons capable of mass destruction still in process. These projects could be small in scale, requiring modest industrial support, sir.'

Truman nodded. 'Go on.'

'There is . . . some evidence they have advanced biological weapons. Um . . . plagues, viruses that could plausibly be released by an agent or added to municipal water supplies, for example. Also they have developed some nasty chemical weaponry. But I believe there is another possibility to consider, though I hasten to add that it is unlikely, sir.'

Truman shrugged and raised his eyebrows.

'We know they have been trying for an atom bomb, sir.'

The announcement caused most of the men around the table to stir uncomfortably. The President however, remained unperturbed, if a little bewildered.

'What the blazes is an *atom bomb*?'

Wallace looked back down at Donovan for help, eager that his department head be the one to explain why such a significant subject should have wholly bypassed Truman while he had been in the role of Vice-President.

Donovan spoke up. 'Mr President, I think with respect to you, sir, this briefing should have come a little earlier. Under the former President's instruction, an enormous research effort known as the Manhattan Project has been put together. It's a programme to produce an atom bomb.'

'Ahh . . . I see, something else that I've yet to be brought up to date on. Colonel Donovan, I might have been informed of this a little sooner.'

Donovan was subdued in his response. 'Yes sir, it was on a list of briefings you were due to receive over the next few days.'

'So then, enough of that for now. Donovan, tell me what the hell an atom bomb is please.'

'An atom bomb is a form of explosive device that is in the order of millions of times more destructive than conventional explosive materials. Although I'm no scientist, sir, I know the destructive potential of one atom bomb is far greater than, for example, all of the combined air raids so far carried out by the 8th Bomber Group in England.'

'My God!' Truman's mouth dropped open. He looked back up to Wallace. 'And young man, you think the Germans have some of these things?'

Wallace cleared his throat.

'No sir, I don't think so. But I know they were attempting to build one. Our troops recently discovered a research laboratory in Strasbourg, and a German scientist called Heisenberg is in our hands. We know from debriefing him that the laboratory was their main research strand, and that this Heisenberg was their leading physicist on the project. At the risk of complicating this with science, I can attempt to explain how we know they can't possibly have an atom bomb.' Wallace raised his eyebrows, a little more relaxed speaking before them all, now that he was approaching familiar territory.

Truman pursed his lips and then nodded. 'Continue. I'll try my best to follow.'

'Okay,' Wallace took a moment to consider how to explain the concept simply. 'Mr President, sir, you know what an atom is?'

Truman frowned. 'Of course, young man, it's those little ball things we're all made of isn't it?'

Wallace smiled, the President was essentially right. 'Yes, sir. Well . . . we know from scientific work carried out in 1939 that splitting one of these releases an immense amount of energy. We also know that some molecules –' Truman frowned '– that some *substances* have atoms that are easier to split than others. One such substance is called uranium 235, or U-235 as we call it for short. Now, to take this idea and turn it into a bomb, one needs to split a whole lot of atoms very quickly. The way one does this is by creating what is known as a chain reaction. When one splits the first atom it sheds energy and a couple of particles known as neutrons. These neutrons in turn smash into neighbouring atoms, split them and release more neutrons. This happens repeatedly, with every new atom that is split two more neutrons are released, and pretty quickly you have billions of neutrons splitting billions of atoms, thus releasing a lot of energy. That is a chain reaction. Are you with me so far, Mr President?'

Truman nodded. 'So far. Keep it like you've just done, as non-scientific as you can.'

'So . . . that is the chain reaction, sir. However, as I mentioned earlier, only one type of substance, U-235, can have its atoms easily split this way, and it is very, very rare and must be very carefully refined and purified. To give you an idea, sir, of how much it has to be refined, it would take five hundred tons of mined uranium ore to produce one ounce of uranium; of this only about one per cent is U-235 while the other ninety-nine per cent is U-238, useless to the process. So, as you can see sir, it takes a lot of work to produce the raw material for a bomb. We have been refining uranium now for nearly a year and I believe we have only just managed enough to make our first bomb.'

'I see,' said Truman. 'But then could they have produced enough of this material for a small bomb?'

'A very good question, sir. And the answer is that there needs to be a minimum amount, mass, of the substance in one place to enable the chain reaction. This is referred to as the critical mass. Once a block of U-235 is put together that exceeds this mass, the chain reaction happens pretty much automatically.'

'Good grief! Do we have more than this amount of uranium? Is it kept apart? Separately I mean?'

Wallace smiled at the President's alarm, charmingly naive, but a sensible concern.

'I believe we have in excess of that amount, and yes, it is stored carefully, sir.'

'So what is this amount? Is it a lot, tons?'

'The critical mass required to produce the chain reaction is calculated as one hundred and ten ounces sir.'

'Ounces!'

'Yes, sir, perhaps about the weight of a saucepan full of water, and about the size of, say, a baseball.'

'Good God, that doesn't sound like a lot! Are you sure the Germans haven't been able to make that amount of the stuff?'

'We are pretty certain, sir.'

'Very certain, sir,' Donovan added. 'The discovery of the laboratory in Strasbourg showed they had only managed to refine much smaller amounts. And as yet, the German scientist, Heisenberg, has not relayed news of any other nuclear research projects. As far as he is concerned, his was the only atom bomb project.'

Truman took a moment to digest the information. He directed his attention towards Wallace. 'Well, thank you, son, what's your name?'

'Wallace, sir.'

'Thank you, Wallace, for bringing me up to date. I'm surprised that I actually understood your description. Well done.'

Wallace took a step back behind Donovan, aware that his moment of glory had passed and his contribution to the conference was more than likely complete.

'I presume that means we can rule out the possibility that the threat is one of these atom bombs, then,' Truman said, displaying a little relief.

Donovan awkwardly corrected the President. 'Not rule out, sir, but it seems highly unlikely.'

'Noted, Colonel Donovan.'

Wallace looked around the men at the table. All of them seemed to some degree comforted by the information he had imparted. One of them, the Chairman of the Joint Chiefs of Staff, Admiral Leahy, stirred.

'Mr President, there appears to be another issue we can perhaps debate here.'

Truman shrugged curiously. 'Yes?'

'Maybe this might represent an opportunity to ... ' the older man scratched the end of his nose awkwardly, ' ... turn the war around against Russia, sir.'

Silence met the end of that sentence. Wallace could see many of the men around the table holding back their reaction to the comment, waiting to see Truman's response and, as important, the response of others around the table. Wallace suspected by the silence that passed, that mixed opinions were waiting to emerge.

'Well sir, I think I know what my predecessor would have made of that suggestion,' Truman said breaking the silence.

Wallace wondered what the President had meant by that comment.

'So ... ? You gentlemen have opinions on this?'

Admiral Leahy decided to further the discussion. 'Mr President, I think Colonel Donovan will agree that the communist state of Russia will be our enemy after Germany is defeated. Maybe not this year, maybe not next year, but pretty soon we'll be fighting in Europe again, this time against Stalin.'

'Donovan?'

Donovan continued. 'He may be right sir. Strategically, this may represent an opportunity to curtail that possible outcome. Pushing the Germans back over the last two years has drained their military resources, if – *if* – we were to turn this around and declare war on Russia, we would probably win, and win quickly.'

Truman nodded as he listened to him and contemplated his words in silence for a full minute before speaking again. 'If we were to do that – and of course gentlemen I am speaking completely hypothetically, as I'm sure we all have been – if we were to do that, we would be extending this war by how long, would you suppose?'

There were no answers.

'A month? A year? Several years?'

Wallace watched the military men at the table shuffle uncomfortably. *Years, that's what they're thinking.*

'In all honesty, this hypothetical debate has run its course. Our people are simply not ready to send their children into the meat grinder for another war. I think I understand the strategic thinking here, and perhaps we need to schedule a briefing to bring me up to date on post-war strategic issues concerning our Russian friends.' Truman directed a firm look towards the generals grouped together at the far end of the conference table. 'But right now this nation is tired, Europe is tired, the world is tired. Perhaps . . . perhaps if this *atom* bomb threat from Germany was a realistic possibility, this might have been an avenue for discussion. But for now I suggest we can treat this communication as nothing more than a futile attempt at a bluff.'

Truman turned to Donovan. 'Have your man there, Wallace, put together a complete report on the Germans' efforts to make one of these bombs. They may not have been able to make one, but I'd like to be sure they haven't left something that the Russians can pick up and use, especially if they are likely to be a worry in the future.'

Donovan nodded and made a note.

Then the meeting was adjourned. Wallace watched as Truman dismissed them all, and they filed out of the conference room in an awkward silence.

Wallace's eyes focused on Chris as his mind swiftly travelled sixty years back to the present.

'Are you all right there?' asked Chris.

Wallace smiled tiredly. 'I'm just tired.' He looked back down at the photographs he still held in his liver-spotted hands. 'A bit of a shock seeing these, and, I'm on some pretty strong medication. It takes it out of you.'

'So what is this all about?' Chris asked, frustrated that the old man had yet to reveal anything that he hadn't already known.

'Are these all the pictures you have?' Wallace asked, looking up from them and ignoring Chris's question. 'Some of them are not very clear.'

'It was very muddy down there, but yeah, I've got others. I'm going to do another dive down there and see if I can get some better shots. But, of course, it would help if I knew *what* to get better shots of.'

'Yes, I understand. But you need to be careful, Chris. Very careful. There could be people watching me, following me. I've been very careful, coming down to meet you, and I'm sure, for now, we are alone. But we do need to be discreet.'

'What people?' asked Chris.

Wallace put a finger to his lips. 'Just be careful who you talk to for now.'

The old man looked down at his watch. It was nine o'clock.

'I'm sorry, but I'm feeling pretty beat up and tired. I've done a lot of travelling today and I could do with some sleep. I think the excitement has taken it out of me.'

'What? You can't leave now!' blurted Chris.

'I'm sorry. I'm tired and I find it hard to concentrate these days when I'm tired. My mind isn't as sharp as it once was.'

Chris looked at the old man's face and noticed for the first time how pale and unwell he looked. His eyes were red-rimmed and puffy, and he wobbled uncertainly as he pushed the chair back to stand up. Chris found himself instinctively helping him out of the chair and up onto his feet as if he were a dutiful grandson to the old man.

'My legs get so stiff if I sit down for too long,' he muttered in a voice that sounded weak and thin.

'Well, can we meet tomorrow for breakfast then?' Chris asked as he helped the old man into his windcheater.

'Yes, yes of course. I should like to come out on the boat with you, if you're planning on another dive . . . you know, to see where she went down.'

'Okay, sure. I'll organise that, but we can do breakfast tomorrow?'

'Of course. I'll be a little more with it, I hope,' Wallace said with a worn smile.

'So, where are you staying?'

'I booked into a place just along up the street. A nice little place, Joe and Jan's I think it's called.'

Chris knew of it. It was a quaint little boarding house with an old-style colonial porch on the front.

'Okay then, Mr Wallace, I'll come by and pick you up tomorrow morning and we'll go and find somewhere quiet to have something cooked.'

Wallace nodded. 'Don't come knocking before nine o'clock.'

Chris would rather it be earlier. As it was, he was going to have a hard enough time waiting for the rest of his story.

'Nine it is, then. Can I help you out –'

Wallace shook his head. 'I'm fine, I'm fine. Just a little stiff and tired is all. I'll see you tomorrow morning.'

Chris watched Wallace leave the bar. He noticed Wallace studying the street outside in both directions before finally shuffling out into the night. The old guy seemed genuinely twitchy. Chris wondered whether he should have warned him about the two men he had spotted down by the jetty, but then decided the old man looked anxious enough. Giving him something extra to worry about would probably finish him off, by the look of him.

'Not a well man,' Chris muttered.

Chapter 27

The Route

8 a.m., 28 April 1945, an airfield south of Stuttgart

'So then, from Lyon I'd suggest we make sure we give Paris a wide berth, duck down and cross over, say . . .' Max's finger traced across the map, 'just north of Limoges.'

'Okay,' said Stef scribbling down the course direction from the previous waypoint.

'You got that?'

'Yes, sir.'

Max yawned and stretched in his seat, arching his tired back. His wrist smacked against the bulkhead as he stretched his arms. 'Ouch, shit,' he said rubbing it. 'There are so many damn edges and corners in this thing. I don't know how many times I've clumped my head or knees against something.'

Stef grinned and pulled his ginger fringe back from his forehead to show a small scab. 'I forgot to duck climbing up the ladder into the cockpit.'

'You idiot,' laughed Pieter.

Max leaned forward once more to study the maps. 'It's basically a dog's leg. South, out of Germany into Swiss airspace, and then a shallow north-westerly climb across France. What's the total distance?'

Stef flattened the map out and measured the distance along the sequence of waypoints he'd plotted across the map.

'About eleven hundred and sixty miles in total to Nantes.'

'And we're talking another four thousand and five hundred across the sea. That's five thousand, six hundred and sixty miles all in,' said Max.

'We should tell Major Rall six thousand miles,' said Pieter

'Agreed . . . let's have a healthy margin.'

Max noted the figure and would inform the Major later on how much capacity the extra tanks inside the bomber would need to have.

'Over France, we'll fly at close to ceiling, then once we're out to sea, we should take her down to about ten thousand to conserve fuel.'

'All right,' said Pieter. The Atlantic would be his part of the flight.

Max looked at both of them. 'All right? That's the route, then. I'll take it over to Rall for him to look over. I'm sure he'll be happy to give this his approval.' He looked at his watch. It was gone one o'clock in the morning. The Major would be awake still and keen to get this information.

'I'm going to piss off, get some sleep, I'm all in,' said Pieter yawning.

Max nodded. 'Fine, go get some rest. We're doing another practice flight tonight.'

Pieter stood up and climbed forward through the bulkhead out of the navigator's compartment.

Stef began inking in the waypoint headings on the map, tidily circling the clusters of numbers on the map and labelling each pocket of information with a waypoint number. He was a tidy, efficient navigator.

'Good work, Stef.'

The lad looked up and smiled. 'Thanks, sir.'

His gaze lingered on Max, as if there was something more he wanted to say.

'What's up?' he said to the boy.

Stef put down his pen. 'I was wondering, sir, do you ever get nervous? It's just that you never seem to be worried or scared, you know, before a sortie.'

If only.

Every man felt it as the time ticked away, and Max knew he was no exception to that rule. The growing sense of dread, those pre-battle nerves, it affected them all … just in different ways. Some men it made feel nauseous, others terribly thirsty. Many of the men he'd commanded in KG-301 suffered a desperate need to shit just before the planes were ready to leave the ground; some of his men had even confessed to feeling sexually aroused just before it was time to go.

Fear really did seem to have a plethora of ways of expressing itself.

With a little knowledge of anthropology, one could explain away most of these symptoms of extreme stress as the body's way of clearing the decks and preparing itself for danger. Nausea? – The body discouraging the ingestion of bulky food that might slow it down, or hamper its performance. Thirst? – A dry mouth was the body asking for water, hoarding it ready to be consumed after a burst of extreme physical exertion. Defecation? – The body ensuring that unnecessary body weight was quickly jettisoned.

Sexual arousal? – That was an odd one.

Max had a suspicion that it was the body's desperate plea to procreate one final time, an attempt at some basic level of instinct to ensure the bloodline continued.

All of these stress-symptoms made sense. They were emergency systems designed to ready the human body to fight, flee or face death. Once upon a time, when men had fought with clubs and rocks, those stress-responses must have been invaluable. But war now wasn't about brute strength, or swiftness of foot. It had much more to do with concentration and patience. And none of these damned symptoms helped at all.

They were made all the worse if there was nothing to do to fill in that dwindling time until zero hour. So he was thankful that for all of them there had been plenty to take care of and plenty more that needed doing in the next couple of days.

Do I get nervous? he asked himself.

More than he would ever let the others know.

'A little bit, maybe, Stef.'

'Oh. You never seem to look it, sir.'

Max smiled. *If only you knew.*

'We're going to be in good hands, thanks to Schröder and his men. We're flying a tough old plane, we're flying in secrecy and we're heading somewhere nobody expects us to go. The wind's in our favour, Stef. We'll do just fine.'

'Yes, I suppose you're right,' replied Stef.

'Don't be too hard on yourself, lad. It's good to be a little jittery, just enough to keep you alert, keep your wits about you.' Max slapped his back. 'You've done us proud over the last year and you'll do just as well tomorrow night.'

Chapter 28

On the Move

11 a.m., 28 April 1945, a suburb in Stuttgart

Schenkelmann found the diffuse glare of the thinly overcast morning almost unbearable after months of living by lamplight below ground. His eyes still hadn't adjusted to the brightness even though he'd been toiling in the daylight for ten minutes now. The little back street he had seen fleetingly all those months ago when they had dragged him into the building under the railway bridge and down below into the cellar did not seem to have taken any bomb damage, it looked unchanged.

He could hear the thudding of artillery shells landing nearby, or perhaps it was bombardment from above, and the sporadic crack of gunfire echoing off the empty streets.

'Hurry up, damn it!' said Hauser, looking up and down the cobbled back street, fear flickering across his narrow face.

Schenkelmann and his two lab assistants had nearly finished loading the weapon components into the back of the truck, where half a dozen of the SS Leibstandarte that Hitler himself had assigned to protect Hauser and the bomb sat guarding the odd-looking collection of crated items.

The U-235 mass and the two U-235 bullets had been carefully transported to the truck separately, but the altimeter trigger was the part of the bomb that needed some degree of protection from the bumping and shaking that lay ahead. This precious cargo was in for a turbulent ride as the truck picked its way over cratered roads to get out of the city. The altimeter was carefully padded in a wooden crate filled with coarse sawdust. The detonators for the two U-235 bullets were also packed away in two separate caskets, safely away from the rest of the bomb.

Schenkelmann slowly finished off sealing one of the caskets, taking his time under the bored gaze of the men in the truck. As he finished up and climbed back out of the truck, he looked around. There was no sign of Zsophia and his mother. Hauser had promised they would be brought along with him when the bomb was to be moved.

A crack of rifle fire sounded nearby, its echo rattled off the stone arches running down one side of the back street. It sounded like it had come from nearby, from behind the furniture workshop that faced the bridge and cast a long squat shadow over the cobbles. Or perhaps it was closer?

Schenkelmann smiled at the obvious discomfort Hauser was experiencing. He resumed the task of packing the second detonator, slowly.

'Hurry up!' Hauser shouted, his nerves beginning to fray.

How close are they? A hundred yards away? Fifty yards away?

Hauser gave an order to two of his SS men to torch the cellar. They had drums of gasoline and immediately jogged into the building and started sloshing the liquid down the stairs into the lab below.

Schenkelmann lifted the casket into the back of the truck, taking his time to place it securely on the floor. Hauser was becoming aware that he was stalling for time.

'Right, that'll do, now get out of the truck.'

Schenkelmann made his way cautiously past the components of the bomb to the open back of the truck and eased himself down. He looked around again, still no sign of them. 'W-where are my sister and mother?'

Hauser smiled. 'Don't worry about them, Joseph, you'll be together soon. You've worked hard for me, and I assure you they're fine.'

'I want to see them.'

'And you will, but first things first.'

There was the sound of a dull 'whump', and they could immediately smell burning. The two SS guards who had been sent down to set the place on fire emerged with their hands over their mouths. They were followed by the first wisps of smoke curling up the steps and out of the corrugated metal doorway.

'Why –?'

'Why are we destroying the lab? Because, Joseph, we're certainly not going to let the Americans have it now, are we?'

Americans? It's American guns I'm hearing, not Russian. Thank God.

Schenkelmann felt a desperate surge of hope that the nightmare was nearly over. In the next street, possibly only hailing distance away, lay his salvation. Perhaps they might just capture the bomb before it was moved . . . capture Hauser before he got away . . . find his mother and sister, and reunite them all. Today it could all be over.

If they were alive still. Hauser should have brought them along, they should be here.

'Dr Hauser, w-where are they?' he asked.

The German smirked like a child about to play a spiteful prank. 'Where are they, eh? Well let me tell –'

Schenkelmann cut him off with a desperate outburst. 'Please . . . I have given you everything, worked hard, please –'

'Oh, do shut up,' Hauser snapped, annoyed that he had been rudely interrupted.

Gunfire again. This time much closer. Schenkelmann cast a glance down the cobbled street.

I could call out, the Americans might hear me.

Hauser looked uneasily at his men.

'We should go now, Doctor,' called out one of the SS guards leaning out of the back of the truck.

'Yes . . . yes, you're right,' he replied, and turned towards the officer in charge of the platoon of regular Wehrmacht soldiers who were going to be left behind to watch that the laboratory was properly destroyed.

'Bösch.' Hauser nodded to the Feldwebel and his men. 'You know what to do. Get on with it, then.'

'Yes, sir,' the soldier answered with a gravelly voice.

He grabbed both the lab assistants by the arms and pulled them towards the corrugated metal wall of the archway. He let go of their arms and walked back a few feet.

'What is going on, Dr Hauser?' Rüd asked in a voice that was breaking with a dawning sense of dread. The technician had realised all too late that they were to be *purged* along with the lab.

'I'm sorry, gentlemen. I can't allow either of you to fall into enemy hands. However, I want to thank you for your diligence over the past few months,' Hauser said with an ill-placed smile. He nodded at Bösch.

The Feldwebel unshouldered his machine gun and, without a moment's delay, fired the entire clip at both men.

Hauser's face flickered with excitement at the sight of the two technicians as they collapsed to the ground; one of them drummed his feet noisily against the base of the corrugated metal door in a post-mortem spasm.

'Give me your gun,' he said. Bösch passed Hauser his weapon.

'And now, about your family, Joseph,' said Hauser walking menacingly towards Schenkelmann, pointing the gun at him.

'You wanted to be with them again didn't you?' He placed a hand on Schenkelmann's shoulder, squeezing it, caressing it.

'You've been a good little Jew, your work has been excellent, and I'm very pleased with you. Now, I made you a promise, didn't I, Joseph? What was it now? I've forgotten,' he said with an empty smile.

Schenkelmann nodded and smiled awkwardly back. 'Yes, we agreed . . . didn't we, my family and I –'

'Oh yes . . . so we did. I'm sorry.'

Hauser shook his head with feigned sadness, pouting his bottom lip with cruel mock-sympathy. 'I'm sorry, they're dead, Joseph. I'm sure you'll understand that we didn't have time to mess around dragging them over here with us. It would've been a nuisance. They died this morning – what?' he turned to the SS men in the truck, 'half an hour ago?'

Schenkelmann started hyperventilating and slumped to his knees. There he began to cry, his voice a weak, warbling high-pitched moan.

Hauser's face curled in disgust at the broken man. He raised the gun and pointed it at his head. 'Oh dear. Well, goodbye, you pathetic Je –'

A loud clatter of gunfire shattered the tableau and a stunned Hauser dropped the weapon as a fleck of stone stung his cheek.

A dozen or more US soldiers had emerged from an archway further down the back street. The American men had instinctively dropped to the ground and leaped for the cover of the doorways opposite them and now lay down a furious volley of gunfire up the street.

Two of Bösch's men dropped, one of them dead instantly. Another four were wounded. One of them lay on the cobbles and shook uncontrollably as blood and air bubbled from a rip in his neck.

Hauser scrambled away from Schenkelmann, on all fours back towards the truck as a storm of bullets zipped down the street at head height. He felt a bullet whistle past his ear with a low hum, and the rattle of a dozen more as they hit the cobbles on the ground around him.

The remaining men of the Wehrmacht platoon scrambled for cover on either side of the vehicle and began to return fire, while the SS men in the truck unslung their weapons and let off a volley from within.

A single bullet thudded into Schenkelmann's back and pushed him over on to his face, where he curled into a foetal position as the gunfight progressed, bullets whizzing in both directions, inches above him.

Hauser managed to make his way back to the truck and opened the cabin door. He waited for a second's lull to shriek an order to Bösch and his men. 'You must hold this position at all costs, the truck must get away!'

Hauser's thin, reedy voice reached Bösch, who reissued the order in a much louder parade-ground voice.

Hauser turned to the driver and screamed as he climbed in. 'Drive, for God's sake!'

Bösch heard the truck's engine stutter to life and it immediately lurched forward as the tyres spun on the cobbles. From his precarious position behind a small sapling he watched the truck rumble down the street and turn a corner before calling out to his men.

'Right, fuck that idiot's order. We'll hold for another minute, no more.'

His voice attracted a burst of gunfire and splinters of wood exploded from the sapling's trunk. He cursed Hauser for dropping the gun he had handed him in the street like a startled old woman. The gunfire died off for a moment. He could hear one of the Americans shouting orders to his men. Bösch had enough street-fighting experience to know that they were trying for a flanking position. The American officer was sending some of his men into the furniture warehouse to find a way up to the windows that overlooked him and his men.

That's what he'd do if the situation were reversed.

'Shit,' he muttered. He looked around and saw two of his men looking to him for instructions. Silently Bösch pointed at a window overlooking them and held up a fist, which he pulled down in a short tugging action and drew a finger across his mouth.

Grenades – through that window – on my command.

Both men nodded and each pulled out a stick grenade, they unscrewed the caps and made ready to tug on the fuse string. The gunfire had stopped. The Americans down the street were waiting for their colleagues to get into position before pressing home the attack.

Bösch studied the windows intently and soon caught a glimpse of the top of a helmet bobbing inside the building. They were making their way along the first floor to the window that looked down on to his position behind the splintered tree trunk. He nodded to his men and both threw their grenades up. One dropped through the window effortlessly whilst the other clattered uselessly against the window frame and dropped back down onto the stones below. He counted to seven before the first grenade went off inside the warehouse, producing a shower of dust from out of the windows and knocking a frame down on to the street. The other grenade exploded on the cobbles, shattering the few windows left intact on the ground floor of the furniture warehouse.

Bösch waited for the cloud of dust to clear. The grenades seemed to have done the trick, it looked like they had stunned, wounded or killed the men up there. Otherwise he'd have expected a retaliatory volley raining down on them by now.

He looked for the Jewish scientist; he was lying in the road, but still moving. A pool of blood had grown around his torso and a small river trickled across the street, meandering through the cracks between the stones.

He's lost too much blood to survive the wound.

If he'd had his gun on him he could have made sure of that with a shot or two to the head. Bösch knew enough that the Americans couldn't be allowed to capture the Jew alive. Hauser had made that quite clear.

Smoke was coming up from the lab below and billowing out through the arched door, thicker than it had been a minute ago, the fire must have caught and already be spreading.

He looked up the street.

The truck must be far enough away by now.

He nodded, assuring himself that they had done enough.

He signalled to his two men across the street that the fight was over, that they should put down their guns. He looked around for the others. It was time to get a quick tally on what had happened to his twelve men. Now that the truck, and the hard cover it afforded them, was gone, they had hastily spread out, seeking safe positions along the street. There were three sheltering in one of the warehouse's doorways further back and another two taking turns to fire short bursts from an archway closer to the Americans. He saw the bodies of five of his men lying in the cobbled street, those that had been caught off guard by the opening exchange. He put two fingers in his mouth and whistled loudly. His men instinctively turned towards him.

'That's it, weapons down,' he bellowed.

The German soldiers tentatively lowered their weapons but none of them moved from their covered positions. Bösch realised he'd have to go first. He loosened the strap of his helmet and then slid it off, he held it one hand by the rim and slowly, very slowly, he eased it out into the open.

Several shots splintered the slender tree trunk still further and it creaked alarmingly as if preparing to topple over. He heard an American call out a ceasefire and the gunfire stopped.

He eased himself out from behind what was left of the tree with both hands raised fully above his head. He called out the only English phrase he knew, one that he and most of his men had taken time to learn in recent months.

'Geneva convention ... Surrendering!' he announced loudly and clearly. He walked cautiously into the middle of the cobbled street, beckoning with one raised hand for his men to do likewise. One by one the seven remaining men of his platoon emerged and joined him.

The American soldiers remained in their positions, guns aimed, ready at a moment's notice to resume firing. One of them, Bösch recognised the stripes of a sergeant, pointed towards the Germans and shouted. 'Levy! Round 'em up and shake 'em down!'

From one of the warehouse doorways a young man emerged, and he trotted at the double towards them, his kit rattling like so many pots and pans in a bag. As Levy passed the Jew's body, the prone form moved and they heard a faint moaning.

'Sir! We got a live one here!'

Amongst the Americans the call for a medic rippled down the street, and moments later a medic appeared through one of the arches and slid to a halt beside Schenkelmann. Levy continued towards the Germans with his rifle raised at them, while the medic began his work.

Bösch watched the medic; he was fumbling with a compress applied to the wound to slow down the blood loss.

The Jew mustn't fall into enemy hands alive.

Hauser had muttered this a countless number of times to him over the last few days, every time he'd heard the sound of artillery, or been spooked by the crack of gunfire.

The young American soldier now stood only feet away from them. 'Okay, you shitheads, get down on the road!' he shouted at them, pointing to the ground.

Bösch and his men stared defiantly at the young man; their eyes drawn to the Star of David pinned prominently on his uniform. Levy jerked his rifle to the ground repeatedly and jabbed one of the prisoners in the ribs to make the point.

'Yeah, that's right, you Nazi shit-holes, I'm Jewish. Now get the fuck down!' he yelled angrily.

Bösch looked anxiously towards Schenkelmann. The medic treating him seemed satisfied that the compress was working and was now applying a bandage to hold it in place. Bösch nodded to his men, and they began to kneel obediently, albeit slowly. Another futile gesture of angry defiance.

The Jew can't fall into their hands alive.

He gritted his teeth and gave one of his men a hard push to the side. The man fell awkwardly to the ground. The young American swung his rifle towards the prone man and Bösch reached for it, yanking hard at the barrel and freeing the gun easily from his hands. He grabbed the waist of the rifle with his other hand and shoved the weapon backwards, the butt smashing into the young man's face with a sickening thud.

Levy dropped to the ground unconscious as Bösch spun the rifle round, aiming it squarely at Schenkelmann.

He had only a fleeting half-second, as he racked the weapon, to register the look of surprise and alarm on the faces of his own men and realise his rash action had doomed them all.

The gunfire from the entire platoon of Americans lasted a little more than fifteen seconds, and many of the young men who emptied their weapons that morning would vividly recall in years to come the bloody mess that was left of the eight German soldiers.

As the smoke cleared, the medic raised himself up off Schenkelmann, whom he'd almost crushed with his own body weight.

'You okay, fella?' he asked.

Schenkelmann nodded in response. His mouth opened and he tried to speak.

'Don't . . . just relax. We'll have you out of here shortly, buddy.'

Schenkelmann tried to speak again, but suddenly he felt light-headed and passed out.

Chapter 29

Via Nantes

4 p.m., 28 April 1945, an airfield south of Stuttgart

The map was spread out on the floor of the hangar and around it sat the fighter pilots, Max and his men and Major Rall. Rall had a length of wood that served adequately as a pointer and was currently indicating the planned route for the bomber and its escort.

'. . . across Lyon, towards the north-west coast of France.'

'Unless my maths is hopelessly inadequate, that's a long way beyond the range of our Me-109s,' announced Schröder backed up by murmurs of agreement from his squadron.

'It is just over one thousand, one hundred and fifty miles, gentlemen. The drop tanks that are being fitted to your planes right now will give you enough fuel to get there.'

As if to confirm his assurance, one of the mechanics fired up a welding torch and a stream of white-hot sparks emerged from among the tightly parked fighter planes.

Schröder nodded. 'So that gets us to the Atlantic, Major. But from the coast out to sea for the first three hundred miles, Max and his men will be on their own. I'm sure the Americans and British must have planes stationed in France now . . . it will only take one unlucky encounter and they will be in trouble.'

Rall's smile caused the burn tissue on the side of his face to wrinkle like parchment. 'Ahh, but you see, you boys will still be with the bomber.'

Schröder looked confused. 'I don't understand how. By the time we hit the coast, that's us done. We'll be empty. Perhaps if we're lucky and fly at a low altitude we can push a few extra miles out to sea, but not the distance we'll need to exceed their fighter range. Not unless we find somewhere to refuel.'

It was clear to Max now why the Major had specifically instructed him to put together a route across France to Nantes on the north-west coastline, instead of taking some other way.

'That's why we're flying across northern France, isn't it?' he said.

'What?' said Schröder.

Rall smiled. 'That's correct. We could have picked a more remote route. An alternative might have been across Norway, and a refill on Bear Island, and then over the North Pole to Greenland, and then down their east coastline. But that would have taken us up through northern Germany, and right now that's not a wise place to be. We're going this way. It's the long way round, but it's safer, and more importantly, we have a place on the north-west coast of France where you and your men can refill your tanks.'

Schröder looked astounded. 'We're landing on a French airfield?'

'A small airfield outside Nantes, it's two miles outside the city and less than one mile from the coast. Our intelligence suggests this airfield has only a custodial presence of Americans. These are mostly support personnel, mechanics, ground crew.'

'Even so, Major, we can't just land there and refill if it's not in our hands. Or am I missing something obvious here?' asked Schröder.

'Probably,' grumbled Pieter quietly.

'For a short time, the airfield will be in German hands.'

Rall paused for effect. He observed the look of confusion on the faces of the men around him.

'A U-boat is presently five miles off shore from Nantes. Tomorrow, before dawn, a platoon of our boys will be dropped ashore. Their instructions are to take up discreet positions just outside the airfield, and while you are less than ten minutes away from your final approach, they will secure it and ready the air fuel for you. Obviously, this is only a narrow window of time. It won't take long before any troops encamped nearby are alerted and attempt to retake the field, but this should buy you enough time to put down and fill up.'

Max exchanged a glance with Pieter; they both subtly shook their heads. This was new to them. Max had wondered about being instructed to pick a course across France, and had wondered how far their fighter escort could stay with them. Now here it was . . . and it sounded foolish.

Rall sensed the mood of the men; this was the part of the plan he knew he'd have difficulty selling to them. Flying over France, possibly fighting their way across some of it was going to be hard enough, but putting down on a strip that could well be in the middle of a hotly contested fire fight was something else entirely.

'Aren't we simply giving away our position, Major?' asked Max. 'Let's assume the B-17 provides us the cover we wanted. We might fly comfortably across France unchallenged, only to find we're attracting unwanted attention by taking this airfield.'

'Flying under cover may get you some of the way. The skies over Germany are filled daily with B-17s. But France? . . . rarely these days. Some way across you surely will attract their attention and then you will be thankful you have Schröder and his men with you. Of course, if that happens, discretion will amount to nothing, and you will need fighter cover for at least a further three hundred miles after you leave France. Refuelling here will give them those extra three hundred miles. Beyond that, no one can touch you.'

The fighter pilots continued to look unhappy with the idea of the landing.

'These soldiers taking the airfield. What are they, Falschirmjäger?' queried Schröder.

'No, not paratroops, Gebirgesjäger,' answered Rall.

Max massaged his temples. *Alpine troops. This only gets better.*

Schröder's eyes widened. 'Snow soldiers? Good God, what do they know about this kind of operation?'

'Leutnant Schröder . . . these are elite soldiers. They are every bit as good as our paratroops. These men have fought in the Metaxas line in Greece, the eastern front near Murmansk. Trust me, those men are the best we have. They'll be dealing with a garrison of engineers and clerks who'll be thinking of nothing more than going back home to America. It will be a quick and easy fight for them.'

Schröder looked at his fellow fighter pilots, seeking their impressions, and then at Max. 'What do you think, Max?'

'I don't know. Flying west across France perhaps is our only option. We can't fly north towards Norway and then over, that's too dangerous. We can only head so far south before we'll need to pull west. I think crossing France is our only choice. But I would think our fighters landing at this airfield . . . we could lose them all there, if the airfield is overrun.'

Schröder nodded in agreement and turned to address the Major.

'These men and I are the best of what's left of the Luftwaffe. We are all decorated men; we've flown with courage and honour. It's not cowardice, believe me . . .' Schröder looked like he was choosing his words carefully. 'I am not prepared, in these last days of the war, to die for a mission that is ill conceived. The stop at this airfield feels like, excuse me, Major . . . a bloody stupid idea. You expect us to refuel our planes on an enemy airstrip, probably amidst a gale of bullets. If we aren't shot to pieces as we come in to land, we certainly will be while we're running around looking for fuel.'

Max studied the Major. It seemed he was going to have to work particularly hard to turn Schröder and his men around. Rall met Schröder's challenging gaze in silence; he took the opportunity to pull out a cigarette and light it up. Max suspected the Major was buying himself time to think up a few well-chosen words that he hoped would win round the fighter pilot.

'Listen . . . you're right. There is no part of this mission which is without risk, from the moment you take off here until the bomb is released over the target, there are a million things that could go wrong.' Rall paused to ensure the point he was about to make had the impact he wanted. 'But this represents the last possible chance we have to save our country. This is it. If this fails, or we don't try, then, gentlemen, the alternative is unthinkable.' Rall looked pointedly at them all. 'We try, and maybe we die . . . we do nothing, and we certainly will.' Rall shrugged. 'Even after Berlin falls, mark my words, the killing will go on.'

He let them dwell on that for a few moments.

It was Schröder who broke the silence eventually. 'So, Major, tell us about this bomb that will be dropped on New York,' he asked quietly, his voice lowered almost to a conspiratorial whisper.

'It is a bomb, gentlemen, that is a thousand times more powerful than *any* bomb dropped in this war so far.'

Max had heard Rall's description of it once before, but he sensed perhaps today the Major would go a little further and reveal more of what he surely must know about it.

'I'm no scientist, so I can't describe in detail how this bomb does what it does. All I do know is that it is a new formula, a new technology that the Americans are only beginning to understand and use. But we have beaten them to it. One bomb, with the explosive potential of one thousand bombs . . . the equivalent of the payloads of fifty of those,' he said pointing towards the bomber.

'My God,' Schröder uttered in response.

Beyond the hangar's closed door, Max could hear the muted rumble of a truck rolling across the concrete and the shrill of poorly serviced brakes bringing the vehicle to a standstill. A moment later the door to the hangar rattled open wide enough to admit Leutnant Höstner. The glare of daylight was momentary and disappeared, as the doors were slid shut again. Max's eyes slowly adjusted as he listened to the approaching click of heels.

Höstner gently touched the Major's elbow. Rall turned round to face him and the Leutnant muttered something under his breath. The Major nodded and then turned back to the men to excuse himself.

'There are risks, gentlemen. The airfield, I agree, is a big one. Why don't you think about this for a while?'

Major Rall followed Leutnant Höstner to the doors of the hangar.

Quite the motivational speaker, thought Max.

Schröder looked towards his men. 'Well, gentlemen . . . what say we give the Major's plan a go?'

Chapter 30

Arrival

Rall blinked at the glaring white sky – his eyes had grown accustomed to the dim interior of the hangar. After weeks of rain, the cloud cover had thinned to form a pale white veil across the sky through which the midday sun shone strongly.

A truck was parked with its rear-end towards the sliding doors. Standing beside the tailgate stood a slight man, pale, thin and with fine, light-coloured hair that was receding. He wore civilian clothing and stood amidst a group of six SS men – *Leibstandarte*, Rall noticed, spotting the insignia on their collars.

Hitler's very own bodyguards.

Rall approached the group of men. 'Dr Hauser, I presume. At last we meet,' Rall said, reaching out a hand and offering what he hoped looked like a sincere welcoming smile.

'Major Rall, is it?' Hauser replied.

'Yes.'

Hauser nodded, glad that he had the right man, and extended his hand to shake the Major's. 'It's a pleasure to meet you at last.'

Both men watched as the truck was driven through the open hangar door, the SS guards walking inside with it. The large sliding door closed hastily afterwards.

'The bomb cradle will need to be built into the plane's bomb bay tonight. I had been hoping for details on the weight and dimensions beforehand, Doctor,' said Rall.

'I know. The assembly was only completed last night. A rushed task, our technicians did an excellent job.'

'Indeed, but we've had to guess the fuel calculations –'

'Major, the bomb is only small. It is heavy, but far less than any normal bomb. I'm sure your calculations will be fine.'

Hauser looked around the airfield. 'Is there somewhere we can talk in private?'

The Major nodded towards the bunker. 'My office is down there.'

He led Hauser into his office and offered him the chair. Hauser sat down.

'Major Rall, you are aware that in recent days there have been many changes in Berlin? You are aware that Albert Speer is no longer overseeing this project?'

Rall nodded, he had heard indirectly, and only within the last couple of days, that the Armaments Minister had been 'relieved' of the duty and assumed Hitler himself was now personally steering things. It had caused him some concern. Speer, he felt, was an intelligent and a rational planner. Rall had spent the last six months reporting directly to him on the setting-up of the operation. There were, however, concerns that had troubled Speer in recent weeks, concerns that the Minister had only mentioned in passing to Rall. Concerns about the design of the bomb itself.

'Yes. I was informed indirectly about Speer. Why did this happen?'

Hauser took his time answering. 'The Führer and Speer did not see eye to eye on this project, Major. And so the Führer has decided to take control of it himself.'

'I believe Speer had some concerns about the design of the bomb, Doctor. He did say that there was an element of risk in the bomb's design.'

Hauser sat stiffly in his chair. He wondered just how much this Major Rall knew. Speer had asked to look through the Jew's research notes – perhaps out of curiosity, but there must have been something he'd seen, read and understood that had worried him. The damned Jew Schenkelmann had made plenty of references throughout his research notes to the potential risk of the infinite chain. Hauser had vetted the man's notes as best he could given the short notice Speer had given him. But it seemed that maybe he hadn't been thorough enough.

'Major, there is always an element of risk in new technology.'

Rall nodded. 'Yes, I understand that. But my question is . . .' he locked his eyes on Hauser, 'this *risk* you mention . . . this *risk* – is *that* why Herr Speer abandoned this project?'

Max stood up, leaving the others to continue studying the map spread out on the floor of the hangar. Stefan was relaying the navigation points to

Schröder and the fighter pilots. The other two, Pieter and Hans, were kicking a ball about with a couple of the ground crew in one corner of the hangar. He decided to head outside now that the gathering darkness of late afternoon made it safe to linger beyond the great sliding doors and enjoy a smoke.

As he walked towards the hangar door he passed by the truck that had recently arrived, guarded by the SS men. Inside, he presumed, must be the weapon, the bomb that Rall had only talked about once or twice since their first meeting. The Major had been surprisingly vague on the weapon itself, while being so specific on all the other details of the operation. It was a 'new technology' was all Rall had been prepared to offer up to Max. Perhaps that was all the Major knew. The Major had been refreshingly candid about everything so far. He suspected that if Rall knew any more about the bomb, he would have told them.

As he approached the truck, the guards warily drew up their guns and watched him carefully as he passed by and headed towards the hangar doors. Max let himself out through a small hatch door and nodded to the guard standing outside.

He wasn't in the mood to make small talk and so he wandered a few dozen yards away from the hangar, across the pitted concrete and grass tufts towards the sandbagged roof of another empty and unused bunker. He sat down heavily and watched the sky to the north flicker and listened to the distant rumble of his country being torn apart.

In about seven or eight hours they would finally be airborne and on their way. It would take at least that long for the engineers to construct an appropriate holding cradle for the weapon. He knew his boys, Schröder and his pilots would all be keen to count those hours down as quickly as possible.

It was the waiting that was the killer.

He pulled out the packet of Russian cigarettes from his breast pocket only to find that it was empty. There weren't so many left now. Rall had done a great job getting in the supplies he had, but there hadn't been any more, and the stash of cigarettes, along with the coffee, were all but exhausted. He decided to try his luck and see if he could find any remaining packets that might have been left in the canteen. The next few hours were going to drag, much more so without some smokes.

'As far as I know, his removal from this operation is nothing to do with the weapon, Major,' Hauser answered testily. 'You have to understand, things are becoming difficult for the Führer. He has been let down by many of the other ministers. They are betraying him. If I'm honest, I suspect Speer is one of them. He has deserted him, fled Berlin.'

Major Rall studied Hauser in silence. The man was lying to him. It was apparent in his demeanour, the way he was holding himself, in his voice. The man was an appalling liar.

'Doctor Hauser, since being called in to work on this project, I have struggled to obtain any meaningful information about this weapon from you. It has been difficult to plan, not knowing the weight or size of this weapon. What is more, the answers I have received from you via Speer's office about the damage potential and blast radius have been vague and inconsistent. So now I hear that Speer has been removed from his role at this late stage, all this fills me with concern.'

Hauser attempted a consoling smile. 'And you have done a commend-able job, Major, with the limited resources at your disposal.'

'You are evading the point. Speer was concerned about the technology of the weapon, this he made known to me. And now I find he has been replaced at this late hour. I respectfully ask that you be honest with me.'

Hauser's smile faded, his patience finally reaching its limit. 'You were charged with planning a way to deploy the weapon over New York, and my responsibility has been to produce the weapon. It is not your business to know how this weapon works –'

'It *is* my business to know everything about this operation!' the Major snapped. 'In the absence of the Armaments Minister, I am the senior military authority, and that means you will –'

'Ahhh, I wondered when it would come to this,' replied Hauser quietly. 'Major, things have changed,' he continued, producing a piece of paper from inside his coat. 'Hitler sends you his gratitude for everything you have done thus far. But he has entrusted it to me to ensure that this operation is concluded in a satisfactory manner.'

He handed the paper to Rall, who studied the brief handwritten order with a growing sense of disbelief and anger.

'As you can see, he has authorised me to act directly on his behalf. On this matter, there is no one with greater authority than myself, other than the Führer, of course. That means, Major, I do not have to explain to you anything at all.'

The hastily scribbled order and the signature were unmistakable. Hauser was right. With this kind of authority, albeit temporarily assigned, Hauser could have him dragged out and shot on a whim. And, of course, the Doctor had been careful enough to bring with him from the bunker half a dozen soldiers.

Leibstandarte.

Knowing Hauser was working on Hitler's direct orders, they would follow any instructions he gave without hesitation.

'However, Major, I will be candid with you. I think you deserve that. The bomb uses an energy that is new, untested and untapped, an energy that lies all around us. We are in the position to be the first men to use it in war. And, if it isn't we that use it, then it will be someone else who does. Be sure of that.'

Hauser stood up and approached the door to the room.

'Of course, there is an element of risk in using this technology, but it is a calculated risk. If we turn our backs on this opportunity now, then we're all dead men. The Russians will finish us all. And in time, they no doubt will attempt to use this energy on the Americans. That is a certainty.'

Hauser turned to face him. 'It will happen, Major. This energy will be discovered and used by someone. Why not let it be us?'

'And how great is the risk?' asked the Major.

'The risk, Major, is small, but remains a possibility.'

'What exactly *is* the risk in using this weapon?' Rall asked again.

Hauser closed the door gently and spoke in a hushed voice. 'That the energy we use to destroy New York will destroy us all.'

In that moment, the cigarettes were forgotten.

Max could hear now only the murmur of voices from inside Rall's study. The last words he'd heard before the door had closed had been Rall's. Max silently left the canteen, walked up the bunker's central corridor, up the stairs and outside into the dark of night.

What exactly is *the risk of using this weapon?* he had heard the Major say. There had been uncertainty in the Major's voice. And that fact alone troubled Max.

Chapter 31

Into the Water

1 a.m., 29 April 1945, off the coast of France

Lündstrom stared silently at the pitch-black form of the coastline. It was silhouetted against a faint orange sky. A low cloud base reflected the night-time amber glow of the city of Nantes. Isolated pinpricks of light dotted the dark landmass and suggested the occasional cottage or farmhouse, but he could see no other detail or definition from the shore. This kind of amphibious deployment of troops was dangerous enough in the daytime, let alone doing it at night with no detailed knowledge of the stretch of shore they intended to land on.

He had no idea what the objectives were for the young captain and his platoon, but whatever the mission, he hoped it was going to be worth the risks they were taking. There was a very real possibility that some of these poor boys might not make it to shore. The sea was lively tonight, with four-foot swells slapping against the side of the sub, and they had no notion of what sort of terrain led down to the sea here.

They could be trying to row ashore onto a lethal barricade of razor-sharp rocks.

Koch and his men were intending to paddle towards the French coast in three inflatable dinghies, across half a mile of choppy sea. He had dared not take the U-boat any closer for fear of grounding her. The men were wearing enough clothing and equipment to sink them like rocks if they fell out, or worse, one of the dinghies was punctured.

He hoped to God this foolish exercise had a point.

Once more he scanned the black world around him and strained his ears to detect any noise other than the chop of water against the sub's hull. There was nothing to be seen or heard; it seemed as if they were safe here in the dark, for now.

Lündstrom called down through the open hatch in the floor of the conning tower. 'All clear.'

Seconds later he was relieved to hear a deep, bass throbbing as the diesel motors started up. The 'all clear' had made its way aft to the engine room in mere seconds, and already the engines had started turning and were recharging the batteries. One of the first things any rating learned in the Kriegsmarine was that a good sub captain never wastes a single solitary second on the surface.

'Tell Hauptman Koch he and his men can come up now.'

He heard the order echoing down the ranks inside the sub, and moments later the hatch on the foredeck was pulled open, and several of Koch's men emerged. They pulled up onto the deck three folded rubber bundles, which they opened out and began to fill with air using foot pumps.

He shook his head. This little venture had the feeling of a disastrous balls-up waiting to happen. These dinghies were all that could be produced at short notice for the mission. They would be a poor offering as a life raft; they were certainly less than adequate for an amphibious landing. And although he had no doubt that the men were fine soldiers, Lündstrom wondered whether these Alpine troops, trained for combat in arctic and mountainous conditions, were ready for this kind of action.

He heard boots on the ladder leading up to the conning tower. Koch emerged beside him and gleefully sucked in a lungful of the chilly, salty air.

'I imagine that tastes pretty good after the last few days below, eh?' said Lündstrom.

The young man nodded. 'Very good. I don't know how you and your men can stand to live in such conditions.'

'Yes, of course, you must be used to the great outdoors, not the inside of a sardine can.'

Koch stretched his arms in front of him, enjoying the space. 'It'll be good to get on with this, least of all so we can stretch our legs.'

Koch had been careful not to reveal a single detail of the mission he and his men were to carry out. Lündstrom guessed that the young man's orders had specified that the nature of their undertaking ashore remain classified. Nonetheless, knowing the war was entering its final days, he felt the imprudence of asking him was forgivable.

'Can I ask what it is you and your men are up to?'

Koch tightened his lips and shook his head. 'I'm sorry, I'm not permitted to reveal the content –'

'– of your orders. I know. I thought as much. Well, I hope whoever's behind this has a damn good reason for throwing you and your lads into the sea. I can't see anything any of us can do right now is going to change the way things will go.'

'We've not had a lot to do but retreat for the last year. My men wouldn't mind one last chance to have a go back at them.'

Lündstrom had on many an occasion in the last year shared a drink with passionate young officers in the bars of Bergen. There were nearly 40,000 servicemen isolated in Norway – soldiers, airmen, sailors, many of them veterans. A large proportion of these men had fought in elite regiments that had served tours of duty in the east. They were good soldiers, the cream of what was left of Germany's fighting forces, but they were stuck where they were, separated by the Baltic from Germany and frustrated that they could do little to help their comrades and defend their country.

He had listened to these young men, soured and embittered by losing the eastern campaign and watching from afar as the war ground to a bitter end. The only opportunity many of these officers had had to prove their leadership was how quickly and efficiently they could withdraw their men and move resources back from the advancing enemy. He pitied the young captain.

The end of the war would bring him only a sense of loss, failure. For Lündstrom, however, it meant only relief. He and his men had already tasted the bitter pill of defeat a year ago. Those feelings had passed, the wounds had healed, and now they were just waiting for the rest of their compatriots to catch up and accept the inevitable, acknowledge the game was up.

'Good night for it, I think,' said Koch studying the dark sky. The cloud cover was total; the full moon would not give them away tonight.

'Yes, but the sea is choppy. Don't let your men sit on the edge of the dinghies or they'll go in.'

Koch nodded.

'And be careful when you start seeing white water. That means you're close to the shore. I've no idea what there is to land on here, sand or rocks. Be careful, eh?'

The men on the foredeck had inflated two out of the three dinghies, and the third was nearly done.

'I should join my men now. Thank you for your hospitality.'

Lündstrom held out his hand. 'Well, I wish you success with whatever it is you hope to achieve.'

'Perhaps our little action will make a minor headline or two in some newspaper somewhere, and then you'll find out what we've been up to.'

'Maybe a footnote in a history book some day, eh?'

Koch smiled. 'That would be nice.' He nodded formally at Lündstrom before descending the ladder to return inside the sub and check one last time that all their field equipment had been bagged up and taken. A few moments later, the rest of his platoon spilled through the hatch on to the foredeck, followed by Koch. They quickly gathered together their firearms and wrapped them up in several waterproof canvas kit bags, then sorted themselves into three groups.

Lündstrom watched them with concern. Unlike seamen, these men were careless in the way they stood on the deck, close to the edge, not holding on to the railings, not keeping an eye on the sea for any approaching swells. They were men unused to the sea, and its ways.

Tonight, however, it seemed the Atlantic wasn't thrashing as unkindly as it had promised. That and the good cloud cover as well. Perhaps fortune had decided to smile on this little endeavour.

Now that his part of the job was done, he wondered if he would hear any more about this operation after reporting back to Bergen. Maybe Koch was right; it would probably amount to no more than a small news item in the provincial newspaper that served this area of France. All eyes were on Berlin now.

'Thirty German bodies washed ashore near Nantes.'

'Poor bastards,' he muttered as he watched the first dinghy slide off the deck into the sea, and begin to bob unhappily as successive swells and troughs raised and dropped it by half a dozen feet.

The other two dinghies followed suit, and awkwardly, their inexperience showing, the men clambered down into them.

The last of Koch's men scrambled down the side of the hull and the three inflatable rafts began to head away into the night, as paddles on all sides sliced into the foaming water.

He watched their painfully slow progress, as they seemed to move more up and down at the mercy of the swells than away towards land.

Ten minutes later, when Lündstrom could no longer make out the pale wake trailing Koch and his men, he ordered the helmsman to turn her around and head due north-west.

He sighed with relief, hoping *this* time he could take the U-1061 home to Bergen to await the end of the war in peace.

Chapter 32

Zero Hour

2.05 a.m., 29 April 1945, an airfield south of Stuttgart

Max had watched as the work assembling the cradle was done and the bomb, under the supervision of the recently arrived civilian, and under the cold gaze of the SS men who had come with him, had been carefully installed aboard the bomber.

The civilian had ordered his SS guards to continue watching the plane; none of the ground crew, nor the crew who were to fly it, were now permitted to approach it. Then the civilian had left the hangar for the bunker.

Max had also noticed the Major watching the whole process from a corner of the hangar, and as the civilian had departed, he had summoned Rall with a flick of his wrist. It appeared that all of a sudden this man was now calling the shots on the airfield. No longer did it seem to be the Major's show.

That had been an hour ago. Max and the others now waited impatiently for the last of the fighters to be fuelled and the extra-large ammo canisters installed. Even carrying the extra ammunition drums, Schröder and his men would need to ensure they were careful to conserve what ammo they had. Yet another thing for them all to keep in mind.

Zero hour, Major Rall had promised, would be midnight, but the cradle had taken longer than planned. That was two hours of wasted night cover.

'Shit!' he muttered to himself. The waiting was getting to him. He slipped out through the hangar hatch-door into the night.

It was playing on his mind, the fact that Rall appeared to have been outranked at this late stage. With the Major's hand at the helm, he had begun to feel confident that the whole operation had a reasonable chance of success. There was a humourless common sense to the Major, a rigid backbone of efficiency and straight-talking that Max had known in some of his previous commanding officers, and he had grown to trust those qualities without question. Now to see the Major sidelined by this civilian, at this final hour ... it was unsettling.

It was cold enough to blow out a cloud of condensation. Max sighed and watched the small plume of steamy breath quickly disperse in the night air. He remembered being a child and doing that on a winter's morning, pretending he was grown up and smoking a cigarette, holding a pencil haughtily between two fingers and puffing on it like a little gentleman of leisure.

'Cold night, eh, Max?' said Pieter as he slipped through the gap between the hangar's sliding door to join Max outside.

Max nodded silently.

'You all right?'

He smiled at Pieter. 'I'm all right, you go and check on the other two. We should be ready to go any time now.'

He watched his co-pilot trot back into the hangar. His crew were in good spirits, ready to get this thing going; all three of them, it seemed, certain that the right choice had been made to volunteer. Schröder and his men too looked eager to mount up and fly into whatever destiny awaited them. It seemed as if only he was having any misgivings.

Those overheard words were playing on his mind. Something was wrong, there was disagreement between Rall and this civilian.

What is *the risk in using this weapon?*

There was a risk, then. Something that rendered the bomb hazardous to Max and his crew? Perhaps this new explosive formula was unstable and could blow up inside the plane? It wouldn't be the first time that an unready weapon prototype had taken lives on its first run. In fact, he'd heard of quite a few test-run disasters recently, unofficially, of course, gossip amongst the officers.

It was yet another thing to worry about, though, as if fighting their way across France wasn't enough. But, in the end, Rall's justification was right. If they managed to get all the way to America and drop this bomb on New York, then there would be millions of German lives saved. The Major's common sense cut through all the shit. A rational transaction.

What is *the risk ... ?*

Perhaps the Major's concern was for *his* men, for Max and his crew. That would explain it. The Major would undoubtedly feel strongly that Max and his men should know exactly what they were handling, expecially if this formula was volatile, prone to blowing up before its time. Max suspected it might be something along those lines, a concern for his airmen that had triggered the angry exchange he had overheard.

All of a sudden, the lights in the hangar were turned out. Moments later, the large sliding doors were wheeled noisily back. By torchlight Max watched as a tractor towed the B-17 out into the open and returned inside the hangar to pull out the fighters one by one.

Pieter and the others emerged from the hangar and joined Max outside.

Max turned to his crew, his troubled mind for now wiped clean of ill-placed worries. 'You gentlemen ready to go, then?'

Pieter yawned and nodded, his face momentarily shrouded by a cloud of vapour. Max knew him well enough to know the yawn was a nervous gesture. Despite the affected sleepy demeanour he knew Pieter was alert and anxious to begin.

Stef shook his head vigorously. 'Ready as ever, sir,' he answered with the slightest hint of tension in his voice.

Hans nodded silently, smoking what was probably the last cigarette on the airfield.

'Good.'

Schröder and his men emerged from the darkness inside the hangar. He heard Schröder's crystal-sharp accent as he finished telling a story that provoked a roar of laughter from his men.

Battlefield laughter.

Max knew the sound well enough, the hysterical laughter, the fluttering of nerves. Before every mission, it seemed almost anything could be funny, and afterwards the same things barely solicited a smile.

'Where's Max and his merry men?' he heard the fighter pilot call out.

'Pompous idiot,' Pieter grumbled as Schröder's voice cut across the general murmuring.

Max nudged Pieter gently. 'Behave.'

Schröder picked Max out of the dark and wandered over. 'Well, Oberleutnant Kleinmann, I presume the finest bomber crew in the Luftwaffe is ready for its final sortie?'

'Perhaps that should be the *last* bomber crew?'

'Yes, I suppose you're right.' Schröder cast his eyes around the group of men. 'This must be all that's left of our airforce now. The only operational squadron.'

'The final flight of the Luftwaffe . . . that has a nice poetic ring about it,' said Max.

'Well, it has been a brief but enriching experience this last week. I wish you and your men the best of luck. Perhaps I'll join you in America after the war and we'll toast the mission and Major Rall.'

'You can buy the first round, then,' replied Max.

Schröder laughed and slapped his shoulder. 'You can buy the last.'

From the entrance to the underground bunker the civilian emerged, flanked by two of his SS guards. Behind them, emerging a few seconds later, Major Rall came out, walking slowly.

The laughter died down as Max and the others watched them make their way across towards the hangar.

'Who *is* that man?' asked Schröder with a hint of distaste in his voice.

'I don't know,' replied Max.

I'd feel a lot happier if I did.

The civilian and his guards approached the men gathered outside the hangar, watching the last of the Me-109s being towed out onto the tarmac. The men quietened down, as the Major finally drew up alongside the civilian.

'Men, this is Doctor Karl Hauser. He is the weapon's designer. I believe he has a few words he wants to say,' Rall announced flatly.

'Thank you, Major. I'm not sure how much the Major has told you about the weapon you have there in that bomber. But it is a new type of weapon, a brand new technology that we have beaten the Americans in developing.'

Hauser turned to Max and his crew.

'When you gentlemen release that bomb over New York, you will be telling the world that we are still a force to be reckoned with.' He offered the men a smile. 'And, of course, you will be making history.'

Several of Schröder's pilots cheered.

'I know you men will find a way to get this bomb to New York. The Führer has asked me to personally convey his admiration and his gratitude to you all for volunteering to carry out this dangerous mission. We have this chance, gentlemen, this one chance, to pull a victory out of the ashes . . .'

Major Rall looked around the pilots listening, in good spirits, to the Doctor's speech. The very same speech Hauser had just been practising down below in the bunker. The man's pomposity, the gestures, the language, reminded him of another man who had brought disaster upon them all, for the sake of his vanity. Rall was reminded of the Hitler of four years ago, on the eve of Operation Barbarossa, the invasion of Russia.

The conclusion was now crystal-clear in his mind. Doctor Hauser was every bit as dangerous. The man had finally conceded, out of sheer arrogance, perhaps aware that there was little the Major could now do to stop things, that there was much more than a *slight* chance that the weapon's blast could be infinite, incinerate everything. He had admitted that, and then summoned his SS guards into the room to escort them both out onto the airfield. The significance of that gesture wasn't wasted on the Major.

One foot out of line now, and he would be a dead man.

'With this bomb, gentlemen . . . with this one bomb, we will destroy the beating heart of America, New York. With one bomb and in one instant, we will turn that entire city and everyone in it to ashes.'

Rall sought out Max amongst the assembled pilots. If there was one man amongst them whom he could possibly get through to in the few seconds that he might have, it was Oberleutnant Kleinmann. There was little chance that this mission could be stopped here and now, he knew that. But if he could present to Max the potential danger, and let the man come to his own conclusion – after all, he had twenty hours in the air in which to think about it – then perhaps this mission could be aborted before it was too late.

He scanned the faces turned towards Hauser, and amongst them he saw Max's eyes locked on to his. The Oberleutnant was studying him intently, curiously.

'We will turn all of New York into Stalingrad with this new weapon. And the Americans will have no choice but to submit to the Führer's terms and join us in the crusade against communism. The Russians will be turned away from Berlin, Germany will survive. And we will make many more of these bombs to ensure our supremacy continues –'

Does Kleinmann sense there's something wrong?

'– and our empire will once more be reclaimed. This weapon is our future, it is our destiny. It is how we will fight wars from now on. Not with tanks or men, but with this all consuming-power. With it we will turn any nation that stands in our way . . . to ashes.'

Rall watched Max frown and shake his head unhappily, and then the pilot glanced back at the Major. There was no mistaking the expression on his face – betrayal.

This weapon is far more powerful than you said. Rall read that accusation in the pilot's eyes.

'And more dangerous than you can imagine,' the Major muttered under his breath. He decided he had to try and talk to Max. By the look of him, it seemed he was already troubled by Hauser's foolish speech. Just a few well-chosen words might be enough to convince the pilot to abort the mission somehow.

Rall began to step through the gathered men towards Max, when Hauser turned sharply towards him. 'Major Rall, are you ready to issue orders?'

He wondered whether he had a chance to tell them all what he knew. What could he say before Hauser ordered his guards to gun him down? They would do it, of course, without a second's hesitation.

'Major Rall? Time is pressing,' added Hauser staring threateningly at the Major.

A single command from this madman – that's all it would take.

'Major?'

'To your planes, men,' Rall ordered flatly.

Schröder's men cheered and turned on their heels towards the Me-109s lined up nearby. Schröder approached Rall and saluted him. 'We will ensure they make it safely across, Herr Major.'

Rall nodded and mumbled weakly, 'Good luck, Schröder.'

He watched the young pilot join his squadron, climbing up onto the nearest fighter with athletic ease. And then the Major's attention turned towards the four men left standing before him, Max and his crew.

Max approached the Major and extended a hand towards him. 'Major?' he offered uncertainly.

Rall grasped the pilot's hand and looked up, met his eyes.

Now man, now! This is your only chance!

'The bomb is dangerous, Max,' he muttered quickly under his breath.

'Sir?'

'Listen! There is a very real poss –'

The engines fired up on the nearest Me-109 and it swiftly began to roll across the grass and tarmac towards the strip. Other engines followed suit and a convoy of fighters began their nose-to-tail procession towards the top of the runway.

Hauser stepped promptly forward to stand beside Rall and presented a sealed envelope to Max. Rall cursed under his breath, the time for whispering was gone.

'Oberleutnant Kleinmann, in this envelope is the arming code for the bomb. It is for your eyes only,' Hauser shouted, competing with the noise of a dozen engines.

Max nodded without a word and took the envelope. He turned back to Rall and saluted him.

'Good luck, Kleinmann,' added Hauser.

Max lingered a moment longer studying the Major's face one final time, but Rall looked down at the ground. He looked beaten, defeated.

Max nodded politely towards Hauser, and then turned on his heels to face his crew.

'Let's go, lads.'

Hauser and Rall watched the four men scramble up through the belly hatch into the bomber and moments later he caught sight of Max through the plexiglas cockpit windows strapping himself into the pilot's seat. The engines on the bomber spluttered and roared to life one after the other, like four sleeping lions roused from their slumber. Moments later, the chocks were removed, and the plane began to roll across the grass towards the strip just as the first of the 109s was taking to the air. In quick succession, the entire squadron took to the air in pairs, making use of the runway's full width, and as each pair reached halfway down the strip, the next pair thundered down the runway after them.

They watched as the B-17 waited her turn for the runway to clear of the last of the fighters, then, finally, the way was clear. The pitch of her engines rose and the large plane began to roll down the tarmac picking up speed as she went.

As the bomber parted from the ground, and her undercarriage swung upwards into the wings, Hauser turned to Rall and shook his head.

'That was very stupid, Major. Really very stupid.'

Rall knew there was no point denying what he had tried to do. The Doctor must have heard him, must even have anticipated some last moment of foolishness. As the sound of the planes receded into the early morning sky, Hauser turned away from Rall and headed towards the truck he had arrived on the previous day. Rall continued to face down the runway, in the direction the planes had departed, standing stiffly and ready for what he knew was coming.

He heard the sound of Hauser's Leibstandarte guards scrambling aboard the truck, the cough and rattle of the vehicle's diesel engine as it started up and a few moments later, the crunch of boots across the shattered and pitted concrete of the ground – coming towards him.

Rall took his cap off and tugged at his Luftwaffe tunic, tidying out the creases, pulling it taut across his chest. He stared resolutely out to the west, a final and futile gesture of defiance. He wasn't going to offer that insane bastard a final anxious glance over his shoulder. If it was coming, then it was coming. The only fear he felt now was not for himself . . . but that he might have done too little to stop this madness from going any further.

Rall took a deep breath, and closed his eyes.

In the end all war is madness ... Who once said that?
Rall's mind never retrieved the answer.

Chapter 33

Observing

From the comfort of the van he watched the photographer coming out of Lenny's. The night lights down this street, which he presumed was the main street for this shitty little seaside town, were poorly maintained, and his driver had easily found a suitable place to park in a pool of dark where one light had failed.

He watched the man walk slowly down the main drag, and then checked his watch.

They should be done by now.

His men had called in to say that there was only a bunch of grainy photographs and the negatives to be found, and asked what should be done.

He had ordered them to take the prints, destroy any equipment and then trash the room. There was a chance this guy might be dumb enough to think he'd just been turned over by some junkie. It was always worth a shot. Not everyone automatically jumped to the conclusion they had been visited by some shady secret agency.

Actually, it was pretty obvious this guy hadn't a clue what he was dealing with and was in well over his head; a rank amateur at best. His clumsy attempts thus far to investigate the story had been made without any caution whatsoever.

The man in the van laughed, not out loud, just a smile.

It was looking good. By first light his dive team should hopefully have been down on the wreck and pulled the thing up, the 'device'. He had been careful to use that word, instead of 'bomb', when briefing them. Neither of the divers had any idea what exactly it was that they were handling, just that it needed to be pulled from the wreck and dropped a little further out to sea where the shallow shelf drops away.

He supposed in all fairness he should have told them they'd be handling degraded fissile material, but then the small amount of uranium that would have been in the bomb should have all but decayed by now. There might be some trace of radiation, but hell, they were being paid extremely well for one night's work, and neither looked like the type to want to settle down any time soon and have a family.

He wouldn't lose any sleep over it.

He let out a muted sigh of relief. Disposing of the 'device' had been the most important thing to take care of. He rubbed his temple once more. The tension was easing, his headache, this kittybitch of a headache, induced he knew by stress, was at last beginning to subside. The most important thing was being sorted out right now.

The other part of the problem was making sure this fool walking down the street hadn't been talking to anybody he shouldn't. It might be sixty years on, but there were one or two people still alive he really didn't want this guy making any associations with. His making contact with the Grady woman, that wasn't good, but it wasn't going to lead anywhere either. The woman knew nothing, nothing at all about what was found on the beach. So that angle wasn't going to help him in any meaningful way.

No, there were far worse people this guy could have spoken to, and if this guy already had ... then he was going to need to think just how thoroughly this little mess needed to be squared away. There was still enough money in the budget to ensure that his silence could be bought. He settled back comfortably in the seat; his men should be done by now in his motel room and faded away into the night. By morning the hard evidence would be gone, the photographs gone ... and just this rank amateur wandering around with an unsubstantiated tale spinning away in his head.

He smiled.

For now, at least tonight, it looked like things were in hand. He could relax, lie down and get a good night's sleep. Tomorrow, when his men reported in, he could decide how to wrap it all up.

Chris looked around Devenster Street as he left the bar; it looked deserted. He was relieved to see there wasn't any sign of those two men he had spotted down by the jetty. Wallace was hardly going to despatch them both with his Kung Fu moves if they had stumbled across each other.

He made his way down Devenster Street and cut through a dimly lit alleyway that led down towards the jetty and his motel. At the end of the alleyway, he peered out at the open gravel parking area in front of the jetty to see if those two men were still there. They were gone.

Feeling a little easier, he walked briskly across the open ground towards his motel. He made his way inside the motel, nodding at the lady who sat behind the reception counter, watching Ricki Lake on an ancient TV set with a picture that was sliding upwards. The old lady banged it once as she waved at him, and the hazy picture momentarily stopped its vertical drift.

'Oh, Mr Roland, isn't it?' she said as he made his way towards the stairs that led to the first floor.

'Yeah?'

'I thought you were in already. I guess you missed them.'

He turned round. 'Who?'

'A couple of gentlemen, they said you were expecting them.'

She studied the expression on his face, and then realised somewhere along the line, she'd screwed up. 'You uh ... *weren't* expecting any visitors, were you?'

Chris shook his head. 'What did they look like?'

'Uhh, middle-thirties, I guess. Short hair, smart, both of them.'

'How long ago?'

She looked at her wristwatch. 'I don't know, earlier this evening.'

Chris looked up the stairs nervously. 'Have they come back down yet?'

'I haven't seen them, but then I've been out the back in the office some of the time, you know?'

He nodded and thanked her, and then took the steps slowly up to the first flight of stairs, his stomach flipping uneasily inside him. There, he warily took a few steps up the second flight until he could see over the lip of the top step and down to the end of the first-floor hallway. There was no one to be seen waiting outside his or Mark's rooms. He allowed himself a small sigh of relief.

Whoever it was, they had been and gone.

He climbed up the last of the steps and walked briskly down the short hallway, his trainers squeaking on the wooden floor. From the smell he guessed it had been recently waxed.

He reached in his pocket for the keys to the motel room while he rested his hand on the brass handle of the door. With a click of the latch, the door drifted ajar.

It's open.

Chris remained frozen, expecting at any second, for the door to be wrenched wide open and one of those two men to pull him roughly inside. A handful of seconds passed and nothing happened.

He remained where he was outside, though, listening intently, one ear close to the gap in the doorway, for subtle sounds of movement; the swish of skin against material, the creak of weight being shifted from one leg to another, the sounds of two well-built men, waiting patiently and readying themselves for Chris to commit to entering.

But he heard nothing, except the muted murmurings of the TV from downstairs, a roar of studio audience laughter and Ricki telling them they were heading for a break.

Sucking in air and puffing it out nervously, he leaned against the door to his room and it swung inwards.

'Shit.'

His room had been thoroughly turned over. Every drawer from the dresser had been pulled out, his travel bag had been emptied on the bed and his clothes and toiletries sifted through. He saw several rolls of unused film had been broken open and the celluloid pulled out and exposed, useless now. He noticed that the roll of dollar notes he kept in his bag for expenses was gone.

He pushed the door open to his bathroom, knowing what he was going to see.

'Oh, for fuck's sake!' he muttered.

The prints were gone, all of them, as were the negatives. For good measure, whoever had been here had smashed his enlarger, and poured all his chemicals down the sink.

'Ahh, that's just great.'

Chris was coming out of the bathroom when someone grabbed him from the side and, roughly pushed him onto the bed. Before he could sit up, he felt something heavy land on his back, and his head was roughly pushed down into the covers on the bed. He could see nothing, and struggled to suck in air through the fabric of his bed's quilt.

'He came back too early!' he heard someone say in a hoarse whisper.

'No, we just took too fucking long processing the room,' a second man said. He sounded older from the deep, grating timbre of his voice, and calmer.

'What do you want?' Chris tried to ask, his voice muffled by the quilt his face was being pushed into. In response he got a painful kick in the ribs, and then a moment later he felt hot, laboured breath against his cheek.

'Be very quiet,' he heard a voice mutter quietly; a younger man by the sound of it. 'What do we do now? This wasn't part of the plan.'

The older man replied calmly, his voice muted, speaking gently. 'I'll call him.'

Chris heard the tones of a mobile phone keypad, and then a pause.

'No signal. Shit. We had a signal earlier, dammit.'

'What are we going to do? Kill him?'

'If we do, it can't be here.'

Chris squirmed in response, his arms flapping around, blindly searching for something to grab on to.

His ribs exploded with pain as another swift kick landed. 'Shut up and stop moving, or we *will* do you right here,' the younger man hissed. 'Try the phone again,' he said. 'Go over by the window, you might get a signal there.'

Chris heard the older man walk across the room towards the small window and once again he heard the key tones. Whoever it was they were trying to get in touch with would presumably decide his fate right now, one way or the other.

Oh Christ, I'm in deep shit.

He wondered where the hell Mark was. These bastards must have made enough noise to alert him from his room next door. Then he remembered, Mark had said he was taking the Cherokee up the coast to refill the air tanks. But surely he should have been back by now? It was gone nine in the evening.

Or maybe these sons of bitches had been next door dealing with him when Chris had entered his room.

'No signal again.'

'We'll have to take him with us, until we meet up for the briefing tomorrow morning,' whispered the man holding Chris down.

'Yeah,' the older one replied. 'But it's getting him out without attracting attention. Shit ... maybe if I open the window and lean out –'

Suddenly, Chris heard the door to the room swing open with a thud, and the sound of three heavy footsteps across the small bedroom followed swiftly by a metallic clang.

The hand that had roughly been holding the back of his head and forcing his face into the quilt went slack, and Chris found he could lift his head up and look to the side.

Just in time to see a lean, middle-aged man, with short, crewcut, greying hair turning round and pulling his gun out. He turned his head to see Mark holding up one of the air cylinders in front of himself.

'Hit this and we're all history!' growled Mark.

Chris could see this stalemate would hold only a second or two. He pushed the unconscious form of the younger man off his back and found another gun lying on the bed beside him. He picked it up and levelled it at the grey-haired man, his hands trembling, fingers fumbling for the trigger.

The older man switched his focus and brought his gun to bear on Chris. 'Put the gun down, son,' he said in his calm voice.

Cool under pressure. The thought raced through Chris's mind. *Very bloody cool*.

Without warning Mark hurled his cylinder at the man, who swung his aim back around towards him just in time to be knocked off balance by the heavy cylinder.

Chris got to his feet in a second and scrambled for the doorway. As he hurled himself out of the room he felt a hum of hot air whistle past his ear and a window overlooking the seafront in the hallway outside his bedroom exploded.

'Fuck! He's shooting!' Chris heard himself shout as he pounded down the hallway after Mark.

He heard the man tumble out into the hallway after him, thudding against the wall opposite, feet crunching on the broken glass.

Another thread of hot air burned past him and the wall ahead erupted with a shower of plaster dust.

'Pissing hell! Run faster, Mark!'

Both of them took the stairs down to the lobby four at a time and hurried outside into the night, gasping cold air into their lungs as they ran across the open parking area of the jetty towards the Cherokee parked up next to the two Runcies trucks.

'Key! You got the key?' Chris yelled.

'Yeah I got it, got it. Lemme just find it.'

As Mark fumbled with the keyring, Chris looked back at the motel entrance. There was no sign of the older man just yet.

'Come on, Mark!'

The doorlocks on the Cherokee popped, and both men dived in. Chris kept his eyes on the motel entrance as Mark fired it up and spun the vehicle round in a hurried loop so that they were facing the exit leading onto the coast road and out of town. With the tyres spinning, sending a cloud of dust and pebbles up into the air, the Cherokee leaped forward and out of the parking lot just as a silhouette appeared in the doorway of their motel.

Chapter 34

Mission Time: 30 Minutes Elapsed

2.35 a.m., 29 April 1945, outside Nantes

The landing had been a bastard. They had paddled towards the sound of waves breaking only to find the bloody things were breaking on a rocky outcrop. All three dinghies had been punctured in quick succession and Koch and his men had had to swim the last few dozen yards and scramble hastily up the razor-sharp rocks to avoid being punished for their reckless landing by the waves. One of his men had drowned during this mad dash, dragged under by the weight of his thick clothes, and two others had received bad gashes clambering ashore; one of them had a broken shinbone. The wounds were bandaged for now, and the broken leg in a makeshift splint, but the men would require medical treatment soon.

That left him twenty-seven effectives.

Koch was cold, wet from the sea and the spattering of rain, chilled by the sporadically gusting wind blowing in from the Atlantic. He stared at the farmhouse from the cover of an apple orchard less than a hundred yards away. It backed onto the airfield; he suspected it would be warm and dry and there was the possibility of some food inside. It looked like it might offer a few hours of relative comfort for his men before the morning's fun and games.

He unslung his MP-40 and turned round to face Feldwebel Büller. 'That looks good for tonight, what do you think?'

The man nodded eagerly. The previous week aboard the U-boat had been a damp and cold hell. A night of dryness and relative comfort sounded like the smartest command decision he'd heard in a long time.

'Okay, let's go.'

Büller passed the word on, and moments later the men jogged across the open ground and scrambled over a low stone wall towards the isolated building.

Remi Boulliard enjoyed the sound of an excited sea tumbling onto the rocky shoreline below. There was something quite delightful about savouring the snug warmth of a plump wife under the comforting spread of a goose-feather quilt while outside the elements did their best to beat their way noisily in; although this smug pleasure was lessened somewhat by the clatter of rotten wood on plaster. The wind tonight was playing mischief with the wooden shutters of their bedroom window. It had worked one of them loose, and every few seconds the damn thing was banging irritatingly against the wall outside. The shutters needed replacing, and the fresh sea breeze was gleefully reminding him of that.

Another job to do.

He shrugged, it was a job for the summer, like whitewashing the old plaster walls of the building; it could wait a couple of months.

He listened to the regular, heavy breathing of his wife; it would take a marching brass band to wake her up. He often found the rhythmic ebb and flow of her deep breathing punctuated by the metronome regularity of her nasal click soporific when he was close to sleep. But on a night like this, when sleep seemed such a remote prospect for him, it was irritating. He slid his bony carpenter's hand under her left shoulder and gently lifted. She obliged automatically in her sleep and rolled onto her side, the nasal clicking stopped.

Remi sighed.

He heard the brittle crash of breaking glass. It sounded as if it had come from the kitchen or the pantry downstairs.

He sat upright in bed, straining to filter the noises from outside the house, to hear only those from inside. He heard the tinkle and scrapes of glass fragments being gently brushed aside, the sound of a footfall on the hard ceramic floor of their kitchen.

'Yvonne! Somebody's in our house,' he whispered hoarsely. She slept on. He shook her shoulder once, and she moaned noisily. He decided it would make too much noise to wake her up and then explain why he'd done so.

Another noise from downstairs!

It sounded like the scraping sound of one of their heavy wooden chairs being nudged an inch across the floor, as a stranger might do accidentally, unfamiliar with the lay of the furniture. It was followed unmistakably by the faintest, barely audible sound of someone 'shushing'.

My God there is someone down there!

Remi climbed out of bed and donned his housecoat. He carefully pulled open the bottom drawer of the bureau he shared with his wife, and from beneath a layer of knitted jumpers he pulled out the only recognisable weapon the Boulliards had in their house. It was an antique blunderbuss, a weapon lethal at short range. He grinned in the darkness, the old pitted metal felt reassuring in his hands and he knew there was a small sachet of gunpowder and shot somewhere . . . downstairs.

Shit!

Another bump from below galvanised him to action. He decided the sight of the weapon alone should be enough to frighten off the intruder (*or intruders . . . who shushes themselves?*) downstairs. It was probably only some kids from the town, perhaps a couple of those gypsies that had migrated north, encouraged by the withdrawal of the Germans. He knew there was a caravan of them nearby, camping just outside Nantes.

Emboldened by the weighty unloaded gun in his hands he began to descend the stairs. Even if the damn thing couldn't fire it would make a fine club if things got a little nasty. He made his way down carefully taking each step close to the wall, where the wood rarely creaked. His bare feet made little noise on each wooden step and as he neared the bottom Remi prepared himself to bellow a loud and terrifying challenge.

As he reached the bottom of the stairs he took the three steps across the hallway to the kitchen. Steadying himself, he extended a hand inside the room and hit the light switch.

The single bulb above the sink lit the kitchen well. Remi's gasp of horror at the sight before him was all but drowned out by the rattling of a dozen or more safety catches being slipped off.

Koch reached a gloved hand out and gently relieved the old man of his antique.

'I think I'd better have that, thank you,' he said in passable French.

Chapter 35

Mission Time: 3 Hours, 10 Minutes Elapsed

5.15 a.m., over France

Outside, above the dark blue bed of clouds, the sky was beginning to lighten. To the east the pale grey sky gave away the approaching dawn with the slightest stain of amber on the horizon. They were at 25,000 feet, high enough to be discreet, but it meant they were now using the oxygen system. The rubber face-piece of his mask was rubbing irritatingly against the bridge of Max's nose. He pulled the mask away from his face, rubbed his nose and placed it back.

'Bad fit,' he muttered.

The oxygen masks they were all wearing were the personal issue of the American crew that had flown this plane and had been adjusted to fit *their* faces when first issued. Max and his crew had had to make do with the masks as best they could. They'd had ten to juggle between the four of them to find the best fits all round. Even so, they each had their own minor irritation to deal with.

Max checked his watch, it was 5.15 a.m. Just over three hours airborne.

They had flown south out of Germany, passing over Swiss airspace, to ensure they were well away from any Allied sorties during the night. Then they'd changed course, heading west into France, just north of Lyon. The detour had added another 300 miles to the journey to Nantes. The bomber had been heavy lifting off, the installed internal tanks just beyond the belly gun had slowed her down, and they'd travelled through the early morning hours at a sluggish 220 miles per hour, to conserve fuel.

'Stef, how're we doing?' he called into the interphone.

'There's a waypoint coming twenty minutes further along this course.'

'Heading north-west?'

'Yes sir, 295 degrees.'

The course would take them in a straight line up to Nantes, south of Paris and the dense Allied air traffic north of the city.

Stef's voice on the interphone again. 'I'll be taking another reading in five minutes, sir.'

'Good, give me a shout when you're about to do it.'

Flying by night and above cloud cover, Stef could only navigate by dead reckoning, backed up with periodic attempts at celestial navigation using a sextant. While he was taking a reading, the plane would need to be as steady as possible. Even the most carefully taken readings could only give them an approximate position and could only be used to confirm Stef's calculation of where he thought they were based on the track, speed of the aircraft and time passed, offset against drift and any head or tail winds. A good navigator working and communicating constantly with the pilot could, in theory, navigate blind from any point to any other point. In reality, minor inaccuracies, as a result of slight calibration errors in the equipment or human error, could inevitably accumulate to throw the dead reckoning calculation off.

But Stef was good. He had a young and alert mind, and was constantly rechecking his work and confirming speed and drift values with Max over the interphone.

By contrast, Schröder and his squadron had only visual contact with the bomber and Max's periodic announcements of direction changes and speed to ensure they remained on course. During the dark hours of the night, they had flown much closer to the B-17 and had been able to maintain a visual by moonlight. The Me-109s had flown slightly higher than the bomber and had been able to see it fairly easily silhouetted against the blue tinged snow-like cloud carpet below. But it was getting lighter now, and they had pulled further away.

Which had been fortunate.

At 4.30 a.m. they had passed within a few miles of a squadron of fighter planes. From that distance they had been unable to work out whether they were American or British. It was most likely they were American. If they had seen them, then undoubtedly the Americans had seen them too. The squadron of fighter planes had not changed course, nor had they attempted to raise them on the radio.

The Allies now owned the sky; no one was expecting to see any German planes in the air. So no one was looking particularly hard, nor would any Allied pilot be particularly suspicious about coming across unexpected planes in the sky.

The flight so far had been uneventful, to the point even that Max had allowed his mind to wander, if only for a few moments at a time.

Pieter took off his flying gloves and rubbed his hands furiously. 'It's bloody freezing! As cold as Bolsch pussy.'

Over the comm. he heard Hans chuckle.

Max pulled the mask away from his mouth and exhaled a cloud of vapour. 'It is. Lads,' he announced to the others, 'make sure you keep squeezing your masks.'

At freezing point the exhaled vapour quickly produced ice crystals within the mask, which could block the oxygen supply pipe.

He watched Pieter trying to warm himself up.

'Go and see how the other two are, Pieter, that should get some blood flowing.'

Pieter nodded. 'Yeah, good idea.' He unplugged himself from the interphone, plugged his regulator into his 'walk-around' oxygen cylinder, pulled himself out of the co-pilot's seat and clambered back through the bulkhead towards the bomb bay, carrying his oxygen cylinder under one arm like a rolled-up newspaper.

Max decided it was time to check in with Schröder and his men. He switched to radio. 'Mother Goose calling, how are my little goslings?'

Max heard the speakers of his earphones crackle as Schröder answered. 'Good morning, Max, we're still here.'

'How's your fuel reading?'

'We're all about the same, just about empty on the drop tanks. What's our position?'

'North-west of Lyon, another four hundred miles or so.'

There was no immediate response from Schröder, the man was obviously doing some quick mental arithmetic or perhaps consulting with his men on another frequency.

The earphones crackled again. 'It looks like it's going to be a bit on the tight side.'

That was no big surprise, they'd all known even with the drop tanks giving them added range that crossing half of Germany, and some of Switzerland and all of France was going to take them to the very limit.

'I can drop altitude a little; not much though,' said Max. It would help marginally.

'No, best to stay up high, we'll do fine, Max. Don't worry about us. It'll be close, but we'll have enough to get us there.'

'Okay. Listen, we have a waypoint coming up in quarter of an hour, the one that takes us north-west for a little while, heading two-nine-five. I'll call in when we're due for that.'

'Good.'

Max studied the horizon again. The amber stain towards the east had grown to colour half the sky, and the first rays of the sun were appearing above the cloud carpet. The cover of night was fast fading.

Now it gets a little trickier.

Pieter ducked through the bomb bay's bulkhead. He stopped to look down at the bomb. It was suspended within a metal cradle just above the bomb hatch. It wobbled slightly as the plane negotiated a brief moment of turbulence. He shook his head in wonder at it.

'So, little man, you're a giant dressed as a midget, eh?' he muttered to himself.

He pulled the glove off one of his hands and reached out towards the rack to touch it. The cold metal was like that of any other bomb, but he sensed inside it immense power, sleeping for now, biding its time.

Something like this should have a name, a big, powerful name, and full of meaning.

Pieter struggled for a moment to think of one . . . his mind focused around the biblical story of David and Goliath, a small being killing a much larger one. The metaphor felt appropriate, but then he reminded himself that David was a Jewish hero. He sighed at his own stupidity, and not for the first time felt a sneaking envy for the kind of education that Max had. He would know what to call it; Max would conjure up an appropriate name, probably something in Latin, something far more fitting without any effort at all.

He pulled his glove back on and ducked through the bulkhead on the other side of the bomb bay to enter the navigator's compartment. Stef was sitting at the radio operator's desk attempting to control several large maps on its tiny surface. He had the sextant out and was preparing to take another reading before the light of dawn totally obliterated the faint light of the stars.

'Morning, Baby Bear,' he shouted through his mask.

Stef frowned angrily at him. 'Ahh, come on, when are you going to stop calling me that, Pieter? I'm nineteen.'

'When you can grow a proper beard, son, then I'll take you to the best whorehouse I know. My treat.'

The young lad lifted his mask to show off the meagre ginger tuft on his chin and attempted to muster a deeper voice. 'You don't think I'd touch anything after your little man's been near it do you?'

'You think it's a "little" man do you? I've put fully grown horses to shame.'

'Yeah, yeah.'

'Anyway,' said Pieter bending his little finger, 'it's got to be bigger than your fanny tickler.'

Stefan's mask was still plugged into the interphone, and over his earphones he heard Hans laughing coarsely once more. Max's voice added to the exchange.

'Tell Pieter to knock it off for me, will you?'

Stef obliged. 'Max says stop arsing around.'

'All right, all right,' said Pieter. He patted Stef on the shoulder to show the kid he was just messing with him and carried on towards the aft bulkhead, leaving Stef and the navigator's compartment behind him. He ducked as he passed through the bulkhead and entered the waist section.

Just ahead on the floor was the bulge of the ball turret, beyond that on either side the openings for both of the waist-guns. It was noticeably colder and noisier in this section of the fuselage, as the wind angrily whistled past the open gun ports. The floor between the two machine guns, offset by a few feet to allow two waist-gunners to operate simultaneously without bumping into each other, was overlaid with wooden planks. It was the only floor space of the plane to have planking to ensure neither gun operator would trip over one of the ribs that ringed the fuselage. Hans was sitting on the wooden floor hugging his knees.

Pieter shouted. 'Hans, what the fuck are you doing down there?'

'Fucking freezing up by the gun. I'm just having a break.'

Pieter wasn't entirely without sympathy for Hans. He was feeling the bitter cold too. They were all used to the sealed comfort of their Heinkel 111.

Pieter pointed at one of the MG-81s that had been installed in place of the Brownings. 'Is it okay to –?'

Hans nodded. 'Sure, you'll freeze your bloody balls off after a few seconds though.'

Pieter climbed onto the planked floor and stood behind the gun. He held it in his hands and stared out through the waist-gun porthole. The wind battered his face as he looked out upon the grey blue world outside and he struggled to keep his eyes open as streams of tears quickly emerged and were blown horizontally across his cheeks. He remembered to pull down his goggles and was able to look out again more comfortably.

He hunkered down behind the gun and, with one eye closed, aimed along the sight and down the barrels. He squeezed the trigger momentarily and let a dozen rounds off. Most of the shells dropped outside and were instantly whisked away by the wind. Three or four rattled down inside onto the wooden floor.

Hans reached out for them and eagerly scooped them up, placing them in the pocket of his flying jacket to savour the fading warmth of the casings through the thick leather.

He placed a hand to his ear and then nodded, Max was on the interphone saying something. 'He's test firing the portside gun, Max,' Hans replied. He nodded and then pulled his mask from his face and shouted out to Pieter. 'He says stop messing around with the guns.'

Pieter nodded back at him and reluctantly let go of the waist-gun.

The curse of the co-pilot . . . fuck all to do.

It angered and frustrated him that he'd been trained as well as any pilot, but rarely had a chance to put those skills into practice. To be fair, Max was better than a lot of pilots who tended to hog the flying time and rarely allowed their co-pilots to refresh their skills. However, on this mission the flying time was too long for one pilot; once they were clear of France, Max would hand over to Pieter to cross the Atlantic, and once they approached America, Max would take over again.

None the less, he resented the hours ahead of them during which he'd have nothing to do but worry, and wait.

Chapter 36

Mission Time: 3 Hours, 55 Minutes Elapsed

6.00 a.m. 300 miles from Nantes

Lieutenant Daniel Ferrelli yawned and as he did so his ears popped. The bright sunlight of early morning reflected brilliantly off the cloud layer below them and he was forced to squint irritably. The overpowering brightness and trapped warmth within the Mustang's cockpit made him feel 'woozy', tired. It was that relaxed, Sunday afternoon feeling, after the pot roast, and in front of a crackling fire, where sleep could come and go easily.

He removed one glove and rubbed his eyes.

You fall asleep, asshole, and they'll be sending what they find of you home in a matchbox.

Daniel Ferrelli, or Danny as he was known by most of the men in his squadron when they were off base, scanned the clouds around him, above and below. It looked like the kind of winter wonderland scene you'd see in the display windows of Macy's come Christmas time: all cotton-wool snow and glitter. Like this, the sky was beautiful. He loved it above the clouds when the white floor beneath him was complete and no sign of the drab green and olive world below could be seen. It was like being in another dimension, a place of ice queens and castles. When his mother had first read him Jack and the Beanstalk he'd seen something like this in his mind. Danny focused on a plateau of cloud with a smooth top and imagined the beanstalk poking up through it, saw a tiny Jack scampering across it, magic harp under one arm and goose under the other and, thundering across the plateau, a giant roaring with anger.

The speakers in his flying cap crackled with the voice of Charles 'Smitty' Brown. 'Uh, Danny?'

'Dammit, Smitty, it's Lieutenant Ferrelli while we're working.'

Smitty bunked with Lieutenant Ferrelli despite being only a rating. He was overflow from the main billet. They'd lost a bed space in there, and Ferrelli had a spare bunk in his room. He'd only agreed to put up with the guy, temporarily, because they'd known each other back home before joining up. Smitty was okay – clean, tidy, but a pain in the ass with the name thing. He wondered whether with him it was a genuine case of forgetting to call him Lieutenant in front of the rest of the men or whether the guy just wanted to look a smart-ass.

'Sorry Dan . . . Lieutenant.'

'What is it anyway?' he asked, cutting Smitty off.

'Well, uhh, I think I saw one of them, errr . . . nine o'clock, above us.'

Ferrelli looked to his left and up. There was a thick layer of cloud above them with occasional gaps between tall cumulus stacks. He looked long and hard, waiting to see a dark form passing the open sky between the cloud stacks.

'I can't see anything, Smitty, you sure?'

'I saw it once, is all, sir.'

Ferrelli's squadron had been sent to escort a wing of B-17s en route across France from Marseille north to an airfield outside Paris. The bombers had served the last two years in Libya and Egypt, and still sported desert colours. They were being relocated back to England. The war was looking like it would be over before they bedded in with the Eighth and did anything useful. Still, Ferrelli figured it made sense to start gathering up the American planes ready to ship them back home.

Things had come unstuck pretty quickly, and he and his men had failed to rendezvous successfully with the B-17s. Not that he thought it mattered too much; it wasn't like there was anything out there they needed escort protection from anyway.

But hey, Danny, it looks bad . . . losing the planes you're meant to be protecting. To lose one is bad luck, but all twelve?

Ferrelli kept his eyes on the clouds above and to the left. 'I don't see anything, Smitty, not a damn –'

He saw it.

A single silhouette way above them at about thirty thousand feet. Unmistakably the outline of a B-17, flitting between the tall white columns, and it was heading west. 'Okay, okay I see it. Looks like these fellas are on their own. If they're the guys we're meant to be looking after, I'd say they are totally, one hundred per cent lost by the look of it. They should be heading north, not west.'

The navigator on that plane needs to go right back to school. Jeeez . . .
Navigation 101.

He knew it was easy enough for even the most experienced crew to drift off course by dozens of miles. Shit, he even knew of bombers that had drifted into the wrong goddamn country. Dumb-ass stuff like that happened all the time. But getting the wrong heading? No matter how lost you are, no matter where you are, the one piece of kit that's always going to work just fine is the compass.

'Okay, boys, let's go take a look-see what these fools are up to.'

'Roger that, Lieutenant,' said Smitty. His response was mirrored by the other ten pilots, most of them bored to distraction by the flight so far and eager for something to see and do.

Ferrelli pulled up and to the left on the yoke and his P51-D swung towards the last place he'd seen the bomber. His squadron followed suit, managing to maintain a recognisable Vee formation as they veered left and climbed steeply.

Ferrelli checked his altimeter. They were at 25,000 feet. He reckoned that bomber was somewhere around thirty. He studied the sky ahead of him, a forest of immensely tall cumulus. There was surely heavy rain down below; a real *roof-rattler* as his mom liked to term the sort of passing downpours that hit them without warning in the spring and ceased just as suddenly.

He saw the plane again. It was higher than he'd thought, now maybe 35,000 feet.

Damn.

Either he was losing his ability to reckon altitudes or the plane had just pulled up steeply since he'd seen it last, only seconds ago.

'You guys see it?' he called out to the squadron.

The voices crackled back in a chorus of confirmation.

'Wasn't that plane at thirty thousand? Or am I losing my touch?'

'Yeah, sir, looked like that to me too,' answered Jake Leonard, one of the youngest guys on the squadron. Even the distortion of radio failed to hide the fact at eighteen his voice still sounded like a kid's. The poor guy hated answering the billet telephones; it got him pissed when people not knowing to whom they were talking referred to him as ma'am.

'You reckon they just climbed?' asked Ferrelli.

'Reckon so, sir.'

Smitty decided to add his two cents. 'It looks like they're playing hide and seek with us, Danny.'

Ferrelli nodded.

It does look that way. What's up with these guys?

'I'm going to try raising them on the radio.'

He flipped the frequency. 'Ahh ... this is Lieutenant Ferrelli, United States Air Force, calling unidentified B-17 due west of me. Are you the guys we're meant to be escorting this morning?'

He waited for a response.

There was none.

'Unidentified B-17, west of my position, that's your seven o'clock. Are you the guys who've flown up from Marseille?'

There was still no answer.

Shit, the radio operator needs to go back to school too.

'You reckon they got problems, sir?' asked Jake.

'Yeah, maybe they have. Maybe they're all asleep.' Hell, five minutes ago *he'd* been ready for a nap. Maybe they were having some technical problems, the radio might be out. He watched the bomber enter a column of cumulus the size of a mountain peak. His eyes followed the predicted course of the plane and half a minute later he spotted it again, but several thousand feet higher. The pilot had just executed a steep climb inside the cloud.

The sonofabitch was trying to lose them.

'Anyone else here reckon this is a little fishy?'

'What're you thinking, sir?' asked Jeff Thomason, a college kid from Boston, as far he could recall.

'I think these boys have tried to shake us off. I reckon it's time we pulled in real close and tried having a talk with them.' Ferrelli smiled and his facemask rustled against his sandpaper chin. All of a sudden today felt like it had just got a little more interesting.

'With me, boys, let's keep the Vee tidy.' He pulled back on the yoke and began to climb. His squadron followed suit. This time the flying formation was a little tidier, as they rode 7000 feet in just under two minutes to match the current altitude of the bomber. He checked the altimeter; it showed 37,000. Their P51-Ds had a ceiling of 41,000, there wasn't much headroom left for them. But then he was pretty sure the ceiling altitude for these brutes was less than their Mustangs. He vaguely recalled the Mustang had about four or five thousand on them.

The only way is down, big fella, no way you're going to out-ceiling us.

The B-17 maintained its course ahead of them, now no more than a quarter of a mile away. It hadn't changed direction now that they were behind it. Neither had it decided to drop. He wondered whether the earlier evasive manoeuvres were because they thought the Mustangs were Krauts. But then you'd have to be one hell of a jittery pilot these days to be worrying about Germans. Those guys were an endangered species, like buffalo.

Ferrelli had been hoping, since his posting to England, to chance across one of their Luftwaffe boys in the skies over Germany. But then he'd arrived at the party way too late to see any of that kind of action. Those poor bastards had been pounded out of the skies of Europe months ago. He had lived in hope though, occasionally fantasising an encounter with a lone rogue ace and duelling to the death in a clear blue sky.

Just one kill, that isn't a lot to ask for, is it?

'You going to try the radio again, sir?' asked Jake.

'Err . . . yup, might as well, I guess.'

Ferrelli flipped the frequency again. 'Unidentified B-17 west of my position, at thirty-seven thousand feet . . . hey! Can you fellas hear me?'

There was still no answer. He found himself wondering once more what the hell was wrong with these guys. Either they were the USAAF's most incompetent bomber crew, ever, period. Or there was some trouble aboard, perhaps multiple equipment failures, or . . . ?

Or that's Adolf Hitler flying a stolen plane and making a run for it.

Ferrelli smiled dreamily like a kid, like some junior league scruff assembling a fantasy baseball team.

'Danny? What do we do now?' asked Smitty.

'Okay, listen up, guys,' he announced. 'I'm going to close in on them, see if I can establish visual contact with the pilot. I want you guys to stay in formation behind them. I've got a real funny feeling about these boys.'

'You reckon they're escaping Nazis, sir?' asked Jake hopefully.

'Don't let's get too excited here, son, I'm just being thorough is all. So let's ease those little thumbs away from the triggers shall we?'

He heard a few of them laugh nervously. They were all as wired as he was. This had to be about the most exciting thing that had happened to them since they had commenced flying as a squadron. Weeks of patrolling empty skies and needlessly escorting cargo planes and bombers, and here they were squealing like kids at a tea party just because some dumb radio operator was probably sleeping on the job.

Chapter 37

Mission Time: 4 Hours Elapsed

6.05 a.m., 300 miles from Nantes

Hans watched the Mustang slowly approaching through the plexiglas of the tail-gunner's blister.

'It's an easy shot Max; he's coming straight up behind us. One burst and I can put half a dozen shells straight into the canopy.'

His voice was loud with excitement, and Max's headphones crackled from the volume. Max shook his head. Hans had a hair-trigger manner about him; fire first, think later.

'We should see if we can bluff our way out of this, before we give ourselves away. They don't look too worked up, they're just curious . . . so we'll play along with them for now.'

Pieter turned to look at him. 'How are we going to do that? You speak English all of a sudden?'

'I'll think of something, just give me a minute.'

The American's voice crackled through their headphones again, a long sentence, entirely unintelligible to them. Pieter was still looking at him. Max knew he wanted to call in Schröder and his men to make a quick clean kill out of this. It wouldn't be hard – these Yanks were probably all green, and it was unlikely that they had seen much action. Schröder and his squadron of seasoned vets would make mincemeat of the poor bastards.

But then the game would be up, and they would end up having to fight the rest of the way across.

Max switched from interphone to radio. 'Schröder? What's your position now?'

Schröder came back almost immediately. 'We've swung in position behind and below their formation, you want us to move in on them?'

Positioned below . . . that was good. Schröder knew his squadron tactics.

The Mustangs would be blind beneath the wing; more importantly, if they were planning to mount an attack on them from behind, they would need to be either coming down or rising up on them to avoid catching the B-17 in their crossfire.

'Not yet . . . I just want to know you're ready in case we need you in a hurry.'

'We're ready.'

'All right, only on my command, is that clear?'

'Absolutely.'

Hans' voice came over the interphone. 'He's closing in, Max, pulling up alongside us on the left.'

'Can you see the pilot?' asked Max.

'Yup.'

'Well that means he can see you, Hans, for Christ's sake smile, or wave at him, or something.' Max turned in his seat and looked out of the left-side cockpit window. After a few seconds he could see the nose of the Mustang slowly edging into view.

'What's the plan, Max?' asked Pieter.

The American's voice could be heard again. From his tone the man was obviously asking them a question. He was probably after their bomber group designation, or enquiring what formation they were meant to be with. Surely at this stage the American fighter pilot could only suspect that they were simply lost. The cloud cover below was complete; it was easy enough in these conditions for a plane to lose its way.

Bluff it.

The Mustang's cockpit slid into view and Max found himself staring directly at the American fighter pilot, only a hundred yards away. The fighter pilot waved, and spoke again. Max responded by waving back at him and tapping the earphone of his flying cap.

He heard Pieter muttering over the interphone. 'That's your bluff? Jesus . . . we're in bloody trouble if that's all you've got.'

The American pilot spoke once more, his voice again sounded like he was asking a question.

Max responded with the same gesture, he backed it up with a shrug of his shoulders. The American didn't say anything more, he studied them, it seemed with a renewed level of suspicion.

'I don't think he's going for it, Max, I really don't.'

Pieter was right.

Max could sense the American was considering the next move. There were perhaps two things he could do next, either report a sighting of them, or attempt to shoot them down. Max had no idea what the state of alertness was amongst the Allied air forces. He knew by now a communication had been sent demanding a surrender. Whether that had trickled down to a heightened state of alertness for their airmen over Europe, he couldn't guess.

If he pulls back into formation behind us, then they're preparing to attack.

The American tried to contact them once more over the radio, this time Max didn't even bother to respond with a gesture. He looked at Max and nodded courteously and then the P51-D gracefully slid backwards out of sight.

'Hans, Stef, man the waist-guns, I think we're going to have to engage these boys.'

Ferrelli eased away from the bomber, wondering what to do next.

'What's up, sir?' asked Jake.

'I got a bad feeling about these guys . . . this ain't one of the planes up from Marseille, that's for sure.'

'We're not going to shoot 'em down, are we, Danny?' asked Smitty.

'I don't know yet . . . lemme see . . . lemme see . . .'

'Maybe their radio's shot, that's why they weren't answering you,' added Smitty.

'Or maybe they're Polish or something?'

'Guys . . . guys! . . . Shut up a second and let me think, will you?' said Ferrelli. He slid back into the leading position of the Vee formation.

What now? There was something wrong about that bomber. Nothing singularly told him that, just a host of little things. They weren't responding to radio contact. They were on their own in an area of sky that didn't normally get B-17 traffic. There seemed to be hardly any crew. He'd seen only the two pilots and the tail-gunner, no belly-gunner, upper-turret-gunner, no bombardier or navigator, neither waist-gun seemed to be manned. Then there were the earlier evasive manoeuvres. It was all suspicious, but Ferrelli wasn't sure he wanted to be the author of a mistake that might cost the lives of at least three of his compatriots.

And what if it is escaping Nazis? You want to be the dope who dropped the ball?

That decided him.

'Okay, boys, here's what we're going to do . . . we're going to wing this bird so she has to ditch. If I've made a stupid mistake here, then at least nobody's killed; on the other hand, if there are Krauts hiding inside, well then I'm sure they'll get picked up quick enough. You guys understand me?'

A chorus of 'Yes sirs' crackled over his earphones.

'You guys with me on this? Because if I'm wrong, I'm going to have to do some explaining why I decided to shoot down one of ours when we land. It's gonna help with the paperwork if you boys can vouch I didn't go all crazy on you.'

Ferrelli's men voiced their support. 'We're with you, Danny,' said Smitty.

'Okay, then let's do it,' said Ferrelli. 'Listen up, boys, I'm going to aim a burst of fire at engine one, then move on to engine two, then three, then four, so she's got no power and they're forced to bail. If the tail-gunner starts popping at me, you have my permission to concentrate fire on that . . . but only if he fires first, you got that?'

The men confirmed the instruction.

'Right . . . here I go.'

Ferrelli swung his Mustang to the left and lined up with the outer port engine of the bomber with his gun sight. His thumb slid onto the trigger on his flight stick and he readied himself to press down.

'Schröder, come and get them,' said Max over the radio.

'Right. We've jettisoned our drop tanks and we're moving in now. When we start firing, dive and pull right so you're well clear of the crossfire,' Schröder responded calmly.

'Understood.' Max turned to Pieter. 'You want to take the roof turret?'

'You bet,' he answered, smiling. He unplugged himself quickly and scrambled out of the cockpit towards the back, eager not to miss the start of the imminent showdown.

'Hans and Stef . . . Schröder and his boys are coming in any second now, when they open fire I'm going to push us into a steep dive and pull out to the right, so be ready to hang on to something.'

Both men confirmed they'd understood.

Chapter 38

Mission Time: 4 Hours, 5 Minutes Elapsed

6.10 a.m., 300 miles from Nantes

Ferrelli looked up at the B-17 in front of him; a last, hasty assessment before committing to his decision to bring her down.

'If I've made a mistake, I'm real sorry, guys,' Ferrelli muttered.

His thumb rested on the trigger and he was preparing to release a short burst of fire when he heard the thud of half a dozen bullets impact the underside of his fuselage.

'What the fu –?'

A Messerschmitt Me-109 roared upwards just in front of him and continued in a steep climb several hundred feet above.

'Where the hell did that come from?' he shouted.

He saw eleven more Me-109s either side of the first rocketing up in front of the vee formation and watched as they banked around for another pass.

'Ahhhhh! shit-shit-shit!' he heard one of his boys shouting.

The P51 to his immediate left lost a wing amidst a shower of fragments and bullets and swerved violently towards him. He had to pull up hard, out of the formation to avoid it. 'Break! Break! Engage targets at will!' he heard himself bellowing.

The vee formation instantly disintegrated as each of the Mustangs pulled out of the formation and attempted to find a valid target, meanwhile the B-17 suddenly dropped into a steep dive leaving the skirmish behind it.

'Bastards! You goddamn Krauty bastards!' he heard Smitty screaming angrily.

Ferrelli's evasive action put him up on the same level as the Me-109s, now curling around to descend on the disorganised P51s below.

Oh my God, my boys are going to be shot to pieces.

He pulled his plane round to follow the banking German fighters and found himself lining up nicely behind one of them.

'No-o-o-o –'

The voice sounded like Jeff's. It cut off suddenly and he saw with his peripheral vision one of the P51s erupt into a ball of fire. Ferrelli let his cannons fire in anger for the first time, and the tracers whipped forward, clipping the right wing of the Me-109 ahead of him. A twisted slither of metal broke away from the wing and spun towards him, clattering noisily off his canopy and thankfully not shattering it. The Me-109 feinted to the left and then pulled sharply to the right. Ferrelli acted quickly enough to keep on the German pilot's tail, but the German had extended the distance between them.

'Fuck! Oh Jesus!' The voice of one of his boys.

'Give us a goddamn chance, you shits.' That was Smitty's voice.

'You okay, Smitty?' he shouted instinctively. There was no answer back, but that probably meant the guy was too busy to talk right now.

He let off a second burst. This time, despite the increased range, some of the bullets found the body of the plane and he was rewarded with another spinning shard of metal hurtling perilously close to the canopy, and a spray of oil that spattered against his glass like greasy rain. The Me-109 was now leaving a faint trail behind it, not smoke unfortunately, but oil.

'Got you, you sonofabitch!' he shouted so loud his throat rasped painfully.

The German dived and broke left, pulling away from the skirmish. Ferrelli decided not to follow him. 'Damaged' was as good as 'out' in this ball game. Instead he decided to see whether he could help any of his boys out. He quickly scanned the sky around him.

Jeeez, it's a fucking massacre.

He could see three planes from his squadron descending away from the epicentre of the battle, trailing thick columns of smoke. Another was being tailed by two Me-109s and as he watched, the combined firepower of both planes disintegrated the tail fin and stabilisers. The Mustang spun along the length of its fuselage and quickly dipped down into a dive, continuing to spin furiously, shedding debris like a wet dog shaking off water, as it began its two-minute journey towards France. He heard a protracted scream over the radio that quickly became a high-pitched whimper of despair and eventually faded into a wash of static.

He hoped that wasn't young Jake, but it had sounded like the kid.

In the distance he saw the B-17 levelling out, at a quick guess, three or four thousand feet below.

These Me-109s are protecting it. Ferrelli decided that his unlikely suspicion had been right, the plane had to be carrying something or someone important. Perhaps carrying some high-ranking Nazis to safety, perhaps even Hitler himself.

I was right, goddammit!

'Who's alive, for fuck's sake? Call in, call in!' he shouted angrily into his radio.

'I'm still here, sir.'

'Who's that?'

'Wally, sir.'

'Me too!'

'Jake?'

'Yessir. I've taken some damage, but I'm okay.'

'Anyone else?'

'Joe here, sir.'

'Smitty? Smitty?' Ferrelli expected the cheeky fella to answer. But the radio remained ominously silent. *Eight of my boys out of action, just like that, in the space of half a minute.*

Ferrelli looked around the sky above him, now smudged with smoke and fading trails. He could see three P51s holding tightly together above the area in which the skirmish had commenced; they reminded him of three little pigs huddled together waiting for the big bad wolf to rip them to shreds.

He leaned over and peered down at the cloud carpet below. The Me-109s were hungrily pursuing two more of his squadron, both of them trailing black cords of burning oil. He watched them all disappear into the clouds, leaving the bomber defended now by only two fighters. The other Me-109s would be back in less than a minute, having finished off those poor bastards.

'Listen ... guys, these fighters are defending the bomber. I reckon there's somebody real important inside ... so that's what we got to go after, capiche?'

'Yes sir.'

'All right, let's do it quickly before those other Krauts realise their mistake.'

Max watched the Messerschmitts dive past them in pursuit of the two Mustangs. 'Where are they going?'

'Stupid bastards. Think they're hunting deer,' said Pieter over the interphone, still manning the roof turret.

Max switched from interphone to radio. 'Schröder! What the hell are you doing?'

'Don't worry, I'm right here, look out of your left window.'

Max did so and saw Schröder sliding into position seventy feet off their left wing tip. 'Erich's on your right-hand side.'

He leaned forward, craning his neck and looked out of the right window to see Erich Köttle waving back at him from a similar flanking position.

'I sent the others after those two . . . we should try and prevent anyone we encounter making it away and raising the alarm . . . yes?' Schröder said.

Max nodded, it made sense.

'Fine. I counted six or seven destroyed. Those two your boys are chasing makes eight or nine, that leaves us a few unaccounted for. Where the hell are they?'

'I'm looking for them,' Schröder answered quickly.

Pieter's voice came through on the interphone, loud, alarmed. 'Max four coming in on our six, high!'

'I see 'em too!' answered Hans.

Max heard the guns in the top turret rattle angrily and brass shell cases cascaded down the ladder from the turret onto the floor just outside the cockpit. Pieter was whooping with joy, or fear.

Seconds after Pieter had started firing he heard a deafening drumming of bullets impacting the fuselage, running from the rear to the front, as if some giant wearing hob-nail boots was sprinting heavily down the spine of the plane. Glass from the roof turret shattered and he heard Pieter yelp in shock.

The machine gun went silent.

With a deafening roar, four P51s swooped low over the bomber's cockpit and out in front. Max found himself instinctively ducking. Two of them banked left, the other two right, climbing up and to the sides, preparing for a second pass.

Schröder and Erich automatically took the opportunity to break their flanking positions and run in pursuit.

'Shit,' Max muttered under his breath. He heard boots on a rung of the ladder leading down from the roof turret. 'Pieter, are you okay?' The regulator on his oxygen mask prevented him from fully turning round; to see if that was him. 'Pieter?' He heard the shuffling of boots at the bottom and then felt a hand grip the back of his seat. He turned to look up; it was

Pieter. His face was darkened by soot and several small cuts, and Max noted his leather flying jacket was ripped and slashed in several places.

'You okay?'

Pieter nodded. 'I'm fine . . . those bastards have wrecked the roof turret. Shit, I manage to fire – what? – twenty, thirty rounds, and then they bloody well break my gun.'

Max, relieved, allowed himself a grin. 'I think they were just trying to tell you you're a shitty gunner.'

Pieter slumped into the co-pilot's seat and plugged himself in. 'Four years I've waited to have a go, and I get to fire one bloody burst,' he grumbled to himself.

Hans watched through the left waist window as two of the Mustangs climbed around the side of them in preparation for another approach from behind. He aimed his MG-81 at a space forty feet in front of the leading fighter plane, but decided the shot would be wasted, they were too far away. In pursuit, and taking a shallower arc, was Schröder. Hans watched with growing respect as the pilot gained on the two American planes, their inexperience showing as they made their way in a lazy, careless curve toward the rear of the bomber.

Hans knew what Schröder was waiting for; he was waiting until they rolled on their sides dipping their left wings to pull them round into a position behind the bomber. It would expose to him the largest possible profile. The leading P51 rolled predictably and began to swerve down and to the right, taking it towards a perfect tailing position, when Schröder opened fire on it.

Hans watched as the glass canopy shattered, and several fragments of plane and pilot showered out of the cockpit. A moment later the entire plane disappeared within a ball of fire and smoke. The flames mushroomed lazily up into the sky, while half a dozen large, tattered portions of the plane spun downwards, trailing spirals of smoke behind them.

'Fuck, Schröder's good!' Hans shouted into the interphone.

'What's up? Have they bagged another?' he heard Max ask.

'Yes, it just ripped open. He must've hit the fuel tank.'

Stef shouted across the noisy waist compartment. 'Hans, the others are coming in again! They're coming in on my side!'

'Swap guns!' Hans shouted back, and shuffled awkwardly past Stef on the floorboards now littered with brass shell casings. He pulled the MG-81 round to face towards the rear and saw three of the P51s lining up behind each other and approaching from the rear. 'I can't bring the gun round on them. They're drifting in right behind us!'

They've worked out there's no one operating the tail gun.

'Okay, Hans, when you think they're close enough, I'll pull to the right –'

'No, left, I'm manning the left waist-gun.'

'The left, then . . . that should bring them round into a position for you to get a clear shot.'

'Right,' Hans replied.

He leaned towards the window, looking back as best he could, but the P51s had drifted behind the tail fin and out of sight.

'Stef, can you see them!'

Stef leaned over the right-hand waist-gun, nearly poking his head out into the roaring wind; he looked back and managed to see the tip of one wing beyond their tail fin. 'They're right on us!'

Max heard Stef's warning and pulled the plane sharply to the left. As he did so the P51s momentarily fell within the arc of fire of the left waist-gun. Hans immediately took the opportunity to fire at the leading fighter as it roared towards them, now no more than a hundred yards away. The heavy-calibre bullets ripped into the underbelly of the fighter and almost immediately smoke began to spout from it. The American pilot fired a responding burst towards the waist-gun and a stream of bullets stitched a row of ragged holes either side of the window as Hans simultaneously let go of the gun and dropped to the wooden floor. The fighter plane screamed close over the top of the bomber's mid-section, the end of the volley over-shooting them.

'Fuck, fuck, fuck!' Hans shouted as he hugged the rough wooden planks, a coarse splinter embedded in one cheek.

That was one of them; there were two more behind it. A second volley raked along the mid-section of the plane and another row of ragged holes appeared along the roof of the fuselage.

Stef dropped to the floor beside Hans, eyes widened with shock. He lay beside Hans, hugging the floor, eyes locked on him.

'You all right?' Hans shouted amidst the roar of whistling air. Stef only blinked.

They heard the volley from the third fighter plane pass over the top of the plane harmlessly, followed by the roar of its passing.

*

His engine was making an unpleasant whining noise, and he could hear the clatter of something loose rattling against the underside of his plane. Ferrelli knew he'd taken some damage, but so far the plane wasn't telling him anything too bad. He just prayed whatever was loose and dangling beneath his Mustang wasn't a part of the landing gear.

He looked back over his shoulder to see the bomber swiftly receding. Jake was behind him, and behind Jake, now passing over the back of the bomber and rising to join them, was Joe Lakeland. His two boys seem to be in good shape, although Jake's left wing was leaking aviation fuel.

Jesus . . . all that's left of my squadron.

Beyond the B-17 he saw the two Me-109s that had been guarding it getting ready to pursue them, and in the distance, emerging from the clouds below, the other German fighters were returning.

Ferrelli clamped his jaw angrily. The whole bloody dogfight had lasted little more than four or five minutes, and nine of his young men were dead or missing. He hoped one or two of them had managed to bail out of their planes, but it seemed unlikely. The attack had been ferocious, the German fighters it seemed had been determined to not just disable them, but ensure none of them got away. They had pursued those two guys relentlessly, at the risk of exposing the bomber. Ferrelli guessed they were keen to ensure that nobody walked away from this exchange alive to spread the word.

Keeping a low profile, it seemed, was pretty high up the agenda for these sons-of-bitches.

Screw this.

'Guys, we're getting the hell out of here,' he muttered into the radio. 'I don't think they want anyone crying wolf.'

'Yes sir,' replied Jake and Joe simultaneously.

'When we hit the clouds, we'll head north . . . let's go.'

Ferrelli pulled his stick hard and rolled over into a steep dive towards the clouds below and the last two men of his squadron swiftly followed suit.

Pieter watched the Mustangs disappear below them. 'You know, I think our bloody cover's blown now,' he said to Max.

Max nodded.

It had been a relatively easy victory for them. Veterans versus raw recruits. Schröder's boys had made a short and ruthless job of them and they'd done well to prevent all but three escaping. But that would be enough to raise the alarm. He wondered how quickly the information would filter back. If the Americans and British were already on some kind of high alert, the news would travel fast. It would all be down to how many planes they had deployed in this part of France as to whether they would have another run-in. Surely, there were very few planes in the area that could respond at short notice to look for them?

Right now, Max decided, they needed to concentrate on making for the airfield outside Nantes. The 109s would be on the last of their fuel by then and, having seen how effective they had been, he didn't want to contemplate flying for long without them close by.

Max switched to radio. 'Schröder, what's your status?'

'We lost one, Jonas. Everyone else is fighting fit.'

They'll have burned a lot of fuel during that dogfight.

'What are you all showing for fuel?'

It was a few seconds before Schröder responded, clearly conferring with his men first. 'We'll make it. It might be a close-run thing, though.'

Max consulted briefly with Stefan on their position; they were about ninety minutes away from the west coast of France. They would arrive sometime around eight in the morning. He hoped those snow soldiers on the ground were in position and ready to go.

Chapter 39

Mission Time: 5 Hours, 25 Minutes Elapsed

7.30 a.m., an airfield outside Nantes

Koch tore another mouthful from the loaf of bread. It was good; the dough was dense and chewy, almost rubbery, while the crust crumbled in a brittle, flaky way, like pastry. It was so different to the bread he was used to, it amazed him how much a basic food substance, such as bread, could vary so much from place to place.

'Good bread,' he managed to say with a full mouth. 'Almost like cake, sponge, you know?'

Büller nodded.

'You want some?' Koch held the mauled loaf out to him.

'No, sir, I'm not too hungry.'

Koch patted Büller's shoulder; he understood.

He checked his watch; the radio signal had been due for a while now. They had received one in the early hours confirming the planes had departed and they would be signalling again when they were half an hour away from the airfield. It had been stressed that Koch and his men should secure the airfield as close as possible to the time of arrival of the planes. Too early and news of the surprise attack might filter to some nearby forces in time for them to respond and take it back before the approaching planes could make their stop for fuel. Timing was going to be everything with this raid.

Koch had sent some of his men out to reconnoitre the airfield at first light. They had come back with good news. It was a small supply strip, mostly occupied by ground crew, there to maintain the occasional Dakotas passing through. A handful of American soldiers guarded the road in, manning a hut and a barricade. These men were just counting the days until they were sent home and certainly not spoiling for a fight. Koch didn't anticipate losing any of his twenty-seven men taking the airfield. In fact, he could see this being done without even a solitary shot being fired. If they were lucky, and everything went to plan, the planes would land, refuel and be gone in a matter of half an hour. However, if it came to it, he knew his men were ready for a scrap. The orders for this mission, which had come directly from Hitler himself, had demanded he and his men fight to the last protecting those planes while they were on the ground; but it looked like it wasn't going to come to that.

Koch decided once the planes were in the air again he would order his men to surrender promptly. There would be no need for heroic sacrifices today if things went smoothly.

He wondered what was so important about these planes . . . a dozen Me-109s and a larger plane he presumed would be a Condor. He'd seen this before, generals appropriating crucial resources to whisk them from some hot spot away to safety. He could imagine, hiding away inside the larger plane, Göring or one of the other stooges that surrounded Hitler. He couldn't envisage Hitler himself scurrying out from Berlin.

Karl, the radio operator, waved his arm, and the men crowded inside the kitchen stirred and looked anxiously to Koch.

'Is it the signal?' Koch asked.

'Yes, sir. They're twenty-five minutes away.'

He nodded and placed the crust of the loaf down on the kitchen table. 'Time to go to work,' he muttered.

He cast a glance at the French couple tied up and gagged, sitting at the kitchen table. They couldn't be left here on their own. If either of them were to wriggle free, they'd most likely raise the alarm. They couldn't be left like this. With some reluctance he had begun to reach for his field knife, when Obergefreiter Schöln gently tapped him on the shoulder.

'Sir, the two wounded men, Paul and Felix . . . what are your orders?'

The two men that had been badly cut during the beach landing last night had been attended to, but neither of them were fit enough to fight. They would be more of a hindrance than a help.

He looked across the kitchen at them. One of them, Paul, had lost a lot of blood, and was weak and tired. The other was grimacing from the agony of a broken shinbone; at least he was alert.

'They can stay here to watch over our friends.' Koch nodded towards the man holding his leg and wincing. 'Tell Felix, if either of them look like they're going to give him some trouble . . .' Koch tapped the hilt of his knife. 'Understand?'

Schöln nodded and turned to pass the orders on while the rest of Koch's platoon grabbed their weapons and made ready to exit the kitchen and head swiftly towards the cover of the apple orchard nearby.

The orchard was small, perhaps only a couple of acres, but the spring blossoms and sprouting leaves would provide a dense enough cover for them to make their way unseen to the perimeter of the airfield.

Koch knelt down beside Felix. 'Did Schöln tell you . . . they give you any grief –?'

'Yes, sir. I don't think they'll be any trouble.'

He turned to look at the French farmer and his wife. Their wide eyes were rolling with fear as they silently watched the men getting ready to move out.

'I'm sorry you couldn't make it along for this one, Felix. Listen, it'll all be over in an hour and a half, so let them both go round about ten o'clock. They'll run into town screaming blue murder, but they'll be back with American soldiers, and hopefully you'll both get some treatment then.'

'Yes, sir, an hour and a half.'

'I'll see you both later,' he said. He nodded towards the farmer. 'Oh, and thank him for the food.'

Koch watched the last few men slip out of the kitchen one after the other.

The last man darted out quietly into the garden, and Koch followed, slipping on wet paving stones just outside the kitchen door.

It was drizzling. Not rain, just a fine mist of moisture descending from a sky as bland and featureless as a sheet of writing paper. He followed the man in front of him into the orchard, and despite his best efforts, made a lot of noise swishing through the tall, wet grass under the trees. He heard several men stumble on concealed roots and the cracking of disconcertingly noisy twigs; but within a minute they were all lying in a ditch at the edge of the orchard, breathing hard from the exertion and looking out onto the small airstrip.

Koch didn't need field glasses, the cluster of tents and huts were only a few hundred yards away. A single hangar was the only building. Inside the hangar was a Dakota DC3, and outside, parked facing the tarmac runway, were three more; beside them was a fuel truck. He could only see a few men milling between the tents, puffs of steam from their mouths drifting up to the cold, wet, grey sky. He watched the men move lethargically around the camp. A canteen was still serving breakfast by the look of it; he could see a queue of men standing in line holding mess trays.

Koch turned to smile at one of the men beside him. 'I can't see these lads giving us much trouble.'

'No, sir.'

It struck him, all of a sudden, how peaceful it was here. After the last few days of being trapped within the noisy confines of the U-boat with the ever-present whine of the electric motors or the chug of the diesel engines, listening to the pattering of drizzle on the leaves, and the occasional rustle of feathered wings amongst the branches around them, he was reluctant to disturb the peace and quiet. It would be nice if this morning's little endeavour could be pulled off without a shot. It really would be a shame to disturb the day's tranquillity with the brittle crack of gunfire.

Koch whistled softly to attract the attention of Feldwebel Büller and Obergefreiter Schöln. The two men immediately recognised their CO's calling sound and shuffled across to join him.

'Okay, Büller, take nine men and head straight for the guard hut. I reckon the lads over there are probably the only ones even close to putting up a fight. Schöln, you take nine and check out the hangar and get the truck and fuel to the side of the airstrip. I'll take whoever's left and do the canteen. We'll rally the prisoners in the hangar. We should do this quietly and quickly; hopefully we can do it with no shots fired. But if any of them look like doing a runner, bring them down. No one is to leave the airfield, you understand?'

Both men nodded.

'Right . . . pick your men and wait for my command.'

Büller and Schöln shuffled off across the ground, wordlessly tapping the shoulders of those men they wanted as they moved down the line. There was little deliberation in their selection; all of the men here were handpicked from Koch's company, all of them good men. He watched as both men gathered their squads in little clusters away from the edge of the orchard and briefly relayed the objectives to them. Koch summoned the men still lying in the ditch, and they gathered around him.

'Lads, this should be easy. We're taking the canteen. I see about thirty men there. None of them are carrying a weapon,' he looked up at the queue of men under the canteen awning waiting tiredly in line for their breakfast. 'Fuck it, some of them aren't even fully dressed!'

The men laughed under their breaths.

'We go in, *quietly*, no shots if you can help it. Once we've got them all, we'll take them to the hangar. Any questions?'

None of his squad could think of any, and they all shook their heads in silence.

'Right, on my command, we're all moving out.'

Koch looked up at his two other squad leaders; they were finished with their briefings and looking at him for the signal.

Here we go.

He nodded, and instantly they were off their knees en masse and sprinting through the long, wet grass of the orchard, out from under the small, squat apple trees and across the shorter grass of the airfield. As they ran the only sound was the grass-softened rustle of boots on the ground and the metallic chatter of buckles and ammo.

Büller and his men veered to the right, towards the guard hut and barricade. Schöln bore left, towards the hangar. Koch and his men continued forward, towards the canteen tent, now only a hundred yards away. Most of the Americans there having breakfast seemed half asleep, and it appeared like none of them had spotted anything yet.

My God, can't they see us?

They were now only thirty feet away and a few of the men sitting down to eat, looked up and seemed to notice the approaching Germans. The initial response didn't seem to be alarm, it looked like curiosity; he could imagine them lazily wondering, 'Who are these guys? Some of ours . . . practising manoeuvres or something?'

Koch sprinted the last few yards and ducked as he entered underneath the awning, MP-40 raised to his shoulder and pointed at the Americans, now it seemed, finally aware that something was amiss.

'Down! Now!' Koch shouted using his limited knowledge of English and gesturing towards the ground with the barrel of his gun. The rest of Koch's squad fanned out around the men in the canteen.

'Andreas, get those over here in the middle of the floor,' he called out.

One of his squad approached the men still standing in line, still holding mess trays, motionless and all staring uncomprehendingly at Koch and his men. He pulled them away from the steaming urns and shoved them towards the middle of the canteen.

'Down!' he hissed.

They finally seemed to wake up and comprehend the situation that had suddenly altered their day. A few moments later they were all lying compliantly on the floor, Koch's men hastily shaking them down for any concealed weapons.

So far so good.

In the meantime, Schöln and his men crossed two hundred yards of open field towards the hangar. It was a relatively small structure, only large enough to house a single transport plane. Outside, parked facing away from the building, were the three DC3s and beside them the fuel truck. As he jogged, he pointed at four of his men and indicated the planes and the fuel truck, they peeled off towards them, weapons at the ready. One of them climbed swiftly into the truck and had it immediately rolling across the field towards the grass landing strip. The other three began checking the planes for anyone hiding inside.

Schöln led the rest of them over towards the hangar and they came to a halt outside the sliding corrugated doors. Schöln took a few seconds to catch his breath.

'Ernst, Dieter, stay here and guard this doorway,' he whispered between ragged gasps. He took the other three men of his squad with him inside the hangar. They fanned out and quickly circled the plane but found no one.

Schöln nodded at one of his men. 'Jan, check inside.'

The soldier slung his MP-40 over one shoulder and pulled himself up inside the cargo hold of the plane. Schöln heard a muffled shout of surprise and a moment later a solitary mechanic emerged from the plane with his hands in the air; behind him Jan emerged intently studying a deck of playing cards. He jogged over to Schöln and showed him the deck.

'Nice . . . very nice,' he nodded appreciatively. The women on this deck weren't just topless. He cast a glance at the American mechanic, who looked as embarrassed as he was frightened. 'I presume he was playing solitaire?'

Jan grinned.

Schöln looked down at the deck. 'When we're done today, I think I'll have another look through these.' He passed the deck back to Jan, who pocketed them quickly.

'Shit,' said Büller as he studied the men twenty yards away, outside the guard hut. There were two of them that he could see, both had rifles slung over their shoulders. There might possibly be a third inside the hut; one of the men seemed to be having a conversation with someone inside. He turned to face his squad, all of them kneeling with him behind a stack of crates and awaiting instructions.

It looked like they were going to have to go in shooting. Büller wasn't so much concerned about any bullets that might whistle towards them, but if the guards weren't taken totally by surprise there was a chance one of them might slip away out of the front entrance and down the dirt track into town.

He cast a glance over his shoulder towards the hangar. He could see several men walking with raised arms away from the parked-up DC3s towards the building, escorted by another, which even at this distance could clearly be seen to be holding a gun. He turned to check out Koch's progress and saw men being pulled unceremoniously to the floor at gunpoint. If either of the guards were to turn towards them, they would see something was wrong.

'Büller?' prompted one of his men. 'What do we do?'

Whatever it is, it's got to be quick.

Büller turned back to study the guards just in time to see one of them pace casually along the length of the barricade and turn round to pace back. He saw the guard look up from his feet tiredly towards the hangar and stop. The guard cocked his head, and then they heard him call out to the other one.

Fuck it, decision's made for me.

'Let's get 'em!' Büller rose from behind the stack of crates and fired a volley from the hip as he ran. His men emerged behind him, quickly spreading out and racing towards the two guards who now were beginning to sluggishly react to the alarming sight of ten German soldiers only a few dozen yards away and rapidly approaching them. One of them was swifter than the others in coming to his senses and swung his rifle down, firing in rapid succession four unaimed shots towards them. All of them missed wildly, thudding harmlessly into the wet ground. The other guard seemed to have woken up now and dived for cover behind a small sandbag bunker beside the barricade. The first guard dropped to his knee and prepared to fire some aimed shots this time. Büller found himself feeling a fleeting instant of sympathy for the guard as he aimed his sub-machine gun at the young man. It seemed like he'd been the only American on the airfield with his wits about him. He squeezed off half a dozen rounds in a short burst. Three puffs of crimson appeared in front of his chest and the young American was pushed backwards off his feet. Büller's men covered the ground quickly and no more than three or four seconds later they were vaulting over the sandbag bunker. The other guard instantly dropped his weapon and threw his arms up quickly.

The hut.

Büller looked towards the open door of the hut and saw a flash of movement from within. The door to the hut slammed shut with a bang.

'Someone inside!' he shouted.

One of his squad, Bergin, rushed the door and kicked it violently open. From inside Büller heard several shots being fired and Bergin dived back out of the doorway.

There were another three shots that followed the direction Bergin had thrown himself in and ragged holes appeared in the flimsy wooden wall of the hut, one of them inches above his head.

Screw this.

'Down!' Büller shouted at Bergin and swung his MP-40 towards the hut. He emptied his magazine at the wall at about waist height. The rest of the squad followed suit while Bergin hugged the ground as a shower of wood splinters fluttered down onto him.

The firing ceased a few seconds later, their ears rung from the noise. The wall of the hut looked like a cheese grater.

Büller took a few steps forward and kicked at the door. It swung in quickly and bounced off a desk inside with a flimsy rattle. Büller raised his weapon and sidestepped into the hut.

As the acrid smoke cleared he could see the body of the third guard slumped over the crackling, hissing remains of a radio. The body slowly slid to the floor with a thump. One hand still holding tightly to the radio receiver.

'Shit . . . I think we're in for some company.'

Chapter 40

Leaving Town

It was a good five miles along the coast road before Mark eased his foot off the pedal and another one before he was happy enough to slow down and pull over. He brought the Cherokee to a standstill down a slip road hidden from the main coastal interstate and applied the handbrake. He left the engine running, though.

'You going to tell me what's going on?' he managed to calmly ask after a while.

'Jesus, Mark. Those bastards were going to kill me!'

'I noticed.'

Chris shook his head. 'My God, if you hadn't come in when you did . . . Jesus.'

'Yup,' Mark answered drily. There was anger bubbling up in his voice. 'You sure you're telling me everything, Chris? Because all of a sudden, this has escalated from being an interesting find to being, well . . . I'll be honest here, a fucking hazardous situation!' He took a deep breath to compose himself once more.

'You're right, there's a little more that's gone on, Mark. I'm sorry, I should've kept you in the picture. But then, I honestly didn't expect something like this to happen. I mean, for crying out loud, whatever happened with that plane out there, it was over half a century ago! Why the fuck does someone want to kill us for finding it?'

'This is America, Chris . . . not good old England. The goons over here don't box by the Marquis of Queensberry rules, if you know what I mean.'

'Shit, yeah, I noticed already.'

Both men sat in silence for a moment, both still recovering from the experience.

'So you going to tell me what's been happening, then?' said Mark finally.

Chris told him as quickly as he could about the call from Wallace, the old man on the beach, McGuire, and then the two men he'd seen down by the jetty. The disjointed events over the last few days, each on their own, had seemed much less disturbing in isolation, but putting them together now for Mark's benefit, they tied together in a chilling way.

'Jesus, Chris, it sounds like we've stumbled on something we probably shouldn't have.'

'I know, and I'll be honest, this is really making me shit myself. Who do you think those guys were working for?'

Mark scratched his beard. 'I dunno. CIA? Some other government agency?'

Chris looked out of the window at the blackness of the night, trying in his mind to colour the whole picture in. But there were so many gaps. It seemed they knew just enough to present a threat to somebody out there, but not enough to know what to do next.

'There's something in that wreck down there that opens a whole can of worms for . . . for someone. And it's that very same someone who's sent in these fucking psychotic hitmen.'

'That's great, Chris, but that isn't telling us a whole lot.'

Mark was right. They were going to need to find out more than they already knew if they were going to walk away from this in one piece. For a start, they needed to know what was in that plane wreck that was so damned important, and maybe then, if they could find that out, they'd have an idea of who the hell had released the rottweilers on them.

He realised there was only one thing they could do right now. 'We have to go back for this guy Wallace,' said Chris.

'No way am I heading back down that road to Port Lawrence. No fucking way,' Mark answered adamantly.

'It's the only way we're going to find out who's after us. I know that wily old bastard knows far more than he let on this evening. I mean, he was really twitchy, like he knew someone was closing in on us. He knows who those guys work for, Mark, I'm sure of that. He knows who they work for, and what's out there under the water.'

Mark drummed his thumbs on the steering wheel. 'So what do you suggest we do?'

'I know where he's staying. We drive right back in and grab him, and then we run like hell.'

'I see. And we happen to run into these guys again?'

'I'll kill them both with my death-ray eyes.'

Mark nodded. 'Great, well that's that covered, then.'

Chris grinned nervously. 'We'll get that old boy ... and then he's going to spill it all even if I have to pull his fingernails out to get him talking.'

A thought occurred to Mark. 'They may have already got to him.'

And if they had, Wallace surely would already be dead. If Chris, with the little that he knew, was a liability worth silencing, then Wallace most definitely was.

'We've got to try, though, Mark. I can't think of anything else to do.'

'We could go to the police.' Mark puffed out air. 'This is some heavy-grade shit you've walked into, Chris.'

'Don't I know it.'

They sat in silence, the only sound the waves from the sea pounding the beach a few hundred yards away, and the gentle idle of the Cherokee's engine.

'And anyway, I've still got this,' said Chris lifting his hand up so that Mark could see from the moonlight what he was holding.

'Sheesh! You got the safety on?' said Mark, reaching out for the weapon and tilting it away from his head. 'That's a Heckler and Koch you got there, and –' his fingers sought out the safety control lever on the left hand side, '– *now* the safety is on.'

Chris drew in a gasp. 'It was off? Shit, I've been fondling the bloody thing since we left my room. Lucky I haven't shot a hole through my bollocks.' He laughed anxiously.

Mark nodded, 'Very lucky. HKs have a light trigger.'

Chris looked at the gun in his hand, wondering if he had the guts to use it. He hadn't fired back at that hitman in the motel, but then he hadn't even been aware that he'd still been holding on to it until now.

Mark must have read his mind. 'No point taking it unless you're prepared to use it. You wave that thing around in front of guys like that, and they *will* take you down in a heartbeat.'

Chris felt the cold, dead weight in his hands, and the odd, overpowering sense of comfort it gave him. 'I'll use it if need be.'

'You ever trained with weapons, Chris? Ever fired a gun?' Mark asked. 'I'm not sure this is one of your better ideas.'

Chris flicked the safety lever upwards and downwards. 'Okay. Safety on

. . . safety off . . . right . . . that's me trained up. We should go now, before I chicken out.'

Mark looked sternly at Chris. 'Grab him and we run?'

Chris nodded. 'Grab him and run, that's the plan.'

Chapter 41

Mission Time: 5 Hours, 42 Minutes Elapsed

7.47 a.m., 2 miles outside Nantes

'We've definitely got a damned leak,' said Max studying the fuel gauge.

Pieter tapped the glass of the display hopefully with his finger; the dial remained resolutely still.

'Shit, that's nearly three-quarters of it gone,' growled Pieter.

Three-quarters of it gone, and we've flown about one-fifth of the distance.

'We must have taken some damage to the internal tanks and we've been leaking fuel since.' Max could have kicked himself; he should have spotted this earlier. If it had been the familiar cockpit of a Heinkel he would have.

'We haven't got enough, Max.'

'I know that,' he answered testily.

There was not enough fuel left to complete the mission. The choices on how to proceed were limited. Either the mission was going to have to be aborted or they were going to have to go down with the fighters to refuel.

'I don't think we've got a lot of alternatives here, Pieter.'

'We abort or we refuel?'

Max nodded. 'If we abort, you know what that means, don't you?'

Pieter knew. Major Rall had instructed them both very carefully on this potential outcome. If damage to the plane meant they would be unable to reach America, they should arm and drop the bomb anyway. At the very least, the detonation of the bomb, albeit not on the required target, would still demonstrate to the world that the Germans had got there first and had a massive destructive capability. That alone *might* still be enough to cause the Americans to think things over.

'What do you think about refuelling?' asked Pieter.

'Let me think, let me think.'

They were approaching the last waypoint before Nantes; from there they should be able to navigate their way by eye to the airfield. It didn't give him much thinking time. Going down with the fighters to refuel hadn't been a part of the plan. It seemed the Major hadn't considered what they should do if fuel became an issue. The extra tanks had been internal. Rall must have assumed they were safe from damage there.

Now Max was alone in having to make the risk assessment of doing this. If they were overrun while they were on the ground, the bomb could fall into the hands of the Americans.

'It's risky, Pieter. They could get their hands on it.'

Max pushed the mask to his face and switched to the radio frequency for their men on the ground.

'*Medusa* calling, what is your status?'

He was about to call again when a reply came back.

'*Medusa* we are ready for you now, come in as quickly as you can.'

'How long can you hold there?'

There was some delay in the answer; when it finally came, it was a different voice that answered. 'Half an hour, possibly as much as an hour if we're lucky.'

'It'll take about twenty-five minutes to refuel the plane, if we forget the extra tanks,' said Pieter. 'Would that get us there?'

Max let his mask fall away again, so that their conversation remained between them. 'It should do, this plane has a 4000-mile one-way range without them. It should get us there, with very little to spare, though.'

He heard Stef's voice over the interphone. 'Approaching waypoint seventeen.'

Pieter looked at Max. 'Come on, we can't throw it away now.'

Time was running out, and Max felt the enormity of this tactical decision resting squarely on his shoulders. He cursed Rall for not anticipating this scenario and giving him a brief for it.

'If we go down, we should refuel first, the fighters will have to wait.'

Pieter sure as hell didn't have a problem with that. 'Fuck . . . yeah, of course.'

Stef was on the interphone again, asking Max to confirm he'd heard the last navigation call.

Pieter shrugged, 'Max? What are we going to do?'

Time is running out.

He tried to visualise Rall, to imagine what the Major would advise him under such circumstances. For what he knew of him, the Major seemed a cautious man, a meticulous planner, Max made a guess that he would reluctantly advise them to return home if they could make it, or if not, to drop the bomb right there. But then he could see Rall's ruined face; a rakish smile on the good side suggested the man had gambled once or twice before in his life.

'If we're overrun, I'll have to detonate it on the ground,' said Max.

Pieter nodded with reluctant agreement. 'You'll have to.'

'You understand what that would mean?'

Pieter nodded. 'Yeah. There are worse ways to go.'

'Fine, we're going down, then.'

Max had made his decision; his hands loosened around the control yoke. He was relieved, almost elated to have cut through the last few moments of indecision.

'All right Pieter, let's get ready.'

He pulled the mask to his face and spoke into the interphone. 'Stef, Hans ... we've got a fuel leak, which means we're landing alongside Schröder and his boys so we can get a top-up.'

Chapter 42

Mission Time: 5 Hours, 50 Minutes Elapsed

12.55 a.m. EST, the White House, Washington, DC

Truman stared silently at those members of his war cabinet and the Joint Chiefs of Staff who had been recalled and able to attend at such short notice. Many of them, with the exception of Donovan and Wallace, looked as if they had been dragged out of their homes, their beds, or reluctantly from some social function.

'Little more than an hour ago, I was informed of something very disturbing, gentlemen, an intelligence report from our people in Europe. Colonel Donovan, will you please . . . ?'

Donovan nodded and picked up a piece of paper; he read from it. 'At 2100 hours, Eastern Standard Time, we received a wire from our OSS operation in Germany. Yesterday, a platoon of our airborne troops discovered a partially destroyed laboratory on the outskirts of Stuttgart.' Donovan looked up from his sheet of notes. 'I should stress that, although these boys passed on news of their discovery promptly to the intelligence people over there, it took them a little time to work out what it was they had, and for the information to make its way back to the OSS over here. So this is nearly twenty hours old. Anyway, the laboratory appears to have been used to refine uranium, a cyclotron was discovered there and –'

'Would you explain to us all what a cyclotron is?' asked Truman.

Donovan turned to Wallace, who stepped forward to address the men at the table. 'A cyclotron is a machine that magnetically separates U-235 from U-238. It's an efficient way to refine on a small scale. We tried it over here, but it was too slow a method, requiring frequent cleaning of the magnetic heads.'

'So then it appears that the Germans have been at it,' interrupted Truman.

The response from around the table was one of quiet discomfort.

Truman nodded at Donovan to carry on.

Donovan cleared his throat and resumed reading his notes. 'One of their technical team was taken prisoner near the lab; he had been wounded. This technician spoke briefly to a field medic before being taken to a field hospital, where he died a few hours later.'

Donovan looked up at the men around the table and finally to Truman. 'The medic reported that this technician talked about working on atomic weapons, and that a bomb had been moved from this installation in preparation for imminent deployment.'

This time, there was only silence from around the table. Truman's face hardened as he studied the faces of his cabinet members and the Chiefs of Staff present. This assembly of middle-aged and distinguished faces around the conference table, faces that still poorly concealed a disapproval of him, cast judgement on him as the man who could *never* replace Roosevelt. They all remained impassive, poker faces, none prepared to offer the vaguest gesture of support or encouragement as he continued to fumble his way through this problem, alone it seemed. None of these wise men seemed to have any advice for him *now*. He turned to the Chairman of the Joint Chiefs, Admiral Leahy. 'Do you have any thoughts on this?'

The Admiral cleared his throat awkwardly. 'That does sound like we're talking a whole new ball game, sir. Perhaps Donovan's young man can let us know if he still thinks it impossible for the Germans to have built at least one of these atom bombs.'

'Mr Donovan, your technical advisor, Mr . . . ?'

'Wallace, Mr President,' Donovan obliged.

'Wallace, you informed me at our last meeting that it was highly unlikely that the Nazis could make an atom bomb due to the amount of this stuff, uranium, that they would need. That is correct, isn't it?'

Wallace nodded. 'Yes sir, Mr President.'

'So if this is an accepted fact, then this new intelligence report withstanding, it remains impossible the Nazis have a bomb. Am I correct again?'

Wallace felt cornered.

There is a remote possibility, one that hasn't been discussed.

'Mr Wallace?'

Bill Donovan looked up at him and frowned, urging him to answer the President. Donovan would be expecting him to confirm the President's assertion. But then Donovan wasn't a physicist, he wouldn't know about . . .

'No sir. It is *theoretically* possible, although very unlikely, that they could have built a bomb.'

Both Donovan and Truman looked sharply at Wallace. 'How come?'

Wallace felt the eyes of all of them boring into him. He should have at least made a mention of this in the previous meeting, no matter how unlikely it was, if only to cover himself. Now it was going to look like he'd deliberately kept information from them. Or that he was simply incompetent.

'It could be a fast-cycle emitter,' he uttered reluctantly.

'Fast-cycle –? What the hell is that supposed to mean?'

'It's a theory, sir. A proposal that accelerating the very start of the nuclear chain reaction and specifically shaping the discharge of neutrons will release enough energy to extend the reaction beyond the fissionable material. Thus much, much less U-235 would be required to produce a bomb, but of course the danger would be that the chain reaction doesn't eventually burn out, but carries on indefinitely.'

Truman shook his head, irritated by the unwelcome return of techno-babble to the conversation.

'In other words, sir, if the theory stands, a bomb made in this way could potentially . . . uhh . . . destroy everything sir. A doomsday weapon of sorts, Mr President.'

Truman paled.

'It's just a theory, sir,' Wallace added. 'There are many men working on the Manhattan Project who have already debunked it as impractical.'

'But it seems the Germans have taken this theory more seriously?'

'Yes sir, it would have been the only way they could have proceeded. If *their* physicists had dismissed the theory as ours have done, they wouldn't have even *begun* the process of making a bomb. They would know that the resources they'd need to muster for a single atom bomb would be well beyond their grasp. So it looks like their people believe the fast-cycle process can work, Mr President. But I must reiterate, sir, that the theory is considered flawed by all of our physicists working with Dr Oppenheimer, including Dr Oppenheimer, who has already described it as a load of nonsense. Any bomb designed along this principle will almost certainly fail to detonate.'

Truman stared long and hard at Wallace. 'And why didn't it occur to you to mention this to me yesterday?'

'It is a flawed theory. It's simply wrong, sir.'

'How certain are you of that, Wallace?'

Wallace swallowed nervously.

'Give me something I can understand . . . one chance in ten, in a hundred, a thousand?'

'It's impossible, sir, to give you a figure like that. All I can say is that it is very unlikely that this kind of bomb will work at all.'

'Unlikely,' repeated Truman.

'Yes, sir.'

'Not "impossible" . . .'

'Highly unlikely, sir,' Wallace added.

'And given they need much less of this *uranium* to make one of these fast-cycle things, is it possible they could have made more than one?'

Wallace nodded, 'If they have taken this theory on board, then yes, sir . . . needing much less uranium than one hundred and ten ounces, it is possible they may have acquired enough U-235 to have made several of these bombs. But I must stress that it is highly improbable –'

Truman raised a finger, 'But, you cannot reassure me and say *impossible*.'

Wallace swallowed nervously as the men around the table studied the young man intently.

'No, sir, I cannot give you that assurance. No atom bomb has yet been tested. In truth, we cannot know for certain what will happen when we eventually test *our* bomb, nor the Germans' much smaller device. As it stands, the science is entirely theoretical, sir. We have only our arithmetic to guide us.'

The colour continued to drain from Truman's face; he was shaken by this young man's reply. The fellow had been unprepared to utter the word 'impossible', leaving Truman to draw small comfort from the young man's assurance that it was highly improbable.

'I think from this point on I would like us all to consider that the threat issued by Adolf Hitler might be a genuine one . . . and given his demand for unconditional surrender expires today, I'd suggest we had better start working out what we're *damn well going to do*.' His words had started out calmly, but a slowly emerging sense of panic and frustration had driven him to shouting by the end of the sentence. The men around the table shuffled awkwardly under his steely gaze.

He looked at his watch. 'If our deadline started from zero hundred hours yesterday, I'd guess we have sixteen and a half hours until it expires. For now, I will presume that this deadline will be when he intends to explode this bomb.'

Chapter 43

Mission Time: 6 Hours, 1 Minute elapsed

8.06 a.m., an airfield outside Nantes

Max cast a quick, anxious glance at his wristwatch; fifteen minutes had passed since they had landed. He checked the pump gauge on the side of the fuel truck; it showed a reading of just under 3000 gallons. They needed to fill the main tanks at least – they took about 3600 gallons. The extra tanks inside the fuselage towards the rear of the plane were useless. Several gashes, caused undoubtedly during the skirmish with the Mustangs, had resulted in their losing the entire load. The gashes were so bad they couldn't even consider patching them. Hans had reported that the back of the plane near the tail-gun reeked of aviation fuel.

Pieter was leaning out of the pilot's window and periodically calling out the fill readings for their tanks, but his attention was caught by movement near the entrance to the airstrip.

'Max!' he shouted down. 'It looks like something –'

The pizzicato rattle of gunfire from the barricaded entrance to the airstrip made both of them jump. It was a quick exchange, no more than a couple of bursts from two different guns. A moment later Koch jogged across the grass field towards them from the direction of the guard hut.

'What's happening?' asked Max.

'It was a jeep-load of American soldiers. They drove up to the barricade and my men opened fire on them.'

'Did they get away?'

'Yes. So, I expect we'll have some more company very soon.' Koch studied the fuel gauge and turned to Max. 'How much longer do you need?'

'Another five, ten minutes.'

The young Captain gestured at the Me-109s parked in a cluster nearby, each pilot awkwardly attempting to fill their wing tanks from five-gallon fuel drums. 'And them?' he said pointing towards the fighter planes.

'They'll leave as soon as we're off the ground.'

Koch nodded. 'If that jeep was on its own, we'll have a while before word spreads, but I've got a feeling that we'll be due some company very soon.'

'Can you hold them away for ten more minutes, though?' Max asked.

Koch turned toward the guard hut and barricade and the small crescent wall of sandbags. It was hardly a great defensive position, and in any case, the airfield wasn't contained. The Americans could easily by-pass the official entrance and enter the strip from any direction via the woods that surrounded it.

'All we can do is fire enough shots to make them keep their heads low, slow them down a little, that's all. I don't suppose any of them want to be heroes today.'

Koch looked around at the collection of planes. The B-17 was parked up beside the grass strip; beside it was the fuel truck, a large container vehicle full of aviation fuel. Nearby, parked in an irregular cluster around a hastily assembled collection of fifty-gallon drums, were the Me-109s. The fighter pilots were sloshing a lot of the fuel onto the grass in their haste to transfer it to their planes.

'It'll take one well-placed shot to take the lot of you out if you're not careful,' Koch said.

Max looked around. The young man wasn't wrong. But there was little they could do about that apart from fill up as quickly as possible and get away. 'Well, if you can keep them off our backs for a few more minutes, I'd be very grateful.'

Koch grinned and nodded. 'We'll do that.' He turned on his heels and jogged across the short grass in the direction of the hangar.

Max looked at Schröder and his men refilling their planes. He'd sent both Stef and Hans across to help them out. Both of them were working hard holding a fifty-gallon drum at an angle to pour the fuel out into the more portable five-gallon drums. The pilots were struggling backwards and forwards between their planes, emptying the fuel into the wing tanks and returning to Stef and Hans to collect another load. They were all soaked in fuel and the air above the central stash of fuel drums danced with gasoline vapours.

It might not even need a bullet, one spark is all it would take . . . and they're all history.

Koch's men or even Schröder's should have been supplied with funnels and pumps; it would have made the task a lot quicker and a lot safer. The sooner they were up and away, the better. Max checked the gauge. It showed just 3050 gallons . . . 550 to go.

Koch entered the hangar and looked around for Schöln. He saw the stocky man on the far side of the hangar overseeing the prisoners now all gathered in there and lying face down on the ground. If it weren't for the movements amongst them one could be forgiven for thinking that these poor men had all been mercilessly gunned down.

'Schöln . . . over here!'

He jogged over towards Koch. 'Yes, sir?'

Koch looked around the hangar; there were six of his men watching over approximately sixty prisoners. Some of these guards could be freed up to help the Luftwaffe pilots with their fuel.

'Is the door to this hangar the only way in or out?'

Schöln looked around. 'Yes sir.'

'Right, well, pick one of your men to remain with the prisoners and send the others over to help those pilots. The quicker they get under way, the better for everyone.'

Schöln looked back at the prisoners lying face down on the ground, hands behind their heads. One man to guard all of them? Under other circumstances he would have considered that as taking a bit of a chance, but looking at them now, none of them were combat soldiers. He couldn't foresee any of them attempting an escape. He nodded and turned to carry out Koch's orders as the first of a series of bursts of small-arms fire could be heard coming from the direction of the guard hut.

Here they come.

Koch headed at the double out of the hangar towards the front entrance. Büller and a dozen of his men were dug in there, the sandbag bunker proving the only sensible place to set up a defensive enclave.

Seconds later he slid to the ground behind the sandbags, and worked his way over to Büller.

'Alright?'

'Hello, sir. Looks like the jeep had some friends with it,' he replied, squinting through a gap between the bags. He made way for Koch to peer through.

Fifty yards beyond the flimsy barricade on a dirt track that led from Nantes to this airfield were four trucks and several more jeeps. As he watched, US soldiers spilled out of the backs of the trucks and spread out to use the cover of poplars that lined both sides of the dirt track.

'I'd say that's a full company they've sent to deal with us,' said Koch to Büller.

'There must be a base nearby . . . it's only been half an hour since we took this strip.'

'Well, I guess we've been a little unlucky. Listen, we've only got to hold 'em here for a few minutes, okay? Nobody needs to do anything stupid. Just keep them busy for a while with some covering fire. It'll probably take them a while to organise something anyway.'

Büller nodded and spread the word amongst the men sheltering behind the sandbags and inside the hut to lay down some suppressing volley fire on the dirt track. The rattle of gunfire increased as the sporadic bursts intensified. Koch watched with satisfaction as the American soldiers, still piling out of the trucks, went to ground. He was right; it was going to be a while before they were fully deployed and ready to retake the airfield.

They won't realise how time-critical this little skirmish was.

We'll do this yet.

The soldiers who had taken cover behind the poplars began moving. Koch watched them as they ducked under some hedges that lined the track and jogged across into an open field beyond. They stopped and dropped several times as Büller's men sprayed a little fire in their direction.

'They're trying to flank us,' he shouted above the clatter of their gunfire. Those Yanks are pretty good, not your average bunch of GIs,' he said to Büller. Büller nodded; these men were almost as good as the Russian convict brigade they'd faced outside of Murmansk. He'd wager a packet of cigarettes that these soldiers had already seen some action.

We spoke too soon.

'They're working their way around to the sides. They'll get to the planes unchallenged unless we pull back. I want you to direct most of your fire on those men moving across the fields to the left there, and those men moving off the track to the right.' Koch pointed towards a copse of trees to the right of the track. The copse extended around to the top end of the airstrip, where it grew a little thicker and became a narrow stretch of wood. The planes and the fuel truck parked there at the bottom of the landing strip were only fifty, perhaps sixty, yards away from this treeline.

That wasn't so good.

'Slow down those ones heading for the trees on the right. If they get to the trees, then keep them ducking with a few shots into the woods. You've got to slow them down.'

'Yes, sir.'

'I'm going to take some of your men and establish a tighter defensive ring nearer the planes. Büller nodded and Koch clapped him on the back. 'Hold your position as long as possible, and then fall back towards me.'

A few dozen yards away from the gathered planes was a stack of supply crates; tinned food, probably destined to be relief for the recently liberated citizens of northern Germany. A typically American gesture, he thought. They bomb the fuck out of us, then shower the poor bastards left alive with food parcels.

The crates were small enough to be manhandled. It would take only a few moments to pull them out across the ground, around the planes to create some reasonable defensive positions.

Koch pointed towards the cluster of planes and the fuel truck to one side of the strip.

'That's where we'll hold them back.'

Büller turned to look. 'That's open ground –'

'Don't worry . . . it won't be.'

Koch was up and quickly tapped five of Büller's squad on the shoulder. They followed him as he ran towards the planes, ducking low as they went.

Max checked the gauge again, it showed only 3270 gallons had been pumped so far. The speed at which it was pumping the fuel was slowing down. The pressure had dropped; the fuel truck must be approaching empty.

Shit.

The sound of gunfire had returned a couple of minutes ago, and now seemed to have intensified. 'What's going on? Can you see anything?' he shouted up to Pieter.

Pieter looked towards the entrance, where a thin haze of blue smoke above the sandbags was developing. He spotted half a dozen of their men running towards them. 'Ah, fuck it, they're running away already!'

Max stood up straight. *Running* away? *So much for 'as good as the Fallschirmjäger'.*

He walked around the end of the fuel truck to see Koch and some of his men approaching them. They veered to the right and headed towards a tarpaulin-covered stack of crates. As soon as they were there they pulled savagely at the boxes and began dragging them across the grass.

'Okay,' said Pieter. 'Maybe they're *not* running away.'

Max watched as Koch slung his MP-40 over one shoulder and struggled with two of the crates, one under each arm, across the ground to a position thirty feet in front of the fuel truck. He threw them unceremoniously to the ground and raced back for some more.

'They're setting up some cover, I think,' he shouted up at Pieter.

He heard the sound of liquid bubbling in the fuel pipe, and then he noticed from the gauge that the pressure from the fuel pump had plummeted. Either the pump was damaged or the fuel pipe had sprung a leak. He worked his way back to the rear of the truck and found a geyser of fuel spraying from a gash in the pipe. Most of the fuel was spurting out of the hole; only a fraction of it was getting to the B-17. Already a large pool of gasoline was spreading across the rain-moistened turf; the thick fumes floating above it, dangerously concentrated.

Dammit.

Max shut off the pump and closed the valve. One spark and the fuel truck, still half full, and their plane would be a smouldering tangle of metal. They needed another 250 gallons to fill the wing tanks. He looked towards the large fifty-gallon drums, there were only four, and they'd need five. Even if there were that many, it was too much fuel to pour manually five gallons at a time.

He called up to Pieter. 'The fuel pipe's severed.'

Pieter ducked inside the cockpit for a moment and then returned. 'Our tank is nearly full, more than three-quarters . . . won't that be enough?'

It could be.

It was a virtually impossible calculation to make. On a full supply of 3900 gallons, they knew the B-17 could achieve a one-way range of about 4500 miles. New York was 4666 miles away. If they flew low, less than say 5000 feet, and flew at a low cruising speed, maybe 200 miles per hour, they could perhaps squeeze an extra couple of hundred miles out. But if they could just lose some weight . . .

'Pieter! Go and remove anything you can, we need to lighten the plane,' Max shouted.

'Like what?'

'Throw out one of the waist-guns, the oxygen cylinders, anything we can afford to lose.'

'We can't throw out the oxygen.'

'We'll do the rest of this journey under 5000 feet. Now do it! Hurry!'

Pieter's head ducked back inside.

Chapter 44

Mission Time: 6 Hours, 9 Minutes Elapsed

8.14 a.m., an airfield outside Nantes

Büller emptied the clip of his MP-40 and ducked back down just as the sandbag above him shuddered under the impact of half a dozen bullets. 'Jesus Christ!' The sand from the shredded bag above him cascaded down onto his head and shoulders. He wiped it irritably from his face and spat out grit from his mouth. 'Fucking sand.'

'Büller, we've got to pull back now!'

'Shut up, we'll run for it when I say so.'

He turned back to see how Koch was doing. They had managed to pull out some of the crates and stack them in twos and threes a few dozen yards in front of the fuel truck, but it was clear they needed some more time to place a few more positions either side in order to build a semi-circle of positions to cover their flanks.

'Another few minutes, boys,' he shouted above the din.

The Americans in front had crept forward, moving from tree to tree. They were now only between twenty or thirty yards away. He'd attempted to keep a mental total of the number of casualties they had inflicted on the Americans. So far he'd seen three, possibly four kills, and maybe another six wounded, it was hard to judge. Two of his men were dead, both instant kills, both head shots, another had been hit in the shoulder, and although it didn't look fatal, the lad could do little more than lie behind the sandbags and hand ammo clips to the other three of his men as they called out for them.

They had done a good enough job slowing them down here at the front, but it was clear the soldiers that had fanned out across the fields either side of the dirt track would soon be emerging from the trees and bushes surrounding the airfield and entering the fray from all angles. The only thing that could sensibly be done in that event would be to pull back and take cover amongst the motley assortment of huts and tents around the canteen. From there they could take pot shots at the Americans as they made their way across the open field towards the planes. If nothing else, that would force them to the ground again. It would slow them down once more.

Büller decided that was the best they could do for now. Their ammo was running low and the increased silences between their volley fire was proving dangerously encouraging to the Americans. They were close enough now to risk a dash across the open ground. Perhaps they'd lose a man in the process, but they'd be able to vault over the sandbags and shoot Büller and his men like dogs in a pit.

He leaned across to the young lad with the shoulder wound. 'Right, we're leaving, Erich. You stay put and make sure you keep your hands away from any guns when they get to you, okay?'

The young lad nodded.

Büller tapped the other three men, and pointed towards the canteen. 'I'll give you covering fire, head for the canteen, we'll pick 'em off from there.'

The three men nodded.

'Right, off you go,' he said quickly before lifting his MP-40 up above his head and firing indiscriminately over the sandbags. The three men, keeping their heads low, sprinted away from him, as a fusillade of return fire thudded into the sandbags above Büller. He heard some of the Americans shouting above the noise of their weapons, and, a moment later, just as Büller was preparing to fire another clipful over the top, they directed their fire at the three fleeing men. Büller felt the displaced air as the bullets whistled over him and a dozen divots of wet soil flicked into the air either side of the fleeing men. One of them, Werner, fell forward, punched hard by a hit in the small of his back, he flopped down with a muted grunt, face buried in the mud, and writhed from side to side for a few moments before another bullet thudded into his prone body to settle the matter. The other two men weaved erratically until they reached the loose arrangement of tents, pursued by raking lines of flying soil.

'Fuck this,' Büller muttered. He readied himself to fire off the clip in his gun, his last clip. Once he'd emptied it he would run after the other two, and hope that he wasn't as unlucky as Werner, now lying motionless on the muddy ground amidst a growing pool of blood.

He winked at Erich. 'Remember; let 'em see your hands clearly. I'll see you later after we're done here.' He propped his gun over the top and emptied the clip before leaping to his feet and running for the canteen as a barrage of bullets peppered the ground behind him.

Schröder was struggling. Like the others, he'd been ferrying five-gallon drums to and from his Me-109 for the last twenty minutes. His spent arms and legs felt like useless lengths of rubber, and his breathing was laboured and ragged from the physical exertion. Gasoline fumes hovered above the small, muddy patch of ground in the midst of the gathered planes, shimmering and undulating like a heat haze. The pilots were all drenched in gasoline, spilled from the drums as they chaotically scrambled to refuel as quickly as possible. The five soldiers that had been drafted in to assist them had no sooner started to help them carry the fuel drums when they were called away by Koch to assist pulling crates out from under a tarpaulin nearby to form a makeshift enclave of cover around the fuel truck and the bomber.

He had no idea how full his tanks were, he'd lost count of the number of five-gallon drums he'd emptied into the wing tanks, and it would take too much valuable time to climb up into the cockpit and take a reading of the fuel gauge. He decided it would be best to just keep filling up until Max and his boys were making ready to go. That thought in his mind, he looked towards the bomber. He could see no sign of Max beside the fuel truck, but then he caught sight of movement beneath the belly of the bomber. Max was underneath the plane working on something.

Fine time to be doing repairs.

'Max!' he shouted across to him as he returned to the central stash of fuel with his empty five-gallon drum. Max couldn't hear him above the increasing din of the skirmish over by the entrance to the airfield.

'What the hell is Max up to?' he shouted to the two young men holding the fifty-gallon drum for his fellow fighter pilots. They both turned towards the bomber and spotted him working busily with a wrench on the belly turret.

'No fucking idea,' said Hans.

Stef saw one of the waist-guns topple out of the plane and land heavily on the ground below. A box of ammunition followed it out a moment later.

'They're chucking out stuff we don't need. Making the plane lighter.'

One of the large fifty-gallon drums clanged noisily and a jet of fuel instantly spurted from a hole near the bottom.

'Shit!' shouted Hans. Their eyes met.

That could have been an end to us all.

Schröder looked up towards the entrance. American soldiers were streaming past the barricade and hunkering down behind the sandbags, firing towards the tents. None of them seemed to have turned towards the planes out on the strip yet. He looked to his left, down to the far end of the strip. He saw about twenty of them emerging from the treeline onto the open field. They were four, maybe five, hundred yards away, and from the hand gestures of the officer leading them, they intended to make their way up the strip towards them. He saw several wisps of blue smoke issue from their guns, and a moment later several dozen more bullets whistled by above them, most harmlessly inaccurate at this range. However, one of the large fuel drums was hit on the side, with a loud metallic clang; the bullet glancing off but producing a small shower of sparks. Schröder watched them flying lazily through the air, biting his lip with relief when the sparks winked out on the rain-moistened grass.

Another hit like that, and it was all going to go up.

'I think now is probably a very good time for you boys to leave,' he said to Stef and Hans. 'You two better report back to Max.'

Both young men nodded eagerly, stood up the drum they'd been pouring fuel from and began to make their way back towards the B-17, ducking as more bullets whistled up from the far end of the landing strip.

Koch watched as one of his men, Dieter, took three hits in the chest and was thrown onto his back. His legs scissored in the mud beside the tarpaulin-covered crates as he struggled for breath. His other men dropped to the ground as still more bullets thudded into the crates and the ground around them.

Koch decided their little enclave of boxes of tinned food was good enough. 'All right, that'll do. Get your heads down,' he shouted to the nine men with him. They scrambled across the ground, each finding a safe place behind one of the small stacks.

The enclave formed an arc of two-and three-crate piles around the fuel truck, like half of a mini Stonehenge. Each pile offered decent enough cover for one or two men lying down from the right side of the strip only. If the Americans were prepared to take their time and work their way across the landing strip to the left hand side and then proceed up the strip towards them, Koch and his men would be successfully flanked, and their hard cover would be useless to them. For now, though, it seemed the Americans were prepared to continue the fight from behind the cover of the sandbags near the entrance and the comparative safety of the far end of the strip.

Koch stuck his head above his pile. He looked for Büller and his men.

They were no longer near the entrance, and he hadn't managed to see which way they had retreated. His other squad leader, Schöln, was curled up behind the next pile of crates along.

The young captain cupped his hands. 'Schöln! Did you see where Büller and his men pulled back to?'

Schöln pointed towards the large canteen tent, and Koch looked for them amongst the mess: overturned wooden tables, the large iron urns, still steaming with tea and coffee and the enormous catering pans and serving plates, now knocked to the ground, their contents of scrambled egg, bacon and sausages spread across the decked floor of the canteen. Amongst this chaos, he saw some movement and a tuft of blond hair.

Good man, Büller, excellent position.

From where they were, Büller and his boys would be able to keep the Americans further down the strip from advancing up towards the planes. It was open terrain, and they would be exposed to any fire coming from Büller's squad and have no cover to dive behind.

The other main group of men by the sandbags near the entrance seemed in no hurry to move in on them either, content to lay down intermittent fire on Koch and his men, now safely tucked behind the crates.

Excellent. It seemed like a temporary stalemate that might last a few more minutes. That would be enough.

But then there were the GIs he'd seen spreading out to the right of the dirt track and heading into the dense foliage and bracken of the woods. They would surely soon emerge from the line of trees that bordered this end, the top, of the strip.

That damned treeline was dangerously close to the parked fighters and the fuel dump in the middle. With hindsight, Koch decided, it would have been smarter of Schöln's squad to have driven the fuel truck *halfway* down the strip and left it there, along with the large fuel drums, well away from the treeline that surrounded the airstrip and any other covered positions that the Americans could use to their advantage. But then, the planes, particularly the American bomber, would still need to taxi up to this end of the strip to have enough running distance to get off the ground, the planes would still be vulnerable from shots coming out of the wood.

His thinking turned out to be timely.

From the trees he caught sight of flickering muzzle flashes and puffs of blue-tinged smoke. The bastards were aiming for the fuel drums.

A moment later one of the large fuel drums erupted. The gasoline-fuelled explosion set off the other large drums. Together they produced a large, bright orange mushroom cloud of flame that wafted lazily up into the sky, slowly turning to black smoke.

Max felt the explosion before he heard it; it was like a hot punch between his shoulders. He turned to see the flame cloud drift upwards. The ground where the drums had been was a sea of flames six or seven feet high, and, swimming through it, arms lashing out, he saw several men staggering to escape the flames.

Stef, Hans.

They'd both been handling one of the large drums.

He watched with horror as several men on fire from head to toe staggered around amidst the inferno before collapsing to their knees, and then with agonising slowness to the ground. He hoped they were dead at that point, rather than enduring the unimaginable agony any longer.

The last he had seen of his lads, they had been holding one of the large fuel drums. The blast would have killed them immediately.

He hoped.

He forced his mind to switch to practical matters. With Stef gone, he'd have to handle the navigation himself. He had undergone basic training for navigation, and had, as a matter of habit, always gone through the flight plan with his navigator before every sortie. The skills were a little rusty, but he could just about get them there. Stef had done the hard work finding their way to this small airfield.

Pieter would fly, and he would navigate. The mission could still be completed.

An image of Stef's face, stretched and contorted by the heat, flickered across his mind. He screwed his eyes shut, pushing the image away. There were fifteen hours of flying time ahead of them. There'd be plenty of time to torment himself and grieve for those two later.

The sea of flames had spread towards several of the Me-109s. He watched as one of Schröder's pilots scrambled up onto the wing of his plane and into the cockpit, as the flames licked hungrily underneath its belly. The pilot had managed to start up the engine and the plane had begun to roll forward, away from the fire, when it exploded. Two other planes followed suit and exploded in a chain reaction, one setting off the other.

The initial eruption had damaged several of the planes parked closest to the fuel drums, and with the other three destroyed, Max could only count four planes as yet undamaged. He feared, as he watched more of Schröder's men succumb to the flames, that there were now even fewer pilots left than planes.

He heard Pieter calling out, he didn't hear the words, but there was a distinct tone of relief in his usually gruff voice. Max loosened the last retaining bolt on the belly-gun blister and it clattered heavily to the ground. He emerged from beneath the bomber's belly to see Stef and Hans loping across the grass, ducking low to avoid the bullets that passed over the top of Koch's improvised defences.

He angrily slapped them on their backs as they passed. 'You two stupid bastards gave me a scare.' He hastily gestured for them to get inside. 'We're leaving, we've got as much fuel as we need,' he shouted, his voice struggling to compete with the deafening gunfight and the roar of the nearby fire.

He waited until Hans had scrambled up through the hatch and then stuck his head up inside. 'Pieter!' he shouted, his voice now beginning to sound hoarse, punished by the fumes of the smoke that was gathering around the plane. 'Start the engines. I'll be up in a second.'

He heard Stef shout, passing the message up to Pieter in the cockpit as he ducked back outside. He dropped down and made his way on all fours across to Koch's position.

'We're going now,' he shouted.

Koch turned round, his face a picture of overwhelming relief. 'About bloody time.'

Max pointed down to the far end of the strip at the Americans who were spread out across it, currently laying down fire on Büller and his men holed up in the canteen. They were going to prevent any of them taking off with the promise of a devastating wall of small-arms fire on any plane stupid enough to rumble down the strip towards them.

'I need them moved. They'll shoot us to shreds before we can get off the ground.'

Koch looked down the strip. There were twenty to thirty of them spread out across it, most of them kneeling on the grass or prone. 'I'm not sure how we can shift them. I've only got a few men left here . . . what am I supposed to do?'

'They've got to be moved, we can't take off otherwise.'

The young Captain looked around. He had seven men here; amongst the overturned tables of the canteen there were a few more men; inside the hangar with the prisoners were perhaps a couple more. He looked back at

Max; ready to shake his head and tell him it couldn't be done when his eyes rested on the fuel truck.

Max followed his gaze. He could guess what the man was thinking. 'Yes, good idea.'

'You get your plane ready to go,' said Koch.

Max held out his hand. 'Thanks. You and your men have done us proud.'

'Last skirmish of the war . . . wouldn't have missed it for anything. Let's just hope whatever it is you're up to is worth it,' Koch said grabbing his hand.

'It'll win us the war.'

Koch's eyes widened, and Max smiled reassuringly. 'Trust me . . . this has been worth it.'

A volley of bullets peppered the ground near both men, and Max decided it was time to move. 'We'll turn, and then you'll hear the engines rev up for take-off speed. That's us ready to go.'

'Understood. You'd better go now,' Koch said, offering Max a hasty salute. Max returned the gesture and then headed back towards the bomber's belly hatch at a sprint. He pulled himself up inside and clambered through the bombardier's compartment to the cockpit.

'What took you so bloody long?' said Pieter.

Chapter 45

Mission Time: 6 Hours, 12 Minutes Elapsed

8.17 a.m., an airfield outside Nantes

Koch watched as the B-17's engines roared to life and all four propellors began spinning. Almost immediately the plane began to roll forward on its wheels. It turned in a tight arc, around one hundred and eighty degrees, to face down the strip towards the GIs, who, even now, were getting ready to deliver a withering barrage of small-arms fire for the plane to hurl itself at.

Koch watched as three of the remaining, undamaged Me-109s began to move too. They pulled away from the flames, which had now subsided a little, and moved to one side to allow the bomber the room to manoeuvre.

He got to his feet and waited for a lull in the firing before scurrying across to Schöln's stack of crates. He slid down beside him as Schöln finished off firing a clip to give him a little covering fire.

'Lovely weather for it,' he said grinning at Koch.

'I'm driving the fuel truck down towards those men,' he said pointing to the Americans at the bottom of the strip. 'We need them moved before the planes can take off. Have you got any grenades?'

Schöln shook his head; he called out to the man on his right. 'Erich . . . you got grenades?' The man shook his head. 'The Captain needs grenades, pass it on.' The man nodded and the message was passed down the line.

Koch could have kicked himself. On his orders, they had shed a lot of their heavier field equipment aboard the U-boat prior to climbing aboard the dinghies. He'd wanted them to travel light. They hadn't been expecting this kind of action today. He'd ordered one or two of his men to keep hold of a couple, just to be on the safe side. He hoped that one of those men was here.

His luck was in, and a moment later he watched as several grenades were tossed gingerly from one man to the next until finally Schöln handed him three. 'Is that enough, sir?'

Koch nodded. 'That'll do.'

The bomber had turned round and was now facing down the strip. He heard the engines rise in pitch, the pilot's sign that they were ready to go.

'Pass this along, I want you all to lay down covering fire on the sandbags while I go for the truck and start it off down the strip. It's still half full of fuel, and enough shots on target by those bastards over there and it'll go up like a torch,' he said, pointing to the Americans by the sandbags, maintaining intermittent fire on them, keeping Koch and his men on the ground behind the crates.

'Yes sir, covering fire.'

The truck was only about thirty feet back from Schöln's position; Koch decided it should be relatively easy to get to the driver's cabin and start her up. Once the truck started rolling, the movement would attract everyone's attention and it would quickly become the Americans' favourite target. He hoped the covering fire would last long enough for him to drive the truck out of range of those bastards up at this end of the airfield.

'Schöln . . . make sure you keep their heads down as long as possible so I can get the truck away, all right?' The man nodded. 'Use up your ammo if you have to, but keep it going as long as possible.'

'Yes sir.'

'Right . . . pass the order on.'

Schöln bellowed the instructions out to the other men nearby, while Koch took a moment to steady his nerves. Running for the truck would be nasty, but bearing down on the men at the far end of the strip in a vehicle still carrying several thousand gallons of aviation fuel while they all concentrated their fire at him . . . that was going to be even nastier.

'We're ready when you are, sir,' said Schöln as he slid another magazine into his MP-40.

Koch slapped him on the shoulder. 'Once the planes are up, the job's done. You make sure you boys surrender, right?'

He nodded.

'Fine. Then I'll see you and Büller later.' He got to his feet, crouching, waiting for a pause in the sporadic fire of the Americans. The pause came, and Koch rose quickly, sprinting towards the truck. He reached the door to the cabin only a few seconds later, having attracted no shots whatsoever.

Just you wait until this thing begins to move.

He tugged the door open and pulled himself up inside. Despite the half a dozen or so dents and bullet holes in the vehicle's engine hood, she still started easily. He threw the truck into gear and the truck began its journey towards the far end of the strip.

'He's off!' said Max.

'What's he going to do?' asked Pieter leaning forward in his seat to look down from the cockpit window.

'I think the plan is to drive it down there and blow it up. If nothing else the smoke will hide us from them until it's too late.'

'Shit, we're taking off through smoke? What if we hit something?'

Max shrugged. 'There isn't much else we can do.'

'True.'

'Let's just get ready.'

Koch threw the truck into third gear and pushed the accelerator to the floor. The truck's suspension bounced him up and down without mercy as the wheels found the occasional dent and bump in the grass strip. Over the laboured whine of the engine he could hear the splashing of gasoline in the fuel tank behind the cabin. Ahead he could see the enemy soldiers pointing towards the truck, bringing their weapons to bear on him. Some of them started firing, but the range as yet was still far enough that most of the shots were off-target. With one hand, Koch pulled the three grenades out of the hip pocket of his camouflage jacket and laid them on the scuffed and torn leather of the passenger seat. He put the truck up another gear, and the whine of the engine dropped to an unforgiving moan that rose in pitch as he pushed the accelerator down again. The truck rolled over another small bump; its flaccid suspension bounced Koch out of his seat and the three grenades up into the air. Two landed back on the passenger seat, the third clattered onto the floor of the cabin. Ahead the Americans were now close enough to fire on him, and in well-trained unison, under the orders of an officer, they let rip.

Koch lay down on his side, still holding the steering wheel with one hand as the windscreen imploded and showered him with glass. He heard the engine hood and the radiator grill clang and shudder as a multitude of bullets began to shred the front of the vehicle. He stole a quick look over the dashboard. The men ahead of him were now the size of a thumb at arm's length, no more than forty or fifty feet away.

Now's as good a time as any.

With his knees he held the steering wheel, with his hands he grabbed one of the grenades, unscrewed the cap and grabbed hold of the fuse-string inside the handle.

Here we go.

He pulled on the string, and the grenade's fuse commenced its ten-second burn. He dropped it on the passenger seat and reached for the handle on the driver-side door.

From where they were at the top of the strip, it looked like the truck was now almost amongst the soldiers at the bottom. Max wasn't sure if the young captain had intended to blow the vehicle up or simply drive it through to distract them momentarily. If he'd intended to blow it up, Max thought he'd have done it by now. Whatever his plan, he decided it would be best that they start their way down the strip *now* and take advantage of the distraction and confusion the truck was currently causing.

Of course, there was the added danger that the truck was going to blow up just as Max lifted the plane over the top of it. The way things had gone here this morning, he wouldn't have been surprised if that was the way this mission was going to come to a messy end.

Go now or not at all.

He set the tail-wheel lock to ON, and turned to look at Pieter.

'We're going,' he said as he eased his foot off the brake and opened the throttle. The plane's four powerful engines roared angrily at 3000 rpm, and the bomber began to roll forward down the grass strip, hungrily consuming the distance between it and whatever consequence lay ahead at the end of the strip.

'Stupid damn thing's stuck!' Koch shouted aloud as he fumbled with the door handle, lying flat across the seats with one foot still down on the accelerator. He pulled hard enough on it to crack the ceramic handle, but the door remained closed.

'Shit!'

The driver-side door had taken a volley of bullets, which had dented and buckled the metal outside. The truck was still bouncing along on suspension that had given in while the truck's hood and cabin rattled and clanked with the impact of small-calibre bullets raining in. He quickly stuck his head up to snatch a glimpse through the shattered windscreen. They were no longer ahead of him; he was now amongst them. Both the passenger and driver-side windows exploded as bullets whistled in from the left and the right of him. He instinctively dropped back down onto the passenger seat as bullets slammed into all sides of the cabin. He looked down at the stick grenade in his hand.

Five . . . six . . .

For a moment he considered throwing it out through the passenger side window and aborting his plan to detonate the truck. But then there was the bomber to think about. Already he could hear it approaching, its engines roaring loudly, pulling the giant plane rapidly towards him, the truck and the American soldiers.

No, the truck needed to go up. There wasn't time now for foolish indecision.

He smiled, it might not have been a Gran Sasso, but today's fun and games had done the regiment proud.

. . . Seven . . . Eight . . .

He was intrigued about the last thing the pilot had said to him. The thing they were doing was going to *win the war for Germany* . . . so, it wasn't just an escape plan for some cowardly general. The pilot hadn't seemed like the kind of man who would part on a lie.

. . . Nine . . .

He was curious, though – how a single stolen American bomber was going to do that, win them the war.

. . . Ten . . .

Ahead, Max could see the fuel truck slowing down amongst the American soldiers. It had almost come to a full stop when it was suddenly ripped apart by an immense explosion.

'Bloody hell,' Pieter muttered, instinctively bringing his hands up to cover his face.

A brilliant ball of flame rolled upwards into the grey overcast sky, while flaming gasoline rained down around the carcass of the truck.

'We're going to fly through that!' cried Pieter.

'Over it, if we're lucky,' answered Max through clenched teeth. He checked their speed; they were running at seventy miles per hour, not fast enough yet. She would lift only over one hundred miles per hour, and they were rapidly running out of strip to achieve that speed.

'We're going to hit that bloody thing!' Pieter shouted.

There was nowhere for him to go with the throttle, and all four engines were screaming at full capacity, the ailerons were fully extended in the vertical position, there was nothing he could do but watch the fireball race towards them and hope to God that the plane lifted off before they smashed into the remains of the fuel truck.

Fifty yards to go.

Some of the Americans had been caught by the blast and had suffered the same agonising end as Schröder's men earlier. The majority, it seemed, had been far enough away to escape that, but nonetheless had been thrown off their feet by the blast. Max watched as some of them had their wits about them to scramble to their feet and grab their weapons in a last-ditch attempt to shoot out the canopy glass and prevent the plane from taking off.

He felt his face contort in anticipation of the bullets that awaited them as they approached the raging wall of fire.

Twenty yards left.

Max checked their speed, ninety-two miles per hour. He sensed the plane beginning to pull upwards, her giant wings grabbing hungrily at the air and forcing it under them.

'Hold on!' he heard himself shout as the burning chassis of the fuel truck raced towards them and disappeared from view beneath the nose of the plane. For the briefest moment the cockpit of the plane was immersed in the churning column of oily flames below.

Max felt the landing gear smash into something below, and the plane shuddered violently as it cleared the smoke.

'Shit!' Pieter shouted once more.

The plane was now at one hundred miles per hour; the lift beneath her wings and the hot air of the inferno below pushed the plane upwards. He felt the lift and pulled back on the yoke. The bomber's nose rose and they were off the ground and climbing steeply.

Schöln watched the B-17 recede to the west, tailed closely by three of the Messerschmitts. The sporadic fire from the Americans had ceased. It seemed everyone, through unconscious collaboration, had agreed to momentarily suspend the fight in order to watch what happened to the bomber as it had charged down towards the flaming truck. Now it was away, it appeared that normal business was ready to be resumed.

Koch's order had been to surrender once the planes were up. The few men that were left were probably ready to do that now; he knew he was. They'd given a good account of themselves, and more importantly the job was done. The planes had made it away.

The gunfire hadn't started up yet; it was silent save for the gentle hiss of drizzling rain, and to his right, the crackling fire amidst the burned carcasses of the 109s. He decided to take advantage of this lull.

'Okay, lads, put your weapons down,' he shouted, his voice echoed loudly across the airfield.

The men huddling behind the crates nearby did as they were ordered, clearly relieved that this particular skirmish was over. He raised his hands above his head and slowly raised his head above the crates.

A single shot rang out, thudding mercifully into the ground nearby and he immediately heard the sharp voice of an officer calling a ceasefire.

Schöln slowly got to his feet and shouted loudly in heavily accented English, 'We surrender!'

There were no further shots, and one by one the men near him rose from behind their crates, hands raised unequivocally. He saw movement from the canteen and movement from the hangar doorway. Only a single man emerged from the canteen, and three others from the hangar. Schöln totalled up the survivors. There were twelve of them left. Twelve out of the original thirty.

He thought there would have been more.

One of the American soldiers stood up from behind the sandbags and walked slowly across the grass towards Schöln, his rifle raised warily. From the uniform and rank insignia Schöln could see he was a captain. The American came to a halt a few feet away and studied him silently for a full minute, his jaw working hard behind sealed lips on a piece of gum. He shook his head and tutted like an adult admonishing a child.

'I mean ... what is it with you guys? The war's over, and yet you people still insist on giving us a hard time here.'

He shook his head once more, 'Jeeeezz ...'

Chapter 46

Getting Wallace

Mark brought the Cherokee to a halt. Devenster Street was empty save for a man walking his dog, and, across the way, three kids dressed in jeans and hooded tracksuits, doing their best to look urban. Other than that, it was deserted.

Chris scanned the road for anyone else, perhaps hiding in a shop doorway, or in the opening of some side street, or watching patiently from one of the many pools of darkness between the sparsely spread streetlights.

'It looks clear, I guess,' Chris uttered quietly, not entirely sure that it was.

'So where's this Wallace guy staying?' asked Mark.

Chris pointed towards a small, traditional-looking wooden house, halfway up the street, with a colonial-style porch in front of it. All it needed was a dinky front lawn surrounded by a white picket fence, he mused, to fit the *olde* New England cliché. 'That place over there. At least, I think that's the one.'

'Okay, how are we going to do this?'

Chris wondered whether he should just have Mark race up the street, stop and drop him outside. With the engine still running he could race inside and hopefully, by knocking on one or two doors, find and rouse the old boy quickly and then hop back into the car and speed out of town. Screw doing this carefully, he thought, just be in and out again in the bat of an eyelid.

But then, on the other hand, it might be wiser to take a more cautious approach. If those men had tracked down Wallace they could be, probably would be, watching from a distance now. They might even be using Wallace as bait, anticipating Chris would come back for him.

'Shit, I don't know Mark. They could be waiting for us,' Chris mumbled unhappily.

Mark sat upright in his seat, and nodded towards the bed and breakfast. 'Hang on! Somebody's coming out of that place,' said Mark quickly.

A door on the porch swung slowly open. Muted amber light from inside spilled out across the whitewashed woodwork momentarily. Chris could see someone coming out, the silhouetted form stooped, tired.

'I think that's him! Wallace.'

The old man shuffled out onto the porch, looking up and down the street warily. Then, he moved away from the single lamp above the door into the darkness of one corner of the porch and settled down on a seat. A moment later, Chris saw the momentary flicker of a cigarette lighter, and, a few seconds later, a cloud of pale blue smoke emerged from the darkness, caught in the amber glow of the porch light.

Having a hard time getting to sleep.

It was not surprising at all, given how jumpy he had been earlier that night in Lenny's. Even if he hadn't been jumped by those two goons in his room, Chris wondered if he would have been able to get much sleep tonight. His mind had begun going to work on the story as he had headed back from Lenny's – which pictures he would use, whether to take the story to any larger publication or dutifully deliver it to *News Fortnite* first.

Wallace was probably just as wound up and twitchy as he was. And right now, Chris could happily have joined him indulging in some nerve-settling cigarette-therapy. The nicotine gum his jaws were industriously working on was doing no bloody good at all.

Why's he sitting outside for a fag? Probably some stringent 'no smoking' policy inside the bed and breakfast, he decided, answering his own question. Then again, maybe the old boy felt a whole lot safer watching the road outside. After this evening's run-in, Chris could empathise with that. Right now there was no way he could see himself curling up in a nice warm quilt somewhere and nodding off, not with some armed psychotic nuts out there roaming the town looking for him.

'Well, that makes our job a whole bunch easier, then. You ready to do this?' said Mark, his hands firmly gripping the steering wheel.

'Okay, mate, nice and easy. Let's not tear up the street and burn rubber in front of him. We'd probably kill him with the shock.'

Mark nodded and had begun to slowly ease the vehicle forward. It was then that Chris spotted something reflective glinting in the darkness towards the other end of the street. 'Hold the phone, what's that?'

'What?' replied Mark.

'I saw something,' said Chris, 'up the other end.'

It emerged out of the darkness, the light from the streetlamp above flickering across the windscreen. A dark, unmarked van approached them from the opposite end of Devenster Street. Like them, it was rolling forward slowly, with the headlights off.

'That doesn't look good,' said Mark.

'Fuck it then, just go!' snapped Chris. 'I'll jump out and grab him.'

Mark pushed the pedal down hard, and with a squeal of rubber that robbed the quiet town of its silence, the Cherokee lurched forward down the narrow road towards the old man. The van, still several hundred yards up the street, further away than them, all of a sudden turned on its headlights and accelerated, the driver obviously aware that he had been spotted and casting caution aside.

Mark slammed the brakes on outside the bed and breakfast, the vehicle slewing to a halt. Chris leaped out of the passenger side and up the steps to the porch, taking the gun with him.

'Wallace! Get up!' he shouted as he approached the old man. Wallace's eyes widened with fear when he saw the handgun. 'What's going –?' he managed to splutter before Chris grabbed him roughly by the arm and pulled him up out of the chair.

The van came to a noisy halt on the opposite side of the street. Chris saw the driver-side and passenger-side doors swing open and the dark shapes of two men emerge. From their profiles, and the way one of them moved, he guessed they were the same two men he had encountered a little earlier. That wasn't so good, since the older guy with the crewcut hadn't seemed too worried last time about using his gun indiscriminately.

'Quick!' he heard Mark shout from the Cherokee.

Chris started down the steps of the porch dragging Wallace after him, half expecting shots from across the road to already be coming at him.

'Stop!' he heard one of the men call out. Both men had their arms raised, and legs spread, both aiming handguns.

Trained firing stance.

The posture was a learned one, Chris noted fleetingly, not the Tarantino posture you see gangsters adopt in the movies. These guys were definitely agency or ex-agency.

Wallace was panicking, struggling, tugging against Chris as best he could. He realised he must have scared the old boy waving the Heckler and Koch in his face.

'Don't piss around. Keep moving!' Chris shouted at him as they hit the pavement. He pulled the back door of the Cherokee open, and then all but hurled the old man across the back seat.

And that was when both men across the road decided to start firing.

This time neither of their guns were fitted with sound suppressors, and the crack of gunfire bounced off the wooden walls down the still street.

Two bullets whistled over the roof of the car as Chris ducked down. '*Shitshitshit*,' he muttered.

The kids up the street started yelling in panic and dropped to the ground. The man walking his dog dived into a shop doorway.

Mark ducked down in his seat, as best his big frame could, at the same time reaching into the back to push Wallace's head down. 'Just stay low!' he shouted, as Wallace, still it seemed bewildered by the sudden and rapid sequence of events, tried to sit up.

Chris stuck his gun over the roof of the car, not aiming, and fired the entire clip of twelve rounds towards the van. Both of the men dropped down behind their open doors as several of the bullets thudded noisily into the side of the van, dislodging a shower of paint flecks.

Chris used the mere seconds of time that he had bought himself as both men cautiously waited for any more follow-up shots to come their way before they stuck their heads back up. Chris raced around the back of the Cherokee and pull open the passenger-side door.

'Go GO GO!' he yelled as he hurled himself in.

Mark once more floored the accelerator and the vehicle rode the pavement before swinging back onto the road and down the street. Chris twisted round in his seat and looked back through the rear window to see one of the men aiming his gun at the retreating vehicle, the other one climbing back into the van.

Wallace looked up at Chris, seeing the gun in his hand. 'What . . . what're you going to –?'

'Just shut up a sec',' he muttered as he watched the van shrink into the distance. It was beginning to turn round, but its size, and the relatively narrow width of the street, meant that it had to do a two-point turn, buying them a few more seconds.

'Mark, get us onto the interstate and then we'll take the next turning off. I really don't give a toss where that takes us!'

'You got it,' replied Mark, his trademark demeanour of calm once more returning. Chris was glad that Mark had a cool head in a tight situation, and that it was him behind the wheel right now. If Chris had been driving, they undoubtedly would have hit every street lamp and post box on the way out of town.

He continued to watch the van through the rear window until, turning the corner at the end of Devenster, he lost sight of it. Then he looked down at the old man, still lying prone across the back seat. 'We ran into those bastards a little earlier. I think they were looking for you.'

Wallace said nothing. Chris couldn't tell if it was unmitigated relief or abject fear that had rendered the old boy speechless.

Chapter 47

Mission Time: 6 Hours, 22 Minutes Elapsed

150 miles across the Atlantic

Max heaved a sigh of relief. The coast of France had been left behind them. The only hint of its presence being a thin, grey line on the horizon, the thick cloudbank that had seemed to end where the Atlantic started. The heavy skies seemed to be for Europe only, blue skies for the rest of the world.

They had been flying on a steady course of two-seventy degrees, due west, at an altitude of 4500 feet, just low enough that they'd been able to do without the oxygen system.

Max was certain that the Americans would have scrambled several squadrons of fighters to deal with them. They surely had to have some stationed near enough to the airfield they'd just left to easily intercept them before they flew beyond fighter range. All of them had kept a silent vigil, scanning the skies behind them intently for the first signs of an avenging vee formation.

'That was bloody hairy,' said Pieter over the interphone.

Hans was the first to reply. 'Whose piece-of-shit idea was that?'

'Well it's not like we had a lot of choice,' Max replied wearily. 'Given the way things turned out, it was lucky we did.'

'I'm sure there must've been an easier way,' grunted Hans.

Stef's voice piped up. 'Sir, I've been doing –'

'For Christ's sake, Stef, you can call me Max now.'

'Yeah,' added Pieter, 'I reckon you've earned that by now, Baby Bear.'

'Ahh, shit, Pieter, can you stop calling me that!' answered Stef, his boyish voice rising angrily.

Max nodded. 'Cut him some slack, eh?'

'Thanks, sir ... Max.'

Pieter cast a sideways glance at him. 'Aha ... the boy's finally learning.'

'He's old enough to fiddle with his balls and scratch his arse now,' Hans added helpfully.

'Hans, you'd know, wouldn't you?' said Stef.

'What're you talking about?'

'You're always scratching and rubbing your arse.'

'Not all the time!'

'Errr ... you do, Hans; we've all seen you at it. You can never leave your arse alone,' contributed Pieter.

'It wouldn't be so bad if you didn't sniff your fingers afterwards.'

'Yeah? Well, you little red-haired weasel-boy, when we're done today I'm going to ram my fist down your throat, then you can taste it for yourself and see.'

The rest of his crew laughed lightly. Max smiled; it was good to hear the banter pass to and fro between them once more. It had been a while since he'd heard them fool around like that. He looked out of his side window to see Schröder's fighter out to one side maintaining a steady position a hundred yards out from their port wingtip.

He switched to radio. 'How're things with you, Schröder?'

'Fine ... fine.' His voice sounded flat, neutral. He knew Schröder was dwelling on those of his men he had lost back on the ground. Certainly they had not long been acquainted, and in no way was it the pilot's fault that they had been caught in that explosion. But as the leader of a group of men it was his burden to feel responsible for them.

'That was a close-run thing,' said Max.

'Yes, very hectic.'

'I'm sorry. You lost a lot of good men, Schröder.'

'Yes ... the best.'

'That's never easy.'

'No.'

Schröder didn't elaborate, but Max knew he was replaying the appalling scene in his mind. The churning sea of flames, those men flailing slowly in agony ... unpleasantly slowly. When he replayed that image in his mind, it struck him that some of those poor bastards had been struggling for thirty seconds before they'd succumbed. It had probably been one of the worst things he'd ever witnessed during this war. And that was saying a lot.

'We needed to make that stop, it was necessary, Schröder.'

'You think so?'

'If it hadn't been for that airfield, this mission would be over. That would have been an end to it. We'd never have made it across on the fuel we had.'

'Well, maybe, we'll see if it's all been worth it when you've dropped your bomb,' Schröder replied tersely.

Right now it sounded like he wanted to be left to himself.

Max couldn't blame him. In the sky, one on one with a squadron of American fighter pilots flying their superior P51s, Schröder and his men had magnificently displayed their skill, their experience and courage, taking only one casualty while inflicting nine. On the ground, amidst the confusion, he had lost nearly all of his men to a single well-aimed bullet.

'What's your fuel situation?'

'Not bad ... let me talk with Günter and Will.'

Just three of the fighters had managed to make it off the ground, bursting through the wall of flames above the fuel truck, only seconds behind them. Just three. If they came across another squadron, Max didn't fancy their chances.

'We all have about the same amount of fuel, approximately a quarter of a tank each ... we didn't have time on the ground to fill up properly.'

'That gives you about two hundred miles, before you need to go back. I'll have Stef call out a warning at one hundred, one-fifty and final warning at one-seventy-five.'

Schröder was some time responding, but he eventually came back just as Max was about to repeat his last message. 'Fine.'

Max had suspected the landing was going to be risky. They all had. But none of them suspected it would be that bad. Rall, starved of good local intelligence, had been forced to make an assumption that there would not be troops stationed close enough to respond so quickly to the airstrip being taken.

It had been bad luck. Koch's men had done well to keep the Americans at bay for so long. He hoped the young captain had managed to bail out of that fuel truck before it went up.

'Max!' Hans shouted over the interphone. 'We've got some coming in on our four o'clock!' Pieter leaned forward and looked out of his window, craning his neck to look backwards.

'He's right, looks like about six or seven of them, fighters ... I can't see what type.'

'Okay, Pieter, this time you better take the bombardier's gun. Stef?'

'Yes sir!'

'I want you on the waist-gun. Hans, you're on the tail-gun.'

Hans had trained himself to use the tail-gun, which was the only gun that had not been replaced with MG-81s, and remained duel Brownings. 'Training' had been little more than reading the tail-gunner section of the B-17 Flight Crew Manual and firing off a few dozen rounds of the limited supply of 0.5 inch ammo the plane carried. But he was ready to use it in anger now.

It was sensible for Stef to be in the comparatively safer waist-gun position, with fuel and range now the most crucial variable of the mission; he needed their navigator alive and well to ensure the most efficient route across. They could scarcely afford to lose him and drift valuable miles off course.

Or maybe he was just trying to keep the young lad out of harm's way.

Both Hans and Stef confirmed their orders and began to scramble to their positions.

'Schröder, bandits, four high.'

'We've seen them. Listen, we will have to engage them close to you, so that you can bring your guns to bear on them. My men and I are low on ammunition.'

Schröder was right. They stood a better chance if the dog fighting went on within range of the B-17's gun positions – the bomber's guns had plenty of ammo to burn, and the additional firepower would go at least some way towards levelling the playing field.

Max debated whether to lock the plane with the autopilot and man the forward-gun position. He had fired an MG-81 several times, but was, by no stretch of the imagination, a good shot. He might not hit anything, but the additional firepower couldn't hurt. But then, if the plane took damage to any of the engines or flaps, there would need to be someone in control to react immediately.

He decided he would be better remaining in his seat.

'Schröder, we jettisoned our belly gun and our starboard waist-gun, you need to lead them in on our port side, or to the rear of the plane, to get the benefit of our guns. Have you got that?' he called to Schröder.

'Uh-huh. I'll try. Good luck.'

Max switched back to the interphone. 'This one's going to be nasty. We've only three of our little friends looking after us, and six of them coming in. Schröder and his men are bringing the fight close to us so that we can back them up with our guns. Hans? You in position yet?'

'Yeah, just about,' he grunted as he squeezed his large frame into the cramped confines of the tail-gunner's position.

'Hans,' called Pieter, 'any tips for me and Stef?'

'Yeah . . . yeah, just make sure you draw a good lead. Ten yards in front of the target for every two hundred yards target range. Fire in bursts no longer than two seconds, the heat causes the guns to lock.'

'Thanks, you big ape. Make sure you save some for me and Stef.'

Max decided to quieten them down. 'Let's keep the comm. clear. I want to hear sightings and confirmed kills, nothing else until we're out of this.'

His crew murmured assent.

A moment later, Hans' voice came across loudly. 'I can see 'em now. Spitfires! Goddamn Spitfires! Three of them are engaging our boys, three splitting off and coming for us!'

Oh shit . . . here we go again.

Chapter 48

Mission Time: 6 Hours, 24 Minutes Elapsed

180 miles across the Atlantic

Schröder pulled up steeply and rolled to his left as the three bandits rose up to meet them. He found himself laughing aloud. This was good, old-style dog fighting. One on one, the sort of duelling he had excelled in during the early days of the war.

He quickly scanned the sky to grab a snapshot of the entire skirmish, momentarily placing all nine other aircraft taking part in this particular exchange.

'Pull these buggers after us down and to the left, and we'll lead them close to Max's lads,' he said, struggling to keep his voice calm and measured.

'Yes sir,' both other fighter pilots replied.

The three Me-109s rolled over and dived down towards the left, one tidily behind the other like the carriages of a train. They raced past the three Spitfires still rising to meet them and all six planes fired speculative bursts in the hope of scoring some early damage. Several hundred bullets whistled angrily through the air between the two formations of advancing planes.

None of them hit anything.

Schröder's guns clattered uselessly as the last of his ammo belts fed through.

I'm out.

He realised all he could do for now was play bait for the Spitfires and lure them in as close as he dared towards the bomber's guns. As Schröder and his men descended to a position several hundred yards behind and to the left of the B-17, the Spitfires mirrored their arc of descent and followed their route around and down. Within a few fleeting seconds they would be lined up behind the Me-109s and in a perfect position to start shredding pieces off of them.

Meanwhile, the other three British fighter planes were ascending towards the bomber from the right. Schröder hoped that Max's boys could see them approaching and had at least one gun trained on them as they came in.

Behind them, Schröder could sense the Spitfires falling into a comfortable tailing position, closing the gap swiftly. Any second now he expected them to commence fire, but not yet. From their tidy manoeuvring he suspected these pilots were experienced. They would want to pull in a little closer before firing to guarantee a more effective opening salvo and avoid wasting rounds. A sensible ploy, but not without its downside, as Schröder had learned from experience. Many a time an enemy plane had escaped him, scrambling out from beneath the lethal gaze of his crosshair because he'd waited a second too long to get a better, cleaner, closer shot.

He hoped those Spitfires behind them were making the same mistake, holding off one or two seconds too long to get a guaranteed kill with the first volley.

Time to move.

'On my command . . . Günter, Will, break right and left, I'll lead the first of them in,' he called out.

'Break!' he shouted a second later.

Both flanking Me-109s rolled in opposite directions and dived, and two of the Spitfires followed in hot pursuit leaving one doggedly following Schröder as he veered to the right and subtly closed the gap, drawing it closer to the B-17. The unfortunate British fighter pilot was about to find out for himself what sort of damage the tail-gun of a flying fortress can deal out.

The bomber grew in size as Schröder led his pursuer in towards the rear of the plane. Just as he'd begun to suspect the tail-gunner was sleeping on the job, the duel barrels suddenly opened up, firing twin streaks of tracers into the empty space between Schröder and the British fighter. The bullets sped past in front of the Spitfire and drifted quickly back as the tail-gunner adjusted his lead. Half a dozen bullets found their mark along the right hand side of the fighter's fuselage and almost immediately a thin whisper of leaking oil trailed out from the Spitfire. The British pilot seemed unperturbed and calmly held position for a few seconds more before firing a burst of gunfire that clipped the tail of Schröder's Messerschmitt.

Schröder pulled up sharply, hoping the Spitfire would follow suit and expose her underbelly to the bomber's left-hand waist-gun, but instead the

British pilot seemed already to have learned the error of his ways and pulled warily away from the bomber.

At the same time, the other three Spitfires that had split away to specifically target the bomber rose one after the other and raked the underside of the flying fortress as they climbed effortlessly past her. The belly of the bomber shed a small shower of fragments that twisted and spun away below her.

As the three fighter planes streamed up past him to his right, less than fifty yards away, Max fleetingly caught sight of one of the British pilots, twisting round in his seat to look back at the bomber as they climbed up into the sky and prepared to come around for another pass.

For some reason they both nodded courteously at each other.

Pieter spun the bombardier's gun upwards and fired a largely ineffective volley at the last of the three planes, his aim insufficiently in advance of his target, the bullets flew harmlessly behind it. Max heard Pieter cursing angrily over the comm.

'Pieter! . . . shut up!' he found himself shouting.

'Sorry,' he answered sheepishly.

Schröder still had that stubborn bastard on his tail. He was good. The Spitfire was proving bloody hard to shake off. Once again he quickly scanned the sky, attempting to grab another updated snapshot of their little skirmish.

He could see one of the Me-109s trailing a thick pall of black smoke and descending in a shallow dive away from the party and down towards the sea in an easterly direction. Schröder couldn't tell if it was Will or Günter. Whoever it was, he presumably was heading back to France in the futile hope that the plane would get him all the way back to land.

One of the Spitfires was also spouting smoke, with the other 109 in hot pursuit. As he watched, the Spitfire was caught by a further well-aimed burst that carved through the starboard wing like a saw through dry wood. A short trail of tumbling debris was left in the plane's wake. Suddenly, the wing ripped off and the plane instantly rolled over and commenced a slow spiralling dive towards the sea.

One of ours and one of theirs.

They needed to do better than that. Schröder pulled his plane up and once more led the obstinate British pilot behind him towards the rear of the bomber again, hoping that whichever one of Max's lads was manning that position could work his magic once again and land a dozen more shots on target.

The three Spitfires that had successfully raked the underside of the bomber had so far been untroubled by either the Me-109s or any fire from the bomber. They turned around in a graceful arc above the B-17 and were now approaching from the front, head on, in a steep predatory dive.

Max looked up in horror as he realised they were lining up to make the cockpit their next target.

'Pieter! Three of them coming fast, twelve-high!'

He imagined what three Spitfires in a tightly formed train, each firing about five seconds worth of .303 millimetre rounds one after the other into the small, enclosed space of the cockpit, would do to him and the plane.

'Pieter! Do you see them!' he called again, this time his voice breaking nervously.

Max could do little but watch their rapid approach. He could pull the bomber into a climb, push her into a dive or roll the plane left or right, but he knew the plane was so slow to manoeuvre that there would be no way they'd avoid the incoming fighters. All he'd be doing is putting his gunners off balance.

'I see 'em Max, I see 'em!'

Pieter swung his gun up and carefully lined the gun sight with the first of the three planes. *Ten yards for every two hundred range.*

He pulled his aim down slightly, anticipating the continued path of the leading Spitfire. 'Come on, you little bastards,' he muttered to himself.

The plane in the lead was holding his shot until the very last moment, two hundred feet away and still Max waited with a face screwed up with anticipation for the first high-calibre round to strike home and begin the process of shredding him and the front of the plane to pieces.

Suddenly, he saw the muzzle flash of the fighters' six guns blazing and tracer lines began to lance down through the air just short of the bombardier's compartment in front of the plane.

At the same instant from the compartment below, Max heard Pieter open fire.

Both Pieter and the pilot appeared to have overdone their target-lead, but in the few seconds that were left before the bomber's cockpit resembled nothing more than the chewed-up knuckle of a dog's bone, Pieter was going to have to pull his aim up and hit the Spitfire first.

'For fuck's sake, draw in the lead!' Max shouted with desperate frustration as the fighter found the nose of the plane and dozens of rounds punctured holes through the metal plate above the bombardier's compartment and below the cockpit.

He winced as loose shards of debris rattled around in the compartment below him with bullet-like velocity. Pieter surely had to have been hit by some of that, a bullet or shrapnel. But he could hear the gun still firing. Max watched as the tracer lines from Pieter's gun rose up from below and found their target.

The duel MG-81s, firing a steady line of tracers, shattered the cockpit glass of the leading Spitfire and the fighter plane ceased its firing immediately, speeding down, missing the nose of the bomber by mere feet. Pieter continued firing towards the same point in space, knowing that the second and third fighters were lined up directly behind where the first one had been. The two other Spitfires cautiously avoided the solid line of fire coming up towards them and broke in different directions, roaring past the cockpit on either side, their attacking dive foiled this time.

Max heard Pieter hooting with pleasure. 'Got ya', you stupid bastards!'

The idiot sounded okay.

He felt a rush of relief and, with a gasp, released a breath that only seconds earlier he'd been convinced would be his last. 'Saved my skin, Pieter . . . are *you* okay?'

'Apart from nearly shitting myself, I'm fine.'

You and me both.

Schröder pulled past the port side, the tip of his wing yards from that of the bomber's, rising upwards in a steep sixty-degree climb, the same damned Spitfire pursuing with single-minded, dogged determination. It fired again; this time the bullets thudded into the underside of his fuselage, one tearing through the flimsy metal plating into his cockpit, where it fractured against the solid metal frame on the under side of his seat, sending a spray of heated shards and sparks up at him past his legs.

He felt a white-hot pain shoot up his right arm as the leather of his flying jacket exploded and a fine spray of crimson appeared on the inside of his canopy.

'Shit! Bitch!' he screamed out in pain.

As the Spitfire rushed hungrily in pursuit of Schröder, sensing the kill was only a volley or two away, it passed carelessly close to the port waist-gun.

Stef jerked back in surprise as it roared upwards, only twenty feet away and he panic-squeezed the trigger, his aiming, at best, erratic. The MG-81 pumped forty-plus rounds at close range into the exposed belly of the British fighter plane. One of the rounds punctured one of the Spitfire's wing tanks and the plane instantly exploded, punching the bomber in the ribs with a powerful shockwave and a fleeting moment later showering the waist section with fragments of shrapnel and burning gasoline.

'Fucking hell! What was that?' shouted Hans over the comm.

'Anyone know what that was? asked Max.

'I think Stef just bagged one. Stef, was that yours?'

There was no answer.

Schröder rolled his plane over, belly up, and pulled back on the yoke so that the plane began a long, graceful arc downwards. He looked 'up' to see the bomber below against the dark blue background of the Atlantic. A mushroom cloud of oily smoke was being left behind it, and beneath the cloud he saw hundreds of tiny fragments each tumbling and fluttering to the sea on its own spiralling path.

There was no sign of the Spitfire any more.

He noticed a fire burning along the bomber's spine and guessed that the Spitfire had exploded and sprayed burning fuel onto the bomber's back. It looked worse than it was. The fuel would burn out in a few seconds.

He hoped whoever it was who'd saved his life hadn't been caught by the blast. It seemed unlikely, though; he could see what looked like hundreds of pebbledash spots along her waist section. Whoever had fired the port waist-gun had probably been shredded by the wall of shrapnel.

He turned his attention to the score sheet . . .

Three of theirs, one of ours. Much better.

Once more his eyes quickly searched the sky around him. He watched as the other Me-109 hung tightly to the tail of a Spitfire that was already in trouble, a white stream of unignited fuel behind it. It fired several short bursts. None found their target, but that seemed academic, the plane was desperately scrambling to find a way out of the skirmish.

'Who is that? Will? Let him go and form up with me behind the bomber.'

The radio crackled and a moment later the pilot replied. 'It's me, sir, Günter.'

'Günter? Well done, man. It's just us now. Let's tighten our position around the bomber.'

'Yes, sir.'

Chapter 49

Mission time: 6 Hours,
28 Minutes Elapsed

200 miles across the Atlantic

There was still no reply from Stef.

'Stef! Are you all right?' Max called once more. Over the interphone he could hear only laboured breathing and the grunting of effort as both Pieter and Hans worked their guns.

Not Stef, please.

'You want me to go back and take a look?' asked Pieter over the comm.

'No, not yet, not until we're done here.'

Max himself wanted to go back and see what had happened to the young lad, but until this exchange was over, he needed every pair of hands busy, holding something useful.

'They've had enough! They're pissing off!' Hans barked loudly.

'You sure? Pieter, can you see?' Max sought confirmation.

'Yup, two of them, plus one limping. They're heading back east.'

'Right, in that case, Pieter, go and see what's happened to Stef.'

Pieter climbed up the metal rungs leading from the bombardier's compartment and hastily made his way through the bomb bay and through the navigation compartment. He stopped in the bulkhead leading into the waist section and studied the damage.

It had been perforated with hundreds of ragged holes. Several small fires were burning on the wood-panelled floor, fuel that had made its way inside from the exploding Spitfire. Stef was sitting on the floor, both hands clasped tightly around one of his legs, holding it desperately. His trouser leg was black and wet with blood. Considering the mess there, the lad looked like he'd got away lightly.

'I think I'm hurt pretty badly,' he said.

'Stef. Let me take a look at that.'

Pieter squatted beside him, ripped the ragged material of his trousers open and moved it out of the way to inspect the wounded leg. There was a triangle of still smoking metal, the size of a packet of cigarettes, lodged into his leg just above the knee. It had clearly severed an artery and Stef had done the best he could with the tight grip of his hands to slow down the blood loss. All the same, the wound was pumping muted jets of blood past his tightly clasped fingers.

'Not too bad, boy,' said Pieter doing his best to sound in charge and calm. 'We'll need to get a tourniquet on that,' he added looking around for something to use. He ripped off the rest of Stef's trouser leg and from that tore a strip long enough to tie around his leg above the knee. He secured it around and tied it up. 'We need something we can use to wind it tighter. Something long and thin.'

'Like your pecker?' Stef grunted painfully.

Pieter smiled and knuckled the lad's head. 'At least it's long.'

He found a socket wrench in a toolbox beneath the port waist-gun. He inserted the wrench between Stef's leg and the tourniquet.

'Now this is going to hurt a lot, sorry.' He twisted it round once and the tourniquet tightened with a creak. Stef let out a scream of agony that he quickly bit down on, turning it into little more than a stifled whimper.

Pieter winced sympathetically. 'It's okay, you can let it out if it hurts.'

Stef shook his head stubbornly, his mouth clamped tightly like a vice, refusing to let out anything more than a grunt.

Pieter patted him roughly on the shoulder. 'So . . . no more of that "Baby Bear" shit, then. I promise.'

The boy smiled. That was about as much praise as he would get from the bastard. But it was more than enough.

'You're not going to pass out, are you?'

Stef shook his head, 'I'm okay,' he hissed painfully.

'You hold that tight for me, right? I'm going to let Max know what's going on back here.'

Stef leaned back against the bulkhead and held the wrench in both hands as Pieter stamped out a couple of the small fires which were still burning on the wooden floor and then made his way forward to update Max.

'We're both fine. Günter didn't take a single scratch, and my plane, amazingly, appears to still be in one piece,' said Schröder, holding the yoke with his right hand, his left clamped tightly over the gash in his right forearm. 'Will didn't make it, though.'

'I know, I saw him go down,' Max replied.

Even if he had managed to bail safely, out at sea, there was little hope for him. If he didn't get pulled under by the parachute and drown immediately after he splashed down, he was unlikely to be picked up by any ship.

'A good thing the three of you made it off the airstrip. They would have had us.'

'Then the refuel was worth it,' Schröder offered.

'I've got to check the damage and get a navigational plotting, and I think one of my crew's hurt. Let me deal with these things and then I'll tell you how we're doing for range.'

'Of course, speak with you soon.'

Schröder checked his fuel gauge. He had lost too much in the last few minutes to be accounted for by the manoeuvres he'd pulled during that skirmish. He must have taken a hit on the fuel tank and was losing it quickly.

'Günter, am I leaving a trail?'

The reply was prompt. 'Yes, sir. Looks like fuel.'

He cursed under his breath. That was that, then, he wouldn't be making it back to France. Günter might be able to make it back, though.

'What's *your* fuel reading?'

'Good, I have about a fifth capacity left sir.'

They were roughly 235 miles out from the French coast and he had a fifth of his fuel left to burn. He could make it back if he turned around right now.

'Günter?'

'Yes, sir?'

'You need to head home now. Fly low, you should make it back to France.'

The young pilot failed to respond.

'Did you hear me? You need to turn around.'

'What about you, sir?'

'I'll be fine for another half an hour, then I'll need to be heading back too.'

There was a pause; the young pilot was going to foolishly object. 'Günter, that's a bloody order, now piss off back to France.'

'Yes, sir . . . Good luck, sir.'

'And you . . . now go!'

Schröder could tell by the tone in Günter's voice that the young man had guessed he was in trouble. He watched as the young pilot pulled his plane around in a roll that arced one-eighty degrees, taking him back east. Günter waggled his wings once in the distance.

Schröder looked back down at his fuel gauge again, the pointer was wobbling unsteadily and indicating that he was virtually empty, with only the unreliable promise of another half an hour's flying time, at best.

Max kneeled beside Stef and inspected the wound.

'We're going to need to tie this wrench in place so the tourniquet doesn't unwind if you lose consciousness. Pieter, go find something we can tie this up with.'

'What?'

'Anything! Just look around.'

Max turned back to Stef. 'How are you feeling?'

'The tourniquet's painful, sir, really hurts,' he said between gritted teeth.

'Well it's got to stay tight, Stef. There's a severed artery in there, which we've got to keep the pressure on for the next thirteen hours. I'm going to tie up this wrench to the side of your leg so this thing doesn't unwind, and you're going to need to sit as still as you can until this thing is done and we can get you to a doctor, all right?'

The young lad nodded.

'We need you to get us there. While you can still focus I need you to navigate. Think you can do that?'

He nodded once more.

'Hans?'

The big man stepped forward. 'Yeah?'

'You'll need to get Stef's things; the map, his navigation tools, and bring them all here.'

Max looked around the waist section. The wind whipped noisily in through the gun portholes and numerous punctures along the metal fuselage. 'And see if you can find something to put over him to keep him warm.'

'Yeah,' he said again and stooped through the bulkhead leading to the navigation compartment.

'What's the damage, sir? Are we going to make it?' asked Stef.

'We're doing fine, don't you worry about the plane, they built these things to take far worse than we've taken today.'

One engine had been hit and begun to splutter and Max had turned it off, fearing the engine might cause the fuel feeding it to ignite. They could make their way across on three. Apart from that, they had fared well, all things considered. The landing gear was damaged, possibly even ripped off completely. None of these things would prevent them completing the mission. Max's only worry now was whether they had the fuel to get them there.

That's *all* that mattered now, fuel . . . everything else was secondary.

Pieter returned with an open parachute bail. 'I found it in the bombardier's compartment. It's useless, cut to ribbons.'

'That'll do,' said Max taking it from him and hastily ripping a long strip from the silky fabric. He held the wrench against Stef's thigh.

'Is that still tight?'

Stef nodded, gritting his teeth. Max wound the parachute fabric firmly around his leg and the wrench binding them tightly together.

'This should hold up if you don't move around. If you start leaking, for God's sake give me a shout and we'll tighten this thing up again.' He patted him on the cheek. 'We need you with us, right?'

'Yes, sir.'

Max's eyebrows knitted in a mock frown. 'Call me "sir" one more time and I'll undo it and let you bleed to death.'

Stef grinned. 'Yes, Max.'

'When Hans has brought you your things, I need you to give me your best guess on our position now. Think you can do that?'

Stef gave Max a thumbs-up. His leather glove was black with drying blood.

'Good lad,' Max replied and then made his way forward, squeezing past Hans in the navigation booth. 'Keep your eye on him, Hans, he's lost a lot of blood,' he muttered under his breath.

'You think he's going to make it?'

'I don't know. If he doesn't lose any more, he might. Just keep an eye on his leg. The blood's drying up now. If it looks wet again, then he needs to be tightened up some more.'

Max passed through the bulkhead into the bomb compartment, and stopped for a moment to look down at the small bomb, still resting snugly in its cradle. It appeared untouched by their skirmishes.

You'd better do what you're supposed to do, you little shit.

He made his way into the cockpit, plugged into the comm. and disengaged the autopilot. He noticed that they had lost one of the Me-109s.

'Schröder? You still there?'

'Yes, Max. Günter had to turn back, his fuel was running low.'

'How are *you* doing? Surely you'll need to head back soon?'

'No . . . it looks like I'll be staying alongside you for the duration.'

Both of them knew what that meant for Schröder.

'How long have you got?' Max asked.

'Just under a half an hour's worth, I would guess. Maybe less.'

'You don't think it's worth a go turning round and trying for land?'

'If I fly slow and low?'

'There's a chance for you, isn't there?'

'No. I think I'd be swimming the last bit, and to be honest with you, Max, I'm not a big fan of swimming.'

'I understand. Anyway, we're still within range of their P51s . . . you might yet need to save our skins one more time.'

'While I've fuel, I'll do my best.'

Ten minutes passed with merciful peace as Max watched Schröder's Messerschmitt hovering to their left, less than a hundred feet away, abreast with the bomber's cockpit. He watched the man checking his instrumentation, occasionally looking up at the sky, around, keeping an eye out for any pursuing planes. Time and fuel ticked away too quickly and presently Max heard the engine of Schröder's Messerschmitt cough and misfire.

Schröder looked across at him, and he heard the pilot's voice. 'I'm all out now. The engine's beginning to skip.'

Pieter looked across at the fighter pilot. His distaste for the man had been replaced with a muted, begrudging respect at some point over the last twelve hours.

'Poor bastard,' he muttered to Max.

'With your permission I'm going to take her up,' said Schröder.

Max knew what the fighter pilot was up to. 'Of course. You do what you have to, Schröder.'

'Thank you. Well, it's been an honour, gentlemen. I should think you're now clear of any trouble from this side, good luck with the rest of it.'

'Thank you. It was our honour too.'

Schröder nodded and waved at them and pulled his plane up and away into a steep climb.

'What's he planning to do?'

'He's going to throw her into a dive. The impact will give him a quick finish, I think that's what he's after.'

They watched him climb above them to 10,000 feet and level out. He held that position for a few seconds and then waggled the wings a couple of times before dropping the nose into a steep dive. The Me-109 plummeted through the sky half a mile away, and twenty seconds later it plunged into the sea. They watched a small, pale plume of water rise and fall, and a circle of foam fade away, leaving no trace of the airplane behind.

Pieter shook his head.

'Better than bailing out here. Freeze or drown, they're not great options.'

Max watched as a dark plume of oil began to stain the water where Schröder had hit. It blossomed on the calm ocean like a dark rose. He hoped it had been the quick finish the pilot was after.

'Just us now, Pieter.'

'Yes,' he replied. His response was muted. 'I suppose we're all that's left of the Luftwaffe – the last operational plane.'

'Probably.'

He checked his watch and their airspeed. They had about twelve hours' flying time to New York ahead of them. They were clear of any fighter threat now, and Pieter deserved a chance to spend some time doing something. It was time to hand over to him, and, in any case, he was suddenly aware of how tired he felt.

'You can take her for a few hours,' he said to Pieter. 'I'm going to try and get some rest, if that's possible.'

'You do that, you look like crap,' said Pieter. 'We're going to make it now, aren't we, Max?'

'I think we are. There's nothing left they can throw in our way now.'

It was nothing but deep blue sea all the way to America.

Max unplugged from the comm. and climbed out of the pilot's seat, suddenly aware of how stiff and drained he felt now that the danger was all behind them, and the adrenalin that had been pounding through his veins since take-off early this morning had finally subsided.

'I'll see how Stef is and get a dead reckoning off him before I get some shut-eye.'

'Alright.'

Max ducked through the bulkhead into the bomb bay and ducked again as he passed from the navigation compartment into the waist section. Stef was sprawled on the floor between the gun portholes where he'd left him, but was now covered in a thick grey blanket.

'I found it in a storage locker,' said Hans, sitting beside Stef, tucked up into a ball and hugging himself to stay warm.

'Go sit up front with Pieter if you want,' he said. It was much warmer in the cockpit, not having any openings to the cold wind outside and bathed in the sunlight streaming in through the cockpit windows.

'Thanks.' Hans clambered forward through the bulkhead.

The young man was still sleeping. Spread across Stef's lap was the map he'd been using since they'd left the airstrip outside Nantes. He'd calculated a dead reckoning and circled it on the map with the time of the estimate. It was only fifteen minutes old.

Good boy.

Max laid the map out flat on the wooden-plank floor and calculated the course to the next waypoint. He then plugged himself into the comm. beside the starboard porthole.

'Pieter, we've drifted north a little, new heading two-fifty-five.'

'Two-five-five.'

He looked at the young lad; he was pale, but breathing steadily. He lifted the blanket and studied the pale silk material of the parachute wrapped around the wound. Some more blood had soaked through, but it looked dark and dry. He could see no new blood.

He might yet make it, if they could get him to a doctor over there.

He felt exhaustion creeping up on him.

When I wake up, it'll be time to ready the bomb.

His hand automatically slid beneath the leather flying jacket and felt anxiously inside his tunic pocket for the envelope Rall had handed him.

Still there.

He slid up beside Stef and pulled the blanket over them both, the heat of his body, for what it was, would help keep the lad warm.

The hardest part of the mission was over. Max realised now how dangerous the decision had been to land the B-17 on the strip. The enemy had nearly overrun those Alpine troops, and the bomb might have fallen into the hands of the Americans. It had all so nearly gone horribly wrong.

He wondered what the Americans would do with such a weapon in their possession. They would study the explosive formula and produce bombs like theirs in the thousands. It was too late in the day for them to drop them on Germany; there was no point. Russia possibly? That seemed probable. He imagined there must be growing fault lines between those two large countries. One capitalist, one communist, such a huge difference there must be in the way both countries, both people would view how the world should be after this war was done. He wondered how long the unlikely alliance between the two would have lasted if Germany had had the resources to hold out for another year.

He wondered what might have happened if they'd never bothered to attack the Russians in the first place.

He found his mind lazily pursuing 'maybes' and 'what ifs', the recreational pastime of historians and history teachers, as his eyes began to feel heavy and his head light, drifting with surprising ease towards sleep. The drone of the three remaining engines, and the roar and whistle of the wind past the portholes and over the ragged punctures in the fuselage, soon became a surprisingly relaxing lullaby.

Chapter 50

Running

Mark drove them for half an hour up the coast. At some instinctive level it had felt safer to them driving north-east out of town, and further into the New England coastal wilderness, rather than head out south-west back through Connecticut towards New York State. Mark drove them along the interstate, following it as it swung north, hugging the coastline where the Atlantic became Narragansett Bay.

They found a small motel just a few miles east of Kingston, beside an intersection coupled with a neon-lit, twenty-four-seven diner. Mark checked in and got them three rooms, while Chris and Wallace found a table inside the diner and ordered some strong coffee. Chris recognised 'Counting Crows' playing in the background. Someone here liked college radio.

When Mark had returned and the waitress had brought them the coffee, Chris turned to study Wallace.

'Okay, Wallace, it's show and tell time,' he said, leaning forward on his elbows. 'I think you can tell me and Mark here what's down in that plane, and why it's so goddamn important that we have a pair of hired killers set loose on us.'

The old man was looking less shaken and upset now as they sat in the diner. Chris hoped it had sunk in that he had been 'rescued', not abducted, that he and Mark meant no harm, that in fact they had put themselves at great risk to save him. Wallace was looking more composed, and Chris decided, frail old man or not, he was going to get the story out of Wallace one way or another, right now. And the old guy had better realise that the time for buggering around was over.

'So? Let's have it,' added Chris.

'Gentlemen,' Wallace replied, 'the less you know the better. Those men in that van, they're after me, not you. It is me that represents a danger to them, or at least, who they work for, not you.'

'Well, you know what? I don't think they're too fussy about taking us guys down alongside you, so I reckon that puts all three of us in the same boat. What do you think?' Chris replied.

Wallace said nothing.

Chris had a gut instinct that the old man *wanted* to tell them what he knew, but something was holding him back. 'Come on, man, both Mark and I are in this up to our balls now. What's this all about?'

Wallace cleared his throat. 'I met up with you only to warn you away from this, *not* to encourage you further. You're in danger now, young man; you'd be in far greater danger if you knew what I knew.'

'I think we're past that point now. Come on, Wallace, what's in that fucking plane?'

Then a thought struck Chris. 'Or was there *someone* aboard that plane? Someone important? A defector perhaps, one of Hitler's top men?'

Wallace said nothing.

'Hitler?'

'The less you know the better,' replied Wallace.

Chris smacked the table with frustration. 'Sorry, I don't buy that shit any more. Those bastards are after all three of us. So just tell me what you know!'

Wallace leaned forward. 'I have to go take a leak.'

Exasperated, Chris watched the old man shuffle out from behind the table and make his way slowly across the diner and through a swing door to the toilets.

'Mark, he's driving me bloody mad!'

'Well, you wanted to rescue him. Maybe he's right though. Maybe we don't want to know what he knows. In fact, the more I think about it, I'd be quite happy to walk away from this not knowing any more. What if we drop him off into the care of the police and just walk away from this ... whatever it is?'

Chris shrugged. 'We could, but aren't you curious?'

'Not if it means being like him, spending the rest of my life jumping at shadows. There's a point at which you've got to be sensible about things and just back off. I think when guys start turning over your room and shooting at you, that's a pretty good sign you've reached that point.'

Chris nodded. 'But you see, I reckon we're already targets now. Don't forget, that bastard in my room was trying to take us down, and Wallace wasn't with us then. I think we're already targets whether we know what he knows, or not. We're targets because we've been down on that wreck, because we've seen someth –'

Chris froze.

'What is it?' asked Mark.

'It's that gadget that was in the bomb bay, isn't it?'

Mark looked puzzled and ran a big hand through his thick, coarse black hair. 'What?'

'You remember the thing I photographed? It was hanging in the bomb bay.'

'Yeah.'

'The bomb-bay doors were ripped off, gone. They must have been knocked away when the plane hit the sea. Think about it . . . they were probably open when it hit the sea.'

'And?'

'And, my friend . . . And? Don't you see? The doors were open. They were planning to drop that thing on America.'

Mark's eyes widened. 'Do you think it was an –?'

'An atom bomb? A German nuke? Shit . . . I bet that's it!' Chris said a little too loudly, and quickly looked around to see if his words had carried across the diner. The only other customers, three truck drivers propping up the counter, seemed lost in individual worlds of their own.

'That's the big deal . . . they got the atom bomb before the Americans, that's got to be it.'

'So why does someone want kill us, and your friend in the toilet?'

'Why? Because . . . because of the political embarrassment? I don't know.'

Mark shook his head. 'No, I can't see the US government wanting to kill us over something like that. It's history for chrissakes, maybe embarrassing history, but it's all in the past.'

'Yeah? I'm pretty sure there have been people *shut up* in this country for less; especially these days, my friend.'

'Not for something like that . . . so the Germans had a nuke, so what?'

'I dunno, maybe there's more to it. We've got to go down and do another dive on the plane. I've got no bloody pictures any more. We have to go down and look at that thing again.'

'If that thing down there is what this is all about, then there could be a risk of radiation leakage,' warned Mark.

'Fine, then we can take down a radiation meter, a Geiger counter. If it starts pinging, then that'll confirm it, all the better,' said Chris. He looked up from the table. There was still no sign of Wallace. 'He's taking his time isn't he?'

At that moment the swing door to the toilets opened, and Wallace appeared.

'Ah, there he is,' said Mark. 'So, you're going to mention the bomb to him? See how he reacts?'

'Yeah, let's see how this wily old bugger responds to that.'

Chapter 51

Surrender: Mission Time: 10 Hours, 6 Minutes Elapsed

5.11 a.m., EST, the White House, Washington, DC

The meeting was still in session and it had been since midnight. The President, the Joint Chiefs and his war cabinet were looking ragged and tired. There had been a break, ostensibly for refreshments, but mainly it had been an opportunity to cool down fraying tempers.

The first hour of the meeting, up until 1.30 a.m., had been spent drafting high-level emergency orders to be despatched directly to General Eisenhower in France. The orders had been wired immediately, and confirmation that Eisenhower had received and read them had returned within the hour. The orders had contained a number of precautionary measures. Many, Wallace suspected, were probably too late to have any effect on whatever plan the Nazis had put in motion. No large planes were permitted to fly for the next twenty-four hours, all fighters based in southern England, France, Holland and Belgium with a suitable range had been issued orders to patrol the Channel and the north-west coast of France. In reality, there were going to be very few fighters they could mobilise at such short notice to cover this kind of area. Wallace considered it a desperate panic-measure, but there was little else Truman could do, so it seemed.

On this side of the Atlantic, there was even less that they could do to prevent it happening, if they were indeed to be the target. There were no anti-aircraft defences along the east coast, and only a few symbolically placed around the White House. There were one or two placed on the rooftops of the tallest buildings around Times Square, more for show than anything else. There was no radar matrix established that could pinpoint any intrusion of airspace approaching America, as was the case for the south coast of England. It seemed obvious now, thought Wallace, why the Germans would pick America as the target for a weapon like this. Separated from the war by thousands of miles of water, the country had allowed itself to become a soft target.

The orders had been sent, but Wallace felt this was no more than a little feel-good medicine for Truman.

Since the despatching of these orders, Truman had used the time to go over once again the validity of the atomic threat. Wallace's scientific contribution was closely questioned, while a senior member of Oppenheimer's team, currently in Washington to prepare a detailed brief of the Manhattan Project for the new President, had been hauled out of bed in a nearby hotel and driven to the White House. The poor man, Dr Frewer, had been hastily fed a breakfast roll and given a black coffee to wake him up. Once he had been roused and brought up to date on events, he, too, had scoffed at the idea that the Germans were capable of making such a bomb and had been dismissive of the fast-cycle emission theory, calling it 'hokum science' at best.

Truman had questioned the man himself and, like Wallace, Frewer could only offer the assurance that the theory was extremely *unlikely* to work. He too had refused to say *impossible*, though.

That had seemed to have a profound effect on the President.

The sun had been up for some hours over DC and flooded into the conference room as the meeting reached a natural break, and Truman allowed them all a chance to step away from the table and visit the staff canteen for a late breakfast. He wanted them all back for half past eleven.

Wallace chose to freshen up and visited the washroom down the hall. He rinsed his face with cold water and stared wearily back at the young man in the mirror, as water dripped from the tip of his hawk-like nose.

He wiped his face dry. Right now, he'd rather return to the secure, comfortable and predictable routine he had been enjoying at Stanford only six short months ago and be blissfully unaware of the chaos here in the White House.

He did up his collar button, picked up his tie and made a quick job of a tidy bow. With a lick of his hand he smoothed down a tuft of hair on his crown and left the washroom, heading up the hallway to the conference room, feeling a little better.

He passed an ornate clock on a walnut side table and it chimed the quarter hour past eleven noisily.

Hitler's deadline was now only a few hours away.

Despite remaining unconvinced that the Germans had the bomb, he was beginning to feel uneasy about the approaching deadline for the *demonstration*. They had exhausted so much valuable time discussing the possibility of an atom bomb that he felt a nagging concern that other possible forms of attack had been inadequately reviewed. Granted they had that garbled message from some alleged technician that the Germans had managed to produce something and move it before it could fall into American hands. Of course, that could easily have been staged for their benefit, to underpin the bluff, a simple attempt at throwing them a curve ball.

But then there had been the exchange this morning between some of their Air Force boys and a Luftwaffe squadron of fighters escorting a B-17.

A B-17 ... that was worrying. A flying fortress was the only plane the Germans might conceivably have got their hands on that had the range to cross the Atlantic. They had no planes of their own with that kind of range, not even their Fokker-Wulf Condor.

He found himself wondering whether that, too, was a part of the bluff. To fly right across French airspace, with every chance they might be discovered, rather than some more discreet route, for example from Norway, across Iceland and down to the US.

Maybe they'd wanted to be discovered?

The more he thought it through, the more it seemed that an atom bomb delivered by plane across the Atlantic was hokum, a theatrical and dramatic bluff, the sort of stunt he could imagine a madman like Hitler would want to pull off. Perhaps it was more than a bluff? Perhaps it was a decoy, to distract their attention from the real threat, whatever that was. Flying openly across French airspace ... ?

It was a goddamn bluff.

Wallace had talked quietly with Dr Frewer about the infinite chain reaction theory while both of them had taken an opportunity to smoke a cigarette in an alcove just outside the conference room. Frewer had said the same as he had in the room, that the possibility of the fast-cycle theory working was minuscule.

And yet there seemed to be some circumstantial evidence building up. Of what, he wasn't sure. But he could understand Truman's growing belief that the atom bomb threat was real. The President didn't understand the science and had the recently assigned responsibility of the office weighing heavily on his shoulders. He was being cautious, waiting as long as he dared before making a decision.

Just a few hours to go.

All of a sudden, Wallace heard the pounding of feet on the thick carpet of the hallway behind him. He turned to see a man in uniform run past him and up the hall to the conference room. He was let in immediately by the marines in dress uniform guarding the double doors.

Jesus Christ, what now?

Wallace quickened his pace up the hall and nodded to the marines, who recognised his face from the several washroom exits he'd made during the morning, and opened the doors for him.

Truman was being handed a slip of paper. He pulled up his glasses to read it as the other men in the room quickly quietened down and studied their President's face for a flicker of reaction.

Truman looked up at them, reading aloud what he'd just digested silently.

'At one o'clock this morning Eastern Standard Time, a small force of German soldiers attacked and captured one of our supply airfields on the west coast of France. The airfield was taken, some planes landed. A squadron of twelve German fighters . . . and a B-17.'

Truman looked up at them. These must be the same planes that had been encountered hours earlier.

'They refuelled and left before the airfield could be recaptured. Nine of the German fighters were disabled on the ground, and the B-17 was seen to have taken some damage. The planes headed west, out to sea.'

He placed the slip of paper on the table. 'That happened several hours ago, gentlemen. Assuming this plane is heading our way, does anyone know how long it takes for a B-17 to cross the Atlantic?'

There was an extended silence. Wallace spotted a junior officer quietly whispering into the ear of General Arnold.

Arnold cleared his throat and leant forward. 'The B-17 has a cruise speed of between two to three hundred miles per hour, Mr President, and the distance across is about four thousand miles, so that would make a journey time of . . .'

Wallace watched as several of the committee closed their eyes in concentration to do the maths.

'Anywhere between thirteen to twenty hours sir,' said Wallace quickly.

Truman looked at Wallace. 'Then it appears that we may have very little time left.'

The President looked down at the conference table, his fingers drummed on its mahogany surface, and the Chiefs and the cabinet looked on in silence as Truman deliberated for a full minute before deciding to voice his thoughts aloud.

'So, according to Hitler's telegram, he intends to make a demonstration of this weapon whatever course of action we take. If he really does have a weapon, that is. And, if we fail to give him what he wants, he'll do it again. Which means, gentlemen,' Truman said, carefully laying out his thoughts, 'that he's telling us he has more than one of these weapons. That's a very frightening claim.'

Truman's gaze drifted to one of the tall, elegant windows that looked out onto the White House lawn. 'So, we know there's a plane on its way over, there's a chance they have something inside that we might have reason to fear. If they can do it once . . .' The President let the men around the table finish the sentence for themselves.

'Despite the fact that Hitler wants to make a demonstration, if we agree promptly to his terms, then perhaps there is time left that he can order this plane around,' Truman added, to the consternation of some of the leading military representatives. 'I'm sorry, gentlemen. I can't afford to delay this any longer. If there's just a chance this bomb is for real, I have only one choice. We will accept his terms.'

The room erupted with a chorus of voices.

'The people of this country won't accept that, sir!' said the Secretary of the Department of the Interior, Harold Ickes. He turned to the man sitting next to him, the Secretary for the Treasury, Henry Morgenthau. 'Harry?'

Morgenthau agreed. 'And what about our allies? We haven't consulted with –'

'Screw our allies! It looks like the Nazi sons-of-bitches are after *us*, not them!' shouted Admiral Leahy. 'And anyway, if the Russians manage to get their hands on this technology, they'll use it on us. We have no choice but to turn this around and square up to Russia. I'm with the President.'

'Mr President?' Wallace called out quietly; his voice was all but lost in the noise. The chorus of responses grew louder, as it escalated to a shouting match between the Joint Chiefs and several of Truman's cabinet.

'That is outrageous!' shouted Morgenthau. 'The people of America will not accept this! Mr President, sir, there is no way that America can be seen to surrender to Germany, not now, not now that they are beaten. For crying out loud, there are Russians in Berlin . . . only miles from Hitler. It's all over –'

'That's right, Russians in Berlin! If they haven't already come across whatever atomic project the Germans have put together, they almost certainly will!'

Wallace surveyed the scene. The President sat back dispassionately and watched the heated debate without any emotion. He looked like a spent force, drained of energy by this act of submission. It seemed everyone else in the room was talking, except the President and Wallace himself, who was beginning to see a possible, although inelegant, way through this mess.

Truman wearily cast his eyes around the assembly of men and advisors who had each, it seemed, been able to offer him little help in his hour of need. He spotted Wallace. The young man had raised his hand like a timid child in a raucous classroom. Truman was touched by the young man's courtesy and grace.

'Mr President, sir?' said Wallace quietly.

Truman raised both his arms to quieten down the meeting. As their voices dropped he turned back to Wallace. 'Since you seem to be the only one here with any manners, young man . . . let's hear what it is you've got to say.'

'Mr President, that communiqué suggested the B-17 was damaged, yes?'

'Yes, I believe it did.'

'With all due respect, may I make a suggestion, sir?' Wallace said. 'That we send Hitler our surrender. But this doesn't pass through normal channels, not through General Eisenhower. Equally, we do not inform Prime Minister Churchill, or, of course, Stalin.'

The noise in the conference room quickly petered out.

'It is a communication *directly* between yourself and him . . . a personal dialogue, a gentleman's agreement, if you will. We know that Adolf Hitler now no longer possesses effective communication with his people or his troops. In fact, the only centre of communication they have left is in Norway. We send our surrender, and we wait. If nothing happens by, say, nine o'clock tonight, we retract it. Hitler will have had our surrender in his hands for only a few hours. I dare say, with the Russians still going about their business in the suburbs of Berlin, he won't be able to stick his head out of the bunker and shout out about winning the war. He will have no one to celebrate this news with other than those people sharing his bunker with him.'

Truman nodded, and Wallace noted Donovan smiling proudly.

'If this does turn out to be a bluff, or this B-17 fails to make it across, then no one need ever know we took this seriously. No one need ever know that the United States of America surrendered to the Germans, even if it was for just a few hours.'

Chapter 52

Mission Time: 20 Hours, 10 Minutes Elapsed

10.15 p.m., the Führer's bunker, Berlin

Dr Hauser sat uncomfortably on a wooden chair in the ante-room outside the Führer's small study. Eva, his wife of only a few hours, was with him inside. The door was closed, but through it he could hear the murmur of her voice, soothing, consoling like a mother to a child. Every now and then he heard his voice, deeper, but high as a man keening. It sounded like he was crying, whimpering. Every time he heard this, her voice quickly followed, swiftly saying whatever it was she needed to say.

Hauser felt his stomach churn, he felt nauseous.

It disturbed him that this magnificent man could sound so frail, so vulnerable. Germany needed him to continue being strong, especially now. It was not the time for tears. The man had the strength of a lion; surely it wasn't possible for these mewling noises to be coming from him, the same whimpering sound that the Jew Schenkelmann had made on his knees.

Hauser had arrived only half an hour ago. The journey up from the airfield had taken much longer than he had anticipated and it had been touch and go as to whether he would be able to safely make it inside the bunker. The few dozen men left of Hitler's Leibstandarte and a pathetic company of boys in oversized Wehrmacht uniforms had been pulled into a tight defensive knot around the ruins of the Reich Chancellery. Hauser's driver had only managed to get the truck within a mile of the bunker, and from there, accompanied by the six SS guards he had brought with him from the airfield, he had picked his way through the ruined maze of buildings towards the bunker. More than once, they had been shot at in the dark and Hauser and his men had had to call out that they weren't Russians. The soldiers guarding the Reich Chancellery had attempted to turn Hauser away, telling him that no one else was being permitted access to the bunker.

Hauser had eventually managed to convince one of them to call through on the entrance phone, and after a few minutes' delay he was told he could make his way down below and into the bunker; his SS guards ordered to help the others defend the perimeter.

The bunker seemed far quieter than he remembered from his visit just over a week ago. As he passed by the Goebbels' rooms he caught a glimpse of the man, recently promoted to General Plenipotentiary for Total War, sitting beside a bed where his wife lay sleeping fitfully. Goebbels had turned to look at him briefly, a drawn look of futility and resignation on his face.

In the second room he could hear the voices of their children talking quietly. This time there were no games going on, no chatter, no laughing. He had noticed, as he had been led towards the Führer's study, that the bunker was starting to look less ordered. He passed in the hallway two generals seated opposite each other in a nook, clearly drunk. They stared in bemusement at him as Frau Jüng led him by. Hauser could only stare back at them with contempt.

The young woman had seated him in the ante-room. She said Hitler had been expecting him since lunchtime to join him in celebration. It was clear from the puzzled look on her face that she had no idea what it was Hitler was planning to celebrate. Now, listening to the murmurings through the wooden door, the Führer's mood seemed to have swung from a positive demeanour only a few hours ago to one of desperation.

Ahead of him he could see through an open door into Eva Braun's sitting room. The German Shepherd he had seen last time was on the bed again, asleep without a care in the world.

He heard movement from inside Hitler's study, and a moment later the door opened, and Eva Braun emerged. She smiled politely at Hauser and then turned and put her head round the door. He heard her inform Hitler that Hauser was waiting outside, and then she drifted past and walked into her sitting room.

'Blondi, out, please,' she muttered, roughly pushing the sleeping dog off and closing the door behind her as it stepped sluggishly outside.

Hauser waited a further minute or so before he heard Hitler mumble, 'Come in'. He stood up and cautiously entered the study.

Hitler was sitting behind his small desk; the light from the desk lamp shone across his tired face and picked out puffy, red eyes. He gestured with his trembling left hand, clearly no longer attempting to conceal it, towards the guest chair opposite the desk.

'Please, sit down.'

'Thank you, my Führer,' said Hauser dutifully as he sat down.

This time Hitler was wearing his uniform, the formal tan tunic Hauser had seen his leader wear in countless movie reels, but it looked scruffy and crumpled with several faint food stains down the front.

'I was hoping we would have received word from the Americans some time this afternoon,' he said, his voice wavering slightly.

'Yes, it would seem they are cutting things a little fine, my Führer.'

Hitler nodded. 'It seems they haven't taken my threat seriously.'

'Then they soon will, I assure you.'

Hitler rubbed his eyes and sighed deeply. 'I think not. They wouldn't leave such a thing to chance. This can only mean they have intercepted the plane . . . it's all over.' He absent-mindedly stroked the decorative braiding on one of his cuffs. 'We shall not be celebrating anything this evening, it seems.'

It was then Hauser realised that Hitler had dressed up for the occasion, worn his finest formal uniform ready to receive the telegram from the Americans. Hauser had little doubt that bottles of champagne lay ready in the pantry, unopened. Hitler looked pitifully like a child dressed for a cancelled birthday party, unwilling to change out of his party-best into his normal workaday things.

'The plane may have been delayed across the ocean; it could even arrive a couple of hours after the deadline, depending on the weather. We will have to –'

'I think you are deceiving yourself . . . if they haven't responded by now it is because they know there is no more threat. They must have intercepted the plane. Your bomb is no longer a threat to them.'

Perhaps he's right.

Hitler inhaled deeply and smoothed down his tunic, aware that as he'd been wearing it all afternoon, it must now look untidy and creased.

'I believe there is a small buffet laid out in the map room; feel free to help yourself,' he muttered. 'Please, leave, there are things I need to attend to now.' He dismissed Hauser with a limp flick of his wrist.

Hauser stood up uncertainly and saluted. Hitler barely acknowledged him, staring with lifeless and empty eyes at a small-scale architectural model of Speer's on the corner of his desk. Hauser nodded curtly and backed out of the study, pulling the door closed behind him.

Frau Jüng was waiting for him in the ante-room, her eyebrows raised curiously. 'How is he?' she asked.

Hauser merely shook his head, unsure of what to say, what to do next, where to go.

'There are spare cots in the Stumpfegger's rooms if you wish to stay, Dr Hauser. I'm not sure it's wise to go outside again –'

Frau Jüng's words were interrupted by a raised voice coming from down the main corridor. The young woman stepped angrily out into the corridor to see what the disturbance was all about. A junior officer approached her, walking briskly down the main corridor holding a single sheet of paper in his hand. 'Frau Jüng, I have a telegram for the Führer.'

'He's not to be disturbed. That's what he told me.'

'It's in English, you speak English do you not?'

'Well, yes, a little. Give it to me.' She took the sheet of paper from the officer and read it briefly.

'Oh my . . .'

'What is it?' asked the officer.

Traudl Jüng looked up at him and snapped angrily. 'It's addressed to your leader, not you!' She stared challengingly at the officer until he turned on his heels and headed back up the corridor towards the telephone exchange room. She angrily muttered something about the slipping standards of discipline around the Führer as she turned smartly around and knocked lightly on the door to Hitler's study. Hauser heard him call her in, and she disappeared inside.

Hauser remained where he was, standing in the small ante-room, staring at the door and straining to hear what was being said beyond. Both Frau Jüng and Hitler must be talking quietly, whispering even. He could hear nothing.

A minute passed before finally the handle of the door turned, and the door swung open, revealing Adolf Hitler. He had changed his tunic to a similar one, freshly laundered. He smiled at Hauser.

Chapter 53

Mission Time: 21 Hours, 20 Minutes Elapsed

4.25 p.m., EST, fifty miles off the east coast of America

He awoke with a start.

'Max, wake up, we're nearly there,' said Hans jabbing his arm insistently.

Max felt the world quickly invade the warmth and comfort of his dream. It faded all too quickly. He hazily recalled images of a long dining table, Lucian beside him, his eyes as wide as saucers staring at the feast arrayed before him. It was a Christmas dinner, and Lucian must have been only seven, nearly eight; it had to have been Christmas 1933, perhaps '34. He had been eighteen that year, and back from his first term at University. Max smiled; what a wonderful time that was, enjoying the novelty of his new life away from home. But he had been surprised at how much he'd missed Lucian during his first term. He had spent some of the money he had saved for several raucous nights down the local beer cellar to mark the end of term on a present that he knew would make that little porcelain face light up with ecstasy . . . a small army of painted soldier figurines. All through that meal he'd teased his brother about what surprise lay within his parcel beneath the Christmas tree.

'Pieter said I should wake you up,' Hans said apologetically.

He would have given anything for another five minutes back there, back then. 'That's all right Hans,' he said stifling a yawn, 'I need to prepare the bomb.'

He turned to look at Stef to see the boy was still unconscious. He lifted the blanket to check his leg wound and found several small patches of wet blood soaking through.

'He's still losing blood.'

It looked like a slow trickle of blood, but it was still leaking out of him.

If they could find him some medical attention as soon as this was all over, he would pull through. The lad had lost a fair bit, but he guessed he still had a chance. It was more likely he was simply sleeping from exhaustion than passed out from lack of blood.

Good, let him sleep. If he's moving around less, the tourniquet will do a better job.

'Hans, what's our position?'

The gunner shook his head like a horse trying to shake off a bridle. 'I don't know, Pieter just told me it was time to wake you up.'

Max pulled the blanket off and stood up stiffly. He plugged into the interphone beside the port waist-gun and lifted his mask. 'Pieter, what's our position?'

'Ahhh, good afternoon Max,' he replied cheerfully. 'We're about forty minutes off the coast.'

'You kept to two-fifty-five degrees?'

'Yeah, and cruising at two hundred and fifty.'

That was fifty miles per hour faster than the minimum cruise speed; the burn from that extra speed had been unnecessary. Fuel, not time, was the important variable. Max wondered anxiously what their reserves were. There couldn't be much left. 'What's the fuel look like?'

'Don't worry, Max; we've probably got an hour, maybe two, of fuel left. Looks like we'll make it with some to spare.'

Max checked his watch: if they hadn't drifted too far north or south they might actually make it to New York after all. He smiled. Not only did it look like, against the odds, they would actually make it, but it looked like they were going to arrive more or less on time. As the hour of midnight struck in Germany, they would be dropping the bomb over New York.

Pieter had done well, flying a little faster than they'd needed to bring them in on time. Max trusted his co-pilot would have calculated the fuel burn before making that kind of decision, and he had calculated well, so it seemed. Drift and head or tail wind would, of course, affect any dead reckoning Pieter could make, but at 5000 feet altitude that wasn't going to throw his reckoning off by too much.

'Well done, Pieter.'

Hans was looking longingly at the thick grey blanket wrapped around Stef.

'Jump in under the blanket,' he said to the gunner, 'it's quite warm under there.'

Hans nodded eagerly and slid along the wooden-panel floor to sit beside Stef. He pulled the thick grey blanket up over himself, up to the chin.

'Keep an eye on that wound, though.'

'Yeah.'

Max climbed through the bulkhead into the navigation compartment, and then through the second bulkhead into the bomb bay. The bomb hung at the bottom of the rack before him, cradled in its metal frame. He sat down on the floor and dangled his legs over the narrow walkway into the darkened bay below. When the bomb bay doors were open, that area would be a dazzling bright abyss. Max was surprised at how little protection there was either side of the narrow walkway, perhaps only eighteen inches wide, and the open space above the bomb bay doors. It would be perilously easy to misplace a foot and fall through. But then he reminded himself that the space above the doors normally would be packed full with 600lb bombs, stacked one above the other in the racks, allowing no room for a clumsy crew member to slip through and fall to his death. He also recalled reading in the manual that while the bay doors were open, the bomb bay was off limits to the crew.

He felt inside his tunic pocket for the envelope and pulled it out. Major Rall had used a normal, unmarked envelope, no insignia. Against his better judgement, Max felt himself injecting this moment with portentous significance. He was about to open the most important envelope in the world. Curiously, it seemed poetically right that such an envelope would be so unremarkable – plain, white, small. He pulled off a leather glove and put a finger under the flap, sliding it along and opening it up.

So, here we are.

He reached in and felt a single sheet of paper and pulled it out. He unfolded it and scanned the words on the paper. It was letter-headed stationery from the Ministry of Armaments, from Albert Speer's office no less. Halfway down the page was a short paragraph and a diagram indicating how the altimeter detonator should be set up. Max glanced down at it. The detonator could only be reached by lining up the correct six-digit code on a thick locking bar that ran over the top. The digits could be set by rotating a series of cylinders with numbers on the side. It reminded him vaguely of the code wheels on an Enigma machine. He looked back at the piece of paper and found the code number at the end of the paragraph.

One . . . five . . . zero . . . eight . . . two . . . seven.

He reached down to the locking bar and carefully rotated each of the number wheels to arrange the six numbers in a line. With the last digit set, the locking bar clicked, and Max lifted it away from the altimeter display.

He glanced back at the paper. The bomb was to detonate 1000 feet above the ground. He wondered why it would be set to explode at such a height. Perhaps the scientists who'd put this weapon together had become paranoid that it might land with a thud on the rooftop of some Manhattan skyscraper and remain there, unexploded indefinitely, undiscovered amongst the rooftop detritus of pipes and boilers.

The altimeter had a similar display of *five* number wheels. He read the instructions one more time before turning the wheels carefully until they displayed: 01000.

One thousand feet.

The last act now was to press a button to the right of the five number wheels, a single blue button. Pressing this would engage the air pressure sensor in the altimeter. Once this was engaged, if the air pressure around the bomb increased to an amount equivalent to that found 1000 feet above sea level, the bomb would detonate. Max would press the blue button, only at the last moment before the bomb was to be released. There would be all manner of localised fluctuations of pressure around the bomb when the bay doors were opened; so they would be opened first, and only then could the bomb be activated safely.

He pulled back from the small device slung within its metal cradle, relieved that the process of preparing it had been simple and straightforward. He folded the paper up, pulled the envelope from his pocket. It was as he was about to place the code back in the envelope, that he noticed another folded sheet of paper nestling inside.

A note from Rall wishing good luck, perhaps? A note even from the Führer, maybe?

Perhaps . . .

He reached in with his ungloved hand, pulled it out and unfolded it. It was the kind of paper you would see in an exercise book or on a writing pad, not the sort of stationery you would expect the Führer to write on. He unfolded it to find a paragraph of handwriting, oblique, spidery strokes. It was the writing of a man in a hurry.

To the one responsible for arming this weapon,

   This is a confession from the man who has built this bomb. This device uses a new energy called atomic energy. We are using a new science that is attempting to harness the energy that holds the very atoms of this world together. The

*weapon I have made will unleash this energy in a way that cannot be predicted.
It has either the potential to destroy a whole city, or, if God has no mercy for us
at all, the whole world.*

*We have taken a dangerous shortcut with this new science to deploy this
weapon ahead of the Americans. There is an even chance that this bomb will
destroy most of this world, perhaps all of it. The risk of this happening is too
great.*

*I implore you, whoever you are, to understand the terrible gamble you are
about to take in arming and dropping this bomb. Think for a moment, what good
is there in winning your war if there is no one left alive to inherit the ashes of
victory?*

Max stared in silence at the note, his mind momentarily locked in
confusion. His first fleeting instinct was to suspect the note to be a poor
attempt to sabotage the mission. Some disgruntled technician, perhaps even
an anti-Nazi? God knows, there were very few Germans left who would
proudly announce allegiance to the swastika. It was a person who had hoped
that the note might bring an end to this endeavour. Misinformation like this
at a crucial moment in time could just be enough to throw someone off their
guard long enough that it might make a difference. That was most probably
what this was. There had been plots before against Hitler, many in fact, and
Max, not a Nazi, never a supporter of the National Socialists, might so
easily have been one of those unfortunate men who had been sucked into
any one of those conspiracies, if he had been approached.

It was possible, Max deliberated, that this might even be the handiwork
of one of those in the highest echelons of power ... Himmler, Göring,
Goebbels? Perhaps an act of sabotage to buy themselves clemency from the
enemy after this war was over.

He looked down at the note once more.

But we're dropping this bomb for Germany, not Hitler.

That was why Max had agreed to carry out the mission. Not for that
insane bastard who had brought this insanity down on all of them.

*I volunteered for those of us poor wretches who are left, not the bastard
who put us here.*

It was their last chance to fight for a truce, that's why he had
volunteered, and for no other reason; not for glory, not for vanity. Whatever
the motive behind the note, whoever had managed to ensure it had made its
way to the last man to lay hands on this weapon, Max decided, the attempt
had been in vain. The mission had to go on. He and his men had managed to

fight their way across France and the Atlantic, he owed it to his men, to Schröder and his pilots, to the millions of civilians across their homeland who would die if the war didn't come to an end right now.

He began to ball the note up in his hands.

And stopped.

What exactly is *the risk of using this weapon?*

He recalled those few words; words he had not been meant to hear. The door had closed on the answer, but the question, Major Rall's question, he had heard.

What is *the risk of using this weapon?*

The civilian, Hauser, had answered quietly, the murmur of his reply for the Major's ears only. Rall had heard the answer to that question only a short time before they had assembled outside the hangar ready to take off.

And how odd the Major had been.

Max recalled those few awkward moments, standing in front of the bomber, watching Schröder and his men climbing into their fighters and preparing to take off ... and the Major's unusual, uncharacteristic behaviour. And then Max recalled the Major had tried to say something, urgently, insistently, quietly.

He was trying to warn me.

Major Rall had attempted to warn Max of something. He had thought the Major was warning him to be careful handling the bomb; that Hauser had imparted to him at this late stage some element of risk that the Major felt in all fairness should have been relayed directly to Max. That particular rationalisation of the Major's odd, hurried last exchange had made sense to Max as he had replayed it in his mind in the few moments he'd had since taking off to reflect upon the matter. The Major, he thought, had been trying to convey one last cautionary piece of advice, but in the haste, the moment, the noise, it had been lost and cast aside as Max had focused on the mission itself.

But this note ... and those overheard words, and the Major's hurried, desperate last-ditch attempt to warn him, interrupted, he now recalled, all too hastily by Hauser ... all of those things gave Max a reason to pause, to unscrew the paper in his hand. He looked once more at the note, rereading the scribbled lines.

The Major must have been informed by the civilian, Hauser, of the bomb's true nature. The discussion he had overheard a mere snippet of was just that: Rall's discovery of the real danger, for the first time. And now, Max replayed those final moments on the airstrip – the haunted look on the

Major's face, his distracted demeanour and the final desperate look of anxiety on his face as he had tried to warn Max with a carefully phrased sentence.

And then there was that civilian, Hauser, his speech . . . perhaps, as he revelled in the moment, he had let slip more than he had intended.

We will turn all of New York into Stalingrad . . .

Max looked down at the crumpled paper in his hands. 'Not just New York,' he muttered.

His mind cruelly began to replay visions of devastation, the horror that he had seen with his own eyes in recent months. The ashes of a city, stretching as far as could be seen, a world of blackened wood, grey rubble and white dust. The bloated, twisted bodies poking from the ground, contorted by heat as they half-cooked from the flames of destruction, yet still raw inside, raw enough to rot, decompose and swell the dark leathery skin to the point of bursting with noxious gases.

Max had briefly struggled with the notion it would be he alone that would be responsible for arming and releasing a weapon that would turn an untouched city, a magnificent city by all that he'd seen of it from newsreels and the occasional movie, into that – that vision of hell upon earth. But now, if this letter was to be believed, if the Major was to be believed, then he might well be the one who would turn the whole world into – and that civilian, Hauser, had put it perfectly – Stalingrad.

Hans took a look at Stef sleeping fitfully beside him. He remembered when Stef had first joined them back in the early months of 1944. He had been a hastily trained recruit, drawn straight out of school to replace Jürgen Dancht, who had died in a field hospital after catching influenza. Stef had been a pain in the arse, too fucking young and stupid to deserve to make it through the war in one piece. But he had, and annoying though the lad could be, it would be a shame to have made it so far and die within sight of the end. Mind you, he thought, if the boy had been drafted into the infantry he wouldn't have lasted long. Stef was too clumsy, too gawky, the kind of poor sod who stands out, whose head always seems to be the one found slap bang in the middle of a sniper's cross-hair. Stef was the kind of poor fool who always died first.

He checked the boy's wound; there was some more fresh blood soaking through, blending with the dark brown patches.

You idiot, stop bloody bleeding.

He cuffed Stef's head lightly, a tress of ginger hair flopped over the boy's pale, ghost-white face. He'd get a doctor soon. Pieter had said they were just over forty minutes away from America, in an hour it would be all done and they'd be finding a safe place to put down. Just another hour or so and they'd get him some help.

Hans wondered whether he would be able to spot the first signs of land. With a surge of curiosity he climbed out from beneath the blanket and leaned toward the starboard porthole. He pulled himself against the roaring, freezing rush of wind to look forward, over the plane's giant wings, for a first glimpse of the continent.

The sky was clear around them and below, the Atlantic ocean was a deep blue. His eyes were drawn to a pale line carved across its glittering surface.

A ship?

New York had a port. They had to be on target, on the right course.

He plugged into the comm. 'Pieter, I can see a ship below us!'

'Yeah? Which way is it headed?'

Hans leaned back out and looked down. It was hard to tell which end of the pale line was the front, and even harder to detect it moving. He squinted tightly as the wind made his eyes water. After a few seconds he picked out the paler line of the ship's wake.

'The ship's heading south-west I think.'

'Then if that's heading into New York, we've drifted a little north,' replied Pieter. 'Max? Are you plugged in?'

There was no answer. Pieter called him again, but he still failed to answer.

'I think he's readying the bomb,' said Hans.

'Well, go tell him I think we need to turn south a little . . . no just go get him to come forward, okay?'

'Yeah.'

Hans took another look at Stef. 'Hang on. We're nearly there,' he muttered. He stooped as he climbed through the bulkhead and again as he entered the bomb bay.

'Pieter needs you up –' He saw Max sitting on the walkway beside the bomb, studying a scrap of paper. 'Hey, Max, is everything all right?'

He looked up at Hans, a look of anguish was stretched across his face.

'Max?'

He held out the piece of paper towards Hans; he said nothing as he did so.

'What is it?'

Max stood up and took a step towards him, the piece of paper still held in front of him. 'Look at this.'

Hans reached for the paper and began to read the handwritten words. *To the one responsible for arming this weapon . . .*

It took the young man only seconds to dismiss it. He looked up at Max. 'What the fuck is this?'

'Read it. Read it all.'

Hans obediently looked back down at it, and Max waited patiently for Hans to finish. Finally, the young man looked up. 'So?'

'We can't go ahead with this.'

Hans looked up at him, confused. 'What're you saying, Max?'

'We can't complete this mission. It's insane to go on, knowing this –'

'Max?'

'Can't you see that? It's insane to do this if there's even the slightest chance.'

'We have orders, not just from some fucking general, but from Hitler himself!' Hans waved the sheet of notepaper in front of him. 'This . . . this shit means nothing. Any fool could have written this.'

'Hans, listen to me. I don't know who wrote this, someone who worked on the bomb maybe, but the Major, just before we took off, I think he was trying to tell me that we shouldn't complete this mission.'

'What?' Hans' face was contorted with uncertainty and panic. 'This is *his* plan! No, not the Major. He . . . he . . . why would *he* want to sabotage it? No, you're wrong, Max, he wouldn't –'

'He was trying to tell me, Hans. He had only a few seconds to –'

'No! No, that's just fucking crazy.'

Max realised he was making a mistake trying to argue with Hans, justifying his thinking. The young man would respond to an order, he always had, and would do so now. The habit was ingrained into his thick skull.

Max straightened his back and pointed towards the bulkhead. 'Get back to your post. We're aborting the mission, Hans, that's all there is to it.'

Hans remained silent, his body frozen with indecision, yet his eyes darting from Max to the note to the bomb, his mind now working hard to make sense of things.

'No . . . I don't underst –'

'Back to the waist-guns. That's an order!'

Hans recoiled slightly, and his mouth clamped shut; it was an automatic response to Max's barked command. He turned to go, beginning to step aft through the bulkhead, and then he stopped.

'No,' he said after a moment, with a quiet and unfamiliar certainty.

Max deliberately ignored the young man's whispered insubordination and began to turn round to climb forward through the bulkhead and into the cockpit.

Hans leaped forward suddenly, moving with a speed and agility that Max would never have imagined him to possess. He tugged Max's Walther from its holster. He held it in both hands and aimed it uncertainly and shakily at Max's head.

'What the hell do you think you're doing? Give me the gun!' shouted Max.

Hans shook his head.

'Give me the gun, Hans, I'm ordering you.'

'I . . . I can't do that.'

'Listen . . . we can't detonate this bomb Hans. It's not going to happen –'

'SHUT UP!' Hans shouted jerking the gun at Max's face. He called out to Pieter at the top of his voice, but there was no answer. 'PIETER!' His voice sounded like a child's plea, breaking with panic.

'What? You think Pieter's going to agree with you, Hans?' said Max.

Hans remained motionless, the gun shaking in his hand, his eyes darting to the bulkhead leading forward, waiting for Pieter to arrive.

Max decided to try a different way to get through to the lad. 'Look, give me the damned gun now, Hans, and I'll forget about this. I know you, you're a good lad and this –'

They heard Pieter calling back through from the cockpit several times, and a few moments later, realising that Hans must not be plugged into the comm. system, Pieter appeared at the bulkhead.

'What's the matter?' He saw Hans pointing the gun at Max. 'Jesus Christ, what the bloody hell are you doing, Hans?'

'He was going to abort the mission, Pieter. He doesn't want to finish it!'

Pieter looked incredulously at Hans. He didn't look like he was buying that for one moment. 'Max, what's up with this fucking idiot?'

Max turned to him and calmly spoke. 'He's right. We've got to abort.'

Pieter frowned, confused. 'Why? What's up? We're there, we've done it.'

'Give him the note, Hans. Let Pieter make up his own mind.'

For one moment Max thought Hans was going to rip the note to shreds.

But the young man remained still, reluctant to pass it on, holding the crumpled sheet of paper tightly in his hands.

'Give it to me, you idiot! We haven't got all day,' said Pieter irritably.

Hans passed the note to Max, keeping the Walther trained on him all the time. Max handed it to Pieter then watched as his co-pilot silently read it.

A minute later Pieter looked up at them with no clear indication on his face as to what he was thinking.

'Pieter?' Hans spoke; there was a note of growing doubt and desperation in his deep voice. He needed Pieter to reassure him that his solo act of mutiny had been the right thing to do, that he wasn't alone in this action.

Pieter passed the note back to Max. 'We should continue, Max. This could be a trick, an attempt to sabotage the mission,' he said evenly.

'I know, I know. I thought the same at first, Pieter. But there's more –'

Pieter shook his head. 'We're nearly there Max, we've done it. This is just a trick.'

'Listen to me. The Major tried to tell me about the bomb, Pieter, on the ground just before we took off.'

'Major Rall? You think *he* would want to abort?'

'Yes. I think he did. And I think he was trying to tell me that.'

Pieter frowned, then laughed, unsure how to respond to such an absurd notion. 'It's *his* fucking mission, he planned it, why would he want to abort it?'

'He knows, Pieter! He knows this bomb could kill us all! And he was trying to tell me.'

Pieter was silent for a moment, his face clouded as he recalled those final moments on the airstrip. 'He did act strange. I heard him too.'

Hans looked indecisively between the two older men. It looked to him as if Pieter now might be having doubts. Hans began to lower the gun to the ground, doubting his decision, his resolve beginning to waver.

Max spotted the weapon drop and decided the time had come to try and wrestle subordination back from Hans. 'Hans, give me the gun, and go and see to Stefan.'

Hans hesitated for only a second before nodding mutely and reaching out to pass Max the weapon.

'Even if this is true, Max,' Pieter suddenly announced, 'we have to go on.'

Max spun to look back at Pieter. 'What? Are you crazy?'

'So . . . there's a risk. What do we lose anyway? The Russians will kill us all if we do nothing. We have to go on.'

Hans looked to Pieter once more, backing away from Max's waiting hand, pulling the gun back and aiming it once more at his commanding officer.

'Give me the bloody gun, Hans,' Max said again, his command sharper.

Hans looked to Pieter, 'Piet? What do I do?'

'Lower the fucking gun, you fool,' Pieter barked at Hans, angered that the young gunner should so readily turn on Max, their friend, their leader. He turned to Max. 'Max, we've got to finish this,' he pleaded.

Max turned to look at him. 'If we go ahead and drop this bomb,' he continued, 'and it *does*, as this notes says, destroy the world, then it's all gone, everything, everyone, just ashes. What kind of a victory is that?'

'And if we drop it, and it just destroys New York, we win. The war ends on our terms, Germany survives, we go on.'

'We go on . . . and what? Another war against the Russians? You think our wonderful Führer is going to think twice about using weapons like this again and again on them?' he said, pointing at the bomb nestled comfortably on the rack, a silent witness to its own fate. 'And every time we use one, we'll be gambling again, until one of these things suddenly goes wrong, and that's it.'

Pieter studied his old friend in silence. He had witnessed Max question orders only once before, and on that occasion Pieter would have stood by him if it had come to court martial. That was a long time ago, when the war had been running their way, when there had been room for an act of high-handed mercy like that amidst the carnage. But the two years since had been a long time. All that was left for them now was the visceral fight for survival, at any cost. The truth was a stark choice, and it was almost certain they would die at the hands of the Russians.

'If we don't complete the mission, then everything we've fought for, you and me, not just today, but the last five bloody years . . . all of that has been for nothing, Come on Max,' Pieter asked. 'Take us to New York. Lead us one last time.'

'You'd risk the whole world for that?'

'Yes,' Pieter answered instantly, with certainty. 'I would.'

The three men stood in silence as the seconds stretched out.

'You've always been there for us, Max,' said Hans with a voice shaking and hesitant. He dropped his aim and extended one hand towards him, open, ready to shake, a final gesture of appeasement, reconciliation. Max knew Hans desperately sought the approval of his commanding officer to make things *right* once more. To have Pieter on his side had certainly helped to firm his resolve, but to have Max *with them* once more would settle the matter. 'We need you now, more than we've ever done. Lead us one last time,' pleaded Hans, echoing Pieter's words.

Max shook his head. 'We shouldn't be doing this.'

He watched Hans, as the young gunner's eyes narrowed and he re-evaluated him, systematically erasing his feelings of loyalty and respect and overwriting them with contempt. Max felt something irreversible had changed in the young man's mind.

For Hans, now, a decision had been made. His commanding officer had become the enemy. 'Then you're a fucking traitor,' he growled.

Max turned back to Pieter, he felt his last chance to swing this around rested with his co-pilot. They had the strongest bond within the four-man crew. Although Max knew their background differed in many ways, they shared a mutual bond of trust. Four years flying side by side had built that trust up into a concrete foundation that surely couldn't possibly be undermined merely by the words they had spoken to each other in the last few minutes.

'Pieter, come on, this is madness.'

Max decided Hans might still succumb if Pieter were to change his mind and agree with him now. The young man would hand the gun over to him and shamefully concede that he had become confused by events *if* he were the only one, *if* Pieter deserted his corner now. Max knew Hans was an insecure young man, still a boy in truth. He had little faith in his view of the world, his opinions, if he held them alone. He needed the corroboration of another; even more, he needed the approval of someone with rank.

It was down to Pieter.

'I'm sorry, Max, but we're going ahead with this, with or without your help.'

Hans looked reassured; pleased that such an important issue had been settled by someone else. 'What do we do now? Do I . . . ?'

Kill him.

All three of them knew those words were what was meant, if not spoken.

Pieter shook his head. 'No, Hans.' He turned to address Max. 'But if you interfere, I will do it myself.'

Max heard the pain in Pieter's voice, it had faltered momentarily. He knew it hadn't been an easy thing for him to say.

Pieter shrugged slightly, and a wan smile spread across his weary face. 'Just don't make me do that, eh?' he muttered to Max, patting his shoulder, the last gesture of friendship. 'Hans, take him back to the waist section and keep your gun on him, I need to get back and fly this plane.'

'How much longer?'

'If we're on course, half an hour, maybe less.'

'Good.' Hans jerked the gun to indicate that Max should lead the way back to the waist section.

Max tried one last time. 'Pieter, do you –'

'SHUT UP!' Pieter shouted in reply. 'Hans, don't let him talk to you, if he talks, then shoot him, okay?'

Max cast one last glance at his co-pilot as he ducked through the bulkhead. His lips were drawn tightly, his eyes narrowed, the burden of the mission weighing heavily on *his* shoulders now. Pieter's face was devoid of emotion, the last residue of warmth he had displayed towards Max had gone. His mind was on the mission, and that was all.

Chapter 54

Mission Time: 21 Hours, 52 Minutes Elapsed

4.57 p.m., EST, the White House, Washington, DC

There was a clock on the wall of the conference room, and Wallace counted the hours. The meeting had been in session now for over fifteen hours. He looked at the other men; many were staring intently at their wristwatches.

An hour ago, one of the marines guarding the conference room door had entered and informed the President that a staff car was waiting for him in front of the White House, ready to remove him to safety outside Washington. After only a moment's consideration Truman had sent the marine away, announcing that he wasn't going to leave his cabinet and the Chiefs of staff behind.

Wallace found he was developing a grudging respect for this new President. He had only been in office a few days. During the last forty-eight hours, and the two meetings which he had attended, Wallace had witnessed the man steadily grow in stature from the unassuming, quietly spoken, unremarkable figure of before to what he was now. Most definitely a leader. Staying with them here, no matter how unknown the risk, was something Wallace would remember about the man for the rest of his long life. It was a true measure of the man.

Truman was sitting motionlessly now, one of the conference room's burgundy- and gold-trimmed telephone handsets held patiently to his ear, everyone else in the room dutifully silent. As the President waited for the call to be put through he looked up at the wall clock. 'My watch shows me two minutes to five, gentlemen. Assuming that is the deadline, just two more minutes to go. I really don't know what is going to happen at five, if anything.' He looked up at them with the faintest hint of a smile on his tight, bookish face. 'I suggest those of you who believe in a God start your praying now.'

There was a murmur of tense laughter from some of the men around the table. Nonetheless, Wallace noticed several of them closing their eyes, their lips moving subtly in silence.

Less than two minutes to go.

Wallace was still certain that the whole thing was an elaborate bluff. The B-17 which had been seen heading out across the Atlantic accompanied by several Messerschmitts was, of course, real, and certainly it sounded, from the garbled and hastily delivered intelligence reports that had come in over the last two days, that the laboratory in Stuttgart with the cyclotron was also real. But the inescapable fact, confirmed now by Dr Frewer and over the phone an hour earlier by Dr Oppenheimer, was that there was very little chance of a viable atomic bomb with critical mass less than they had calculated – enough U-235 to produce a mass the size of a baseball – and there was no conceivable way the Germans could have got their hands on that much uranium.

No possible way, unless they'd discovered another form of isotope?
Unlikely.

At five o'clock only one possible thing could happen. The bomber would drop a device that would fail to detonate.

But there was a remote chance . . . Wallace noticed his mouth drying and the slightest tremble coming and going. *There's a chance.*

He allowed himself to indulge the improbable notion for a moment, that on this day the world would end with a bang. He wondered how fast this theoretical chain reaction would travel if it happened. If the bomb were to be dropped on them here in Washington, it would presumably be an instant death. But if it were dropped on New York, he wondered what vision they would behold as the explosive ripple of separating atoms approached them here, 300 miles away. A wall of brilliant light sweeping across the world, the light of a thousand suns bearing down on them, consuming all matter in front of it, and leaving behind it only superheated sub-atomic fragments?

'One minute,' Truman announced drily. Then, all of sudden, the call connection came through. 'Gentlemen,' Truman continued, 'I've got the company commander of the Times Square anti-aircraft battery on the phone.'

They heard an indistinct noise over the speaker-phone on the table in front of Truman, a hiss and a warble, the rumble of wind and of distant traffic and the muffled sound of a voice.

'Is this Captain Delaware?' Truman asked, speaking loudly into the mouthpiece.

'Captain Eugene Delaware,' they heard someone answer equally loudly. 'Who's this?'

'This is President Truman.'

The Captain laughed, 'Steve, you trying that shit on me again? I told you this kind of crap don't –'

'Captain Delaware, this is your President, and I don't have the time nor am I in the mood to play games with you, son.'

The President had struck the right tone.

'Uh?' Delaware responded. The noise over the speaker was suddenly muted, as if a hand had been placed over the mouthpiece and they heard the frantic exchange of muffled voices.

'Captain Delaware, I was directed to this line via Colonel Smithson. When we're done here you can check on that,' added Truman impatiently.

The noise of wind and distant traffic returned as, presumably, the young captain had removed his hand. 'Mr President . . . I'm really s-sorry, sir.'

'Don't worry about it, son. Listen now. We have had a report that one of our B-17 bomber planes is inbound to New York,' Truman looked up at General Arnold, who nodded. 'It's carrying an important guest . . . but, we think it may be in some trouble.'

'Yes, sir. A B-17, sir.'

'We think it should be arriving any time soon. I want you to stay on the line with me, Captain, and let me know what you can see or hear. You got that?'

'Y-yes sir. I got that, sir.'

The conference room was utterly silent as all of them strained to listen to the confusion of noises coming from the small table-top speaker. Wallace wondered, if New York was the target, whether they would actually be able to hear the distant drone of the flying fortress's engines moments before this bomb was to be dropped.

Truman broke the silence. 'So, is there anything in the skies, son? Anything you can see or hear?'

'It's very noisy, sir. A lot of noise up here. I'm just looking around. There's patchy cloud cover, sir. Broken clouds, so anything approaching could be hidden from us until it's quite close.'

'Just keep looking, Captain, and stay with us,' said Truman.

The President looked down at his watch. 'By my timepiece, we have under a minute left, gentlemen. In case I'm not around to say so . . . thank you for attending these last two days.' Almost as an afterthought, Truman added: 'God bless America.'

Wallace smiled at the President's words, and he found himself marvelling at Truman's composure. The man must be as nervous as him, probably much more so, given that he had no understanding of the science that confidently assured Wallace that this day would not be their last. Only Wallace and Frewer could see the numbers that made this bomb a nonsense. Their eyes met across the conference room and Frewer shook his head in a relaxed manner and smiled to reassure Wallace.

Nothing's going to happen, kid.

Even so, Wallace couldn't help but feel the cold draft of fate rushing towards them all.

The second hand on the wall clock passed by the nine and now pulled upwards towards the twelve in a languid arc.

Chapter 55

Mission Time: 22 Hours, 5 Minutes Elapsed

5.10 p.m., EST, approaching New York

Pieter saw the continent ahead of them at first as a series of indistinct smudges, appearing fleetingly behind the thick bank of clouds on the horizon. It seemed like America was having a dull, wet day as well as Europe. The smudges eventually merged into a solid dark mass of land on the horizon as he brought the plane down to 3000 feet.

'Hans, I can see America!' he shouted excitedly into his mask.

There was a moment before Hans replied as he scrambled to look out of one of the portholes to confirm the sighting. 'My God, we made it!'

The low cloud had shrouded the coastline, hiding it from them until the last moment, and now he could see it approaching swiftly. Below, he could see several ships heading out to sea, leaving behind them long wakes that pointed like pale fingers north-west towards New York.

'We've come too far south. I'm going to bring us up to two-ninety,' he said, thinking aloud. 'How's Stef?'

'Still out cold. He doesn't look too good.'

Poor lad.

It would have been good to have his help finding their way to New York, but it was clear from the traffic on the sea they weren't too far off. Pieter smiled to himself. He just had to follow the ships; that was all he'd need to guide them in now. He checked their fuel. It was low, uncomfortably so. He estimated there was enough left for maybe another twenty minutes' flying time. That was enough. Fifteen minutes or so to find New York, and five minutes to get some distance from it after they had dropped the bomb. If they couldn't find anywhere suitable to land, they could bail out. Stef might be a problem if they had to do that, especially if he couldn't be roused. In that case they'd just have to push him out, pull the cord and hope for the best.

And what about Max?

He suspected Hans would be happy enough to leave him aboard to go down with the plane. His snarling decision that Max was a traitor had sounded final. His own feelings were a little less certain. Max was no traitor, that much was for sure, but that strange note had clearly shaken him. He suspected that there was more to his odd behaviour than just that. Pieter had seen officers break down before, men that could seemingly endure an infinite amount of battlefield stress, and yet who suddenly seemed to suffer total emotional collapse. Several squadron leaders from KG-301 had suffered that fate, but for some reason he'd thought Max would never crumble like that. He wasn't a traitor, and nor did he deserve to die. If it came to bailing, he'd make sure they *all* got out. Once they'd dropped the bomb, one way or another, this rift between them would no longer have any relevance.

The note?

The bloody thing had to be an attempt at sabotage, or a last-minute change of heart by some paranoid technician working on the project. But he wondered, for a moment, if the damn thing was for real, would that change anything?

Of course not.

If there *really* was a risk involved in dropping this bomb, a risk that the entire world could be incinerated, then it was the world's fault for cornering them like this. The Russians were going to obliterate Germany anyway – better to bring them all down with them than for the Fatherland to die alone.

Pieter nodded; he was satisfied with that justification. It would be *everyone*'s fault if it all ended in ashes; after all, they were just trying to defend themselves. What other country wouldn't do the same if they had the chance? And anyway, who would be left to point an accusatory finger?

No one.

He smiled grimly. To have got this far required the intervention of fate. To turn back now would be an unforgivable act of weakness. Pieter knew that fate, destiny, or whatever you wanted to call it, was with him, with them. Now was not the time for doubts or second thoughts.

He decided that that was the last of the thinking he should do on the subject. The only thing to do now was to concentrate on the job in hand.

Max watched Hans as he kept the gun squarely aimed at him. However, the young man's eyes darted frequently to the starboard porthole, anxious to watch America approach, to see the country first hand that he'd only so far seen in the occasional newsreel, and once in a film about cowboys and Indians. Hans saw the clouds and the dark coastline, surprised at how much like the coast of Normandy it looked. He'd always thought America was a hot place – blue skies, golden beaches and large, beautiful, snow-tipped mountain ranges. But it looked like yet another cold, dark and wet country. He decided with a silent nod that it would make it that much easier to blow up a large chunk of it.

'It's not like you imagined it, eh?' said Max.

'No,' Hans replied automatically.

Pieter's voice came over the interphone. 'Hans . . . tell him to be quiet, we need to concentrate.'

Hans reminded himself of the new situation; Max was no longer the plane's commander, no longer a comrade, a friend. He jerked the gun towards him angrily. 'Shut up, Max, I told you to stay quiet.'

Max raised his hands submissively.

How in God's name am I going to stop this?

Time was running out for him to find a way to put an end to the mission.

He wondered why it had been so easy for him to believe there was some truth in that note, and for Pieter and Hans to dismiss it so readily. There might have been a time, maybe two or three years ago, before their posting to the eastern front, before this war had become so barbaric, that he too might have sided with them and considered it a Jew's attempt to sabotage things.

But now? Maybe deep down, a suspicion as yet unspoken, he'd decided that their home wasn't worth killing so many innocent people for. Maybe the world would be a safer place without someone like Hitler in it, who would gamble the world for his own ambitions; without easily-led people like Pieter and Hans, who would do the same out of blind fealty to such a recklessly dangerous leader.

As a country, Germany would vanish, and her people would become – what? Russian citizens. Some might argue, losing a flag and a language . . . they deserved a great deal worse than just that.

Pieter leaned forward in his seat and looked out of the cockpit window. Below and ahead of them the coastline of America was upon them. He watched as greyish beaches, awash with the rolling surf of the Atlantic, slid beneath the nose of the B-17. There had been no more ships to follow in the last few minutes, so he had decided to hold his oblique north-westerly course until they crossed over the coastline and then he would pull round to the right and head due north, following the coastline until either they were nearly dry or he came across the city.

The gauge was now showing empty; it wasn't a precise display, a needle hovering over a crudely marked dial showing hundreds of pounds of fuel, it was an approximate reading at best. His watch showed the time was twelve minutes past the hour. Another eight minutes, he decided, and then the bomb would have to go, New York or no New York.

'I'm pulling around to the north now, Hans, and we'll follow the coast. Eight minutes to go.' Hans acknowledged, and Pieter began to bring the plane smoothly around to the right.

Chapter 56

Question

'The device in the bomber, it's an atom bomb, isn't it?' asked Chris.

Wallace made no discernible response.

'The Germans beat you guys to it, and right at the end of the war they were about to bomb America,' Chris added, hoping to prod him for a reaction. 'They used an American plane, I guess captured sometime earlier, because it was the only thing big enough to make it across, and because it would be a disguise. And they nearly did it, didn't they? They got within a few miles.'

Wallace said nothing, he simply sipped at his coffee.

Chris knew that he had it right there. No response was no denial. The old man was telling him all without uttering a word.

'Jesus! Oh, for fuck's sake, that's bloody amazing!' he laughed aloud.

Wallace looked up from his coffee and smiled. 'Congratulations, so now you know, I might as well give you and your friend the whole tour, then. But not tonight.'

Chris shook his head. 'No, no way. I want to hear what you've got, Wallace. I let you go earlier this evening, and we nearly lost you. I'm not doing that again.'

Wallace smiled. 'Very touching,' he said drily. 'Tomorrow, if you can drive me back to my home, not far from Queens, I'll tell you it all. I have notebooks, evidence that you could use if you wanted to go public with this. I've been waiting a long time to find that old bomber and to know whether they really did manage to build the bomb. So now I finally know for sure . . . it's time you and I show the world what we know, eh?' said Wallace quietly, with a wry smile and a wink. 'But that's for tomorrow. Right now, I need to sleep. I think we all should get some sleep.'

Mark nodded. 'That's probably good advice. I feel wasted after this evening's goosing around.'

Chris shrugged. 'Yeah, sure . . . okay. Anyway, I need to make some calls tonight. If we're going down on that wreck again –'

Wallace placed a hand on Chris's arm. 'No calls tonight,' he said, 'please. Let's be careful about that. They can be traced. Right now, I think we've safely lost them. Please let's keep it that way.'

Chris patted his hand reassuringly. 'Okay, no calls . . . it'll wait another night.' He looked at his watch. 'It's gone two in the morning. Shall we make it an early start tomorrow, then, chaps?'

'Sounds good,' Mark replied. 'The sooner we clear out of here, the better.'

Chris pulled out some bills and left them on the table, while Mark helped the old man up out of his chair. The three of them wandered out into the cool night.

Mark handed them both the motel room keys he'd picked up earlier. 'Rooms four, five and six. I'm hitting the sack, guys; too much fun for one day. Good night.'

'Good night, mate,' Chris replied slapping him gently on the back. 'I'll come knocking at nine.'

Mark waved as he walked tiredly across the neon-lit tarmac forecourt towards the motel rooms, a dozen quaint wooden cabins arranged in a tidy row.

Wallace watched him go. 'He's a good friend to you?'

'The best,' replied Chris.

'You trust him with this story?' the old man asked carefully.

'With my life, actually. Yeah, I trust him.'

Wallace nodded and smiled. 'That's good,' he said, raising one hand to massage his temple. 'Please excuse me, I really must rest now.'

'Sure. I think we lost those spooks. You go and rest up.'

He watched the old man walk wearily towards his cabin. 'See you tomorrow,' he called out to him.

Chapter 57

Mission Time: 22 Hours, 12 Minutes Elapsed

5.17 p.m., EST over the outskirts of New York

'There it is! I can bloody well see it! Hans!'

Hans jumped a little as Pieter's voice crackled over the interphone.

'We're there! Look out the port side!'

Hans kept the gun trained on Max as he leaned across to peer out of the porthole. Ahead he could see the faint silhouette of a cluster of tall buildings against a darkening grey sky. He guessed it was about fifteen miles away. A few thousand feet below he could see the start of an intermittent carpet of low buildings. By the look of them they were homes, a belt of suburbia.

'Are we there?' said Max quietly.

'Yeah,' replied Hans with a grin, too elated to feel the need to chastise him for talking. 'We're here, Max. We did it!'

Pieter's voice came over the intercom again 'Alright, Hans, time to get things ready. We need to drop this bomb as quickly as we can. I've got no idea how much time we have left before we're dry.'

'What do you want me to do?' he replied, pulling his mask up and shouting excitedly into it.

'Max knows, he's already put in the code . . . it just needs arming. Get him into the bomb bay . . .'

Hans nodded and turned to Max. 'Time to get it done. Up you get,' he said nodding towards the bulkhead leading to the bomb bay.

Max pulled himself up, stiff and sore from the cold and the inactivity.

'I'm not going to do it, Hans, if that's what you're thinking.'

'Just fucking MOVE!' he shouted, his voice breaking hoarsely.

Max slowly ducked through into the bulkhead and held on to the bomb rack beside the walkway. Hans followed, squeezing through after him, the Walther aimed at Max all the time.

'You've made the bomb ready, Max, but Pieter says you've got to arm it ... so do that now.'

Max shook his head. 'You know I won't, Hans. We have got to take this bomb out to sea and ditch it.'

Hans raised the gun and banged it roughly against the bomb rack out of frustration. 'Shut up and do it, or I'll bloody well shoot you right now!'

'Hans. I'm going to open the bomb bay doors, make sure you're holding on to something,' Pieter shouted down from the cockpit into the bay.

Hans held tightly on to the bulkhead, while Max tightened his grip on the bomb rack. With a loud clunk and a whir of motors, the bomb-bay doors cracked open. A slither of brightness widened beneath them as the doors juddered open. The bay was quickly bathed with the sepia light of the waning evening sun. The wind rushed noisily below them, a roar and a high-pitched whistling together, and both men stared in awe down at the passing suburban tapestry.

Hans cast a glance at the bomb. There appeared to be only one button on the whole contraption, a blue button beside a row of numbers.

'It's the blue button you need to press, isn't it?' he shouted against the roar of the wind.

Max said nothing, certain that a denial would sound like an obvious lie.

'It's the blue button, isn't it?' Hans asked again, his voice rattling with anger.

He remained silent.

Hans nodded, all of a sudden certain that Max's silence was nothing but an affirmative. There was nothing else on the bomb that looked like a switch or button.

'I'll arm the bomb myself then. It looks like we don't need you now,' he said smiling coldly.

'God have mercy on you, Hans, because those people down there won't if they get hold of you.'

Hans once more aimed the barrel of the gun at his head. 'I never thought you'd let us down Max, never. But you have, and now you're the fucking enemy ... it's just me and Pieter left.'

Max looked into his eyes, desperately searching for a trace of mercy. 'Hans, don't do this.'

Captain Eugene Delaware caught the faint hum first, above the crumple of wind and the rumble of traffic and activity from down below. In the streets below, full of cars accelerating and braking in concert with the myriad of pedestrian crossings and traffic lights, the faint hum of the B-17 was the only engine on a steady note.

'I can hear something, Mr President, sir,' he blurted into the phone. 'I think it's coming from the south-east. Definitely a plane, sir.'

Delaware pulled the binoculars up to his face and scanned the broken clouds in the distance over Brooklyn. He scanned systematically, sweeping from left to right, as the faint hum, every now and then fading behind the downtown symphony from below, emerged, a little louder, a little more distinct, a little closer.

'It's definitely approaching our position, sir. But I can't see it just yet.'

President Truman's voice crackled over the phone, 'Just keep looking, Captain.'

'Sorry, Max, goodbye.'

Max closed his eyes and waited for the bullet.

'What's going on!?' shouted Stef.

He opened his eyes to see Hans half turn in surprise, the gun pulling a couple of inches off target, away from his head. Leaning through the bulkhead, the young lad appeared groggy and confused by the sight of the handgun.

Max, still holding tightly to the bomb rack, reached out with one hand for the gun and twisted it sharply in Hans' hand.

'Fuck!' Hans bawled with surprise, squeezing the trigger three times in rapid succession. Even with the roaring of the wind below them, the report of the Walther was deafeningly loud. The barrel was close enough to Max's cheek that he felt the sting of burning gunpowder from the muzzle flash. Two of the bullets rattled around chaotically inside the bomb bay, ricocheting off the metal spars of the rack. The third bullet was aimed upwards, and left the bomb bay via the forward bulkhead into the cockpit.

'What's going on?' Stef shouted once more, as both Hans and Max wrestled one-handed to gain possession of the firearm, each of them holding on desperately with the other hand to avoid being pulled off-balance and pitched into the gaping chasm below.

All of a sudden the bomber lurched and started to roll to the left. Through the open hatch both struggling men paused in their efforts as they stared down to see the suburbs of Brooklyn slide away and the steely grey of the Atlantic begin to drift into view. The plane was rolling hard to port, taking them inland. If it continued much further it would roll over onto its back and begin an irrecoverable dive.

Hans suddenly screamed as he lost his grip on the bulkhead and swung out over the open chasm. The only thing keeping him from falling was his grip on the gun. His legs seesawed desperately as he tried in vain to swing them up onto the walkway above.

'SHITshitshitshit!' he gasped up at Max.

Max held on to the gun with grim determination. 'Hold on! Hans, grab my arm with your other hand!' he shouted down to him.

The bomber pulled out of the roll, momentarily levelling, before beginning to roll to starboard.

Hans reached up with his other hand and grabbed hold of Max's sleeve. Max was struggling hard to keep from tumbling out, his one-handed hold on the bomb rack weakening fast.

'Get your legs up on the walkway! I can't hold on to you much longer!' he shouted down to Hans.

His long legs swung several times, but came nowhere near close to the metal grating. He shook his head. 'I can't do it.'

Max looked to Stef for help. The lad was making his way towards them on his hands and knees, groaning with the effort, but he looked too weak to be of any use. Max's grip was weakening rapidly; another ten seconds and he could see both himself and Hans tumbling side by side down to earth.

'Hans, I can't pull you in, you've got to get your legs up!'

The big German tried again. This time his left heel swung high enough to hook over the top of the walkway.

'That's it! Come on you big idiot!' called Stef weakly, lying on the walkway beside Max.

Hans dug his heel into the metal grating and pulled upwards with his lower leg and his two arms. He hefted himself up enough that his hands could reach up past the gun and grab the walkway.

'Good boy, keep pulling,' encouraged Max, relieved that Hans was bearing some of his own weight.

Hans began pulling himself up and grinned foolishly at them. 'Nearly fucking well lost it th –'

The plane lurched hard to port once more, the left wing dropping almost ninety degrees. Without a sound Hans vanished.

'Oh no!' whispered Stef.

And all of a sudden he saw it, little more than a black dot appearing, then disappearing amidst the rolling clouds. He quickly raised his binoculars and studied the portion of sky in which he had last seen the plane.

'Dammit!' he whispered to himself. 'Where's it gone?'

'Delaware!' Truman called out. 'You see anything yet?'

'Uh . . . I thought I saw something sir.'

And then the clouds broke. Through his binoculars Captain Eugene Delaware caught sight of the flying fortress, as the plane bore down on Manhattan Island. By the look of it, the plane was already over the Hudson and now on its way northwards, running parallel with Broadway and up to Times Square.

'Oh, yeah! There it is, sir! It's coming right towards us now!'

Truman looked up at the men in the room with him. 'My God, they've made it all the way over, then,' he uttered, the conceit of measured calm he had managed to maintain throughout the day finally beginning to show the first signs of slipping away from him.

The young battery captain's voice came over the speaker once more. 'Mr President, something's happening!'

Wallace found his legs beginning to tremble uncontrollably. Once more he shot a glance up at Dr Frewer, the only other person in the room whom he felt he could draw comfort from. Frewer met his eyes, but this time he didn't offer a reassuring shake of the head or a knowing smile; the tension was played out across his face as well.

Oh-my-god, this is it. Even Oppenheimer's man is having doubts.

Truman put his hand over the phone and his gaze travelled around the room. 'And now, gentlemen, we're going to know, one way or the other.'

'The plane is turning now, sir! She's . . . yeah, she's banking pretty steeply, sir. I'd say it looks like they're in trouble,' Delaware continued. 'She's heading due west now! It's a steep turn, sir!'

Max stared into the chasm. The ground below was rotating slowly now, but he could see it gradually increasing in speed.

It's going into a spin.

He pulled himself up, holstering the pistol, and clambered through the bulkhead up into the cockpit. Pieter was slumped over the pilot's flight stick. There was blood under his jaw and down his neck; he was either unconscious or dead by the look of him. He must have been caught by one of the Walther's bullets during the struggle. It looked like he'd received a wound to his throat.

Max saw that Pieter had managed to pull out his own sidearm. He must have been getting ready to come back and settle the issue when the bullet had caught him.

So, for this mission, for your beloved Führer, you would have shot me too?

He shook his head sadly. Both Pieter and Hans had been the better soldiers, prepared to do anything to see the job done, too damned stupid to question whether it should be.

He pulled Pieter's body back and grabbed hold of the flight stick, pulling against the lazy downward spiral that the bomber had settled into. The altimeter displayed an altitude of only 2000 feet, and that was slipping away steadily. He pulled back and to the right and within a few seconds the B-17 had straightened out and levelled. With the plane on an even keel, he momentarily released the pilot's flight stick, settled into the co-pilot's seat and grabbed the flight stick there.

Below them now he could see the central island of New York, Manhattan, its tall structures clustered together like giant chess pieces on an enormous metropolitan chess board.

Max had flown over Berlin several times, but the size and scale of the city he saw now below him was a poignant demonstration of the sheer might and muscle of America. While Speer had dreamed of a gigantic trophy structure in the heart of Germany, over here it looked like they'd been routinely building them for decades.

And we thought a single bomb would make them surrender.

Even if the bomb worked as it was hoped, and destroyed only this city, he wondered if a country capable of such impressive scale could be beaten so easily. America was a giant, a leviathan, a Goliath of economic muscle and might. Perhaps back in 1942, when the German empire stretched from the Atlantic to the Urals, the Baltic to the Black Sea, before things had ground to a halt outside Stalingrad, perhaps back then Germany had stood only shoulder high to them; a vain midget standing on tip-toes.

He pulled the B-17 to the right and the Atlantic swung into view once more. Below, he could see the large pale green statue of the crowned lady holding aloft a torch. For a few seconds he struggled to recall its name, and then it came to him: Liberty. He watched as the statue passed beyond sight of the cockpit canopy and the buildings of New York slid away beneath him.

The fuel gauge showed empty. It had done so for some time now, he guessed. Pieter had been flying on the margin of safety, the extra fuel capacity the tanks could hold over and above the dial reading. But that too must be all but exhausted. One of the engines had begun to stutter, the last one on the starboard wing that was still functioning. That left two engines on the port side still going strong. He decided to reduce the throttle on them to even things out a little. The plane was still going to pull gently to the right, and he would need to constantly correct the plane's course to keep it going in a straight line . . .

A straight line where?

The plane had to be ditched, far enough out that it would be deep, but not so far they had no hope of making it ashore.

He heard movement beside him and turned to see Stef leaning over Pieter's seat. 'Is he dead too?' he asked with a weak voice.

'I think so.'

'What happened, Max?' he asked groggily.

For a moment he toyed with feeding the lad some untruth, that the mission had been recalled, or that Hans and Pieter had decided to surrender the bomb to the Americans, but he decided Stef was clever enough to sense he was being lied to.

'The mission is to be aborted.'

Stef seemed unsurprised, as if he'd expected all along this sort of outcome, or perhaps he was too far gone and light-headed to muster a response of shock. 'Right,' he said listlessly.

'We're going to ditch the plane out at sea and then make our way ashore, understand Stef?'

The lad nodded, swaying unsteadily.

Max looked down at his wounded leg and saw that the wound had been leaking again. Badly. He knew Stef wouldn't last long in the water.

'Why . . . why is it being aborted, Max?' he asked hazily.

He wondered whether he should try and tell Stef about the letter, but that had been sucked out during the struggle, or economise on the story, simplify it in a way a foggy head could understand. He decided neither would do. A simple lie was the best thing he could come up with for now.

'Because, lad . . . the Americans have surrendered,' he said raising a smile. 'It's all over.'

Stefan grinned like a drunkard. 'We did it? We won?'

'Yeah, Stef, we won. But we've still got a job to do.'

'What?'

'The bomb has to be lost at sea, you understand? We wouldn't want the

Americans to get a hold of it now. So sit tight, lad, we're taking her out east as far as she'll go.'

'Okay, Max, let's complete the mission,' Stef nodded, his words slurring.

Captain Delaware watched as the bomber straightened out and headed in an easterly direction, passing once more over the Hudson River and, as its form dwindled to no more than a speck appearing and disappearing between the rolling grey clouds, he pulled the binoculars away from his eyes.

'Damndest thing . . . it's heading away again, sir.'

There was a long pause before the President replied. Even above the cacophony of rush-hour New York, he could sense the obvious relief in the President's voice. 'Which way, Captain, where's it headed?'

'It's due east sir. The plane is back over Brooklyn, sir. If it keeps on that course, sir, it will be heading out to sea again.'

The Captain could hear other noises over the phone, a chorus of voices in the background. Truman's voice came on again. 'Good work, Captain. Keep your eyes peeled, though, son. If there's any further sign of that plane you pipe up, understand?'

'Yessir!' replied Delaware.

'Let's keep this line open,' added Truman, 'but for now, this call will be kept on hold. Thank you for your help this evening, Captain.'

There was a click followed by a steady tone and Eugene Delaware pulled the phone away from his ear and turned to his gunnery sergeant.

'Well, that was just about the weirdest fucking five minutes of my life.'

Chapter 58

Ditched

5.27 p.m., EST, several miles off the coast of Rhode Island

The empty fuel tank gave them only five more minutes before the last engine stuttered and died. They were gliding now.

'Stef . . . go and strap yourself in, it's going to be a hard landing.'

Stef pulled himself up slowly, groaning with the effort, and staggered back through the bomb bay towards the navigation compartment. He slumped down in his chair and, with the last of his strength, pulled the harness around him and buckled it.

Max checked their altitude, it was dropping past 1000 feet and falling quickly, they were going to hit the sea hard. It would be critical that the nose of the plane should need to be pulled up at the last possible moment; too soon and they would lose the forward momentum and stall, the bomber would drop the rest of the way like a stone; too late and the nose could catch a wave and the plane would flip. If he could land her smoothly and she stayed in one piece, they'd have a minute, maybe two, before the bomber was flooded and sank. Two minutes was time enough to release themselves, inflate their life-vests, possibly even retrieve and inflate the life-raft. Max knew how important the raft was for both of them. They'd die of exposure in less than an hour if they couldn't get themselves out of the water.

Four hundred feet.

Below, the sea looked calmer than he thought it would be. He could see the faint feathery crests of white horses punctuating the rippled grey of the sea. It looked like a light chop only.

The rate of descent was increasing. The bomber was gliding, now there was nothing but the rush of air under her shuddering wings to keep them from tumbling down. Max fought an almost overpowering urge to pull up, away from the swiftly ascending sea; without engine power, that would be the death of them.

Save the pull back for the last moment before she touches down. She'll splash heavily; she'll skid along the surface. And then it's just a swim for shore.

He wondered how far they had flown out from New York. He had lost track of how long they had been flying away . . . ten minutes, twenty, thirty? He had fought with the plane's desire to pull to the right. Both engines on the port wing had been dutifully running until they'd started to misfire and eventually failed minutes ago. Max had been pulling against the starboard lean, steering the bomber reluctantly north-east to counteract it. He hoped he had not overdone it, and the plane had been heading more east than north. According to the map, the coastline above New York curved round to the right as New York State gave way to Connecticut and then Rhode Island. He hoped the fluctuating course he'd attempted to hold had not drawn him too close to that coastline. It would be the cruellest irony if, despite his best efforts to seek the deep water of the Atlantic, he found himself splashing down on some shallow shelf.

He had no idea how far out from the shore they were.

Three hundred feet.

Pieter's lifeless head lolled forward as the plane's nose continued to drop and their angle of descent steepened. Max felt a stab of guilt and anger towards the body in the seat beside him. They had flown together for nearly five years, survived some of the worst times of the war together, and in the end the bond he thought had existed between them had counted for nothing. When it came to the crunch for Pieter, their partnership played second fiddle to his sense of duty.

He had proven himself to be a better soldier than Max in the end. Unthinking, unquestioning.

Two hundred feet.

The evening light was beginning to fade below the low cloud ceiling above. To the west, the sun poked out beneath it and picked out the suds at the top of each shallow swell as a glittering amber highlight. For some crazy reason the water looked warm.

One hundred . . .

Max readied himself for the splash-down, tightening his harness. He shouted back over his shoulder, 'Stef! Brace yourself!' The sea suddenly seemed to accelerate towards them as the last few dozen feet slipped from beneath the plane.

Now . . .

He pulled back on the yoke in a last-second attempt to prevent the nose of the plane catching a swell that would turn it over. The flaps on both wings and the tail fins swung upwards, and the nose of the plane lifted only slightly.

The light of day vanished instantly as all of the windows in the cockpit were shrouded by churning water and the nose of the plane buried itself beneath the sea. Max felt as if the plane had hit a wall – he was thrown hard against the harness, his head snapped forward, and he banged his forehead against the yoke.

The darkness was only momentary, and light returned to the cockpit once more as the seawater swiftly drained away.

For a few short seconds it was silent except for the sound of the sea slapping against the bomber's fuselage.

Max felt a warm stream of liquid rolling down his forehead. He put his hand to it and felt a gash above his right eye, just below the hairline. He wiped the slow trickle of blood away before it got in his eye.

The plane's floating.

He fumbled frantically to undo his harness; aware that the valuable time she would give them both as she filled with water would disappear quickly.

He heard the sound of water cascading inside from below. It was coming in through the shattered plexiglas canopy of the bombardier's compartment directly underneath him. He climbed out of the pilot's seat shakily and made his way through the bomb bay, sparing a glance at the bomb.

Goodbye, you piece of shit; may you rot at the bottom of the ocean.

He felt an irrational loathing towards the little beer-keg-shaped device, and a grim sense of satisfaction that it was destined for an eternal, dark grave.

He entered the navigator's compartment. Stef was struggling to undo his harness, his hand slipped and flapped around the buckle like a drunkard hunting desperately for his zipper down a back street.

'Here, let me help you,' said Max leaning over and releasing the strap. Stef remained seated, close to losing consciousness.

There was a storage locker above the navigation desk in which the emergency kit was supposed to be stored, according to the flight manual. He pulled it open and the raft rolled out into his hands, a tightly packed cylinder of rubber. As he spread it out on the floor it was immediately obvious the thing was going to be no good to them. One side of the raft had been shredded. He looked up at the locker to see a shaft of light beaming in from the outside. Another of the fragments of debris that had peppered the side of the plane during the last dogfight had cruelly found the compartment.

'Shit,' he muttered.

Water rolled across the floor of the navigation compartment, just an inch deep, followed quickly by more coming from the waist section. A small wave lapped inside through the bulkhead along the floor. It was ankle-deep. By the look of it they were going down tail first.

'Stef! We've got to get out now!'

The young lad stirred, his heavy-lidded eyes opened quickly, roused by the icy cold water that had found his feet.

'Oh God, no!' he whispered.

'Stef, we've got life-vests, we'll be alright, but we need to leave now.'

We'll be all right? No, we won't. Stef sure as hell won't.

Stef looked up at Max, as if he'd heard his thoughts, his eyes wide with fear. 'Max . . . I can't swim, my leg . . .'

'Yes you can.'

'No! I don't want to drown . . . that's the worst way –'

'I won't let you drown, Stef.'

Stef shook his head. 'I'll drown . . . I don't want to go that way.' His eyes focused on Max's pistol. 'Please?'

Max looked down and understood what the young lad was asking of him. Stef was right. There was no way he would make it ashore. He would die of hypothermia if he didn't drown first.

The water had quickly risen to just below his knees, and he could feel the ice-cold water starting to get a grip on him.

'Please Max?' whispered Stef, already his lips were turning blue and a puff of evaporation escaped from his mouth. 'Don't let me drown.'

A memory of a conversation they had all had months ago flashed through Max's mind. The four of them huddled around a paraffin heater in some hastily assembled camp, back when KG-301 was still a functional squadron, sombrely discussing ways they might die. They had all agreed that burning to death had to be the worst way to go. Stef had confessed to a terrible fear of drowning.

'Okay, lad . . . okay.'

He reached down for the gun and pulled it out of its holster, his hand trembling almost uncontrollably from the cold.

'Please Max . . . please hurry, just do it.'

He reached out with one hand and rested it on the top of Stef's head and patted his ginger hair.

'I'm sorry. Stef . . . I couldn't land the plane ashore, I couldn't let them have it.'

'I kn-know,' the boy said, his lips trembling. 'It's all right Max. That w-was the mission.'

The water was thigh-deep now, but for Stef still seated, it was around his stomach, and rising swiftly up his chest. 'P-please . . .' he muttered shaking uncontrollably.

Max slid his hand around the back of the boy's head and embraced him with a rough and clumsy hold.

He wondered whether he could have done this for Lucian. Probably.

For a moment they both gasped and shivered in silence as the water quickly rose noisily around them, and then Max placed the barrel of the gun against the side of the boy's head and pulled the trigger. Stef jerked once, violently, his hands clawed against Max's back for a second before slackening.

Max let his limp body drop from his arms and slowly slide beneath the water. He held back the grief behind gritted teeth and smacked the sea angrily with one hand.

Only an inch of the little window in the navigation compartment remained above water, and through it the faint glow of the gathering dusk outside was fading fast. For a moment he considered turning the gun on himself and joining Stef and Pieter below the waves. Now the mission was over, they could once more be comrades, if only in death. One quick movement of the arm and another of his index finger and it would be over, no more struggling, it would be the easiest thing.

There's still time to get out.

He dropped the gun, suddenly galvanised into action.

'All right then,' he muttered through trembling blue lips amidst a cloud of vapour. There were two ways to exit, both of them were underwater now and he would have to dive down and feel his way out blindly. He could either go back down into the waist section and out through one of the gun portholes. There might be enough room to squeeze his way out, since the port side gun had been jettisoned. Or he could climb forward, down through the flooded bombardier's compartment and out through the belly hatch.

He decided to head for the waist section.

He waded towards the bulkhead leading to the waist. There was now a gap of only inches at the top, the water was around his chest and rising fast.

It's flooded beyond the bulkhead, no air until you're outside again . . . you ready for that?

Max breathed deeply several times. Each time he exhaled the dwindling space in front of him between the water and the roof of the fuselage filled with his foggy breath. Water bubbled and spat as trapped air from the aft of the plane hissed out through the last inches of the bulkhead doorway above the water line.

He watched the top of the bulkhead dip below the water and felt the rear of the plane beginning to swing downwards, the plane now held above the sea by the air trapped in the front half. His ears popped from the build-up of pressure.

There was a loud, deep metallic groan. It sounded like the mournful cry of a whale.

She's sliding under . . . go now!

He filled his lungs quickly and ducked through the bulkhead. Under the icy water he could hear a whole new world of sounds, the sound of metal straining and contorting, the roar of expelled air and incoming water, the click and clatter of debris spinning in circles and eddies. He pulled himself deeper and forwards, down towards where both waist-guns had once spewed bullets in anger. He was encumbered by his uniform and the thick leather flying jacket. His progress was torturously slow, but there was no time to tread water while he struggled to unzip it and shrug it off. He worked desperately with his arms, grabbing hold of the internal ribs of the fuselage and pulling himself forward to the next. His hand scraped a jagged bullet hole, one of a row that had stitched a line diagonally above the starboard waist-gun. Frantically his hand felt along the metal, seeking the edge of the porthole, as he felt his body urgently commanding him to take another breath.

He found the top rim of the porthole and with one frantic exertion he pulled himself down deeper into the flooded waist section, down and through the porthole. His legs now kicked desperately as he struggled to rise to the surface, but his flying jacket was weighing him down, and he had precious little energy left to fight the drag.

Life-vest, you idiot! Life-vest.

He felt for the pull-cord, patting his chest to find it, all the while feeling himself sinking slowly. He heard the painful groan of metal under stress below him. The plane was going down. The noise began to diminish as it pulled away from him, sinking at a greater speed than he was. He saw the bomber's tailfin pass by closely. As it descended and faded from view he felt a rush of bubbles rising swiftly past him and the tug of the backwash from the plane plummeting below.

He felt the tickle of string against the back of his hand – the cord – and frantically waved his hand to find it again. He made contact, grasped the cord in his hand and pulled.

The vest inflated violently with a roar of bubbles and Max felt himself pulled rapidly up through little more than twenty feet of water.

He broke the surface with a roar of expelled air and gasped for a fresh lungful.

The plane was gone, marked now only by a handful of floating items of debris. The sea was kind this evening, only small swells, but it was painfully cold. The sun shone weakly; a few hours more and it would be gone. Max turned towards it.

Rises in the east, sets in the west.

West was where he was headed. He started to swim, in his heart knowing the cold would get him before long.

Chapter 59

Burning the Bodies

5 a.m., 30 April, Berlin

It was easy to lose track of the time, down there, down in that dimly lit warren of concrete rooms. For some inexplicable reason he had thought it was five o'clock in the evening, not five o'clock in the morning.

He looked up at the early-morning sky. It was a pale grey, and, for once, it was silent in Berlin. The Russian artillery was sleeping. The featureless clouds above were letting go of a light drizzle of rain, and delicate drops, like cold pinpricks, touched his cheeks. He closed his eyes and felt the raindrops on his eyelids and tasted the still, cold, morning air. It felt good, to drift away from this messy end to things, if only for a few moments, to savour something as simple as the coolness of rain on his face.

He heard the sound of boots scraping on wet concrete. Someone coughed awkwardly, dispelling the quiet, and he was immediately back where he would rather not be.

Hauser opened his eyes.

He stood in the small courtyard beyond the western emergency exit. Goebbels, Frau Jüng and a few of the remaining staff officers looked on as four of Hitler's personal guards brought the bodies outside. They carried them out on white, linen bed-sheets – improvised stretchers. He watched in silence as they carried both bodies across the courtyard to a corner where the brick walls were at their highest. The bodyguards placed both of them on the ground with surprisingly little ceremony or deference; almost dropped them, like two sacks of grain.

There were no words spoken, and Hauser noticed very little grief displayed on the grim line of faces watching both Adolf and Eva Hitler being doused with petrol.

The sheets had fallen aside as the bodies had settled and both Hitler's and Eva's heads had emerged. Eva looked asleep. Her face looked peaceful, as if the cyanide had been mercifully quick. By contrast, Hitler's face looked like that of a man who had died badly, violently. Blood coated the right side of it, from a bullet wound to his temple, and his mouth was pulled back in a vicious snarl of agony.

Otto Gunsch, Hitler's adjutant, brought out the body of the German Shepherd, Blondi, and placed it carefully beside them with a tenderness than had not been afforded to the two bodies. Gunsch, who had the impassive face of a brutal and ruthless killer, kneeled down and stroked the dog's head gently. He muttered a few words too, before stepping back as the last of the fuel was emptied over the three bodies.

Hauser rubbed his eyes tiredly.

The communication from the Americans had arrived only three hours ago, at two in the morning. That was when everything had come tumbling down for Hitler and, Hauser reflected, for himself too. The preceding hours, however, since the telegram from President Truman had arrived and confirmed that he agreed to the terms ... they had been the happiest of Hauser's life.

He had shared several glasses of brandy with Hitler and Eva and his three personal secretaries. Only two or three of the officers in the bunker had joined in; the others had stayed warily away from the sudden and unplanned eruption of joy and celebrations.

It had been an impromptu party, of sorts, in the map room.

Hitler had announced to the few present that the war was over, and that the Americans had announced they were to step in to help what was left of their army expel the Russians from Berlin. The ladies, although bemused by this announcement, had cheered gleefully and raised their glasses, and Hitler had sought out Hauser with his eyes.

He had winked at him, like a friendly uncle.

They had sung along to some records, and Hitler had talked to Eva about urgent things that would need to be done first thing in the morning. He had cornered Hauser before he prepared to turn in for the night, as the party was winding down, and embraced him without warning.

He had let Hauser go and patted him awkwardly on the shoulder, as if embarrassed by the emotional gesture. He had said one last thing to Hauser as he held the door of the map room open and Eva brushed past him into the passage heading for their quarters.

'There's a lot both you and I will need to do tomorrow. We have a busy time ahead. Get some sleep, Karl.'

Bormann stepped forward and produced a cigarette lighter. He lit one end of a rolled-up cone of paper. He waited until the flames had firmly taken hold of it before stepping back and tossing it onto the bodies. The flames engulfed Hitler, his wife and his dog, with a dull *thump*, and Hauser felt the warmth on his face from the other side of the courtyard.

The second communication from President Truman had been a simple statement that Hitler should surrender now, or suffer dire consequences. There had been no mention at all of the previous communication. And twenty minutes after Hitler had been handed the telegram, he had bid farewell to his staff and retired to his personal rooms with Eva. As Gunsch had stood guard outside, it was clear to all that the final moment had arrived. Hauser had heard many of them muttering that they were surprised that Hitler had left it so long, wondering what miracle it was that the Führer had been doggedly hanging on for. And then the muted conversations amongst the officers had swiftly moved on to the subject of the breakout that they were planning.

They all heard the single shot fired inside Eva's bedroom.

Hauser had felt strangely immobilised by events, unable to think or do anything, other than follow the others outside shortly after the deaths had been confirmed, as they prepared to have the bodies promptly destroyed.

He watched as the flames caught the dog's fur, and the animal seemed to shrink before his eyes.

Hauser wondered what happened next for him.

Some of those here planned on leaving; others, fearful of the fighting around the Chancellery, were for staying. Most of them appeared locked into a state of indecision. Perhaps they were to just wait until someone from the outside world knocked on the door of the bunker and told them the war was finally over.

To Hauser they looked pitiful. Goebbels, Bormann, the staff officers, even Hitler's bodyguards. They looked like a group of children left unattended, unsupervised for too long – lost, confused, and those in uniform like little boys playing at being soldiers.

Hauser shook his head with disgust. Even Hitler, ultimately, had disappointed him.

In the last few days he had begun to see how weak and frail the man was. Only last night as they celebrated, had he returned, briefly, to the powerful and charismatic figure he once was. But even then, his jokes and his stories had solicited tired, long-suffering smiles from those around him. He had become like the drunken, awkward party guest that everyone wished would leave.

The flames had engulfed Hitler's head, and now, amidst the popping and hissing, he imagined he could hear the man's mewling cry, like Schenkelmann's. Pathetic.

The Jew's research notes and Hauser's project data for the bomb were in a box in the bunker. That was a box of incredibly valuable information. And, he reflected, he too was going to be valuable.

His work could go on. His knowledge and his skills would be of extreme interest to the Russians, of that he was sure.

When they arrived, all of these people standing with him out in the courtyard and watching the flames would be unimportant, superfluous. He could well imagine the first Russians to arrive being trigger-happy, hungry to exact a little vengeance upon the first faces they stumbled across.

It would be important, he decided, to lie low, to remain unfound until their intelligence officers arrived at the scene later on, and then . . . *then*, he could make himself known, and humbly offer his services.

While every other face in the courtyard remained impassive, emotionless and still, there was a smile spreading across his.

Hauser could see in the time ahead, after this war was brought to a conclusion, that there were going to be great opportunities for a man like him. He turned away from the flames and headed back inside the bunker to collect his box of notes. Those papers were going to be his passport out of here when the Russians came.

Chapter 60

Decision

He studied their motel rooms from across the parking lot. There had been a light on in one of them until just now. He looked at his watch – it was approaching four in the morning. He would love to be tucked up in bed like them, but there was some thinking to do and perhaps a final job to be done.

It was decision time.

As he stood silently in the darkness, lit only faintly by the flickering neon light outside the diner, he allowed his mind to wander, to start gathering up all the loose ends into a manageable knot; loose ends that spanned over sixty years, all of his professional life, in fact.

His mind drifted back to the end of that last meeting with Truman. There had been an almost tangible sense of relief in the conference room as Hitler's implied deadline came and went. Hours had passed and nothing had happened. Then Truman drafted a second, cautiously worded telegram to Hitler, calling for his surrender once more. It was over.

Then the work, *his* work, began.

The worst of it had all been a long time ago, the killings. Some of them were still fresh in his mind. He sometimes thought he saw their faces in a crowd, or on the evening news, or at least faces that reminded him of them; the faces of those innocent witnesses whose deaths he had calmly ordered.

The whole thing had been a nasty, unpleasant business, but a necessary job that had been passed his way to organise. In the weeks that had followed that meeting at the White House in the last days of the war, in fact for several months afterwards, he had been put in sole charge of the hastily assembled little department as it went about cleaning up many of the scattered breadcrumbs.

It had needed to be done quickly with the minimum of fuss, and certainly without the unnecessary involvement of any other departments. The President had decided that a small, ring-fenced mini-agency with a lean head-count of dependable, well-remunerated and experienced agents was the perfect tool for the job. The breadcrumbs had needed tidying up, therefore it was he, and his little task force, who'd had to ensure that all seventeen of the civilian witnesses simply vanished, with no one left to make a noise.

There were some *vanishings* that had stuck in his mind more than others; the truly unpleasant ones. They were the ones that, even today, could disturb his sleep and keep him up until the first pale shades of dawn. There were other ones, though, that he'd found comparatively easy to organise. For example, there had been that obnoxious Brooklyn janitor who had discovered the decomposing remains of a body on the roof of his tenement building late in the summer of '45. He could still remember the janitor's name – Bradley Donegan. The body he had accidentally stumbled upon was grostesquely distorted by both the fall impact and several months of decomposition and would have passed as just another John Doe in a city that served them up every day.

It would have passed for a John Doe, that is, except for the fact that Donegan had seen the German uniform and was asking a lot of awkward questions. The mess, of course, had been quickly cleared up by the Department. The body never made it to a morgue, and the uniform was hastily incinerated in the building's basement boiler room. His report to the local police went missing, and Bradley Donegan, a single, middle-aged man with a legacy of violent offences against his ex-wife and a taste for under-aged hookers, was found hanging in his apartment a few days later.

He smiled.

Never lost a single night's sleep over that piece of shit.

The world was most definitely a better place without Bradley Donegan in it.

But then, to counter that, there were those ones that had troubled him deeply.

For example, the young elementary school teacher, Ms Elaine Scherbaum, who had spotted the erratic behaviour of 'a large military-looking aircraft' over the Prospect Park area. There had been children in her care at the time. That had complicated things further.

He had struggled with that one, long and hard, allowing himself much more time than was prudent to wrestle with the decision of what to do. Most of the children he was prepared to let go. None of them had seen the plane themselves, and had only heard their teacher comment on it briefly. It would have been an unnecessary risk to consider these children as liabilities. Children tell stories all the time. No one ever listens to them.

But it turned out that one of them, a twelve-year-old girl, had seen the plane along with Miss Scherbaum. Worse still, the girl had made a big deal about seeing something that looked like a body fall from the plane. Deciding what to do with them had been a very tough call, but there was no way he could afford to let them go around talking. The young teacher had family, sisters and parents in New York, and the longer she was left the more it looked like she would share her story with them. With some regret, there had been strings that needed pulling, quite a few in fact, to ensure both the little girl and the teacher were held longer than they should have been at the precinct station and then driven back home in the early hours by a squad car that met with an unfortunate end off the Brooklyn Bridge. The policeman driving the car had drowned along with them, and the next day the vehicle and all three bodies were recovered. The police discovered one of the car's tyres had blown, and a curiously weak section of guard rail on the bridge, it appeared, had failed to prevent the car from going over.

That one had been unpleasant. But it had been by no means the worst. He shuddered at memories that crept insidiously forward into the light. *What about the young boy?*

They are taking the boy and his father, the only two people from this small coastal town to have seen the body on the beach, taking them back to Washington to be properly debriefed. At least, that's what he's told them. And, being patriotic Americans, they're eager to help in any way they can.

It's just him and Blaine in the car with them. He doesn't know Blaine well. The man is older than him, has served in the OSS for some time. He had helped in the round-up of Japanese-Americans back in '41. Blaine looks like a hard sonofabitch, and there are no black marks on his record. He comes across as the kind of guy that doesn't ask questions, just gets the job done with as little fuss and fanfare as possible. That's why he was one of the first to be hastily headhunted and recruited by the Department. A safe pair of hands.

They're driving south along the coast road, looking for somewhere remote enough to pull over and do this thing. Blaine spots a track off the road, leading into woods. It's perfect. Blaine looks at him, and he nods back. The car pulls off the road and bounces uncomfortably along the rutted track into a tree-shrouded twilight. He turns round to the father and the boy and tells them it's probably a good point for them to take a toilet break, as they won't be stopping for some time. Even then, odd and unlikely as that is, they nod, trusting him unquestioningly because he wears a suit and has shown them an ID card with the American eagle embossed in tin across it.

He suggests the father goes first, and nods to Blaine to go with him. The men both leave the car and stumble through knee-high ferns into the woods to seek their own private spots. Only, Blaine isn't going for a toilet break. He watches them until both men vanish, then smiles reassuringly at the boy.

'Are we going to see the President?' the boy asks.

'He's a busy man right now. Even though we've finished up in Europe, our boys're still fighting the Japs. There's a lot still to do.'

'Yeah,' says the boy thoughtfully. 'How do you think that German ended up over here?'

'I don't really know. That's why we're taking you and your father back to our headquarters so we can puzzle this thing out together. You did the right thing telling the authorities.'

The boy smiles, proud that he's done his bit.

He knows this is going to be hard.

He thanks God he can delegate the messy business to Blaine. It's one thing to remotely give the go-ahead for some innocent to be discreetly removed, quite another to have to pull the trigger oneself.

Through the trees, he can see movement. It's Blaine returning alone. The boy's father is dead. Now it's the kid's turn.

The boy turns to follow his gaze. 'Where's my dad?'

He wonders whether there's any point keeping up the pretence now. The lad may struggle, or try to run if he works out what's about to happen, but he won't outrun a bullet.

The boy looks back at him. 'What's happened to my dad?'

'I'm sorry, boy, but we've got to do this.' He gestures to Blaine to grab the lad and pull him out of the car, and finish off this unpleasant job. But Blaine remains fixed to the spot, shaking his head.

The boy is beginning to panic. 'What have you done with my daddy?' he begins to whimper.

'Blaine, get the boy!' he orders the man.

Blaine shakes his head again. 'I can't do it. Not a kid.'

'What? Just fucking well do it!'

The boy, now sobbing, turns to Blaine, standing outside the car. 'Please don't hurt me!'

Blaine, the 'hard' man, is crumbling – not so hard after all it seems. 'I can't do it, sir. There must be another way.'

'You know we have to do them both, now get on with it!'

The man grimaces and pulls his silenced handgun out. He raises it uncertainly, lining the gun up on the boy in the car.

'I'm really sorry, kid,' he mumbles. 'You have to get out of the car now.'

The boy opens the rear door and steps outside, his eyes fearfully locked on the pistol. He whispers 'please', his hands involuntarily clasped together like he's praying.

'Do it, Blaine!'

The man fires a wavering shot that hits the boy in the arm. The boy's startled face looks down at the growing crimson stain on his sleeve. He looks up from the wound and without a word of warning turns on his heels and runs from the car, up the dirt lane towards the main coast road.

The boy has to be stopped . . . but the useless fool Blaine is not giving chase. He's staring after the boy, his gun arm isn't raised to finish the boy off. It's hanging uselessly by his side.

He climbs out of the car and grabs Blaine's gun and turns round to take aim. But the boy has stumbled, and lies on the ground shaking, trembling, sobbing. His momentary bid to escape spent.

The dozen or so strides he takes towards the boy cowering on the floor have been replayed time and time again in his mind. The final shot he has managed, over time, to blank out.

He shuddered, the boy had definitely been the worst of them.

There had been seventeen in total. Seventeen civilians whose deaths he'd had to arrange in the months after the end of the war. And then after that, after the civilian liabilities had all been disposed of, there had been another job for him and the Department – ensuring that those men who had attended Truman's crisis conference had remained silent on the matter, for the rest of their lives.

Being the youngest man who had attended during those two days at the White House had most definitely been a factor in Truman's decision to entrust him with keeping the whole incident under wraps; he would outlive them all.

For the last sixty years, he alone had overseen the task entrusted to the Department – collating data on those men, powerful men who lived very political and complicated lives; watching closely those who looked wobbly, those whom he had a hunch might just talk.

And, oh yes . . . there had been a few.

Several of the most senior men who had been with Truman on those two days had come dangerously close to looking like they might spill it all as they entered the autumn years of their lives. Of course, that was when they became most worrying: old men, facing their inevitable mortality and wondering if now, after so many years, it might just be safe enough to tell a favourite grandchild or nephew an incredible story from way back.

He smiled with satisfaction as he recalled the discreet and not so veiled warnings he had made to some very powerful and influential men from time to time throughout his long vigil. Men who had recoiled with shock that they should be under surveillance so many decades after the event.

Men who should have known better.

Wallace smiled with pride. Truman had turned to him on that final day, as men great and powerful filed dutifully and silently out of the conference room. Truman had quietly asked *him* to stay, and no one else.

President Truman took off his glasses and rubbed his tired and red-rimmed eyes. The last forty-eight hours had clearly taken a lot out of him. 'I'm the new boy, here, Wallace. I don't know who to trust, who are the sharks. All I know is that amongst all these supposedly wise men, it was your advice that seemed to make the most sense. It was your counsel I took in the end, not theirs.'

'Thank you, Mr President,' replied Wallace.

'I'm going to need someone I can trust, someone with a lot of smarts, someone who can work quickly, think on his feet like you did today, to make sure this whole sorry episode stays buried. Think you're up to it?'

'Me sir?'

'Yes, lad, you.'

'I've not been in intelligence long sir . . . just a few months –'

'Then perhaps you're untainted. You're not habitually used to proce-dures, ways of doing things that might slow you down . . . red tape that might prevent you from acting quickly, if it was required. Do you understand me?'

'I'm not sure I do, sir.'

'This must never, ever become known to the public. And I'd like you to take charge of that. I'll make sure you have everything you need – money, men, materials, your own little secret agency . . . just make sure this thing

never surfaces. Whatever it takes ... you understand me? Whatever it takes. *Whatever you need to do, I don't care what it is, and I won't want to know either, you make sure this remains a secret.'*

Truman's eyes remained on Wallace, studying his reaction, looking for uncertainty in the young man's response. If there was doubt or any indecision in his response, he supposed the young man would not be suitable ... and he too would be a potential liability to deal with.

'Whatever it takes, sir?'

Truman nodded. 'Well? Do you think you're up to it?'

In the darkness, outside the motel rooms, in response to that question asked over sixty years earlier, Wallace nodded with satisfaction. He *had* been up to it.

His eyes picked out the headlights of the van as it exited the interstate off the slip road, disappeared momentarily behind some trees and then, seconds later, cruised quietly past the diner and on to the parking lot in front of the motel rooms. The headlights winked off and the van rolled silently forward, the engine switched off, using the last of the vehicle's momentum. It came to a rest a few yards from where Wallace waited in the shadows.

His men had taken their damned time.

He had called them from the diner's toilet over two hours ago. He was lucky this man Chris and his friend hadn't a clue who they had in their care. In fact, after his initial fear of the impromptu 'rescuing' had passed, Wallace had begun to find the whole situation rather amusing.

It had been an appalling *fuck-up*, his men being caught out like that, allowing these two amateurs to best them and escape into the night. And then, to make matters worse, abduct him shortly afterwards, right under their noses. But, despite the fact that shots had been fired, and there were some people who had witnessed what had happened, it had worked itself out all right. Here they were, somewhere remote and quiet, and now it was time to tidy things up once more.

As he had waited for his men to arrive, Wallace had contacted the dive team. The deed was done, the *package* had been dropped into deeper waters. So, it was finally done, the only *real* evidence of the event was gone. All that was left now to think about was what these two amateurs might decide to say and do.

Wallace beckoned to the two men sitting inside the van to follow him and approached the motel rooms. Both men gently stepped out of the van, leaving the doors open rather than make a noise closing them. They came to a halt outside cabin five and Wallace raised a hand, an indication that they should wait right there.

It was silent now, except for the occasional whisper of a passing car on the nearby interstate, and the hum of the neon light above the motel cabins. There were no other guests tonight, only Chris Roland's car in the parking lot . . . and the anonymous-looking black van.

Wallace studied the door in front of him. It had a flat-key lock, little more than a springed-latch.

He turned to his men, motionless silhouettes in the dark poised for action, and pointed to the lock. The older of his two men, the grey-haired man who used the name 'Jimmy' for this particular contract, approached the lock and quietly produced an adjustable lock-pick, cradling it carefully so that the metal parts didn't jangle. Deftly he inserted it into the lock and twisted it, feeling the resistance and adjusting the spacing of the teeth until the pick approximated the profile of the lock. It opened with the lightest of clicks. He nodded to Wallace to let him know that it was done and then took a step back.

Inside, Wallace could hear the faint rustling of rhythmic breathing. Chris Roland was in a deep sleep.

All the better, then.

He didn't want a discussion with the guy, he needed time to think, not talk. If he was going to do it himself once more, he'd rather put a single cap into his unconscious head than endure a startled plea for mercy. Not something he was particularly keen to experience again.

He approached the side of the bed, feeling his way cautiously with one foot in front of the other. A shard of amber light from the arc lamp outside fell across the bed and picked out the English guy's face.

Wallace smiled as he looked down on Chris sleeping deeply, no doubt dreaming of fame and glory and journalistic prizes. A smile spread across Wallace's lips, not of compassion, but of satisfaction. The job was nearly done . . . just this last thing.

Truman had asked him all those years ago if he thought he could do the job.

Damned right he could. He had seen it through right up until now. There was only one name left on that list of Those Who Knew, one person left alive who had lived through the events of that day, and that last name was *his*. When his time was up, and if he was honest with himself, that wasn't going to be too much longer now, there really would be no one left to tell the story.

It would die right alongside him. He had fulfilled Truman's brief absolutely to the letter.

There was something about that thought that filled Wallace with an odd feeling of loss. The job needed finishing up with a single bullet into this man's head, and that of his friend's, and their bodies disposed of. That would be the end of it all. And then, with the few months he had left, he would need to close down the Department, shred what was left of file n-27, empty the safe that sat in the corner of his now rarely used office of the last of the money and close the door once and for all on that mezzanine floor.

There would be something poetically final about that; finishing off a job well done.

But it was the finality that troubled him. Once he had done away with these two young men, it would just be him once more. The last person . . . the only person to know.

A very lonely responsibility.

Chris stirred and muttered in his sleep and turned over. Wallace raised his gun and lined it up on the back of Chris's head.

There was something else to bear in mind. Killing him now, after the unfortunately noisy skirmish earlier this evening, might result in some awkward complications he wasn't sure he could square away with the money he had left. Making these two men vanish wasn't going to be as easy as it once was. Those gunshots in the dark back in that sleepy little seaside town might attract the interest of some slack-jawed local law enforcement officer. But a murder? That would mean the FBI would get to stick its nose in, and frankly, with whatever time he had left, Wallace didn't want to be worrying about a knock on his door and a visit from the G-men.

I could let him go.

There was nothing left of the story for Chris Roland. No bomb, no photographs of a bomb, no eye witnesses, no testimonies, nothing. There was now just the plane and two skeletons dressed in shreds that might possibly be recognised as a Luftwaffe uniform; an intriguing story perhaps, but nothing that would lead anywhere. There was nothing that could be substantiated.

With a shudder of dawning realisation, the old man could see the job was already done. The secret was now safe. He decided that leaving it like this was tidy enough as far as he was concerned. And anyway, there was something about this bumbling British amateur he had grown to like.

He lowered his gun.

Your lucky night.

Wallace reached into his jacket pocket and pulled something out, something he had kept close to himself for sixty years, something he had once upon a time prised loose from the stiff grasp of a dead boy called Sean Grady, lying amidst blood-spattered ferns. It jingled ever so slightly, as he lifted it carefully out and placed it softly on the bedside table.

You can have that, my young friend.

Wallace felt strangely light, as if the small metal disc and the chain attached to it had been a weighty shackle. It glinted in the amber light streaking in from the lamp outside. Wallace had never really understood why he had taken it off the dead boy. It was evidence, of course, something that really shouldn't be found. He should have destroyed it. But instead he had kept it all these years, perhaps as a reminder of how ruthless he had once been, and might need to be again? Perhaps out of a sense of guilt – that boy, the young girl and her teacher in New York, none of them deserved to die . . . but they really had to.

Wallace felt his throat tighten and a momentary welling of a confused, unidentifiable emotion. He struggled to fight it down and put a lid back on it.

This young man can have it, he thought. On its own, the little disc could tell no one anything, but in some odd way, to the old man, it felt like he was passing on the baton, the secret, to someone else to keep close, to cherish.

Wallace eased his way back towards the door and slipped quietly outside. He turned to the motionless dark shapes of his hired men gathered by the doorway.

'We're done here,' he whispered. 'Let's go.'

Chapter 61

Going Home

The surf rolled across the pebbles and came to a reluctant halt a few inches away from his trainers, before drawing back with a hiss of frustration. Chris looked up at grey clouds rolling across the mid-morning sky. It was going to rain pretty soon. Another rainy day to join the other seven he'd endured out here amidst the coastal wilderness of Rhode Island.

He looked down at the object in his hand, the dog tag with the serial number on it, and the German name: OberLt Kleinmann M. That's all he had left now.

'Fuck it.'

That bastard Wallace had stitched him up. He had discovered that fantastic bit of news first thing this morning when he had gone to open his door to step outside and spotted the note pushed through underneath the draft flap.

It's not going to make a great news story without any pictures or evidence is it? By now, what you discovered beneath the sea will be long gone. So why not let it go? It's no longer a news story . . . it's just a story now. Hell, it might even make a good book one day. I'll be watching you. W.

The wily old bastard had played Chris like a fiddle – cosying up and playing new-best-friend, while all the time, behind his back, his bloody hired thugs were hoovering up the evidence. Now he was starting to wonder how much of what Wallace had told him was the truth anyway, and how much of it was just a yarn he had spun to keep Chris out of his motel room long enough for his men to sweep it thoroughly.

He could dive again on the wreck, but something told him that all he would find this time would be the plane . . . he was sure even the bodies would be gone.

He kicked at the sand with frustration. It would have been a great story. Better than Nixon and Watergate, better than Bush and Bin Laden, the Hitler Diaries. It would have set him up for life.

Nazi Germany Came Within an Ace of Nuking New York – the sort of tagline that would give a tabloid editor a permanent hard-on. He could have licensed the picture of the bomb itself for hundreds of thousands to the right publication.

But it was pointless beating himself up like this. There were no pictures now, thanks to that old bastard. It was game over.

How about counting your blessings, Chris me old mate?

'Yeah? And what blessings would those be, exactly?' he muttered.

People have been known to go missing for knowing a whole lot less.

Perhaps there was some truth in that. If that shit Wallace really had been a government spook he could surely have made him and Mark just vanish. Those men who had jumped him in his motel room had come within a few moments of wasting him. The thought sent a shiver down his spine. If that old man Wallace – if that was his name – had really been their boss, *shit* . . . he and Mark were pretty lucky to have woken up this morning.

And they had been in his room last night. God knows, while he'd been sleeping like a baby, they must have been standing over him, guns raised, aimed at his face, and he could imagine Wallace silently doing an *eeny-meeny-miny-mo*.

Chris heard the Cherokee's horn. Mark was getting impatient. He wanted to get the hell out of here. Chris didn't couldn't blame him.

It was time to head back to New York. Elaine Swisson was going to go ballistic when he turned up empty-handed. He knew damn well if he switched his mobile back on, there would be a dozen frantic messages from her, that deadline almost upon them. He wondered what exactly he was going to tell the woman. Perhaps he could come up with something between now and hitting New York.

Well, Elaine I'll tell you what happened. A legal eagle from the US Air Force paid me a visit and asked me not to exploit what they consider to be a war grave . . . and they suggested they might take legal action if the pictures appeared in the public domain. So I guess we're screwed.

Chris nodded. That would probably do it. *News Fortnite* readers generally seemed to be of the blue-rinse variety or elderly, medal-wearing vets. If the mention of legal action didn't cool her enthusiasm, the possibility of alienating her readers would. He wasn't looking forward to lying to her. He respected Elaine, but the lie would keep things uncomplicated.

Chris decided he would hand some of the advance back to the magazine, and keep a couple of thousand to cover the costs he had incurred in the last week, including paying Mark. That seemed to be the best he could do in the circumstances. And once he'd dealt with Elaine, he was going to have to drop Mark back home in Queens and then return the car to Hertz.

After that, he fancied maybe he would grab a plane at JFK and go back home to London. The old man, Wallace, was right about one thing, though – it might make for a good book. He could always have a go, write up the tale Wallace had told him, as a work of fiction, of course.

Chris turned the dog tags over in his hand and studied the name stamped into the brass surface. He had found them on his bedside table, a parting gift from Wallace.

'M. Kleinmann, I guess whatever it is you did, or didn't do, is . . . well I suppose it just never happened.'

He turned away from the sea, as rolling surf once more reached out for his feet. He began to make his way back across wet pebbles and drying sand towards grass-topped dunes and the road side beyond, where Mark was gunning the engine impatiently.

Without a story behind it, it was nothing but a disc of brass with a name stamped in it. He ran his finger across the indented name one last time before tossing it away as he took a step up out of the dunes and headed across hard gravel towards the jeep.

The little brass disc rolled down the side of the dune, gathering a miniature avalanche of loose sand in its wake. With a gentle tap, it came to rest against the base of a weathered, old, wooden cross that poked out of the sand and was embraced by the coarse grass. The cross had been crudely fashioned from two pieces of driftwood nailed together a long time ago, but had stood the test of time. Engraved on the coarse wood by a boy with a penknife was a simple sentence. The letters now were worn by the elements, scoured by wind-borne sand, but still legible, just:

Here was found the body of an unknown airman.
Died April, 1945.

Author's Note

There's an old tale I was told, a long long time ago. It concerned one Enrico Fermi, if I recall correctly, an Italian-born physicist who had emigrated to America during the war and produced the first artificial nuclear fission chain reaction. The story goes that, as he readied himself to initiate the experiment, he turned to his assistant and nervously confessed he wasn't sure whether the chain reaction would go on indefinitely or quickly come to a halt.

And then of course, he went and hit the button anyway.

I've never been able to confirm that story, and perhaps it's urban myth, but it's a story that stuck in my mind for many years afterwards ... that a scientist might theoretically gamble the world on the back of an experiment.

In 1945 when J. Robert Oppenheimer and his team prepared Trinity, the first American atom bomb, to let rip with a test blast in the deserts of New Mexico on 16 July, it was known that he was intensely wary of what would happen at the moment of detonation. And as the mushroom cloud of flame and churning destruction rose up into the sky, he was seen to exhale a long-held breath and mutter those few words, 'I am Vishnu, become death, Destroyer of worlds, Shatterer of worlds, The Mighty One ... A thousand suns Bursting in the sky.'

At the time they were dabbling with this new technology, nothing was certain, and until the day of Trinity, over two months after Germany's surrender, there was a chance, in their minds, a remote chance, that they were meddling with something they might not be able to control.

With regard to Schenkelmann's fast-cycle emitter, as any physics student will know, the idea is mere fancy. Fission only continues as long as there is fissionable material to burn up. Perhaps back in 1945 a theory like that might have sounded convincing; after all, there was some disagreement amongst the leading minds in this field as to how much U-235 would need to be in one place to initiate a chain reaction.

A good example of this uncertainty amongst brilliant minds is Werner Heisenberg, the man in charge of the German attempt to build an atom bomb. He initially miscalculated the amount of pure, refined uranium needed as being in the hundreds of tons, as opposed to ounces! When Heisenberg made that miscalculation and reported his findings to the German Army Weapons Department, the Nazis effectively back-pedalled their efforts to produce an atom bomb, thinking that it was impractical if not impossible to refine enough uranium to produce even a solitary bomb. The German nuclear effort was further hampered by Adolf Hitler's lack of enthusiasm for what he called the 'Jewish science'.

It was worryingly close, though. If Heisenberg had done the maths correctly, the Germans might well have beaten the Americans to the bomb.

After the war Heisenberg maintained that he understood the principles of the atomic bomb, but that he had deliberately misled the German programme into concentrating on reactors instead of building a weapon. Shortly after the war, Heisenberg and nine of his colleagues were being held and debriefed at Farm Hall, a British country house, when news of the bombing of Hiroshima with an atomic bomb was relayed to them. Hidden microphones recorded their reactions, and Heisenberg condemned his reputation when he exclaimed that the Hiroshima announcement was simply not possible.

On a completely separate note, Chris Roland was based entirely on a bloke I used to work with – the mannerisms, his description, the way he talked. I liked the guy, his self-effacing charm, his gangly frame and unflattering ginger hair, buzz-cut like a marine's. The last I heard, he's doing really well in the computer games industry. But he'll never know I used him as a character, and hopefully no one will ever spot my character is him.

Acknowledgements

Perhaps this kind of thing is best done in some sort of chronological order. I owe thanks to Frances, backdated, for seventeen years of love and support – most of those misguided years spent making music and computer games. I really should've started writing earlier. I owe her for all of that first-class proof reading and the copious red ink in the margins, and for helping me make some pretty critical plot choices.

Thanks also due to my author-brother Simon, and my dad, Tony. You see, both of them read a screenplay of mine a few years back, entitled *Silent Tide*. I never finished the damned thing. I think I got about three quarters of the way through and couldn't decide whether the Germans should . . . tsk tsk, nearly . . . anyway, both agreed it would make a fine book and I should pull my finger out and get on and write it. Well here it is guys, several revisions later. Thanks for nudging me towards writing the novel. And Dad, thanks for the help on the research side, and boy, was there was a lot of it, painstaking fact-checking. You pointed me in the right direction more than once.

Merric Davidson, I thank you. You spotted the potential in that first draft and nursed it through some early surgery, and of course, found an excellent home for it with Orion.

I also owe a debt of gratitude to my editor Jon Wood and assistant editor, Genevieve Pegg over at Orion for truly taking the story to another level and holding down our patient whilst I indulged in a little more keyhole surgery. Thanks also due to them for showing such unstinting enthusiasm for the book and for Jon's infectious evangelizing.

And of course Eugenie Furniss at William Morris; a good agency, a great agent.

Finally . . . a little thank you to that piece of cheese I had the night before *that* dream . . . the one that led to the screenplay that ultimately led to the book. Cheers bud.